Copyright © 2019 Rack

All rights reserv

ISBN-13: 979-8698334323
ASIN: B07Q4294XX

For avoidance of doubt, the author reserves the rights, and no publisher/platform/individual has the rights to, reproduce and/or otherwise use the Work in any manner for purposes of training artificial intelligence technologies to generate text, including without limitation, technologies that are capable of generating works in the same style or genre as the Work, unless the publisher/platform/individual obtains the author's specific and express permission to do so. Nor does any publisher/platform/individual have the right to sublicense others to reproduce and/or otherwise use the Work in any manner for purposes of training artificial intelligence technologies to generate text without the author's specific and express permission.

THE LOCKET

Magician's Prophecy

Small print
All rights reserved. No part of this book may be reproduced or distributed in any form without prior written permission from the author, with the exception of non-commercial uses permitted by copyright law.

CONTENTS

Copyright	
The Locket	2
Chapter 1	6
Chapter 2	15
Chapter 3	29
Chapter 4	41
Chapter 5	48
Chapter 6	59
Chapter 7	65
Chapter 8	72
Chapter 9	81
Chapter 10	89
Chapter 11	97
Chapter 12	105
Chapter 13	115
Chapter 14	127
Chapter 15	135
Chapter 16	143
Chapter 17	150
Chapter 18	158

Chapter 19	167
Chapter 20	174
Chapter 21	183
Chapter 22	190
Chapter 23	197
Chapter 24	203
Chapter 25	211
Chapter 26	219
Chapter 27	227
Chapter 28	237
Chapter 29	246
Chapter 30	260
Chapter 31	270
Chapter 32	278
Chapter 33	287
Chapter 34	296
Chapter 35	304
Chapter 36	313
Chapter 37	321
Chapter 38	332
Chapter 39	341
Chapter 40	347
Chapter 41	354
Chapter 42	360
Chapter 43	369
Chapter 44	376
Chapter 45 - Epilogue	387

CHAPTER 1

Carra's eyes burned from the smoke, and blinking did little to soothe them. Only when a shack to the side of the path collapsed in on itself, was she distracted from the irritation. Pausing from her run, she attempted to see whether anyone had been crushed underneath.

There was no one in sight.

Having reached the village border – its most westerly point – she reckoned she would be okay sparing a couple of minutes to check the ruined shanty more thoroughly. The collapse had mostly smothered the flames, meaning she was able to approach the wreckage, but she still did so cautiously.

Pulling her cloth jerkin over her sleeves to shield her hands from the hot wood, she tried to pry the planks aside. Her attempts to lift up the wooden beams however, proved futile; she was already panting from her run, short of breath from being exposed to smoke from the burning village, and had little upper body strength regardless.

Giving up, she walked around the outside of the rubble, calling out to anyone who might be trapped within. It was with some embarrassment she realised she didn't know the names of its former residents.

Frustrated, she stopped. Stooping over, with her hands on her knees, she considered her surroundings while she attempted to get her breath back. The chaos of the last hour had been replaced by an eerie, almost unnerving quiet.

From what she could see, the village was mostly still aflame. Maybe around half of the structures were still standing. A wave of sadness passed over her, the realisation of what had happened suddenly hitting her.

The screaming had ceased, and it appeared she was now completely alone. *Where was everyone?* Unpleasant scenarios flashed through her mind. She worried the people had been taken captive, or worse, slain. She wished she knew if anyone was still hiding. Had anyone else run like her? *What had happened to her home...*

✩ ✩ ✩

Carra had been running an errand on the less populated, west side of Astonelay village, and in some ways she had been lucky, because the raiders had come from the south-east. Yet now she was over her panic and her mind had cleared, guilt was beginning to set in. *Her family – what had become of them?*

After contemplating her options, she remained unsure what her next move should be. It was tempting to go back home, but common sense said she should find somewhere to hide. The next village was six miles to the north. Much too far to run to for help, or at least, for it to be in time to be of any use.

The north of Florinyn consisted of lots of small hamlets indistinguishable from Carra's. A largely flat, forested expanse stretching for 120 miles or more east to west, Florinyn's villages and towns lay sparsely situated and many of them were fifteen, even twenty, miles away from the next area of civilisation. There was some communication between villages but not much; runners who came and went, or occasionally messengers on horses if the sender was willing to pay.

Sawmills had been set up – predominantly by

southerners looking for isolated areas to continue trading, having made their initial fortune through more iniquitous means. Their founders had felled trees by the hundreds, thereby clearing the areas, and the villages had popped up around these.

Unlike the original settlers, these peasants had flocked north to escape poverty with the hope of self-sufficiency mostly through farming their own land, availability of which was plentiful in the north. They built their own wooden shanties in clusters, which had gradually been knocked down and rebuilt over the years, until the standard of living had become more comfortable. They were still made of wood, though, and susceptible to burning. No one would have considered it worth the cost to have stone hauled from the cities in South Florinyn.

Carra's family had a modest house, better than many, due to the prominent position her father held as the town's alderman. Except... it was situated right in the heart of the village. At the centre of the attack.

There had been a rumour passed around the village that an inn on the eastern border had been raided a couple of moons ago. They should have known the information must have had some founding. Maybe, deep down she *had* known, but of course it had been easier to be dismissive. Village gossip claimed the inn had been cheating its residents, that the raid was just a few disgruntled locals, and even that only one or two people were actually hurt. She sighed. *People believe what they want to. Until it affects them personally, that is.*

There had been nothing even remotely covert about the attack on Astonelay. Armed leather-clad men had walked into the city on foot, during the hottest part of the midday sun. She wanted to hate them for it but right now, there were too many conflicting emotions for her to parse out any one. Holding torches, they'd walked – almost casually

– between buildings setting them alight. She had heard their primitive grunts but had no idea how many of them there were in total.

Screams had followed. They'd echo in her ears the rest of her life.

Some of the villagers had run, others had huddled with their children in prayer. The more practical ones had tried to stop the flames using their cloaks or anything to hand. Carra herself had started running for the well. The only semi-rational thought she'd been able to find had been to fill a bucket with water and try to douse the fire. By the time she had reached it, the whole village had seemed to be alight, and her intended efforts reduced to futility.

The men had started attacking villagers. Either grabbing anyone close to them, or using the torches as clubs. Carra had found the body of an elderly male sprawled against the side of the well. Bending down to try and find a pulse, he had turned his head towards her and whispered, "run" with what could well have been his last breath. Was she selfish for listening? It was too late to change that decision now.

☆ ☆ ☆

Carra managed to calm her breathing. There was still no one else in sight, but she was too far away to grasp any clues as to what was happening. She decided she would track the village border, and circle back on herself. Maybe she'd be able to spot her family, or observe where the raiders headed next. The forest would provide her quite good cover, and the village air was thick with smoke, which might help – but really, she hoped her biggest advantage was simply that nobody would be looking for her.

She estimated her position as quarter of a mile from where she needed to be to get a good enough vantage, and she had to resist the urge to run it. The sound of running would surely be loud enough to attract some unwanted attention. Even still, the patter of every footstep, crisp leaves crunching under her feet, made her wince.

She stopped and tried to gain composure, then realised she was shaking. Not with fear, but the adrenaline had built up gradually, and now she was no longer in panic mode, it had all caught up with her. *Breathe, remember to breathe.*

She resisted the urge to wipe away the sweat dripping from her forehead. The sun was particularly hot that day and she regretted her foolishness of having not bothered to fill her water flask on her way out this morning.

Carra still lived with her father and sister, but since she had recently turned nineteen, that had been about to change. She had been planning to join the next convoy to the central market, where she was now eligible to obtain an apprenticeship. Unlike around three-quarters of candidates, she could read and write, and was therefore likely to be desirable as a scribe, a messenger or as a mayor's assistant.

Secretly her interests lay elsewhere. She'd been hoping to do something more hands-on like building or carpentry, although she didn't have enough experience of either to be entirely confident what she wanted. Mainly she'd wanted to secure *something*, and have a better idea what her future was going to hold. The waiting and uncertainty didn't sit well with her. At least she was self-aware – she knew her biggest flaw was impatience!

In the meantime, she had been spending her days running errands to help her father. This day in particular, had started just like any other day. Firstly, Alliana had wanted to go fishing by the river – Carra didn't fish, but she was happy to watch and bathe her feet. Before joining her, she'd had to deliver a letter and read it to her neighbour across the village – which is where she had been when the attack struck.

She really hoped her little sister had still gone

fishing. *Please let her be okay.* They might bicker and tease each other, basically the same as all sisters did, but she was still strongly protective of both her ageing father and little Ally, who was almost two years her junior.

She reached a gap in the trees. To get to the next area with dense enough cover was a distance of several strides. Taking a deep breath, she stepped out – and an arm clasped around her waist. She hit her arms up and down against the foreign arm. "Let go, let me go!" There was no response, but the arm lifted her off the ground, and whoever was carrying her started walking. She kicked backwards, still thrashing about with her arms. She felt sure of her own strength, but nothing was happening. She was being overpowered by just an arm.

She tried to turn her head to catch a glimpse of her captor but he had her in a vice. "What do you want?" she shouted, and then, although not really expecting a response, "Do you understand me?" He grunted. *Well, that could be taken either way.*

She stopped hitting him. She was going to leave it a minute, and then, when he thought she was done resisting, she would surprise him and break free. He relaxed his arm as she relaxed – so far so good.

He continued walking her back towards the village; she was quickly running out of time to escape. Carra could see his feet now – leather shoes caked with mud, and his arm – muscular with dark hair – and… neither of those told her anything helpful. Although, on the other hand, she actually couldn't see any indication he had a weapon.

Only about thirty seconds had passed when he turned direction and she was forced to make her move – it was then or never. She grabbed the arm at the wrist and twisted, whilst at the same time, she threw her head backwards aiming for a headbutt and kicked his right leg just below the knee – being the only place she could reach with her foot.

She made contact with all three but that was where her luck ended. He simply threw her over his shoulder and kept walking, this time trapping her upper arms in his grip as well. Her head was now angled towards his back and the ground. So, not only was the whole thing embarrassing, but she was also no longer able to see what was going on around her. She was really stuffing this up.

It wasn't long before they got close to the village, and Carra started coughing from the smoke, which only worsened the discomfort she already felt from the sensation of blood rushing to her head. She expected him to stop, but he continued walking. He walked past the outskirts of the village, and kept going into the forest the other side, only stopping just before he reached the sawmill.

Entering the clearing, Carra could see what had happened to the residents of her village – or at least, she reflected, the surviving occupants. Lined up in two long rows were any people she supposed they classed as 'able-bodied' men. The raiders were pacing up and down both sides of these lines, with their clubs held out ready to prevent any insurgence.

On their right, there were two dozen children huddled together on the back of a wagon inside a large cage, and on the back of two other caged wagons, there were women sitting around the edges, with their hands tied behind them. Her heart sank. She needed to do something, but the seriousness of the situation has suddenly hit her; she was scared.

Having been dropped back on her feet, she found herself shoved to the ground on her knees. She immediately tried to stand up, but a steadying hand was placed on her shoulder, effectively pinning her down. She applied some pressure against it, but this was met by resistance from the hand clamping onto her shoulder. Squeezing. It started to hurt, but she would not deign to show as such on her face – right then, that was the most rebellion she could muster.

Looking around, at least half of the village men were sporting cuts or minor injuries. A few looked worse – Carra spotted a neighbour, Sam, who was grimacing whilst trying to stay upright on his knees and not fall over. She couldn't see her father anywhere, but Alliana was there, tied up among the women.

Despite trying to remain impassive, a frown formed on Carra's face. The other raiders, any who weren't watching the captives, were sitting around a fire boiling some soup or stew in a large pot. They were laughing with each other, holding conversations as if they were going about their normal business and today was an ordinary day. It made her even angrier.

She clenched her fists to try and release some of the emotion building up inside her. A favourite concentration technique, she pictured the pain leaving her through her knees and fingers down into the ground, and after a short while she could imagine she felt lighter.

She could see now that the raiders numbered about twenty in total – it was so few to take a village of three hundred occupants. They were all male, aged between their mid-twenties and early forties. Whereas mostly of a similar height, they were much stockier than her people. It wasn't just that her people were lean as a result of limited food, they were generally more petite somehow – the raiders all had broad shoulders and muscular arms.

Carra didn't know much about geography; her family had not kept any maps other than a hand drawn diagram showing the positioning of nearby villages. She had little knowledge of the surrounding lands and waters, and couldn't even hazard a guess as to how far away the lands of these invaders lay.

One of the raiders walked towards Carra and she dropped her head, with her eyes on the ground. Her intention wasn't to demonstrate obsequience, she was meaning to project disinterest – but too late she realised they probably assumed it was the former.

Even with her head bowed, she could see the feet walk towards her and legs stop inches before her nose. A hand reached for her, and she couldn't help but flinch.

Fingers grabbed her underneath her chin and lifted her face upwards. She stared back, directly into his eyes, refusing to look away. He held her gaze for several seconds. Before she could feel any relief that he'd at last let go, he hauled her off her knees and dragged her away.

Walking her onto one of the wagons, he commanded her to 'sit'. She did as she was told. Her back was to the bars, and someone who must have been standing watching the wagon behind her grabbed her hands, before tying them around one of the cage bars. They used a thick rope and wrapped it round several times. Surveying those who shared her fate, Carra saw several faces she recognised.

CHAPTER 2

Carra smiled as Alliana turned towards her, but her sister's words were harsh. "When you weren't with the rest of us, I was hoping you'd escaped and, I don't know, made it to find someone to help us."

Her first instinct was to feel affronted. Okay, so she'd gone back to check on her family instead of running to the next village - Alliana of all people should see that it was *her* she'd been worried for. But she was right. Carra might have condemned people she instead could have helped. Guilt set in like a heavy weight. "I... I nearly did but they caught me. I tried. Have they said anything? At all? To anyone?"

"No," sighed Alliana, "I mean, some people were speculating, but none of it was optimistic."

"And father?" She asked hopefully.

Alliana looked away and took a deep breath, "No." Another sigh. "He... well, he got hit badly while he was trying to smother the fire in our dining room. I don't know if he... they dragged me away when I tried to go to him. I don't know if he is okay."

"You couldn't have done anything else. It'll be okay, we'll work it out." She forced the words out, knowing they were what Alliana needed to hear.

It was at that moment, Carra saw one of the other women trying to catch her eye. She was looking over and making a pointing gesture with her head. As Carra tried to work out what message she was communicating, a club came down hard on her hands. Being tied behind her back outside of the cage as they were, she hadn't seen it coming, and it was so sudden she had to try and choke back a tear. She failed. It fell slowly down her cheek. Tilting her head, she wiped it dry using her shoulder. "Quiet!" the man growled. *She'd already got the message by that point.* Alliana was looking at her sympathetically at least, and even mouthed, "sorry" across at her.

Carra wiggled her fingers. They hurt awfully, but it felt like bruising, and she didn't think they were actually broken – maybe one of her little fingers could be, as she couldn't currently move it, but that was minor. She had been lucky.

They sat in silence, from mid-afternoon until dusk fell. The ropes chafed around Carra's wrists, which were now swollen from her injury. She could hear muted sobbing coming from the children, as well as shivering from more people than not. Night-time in the forest brought cold air – especially uncomfortable for people who were still outside in their summer vests and dresses. People who were also unable to move to keep warm.

Aching hands and her concerns over her father were enough to distract Carra from the falling temperature, although her jerkin did provide her with some welcome extra protection compared to many others.

There were things in the forests that only moved about at night; critters and scavengers that would stay away from inhabited areas but harass travellers when it was dark. Carra distracted herself by imagining some of the creatures the raiders might encounter, attracted by their fire, and the unpleasant situations which would result. She shortly had a new distraction however, as the campfire was dampened, followed by which some of the men walked over to the wagons.

Soon they were moving, with three raiders at the

helm. The second women's wagon set off too, but not the others, and it was only a short while before Carra could no longer see them. She supposed they had been waiting until dark to set off and guessed that they were planning on keeping the men separate.

***

Carra watched her surroundings wide-eyed, she'd actually never been more than fifteen miles east of the village before now. She would have enjoyed this trip if it wasn't for the circumstances. The wagons had quickly covered that distance overnight and she had even dozed off briefly, missing much of the journey so far.

The practical part of her brain said she should be watching and memorising where they went, so that should she ever succeed in escaping, she'd be able to make her way home.

The morning brought warmth with a cool breeze that blew her long dark chestnut curls away from her face. The rising sun provided a spectrum of summer colours, the forest whistling with the wind passing through the leaves.

She'd never felt more alive, and Carra wasn't sure if it was because she was worried about what was coming next, or whether she'd just never appreciated her surroundings enough before.

Although they were following a well-used path, they didn't pass closely enough to any settlements for her to be able to see them; presumably that was intentional. She wondered whether news of the raid would even have spread yet. Given they had found her lurking outside of the village, they must have been fairly thorough despite their brutish, unintelligent appearance, so she didn't dare hope that anyone had managed to escape and pass on the message.

: THE LOCKET

The more she thought about it, she wondered if anyone would even care. Perhaps nearby villages would prefer to spend time on their own fortifications, as opposed to rescuing another. However she looked at it, unless someone had strong familial links with Astonelay, she couldn't see what incentive they would have to come looking for them.

As pretty as the scenery was, miles of forest did all look the same after a while. The trees and plants were fairly repetitive in appearance, and as it passed midday, the sun burned down on them making it difficult to find any enjoyment in the landscape. It was a shame as they'd been a welcome distraction from her discomfort. The feeling in her fingers was now beginning to return a bit, but as the numbness had reduced, they'd become more painful. *Maybe she should be glad she couldn't see the damage!*

Sometime just after the middle of the day, the kidnappers stopped and lit a fire to make some food. The smell wafted over to where they had been stationed, and Carra salivated despite herself. Once they'd dismounted the wagon, she was able to get a better look at the three men. There was an older-looking man whose expression she couldn't read, and two younger, angry-looking men both with broad stubbled jaws and dark-hazel eyes.

They were maybe a few years older than she was, and both looked fairly similar facially, although one was clearly much cockier and slightly broader whereas the other, whilst still muscular, was leaner. They sat and ate, not even talking much among themselves. Instead, their eyes kept flickering over to the wagon, watching for signs of movement.

After they had eaten, they filled one of the wooden bowls and carried it round their captives one by one, stopping to refill it a couple of times. Carra had been determined to refuse it, but when they lifted the bowl to her mouth, she found she used the few seconds to drink as much broth as she could.

Something about surrendering to the food made her realise she'd been trying to stay strong in front of Alliana. She was kidding herself really. Alliana wasn't daft – she knew as well as she did that their current prospects weren't good.

She was still none the wiser where they were going or what these men wanted with them. She hadn't even noticed them scavenging, or piling up anything they planned to pilfer, but she supposed that didn't mean they definitely hadn't. Yet, their village didn't exactly have much to offer – any 'wealth' they had held was in their comfortable abodes, which these jerks had burnt down. *They haven't killed everyone so they must want us for* something, she thought to herself, optimistically.

Now they'd refreshed themselves, they set off again. Before long, the path ended, and instead, they were met by a more densely forested region – which they foolishly tried to navigate the wagon through, taking longer than Carra would have expected to realise this wasn't feasible. In the end they had to backtrack as far back as where they had rested. They were left waiting whilst one of the men went to scout another path.

Carra shifted about uncomfortably, switching between sitting on her feet – which made her legs feel dead – and stretching out her legs, which made her backside ache. She wondered how the other girls were faring, as even though she was slender otherwise, she had more padding there than most.

Flies buzzed around them in swarms, landing on the sweat on their faces and shoulders. Carra tried to ignore them, but found herself shaking her upper body and head to try and rid herself of them. They weren't as bad as this when they were moving, and she felt impatient to get going. Their destination might well be worse, she wasn't fooling herself, but known still seemed better than unknown.

It wasn't until long after the sun had set that they

continued on their way. They weren't following a proper path like they had been before and although the trees in this area were sparser, there were still plenty of thickets. The going was slow, and the wagon frequently ricocheted up and down, jolting them. Each time they bounced, she was thrown forwards and her arms were strained, trying to pull away from where her hands were tied.

Carra, who normally could nap any-time, anywhere, didn't get to sleep that night, and she could see she wasn't the only one. In the early hours, the terrain seemed to improve, and they sped up a little at last.

The next day continued with more of the same. Predictably, the sun burned hot in the sky once again, and there was almost no cloud cover to relieve the heat. The lack of clouds seemed to cancel out the effect of the decrease in humidity she'd noticed. Yet the dawn also brought a couple of new advantages.

Firstly, the guards seemed to relax a bit, likely given there had been an absence of any revolt from their quarry. But even better, the swelling on her wrists had gone down, which had in turn resulted in her realising that the rope had stretched slightly. She now had a bit more room to manoeuvre her hands.

The less mean, more indifferent looking of the two younger guards was sitting backwards watching them, so as much as she wanted to test the ropes, she was reluctant to move her hands about too much.

She settled for massaging each of her fingers in turn – and was relieved to find that some feeling returned. Wiggling her fingers as much as she could bear, she persisted through the onset of the pins and needles, until eventually, the pain relieved.

It was difficult to tell whether her female companions were faring any better. She'd been studying her regularly, but Ally certainly wasn't conveying much emotion.

Her sister's dark hair, a similar chocolate-cherry colour to her own – although Ally had straight locks compared to Carra's curls – stood in contrast to the blonde and light, mousy brown locks of the other nine women they shared the cart with.

Her father had never talked about his life before she was born. Carra had gathered from her paler skin and darker hair that she had not been born in Astonelay, but she knew little else. She did have some faint memories of her mother, but not many, and Alliana did not remember her at all. As far as she knew, Alliana had never shown much curiosity. On Carra's part, she'd sensed her father's grief had run deep, and had never pushed the matter. She supposed now she'd never know, but the thought didn't upset her like it once might have.

Cassie and Sandria – close friends, who were only a couple of years older than Carra – had spent most of the journey huddled together,. Carra noticed they had moved away from each other slightly now the sun had reached its peak, but they had been whispering between themselves most of the morning. The guard either hadn't deigned to notice or had ignored it.

The twins, Rosie and Fi, were around Alliana's age and she knew them quite well. Whilst, unsurprisingly, they looked downcast, their rosy cheeks suggested they were well. There were another three girls who were younger still. Carra had spoken to their parents while running errands but not had much to do with the girls themselves.

The two remaining women, who were placed either side of Alliana, she didn't know. They both seemed to be in their early twenties, and Carra recalled that the older women had all been on the other wagon. The person on Ally's right had her head bent forward, giving the impression she was asleep. Alliana caught her looking and nudged the dozer, who flopped sideways slightly. Alliana nudged her again, but she still didn't wake up.

Carra looked to their watcher for assistance, but he had his head turned outside of the wagon, seemingly oblivious. She resorted to coughing to get his attention, but he ignored her. There was nothing else for it. "Water" she called out, "Look at her. She needs help." The man slowly stood up, then walked towards Carra menacingly. Narrowing her eyes at him, she forgot herself for a second, and struggled against her bonds. He glared at her. *Maybe she'd been wrong when she imagined him indifferent.*

Just as he approached and things might have turned sour, Alliana said tenderly, "Over here please, she looks to be in a poor way, please help her." Alliana's softer tone obviously having a soothing effect, he immediately turned, instead making towards the semi-conscious woman.

From where Carra sat, it appeared as though he forced her mouth open, before pouring some water down it. She stirred slightly, and seeming to have assessed the situation as under control, he sat back down.

Opposite her, Carra could see that Alliana looked unimpressed. The woman was still struggling to breathe and was clearly not hale. "What is your name?" She whispered to her. Carra could just about make out that 'Anna' was her choked response. "Anna, you let me know if you feel worse. Just try to relax and keep breathing." It was obvious to Carra that she hadn't had nearly enough water and worryingly, as Alliana removed the woman's shawl to help her cool down, she could see there were large bruises all down her left arm.

They stopped again for food not long after. To Carra's astonishment, they brought the bowl round the wagon first this time. Everyone partook except for Anna, who Carra noticed did not swallow anything when the bowl was brought to her lips. It was fairly obvious she hadn't eaten and Carra was annoyed that this had apparently just been accepted and ignored.

While the men sat and ate their fill, she wriggled her hands, finding that her wrists were significantly smaller. The rope rubbed against her raw skin, where her swollen wrists had been cut by the tight rope on that first day. A shooting pain hit her as the rope rubbed against her, and then again when she reopened one of the cuts.

She persisted.

In the end, her efforts paid off and she felt her right hand fall free of the ropes. After a quick look to establish the men weren't watching, she brought her hand forward to show Alliana. It took her a couple of seconds to get Alliana's attention as she didn't want to make a sound in case their kidnappers heard. It felt like a long two seconds, but eventually Alliana looked up... and straight away shook her head, wide-eyed. Carra almost laughed at Alliana's 'disapproving' face, which in the past she had found so annoying. She swiftly put her hand back behind her and grinned back at her sister.

Carra quickly checked to see who else had noticed she was free. The men certainly hadn't, and she breathed a deep sigh of relief. A couple of the girls seemed to have seen, and she thought Cassie had too, though she was feigning disinterest. Carra rolled her eyes. Cassie irritated her, and she'd always disliked her attitude – a superiority seemingly arising because she was incredibly pretty.

That afternoon's ride seemed much more pleasant than both the morning's, and the previous day's before that. Carra tried to use the time wisely, thinking about how she could make her escape. There weren't too many options as to 'when'. Either she planned it for the next meal break, she waited until she saw a reasonably fast moving stream she could make a run for, or she made a break for it at nightfall.

The last option seemed the most appealing - she

figured that in the dark they may find it difficult to track her; if they even bothered to attempt it - possibly, they'd decide not to leave the rest of the girls unaccompanied. They might not fancy wandering in the dark forest alone looking for her either! The more she thought about it, the more she had herself convinced that, once she was far enough away to be out of sight, pursuing her any further wouldn't be worth their effort.

Her success did somewhat depend on whether she reckoned she could run faster than them – as otherwise, she'd need the slight head-start that mealtime would give her above making a dash for it while they were on board the moving wagon. Of course, it may take a while for them to mobilise themselves to take action whichever course she took. *She couldn't rely on that though.* Finding a stream seemed unlikely, plus that option would prohibit her coming back for Alliana. On the other hand, if she did find a stream, she could go back to her father and get help.

Leaving under the cover of night had the most advantages, but she wasn't sure she fancied the dark alone; although if she successfully escaped, she would have to spend at least one night alone in the dark regardless. Just the thought was enough to make her shiver.

Her conviction was still lacking by the next mealtime stop. When they brought the meal bowl round the wagon first again, before taking any food themselves, that decided it for her. She could have as much as a fifteen minutes' head start if she managed to time it right – and at least some food in her stomach. Dusk was fast approaching, so that might also work in her favour.

After she had partaken of the food, the man returned to his comrades. As usual, they spared frequent looks in the direction of the wagon but, in this low light, Carra doubted they could tell exactly how many women were on-board.

She slid her right hand free. Her heart was pounding fast, and Carra felt her resolve wavering again – but as she looked around, she saw that Anna still hadn't stirred, which renewed her determination to go find help. She used her right hand to pry free the rope around her left, did a quick check the men weren't looking, and she was up. She fleet-footed over to the edge of the cage, tried to jump down as quietly as possible, and then ran for the nearest tree cover. *Drat, I'm certain they heard that. Better make sure I get out of sight. And quickly!*

She called to mind the old map of her father's, picturing it to the best of her ability. The cart had been moving mostly east or southeast, meaning most of the villages were north of where they currently were. She headed the way she thought was north-west. Her village had to be at least fifty miles away from two days' travelling, but she hoped she'd encounter another village on the way who could provide help and lend her a horse. It was wishful thinking – horses were expensive – but she really hoped she'd manage to persuade them to see why the unusual circumstances required it.

In the low light, she could just about see well enough to place her feet without tripping. Weaving in and out of the trees, she ran as fast as she could, but also as lightly. She clambered over bushes to avoid wasting time looking for a clear route; jumping in surprise as an owl hooted somewhere in the distance.

Having only traversed around half a mile, she realised she was incredibly short of breath from her scramble. She could hear the sound of her own breathing contrasting loudly against the other noises of the forest. Two and a half days of sitting in the same position meant her legs felt more than a bit like jelly. She could only pray they hadn't noticed she was missing yet.

After another mile or so, half jogging, half walking, she paused and listened. She thought she could hear footsteps. Another owl hooted, and then a third. Unable to run any further, she climbed up a tree. From the lowest hanging branch, she went up two more, and obscured herself using the foliage. Only now did she spot a gorse bush, which probably would have provided better cover if she had climbed inside it. Before she could change position the footsteps became louder. She held her breath. Another owl hoot. *Of course, they're using owl hoots as signals.* She could've kicked herself for not realising that sooner.

A man approached that she didn't recognise. It probably hadn't even required much skill to track her with all the noise she had been making. She watched him with trepidation as he walked around her footprints, which, she noted, even in the low dusk light were clearly visible in the mud. He looked up. She'd place him as about twenty-five, he was clean-shaven – unlike the other raiders – and had an unusual gold chain which fastened his cloak. The cloak, as well as his trousers and shirt were all black, matching his short black hair.

"Gotcha," he said, a villainous grin on his face. Carra looked around for another tree to jump across to, but the nearest one was still a bit of a leap. Meanwhile, he had started climbing up the tree. Panicking, she dropped down onto the second branch, and then jumped for the floor, missing out the branch that he was clambering up. It was a bit of a jolt, but she managed stay on her feet. As he tried to reach for her, his cloak appeared to catch on the branch. She heard him muttering expletives as she began running.

Her legs seemed to be cooperating again now she was feeling threatened. She couldn't catch a glimpse of him but fancied she could hear him chasing her. Full night had set in now, so it was difficult to see where she was going, never mind whether anyone was nearby.

Eventually, she reached a stream. It was welcome in more ways than one. She was covered in dirt and brambles, as well as no small amount of sweat, and everything ached. The water was still fairly warm from the sun's rays during the day. She bent down and drank some, having not had any since she'd last been in her own home. Once she'd taken the edge off the worst of her thirst, she sloshed the water over her arms and face, trying to clear away some of the mud, and then she dove in. There wasn't as much of a current as she'd have liked, but it was heading west, so in the right direction.

As she started to swim with the flow, she saw the cloaked man reach the bank. She was so busy watching him catch up with her from behind, that she didn't see the other man grab her arm and drag her out of the stream. Again she struggled, but he was far stronger than her. This also wasn't a man she recognised, but by his clothing, he was clearly from the party of raiders.

She saw the cloaked man slink off and hide behind a tree – the raider didn't seem to notice him. He was still watching them though; a hand to his chin, pensively. Carra wondered who he was – but, distracted by her current predicament, soon forgot all about him.

The raider carried her back to his own camp, where she saw the children from her village on board a wagon. They weren't tied up as she and the other women had been, so they had huddled together, and a couple of the younger ones were sobbing. "Shhh," she said "It's okay, it'll be okay." They looked up at her as a group, expectantly. The man holding her backhanded her across her cheek. Carrying her across to a horse, he sat her atop, and tied her arms around its neck.

Holding the reins, he walked her over to the fire, where his cronies were waiting. Telling them he'd be back as soon as possible, he jumped on the horse behind her and kicked the horse into action. It couldn't have been more than ten minutes before Carra found herself back where she'd started.

The scene she returned to was much as she'd left it several hours earlier. On spotting her, two of the raiders stomped over to the horse and an argument quickly ensued. Accusations of carelessness were being thrown around, to which of course they had no defence, so they responded by becoming angry instead. He called the older raider Simeon, and the cockier of the younger two's name was Saul. Carra was thrown from the horse, and Simeon carried her back over to the wagon, muttering to himself about her being a nuisance. She was too tired at this point to put up a fight.

As they got closer, she noticed Alliana was sporting a black eye. *Oh great, I've managed to go and make things worse.* The others looked okay, so they must've seen her and Alliana communicating, likely guessing they were related by the dark hair.

Reunited with her rope – she knew it was the same from the blood stains on it – Carra soon found her wrists were tied behind her back once again. However, this time, they were not tied to the wagon. *Curious.* They procured some more rope and tied her ankles as well. *Oh great.* She nearly fell, but both Simeon and now Saul too had hold of her.

Dragging her over to the front of the wagon, they opened a box in the floor. When they drove the wagon, this compartment would be where their feet were resting. At the moment, their cooking equipment was inside and removing it, they piled it all into a large sack, which they tied to one of the horses. Carra only had a moment to properly admire the two large brown mares before they shoved her into the now empty compartment, and closed the lid.

CHAPTER 3

There was just about enough room for her to curl up inside. She couldn't quite straighten her legs, and she couldn't do anything to try and rearrange her arms so they were in front of her instead of behind. Carra was glad she wasn't claustrophobic. It was dark, but then it was still night, and the only light outside was from the new moon and a few stars.

She heard the three raiders climb aboard the wagon and sit down. The lid of her cabin bucked slightly under their weight and for a horrible second, she thought she might be crushed.

She tested the lid, pushing it upwards with both her feet, and could feel that she was trapped in by the weight of their feet holding it down. *Not that she'd be able to stand up even if the lid was lifted,* she mused. She had already twisted every which way she could and determined there was no way she was going to be able to remove the ropes again this time.

As they started travelling, she became even more uncomfortable. The box shook with the movement of the horses, jolting whenever either of the wagon wheels went over a stone. Not being able to see where they were going meant made the jostles from the uneven lay of the path feel far more extreme.

It wasn't long before her arms and legs began to ache from the lack of movement either. She was desperate for some fresh air. The more she thought about not being able to breathe properly, the more she imagined she couldn't. The night cold seeped through into her bones. She could feel she was beginning to lose herself.

Carra didn't know how long she'd been in there when she snapped. Usually she had remarkably good control over her emotions, but this time she decided she didn't want to. With a single thought, she ceased trying to keep herself in check. In these circumstances she'd earned the right, no she *deserved*, to let it all out.

She banged her feet up, moving her arms as much as she could, which admittedly wasn't much, and she shouted, shouted anything at all – demands to the raiders interspersed with cursing – anything to try and let out her frustration. The box suddenly seemed even smaller than it had before, the air even thinner.

If she stopped ranting, then she thought she would end up in tears instead – she couldn't stop. There was no response from above, she was being ignored. Not surprisingly given that evening's exertion, the outburst wore her out, and soon she dozed off.

✩ ✩ ✩

When she awoke, it was still mostly to darkness. She could see a slither of light filtering through a crack in one of the wooden planks, but it wasn't enough to make her surroundings even remotely more pleasant. Something itchy, likely a spider, crawled across her nose and she sneezed. *Don't think about it. Do* not *think about it.*

The wagon was still moving – happily, the current road was perhaps a little less bumpy – when she heard a voice from above her. They were discussing the mid-morning food break. "We'll have to wake up Eron if we stop, but he hasn't had much kip yet." That must've been the name of the other younger one; the mean-spirited one. The need for him to nap must have won out as they didn't stop for a while after that but, to Carra's disappointment, there wasn't any further conversation either.

When they did stop, Carra's stomach started rumbling. *I hope they don't forget about me!* She wasn't exactly optimistic she'd be fed, so tried not to think about her hunger; but as the three men disembarked, they actually opened the lid!

Eron lifted her up, carried her over to a tree, and sat her against it. Using another rope, he extended it around her stomach and the tree trunk, circling three times before tying it and testing how secure she was. The sunlight hurt her eyes and her limbs tingled with the renewed sensation, but she was so glad to be back outdoors again - and about to replenish her energy.

They fed their captives first again, taking the bowl around the wagon. She anticipated she was next, but much to Carra's dismay they went straight to feeding themselves. Being constrained only a few feet away, she could both smell the stew and see the men as they ate. They ignored her as she wriggled between the ropes and the tree.

Before long they finished, and Eron walked over to her. "We're behind because of you," was all he said as he carried her back over to the compartment and shoved her back in it. He didn't place her in as carefully this time, and actually kicked her legs down so that they fit. She whimpered slightly, but he didn't acknowledge he had heard her.

On the bright side, at least if she hadn't eaten, she probably wouldn't need to relieve herself anytime soon. *This was what they had reduced her to.* Sometime, maybe a couple of hours, after they had set off again, they must have forgotten she was there – or at least not realised she could hear them – as they started up a conversation. They spoke in semi-hushed whispers so that the girls in the wagon wouldn't hear, which made it difficult for Carra to make out several of the words.

Even so, she listened intently in case they revealed anything that might impact her.

Eron was talking about their share of something, maybe gold. They referred to some things she didn't understand and guessed must be place names – from the context that seemed to fit. There were two words though that, disturbingly, she did think she had correctly made out – 'slaves' and 'blackmail'. She had strained even harder to make out the rest of the sentence whenever those were mentioned.

It sounded like they were going to a market for a slave auction. Whilst it would explain how they expected to make gold out of the raid, as far as Carra knew, there weren't any slaves in Florinyn, north or south anymore – and there hadn't been for the last two centuries since the Peasant Revolt. In the southern cities, yes there *had* been slaves, but the poor conditions had led to insurrection, followed by widescale migration of those newly liberated, but poor, folk to the northern sawmills. Those that had fled north had helped establish villages such as her own. Anyone who remained had been left to find work as a paid servant.

The realisation therefore hit her, that they were going to be crossing the border. She cursed her lack of geographical knowledge once again. They were all going to be sold as slaves, in some unknown land, to make coin for these raiders. Carra had begun to feel more than a little nauseated and was certain she was going to throw up. She swallowed the bile rising in her throat, not wanting the men to know she'd heard them. Carra never would have anticipated it but somehow knowing their fate was worse than not knowing, even if she supposed the alternatives could perhaps have been worse. She had a feeling she wasn't going to get any sleep that night.

✧✦✧✦✧

The routine continued. She was let out of her box again, this time at dusk, and they tied her to another tree. Eron still didn't bring her any food but at least she was able to stretch her legs. She noticed this time that Anna was missing from the wagon. That really didn't bode well.

She tried to catch Alliana's eye but failed to get her attention. She'd been too far away to get a proper look last time they'd stopped, but Carra could see now that her black eye had gone a deep shade of purple and spread right down to her cheekbone. *Oh Alliana.* Carra wished she would look her way.

Although she thought her sister was deliberately not looking her way, she also looked deep in thought. Carra tried to remember whether she had seen what happened to Niall - Alliana's intended - during the raid, but she couldn't recall seeing him.

Whilst she had no experience with men, her little sister had possibly lost a lot more in that respect. Alliana was quite mature for her age despite her sweet, naive countenance, but even so, it had been a long betrothal as traditionally they were young to be married, and the ceremony would have taken place next autumn once they had both turned seventeen.

Once married, Alliana would have probably helped in managing their family's wheat farms, rather than following in Carra's footsteps and seeking an apprenticeship.

☆✧☆✧☆
✧✧✧

Back in her box with no food once again, Carra tried to sleep but couldn't silence the concerns running through her head. At some point she must have eventually drifted off, because before she knew it, she was being dragged up again for the mid-morning stop.

Straight away she could see they were no longer in North Florinyn. The trees and vegetation had given way to grassy plains. The ground was slightly boggy, it had obviously rained recently, and when Eron placed her on the ground by the campsite she squelched into the mud. In the absence of a tree, he tied the rope around her waist and then the other end around Saul's wrist. It was humiliating.

Eron went to feed the others, and she noticed he was taking longer about it than previously, leering at the girls. She rolled her eyes angrily. Her stomach rumbled loudly at the smell of food, and much to her shock, Saul actually gave her some from his bowl. *Maybe he wasn't that awful,* she supposed. Then, w*hat am I thinking, being grateful just for a bit of food – it's their horrid fault I'm unable to get myself food*!

While Eron was still preoccupied, and Simeon had stepped away to give the horses some water, Saul retied her hands, so they were in front of her. Another small mercy she was thankful for.

Except… when she looked round, she saw that Eron had untied Sandria and was carrying her off the wagon. She immediately tried to push herself up, but Saul kept a hand on her. She growled at him. "He is taking her down to the river. He is going to let you all wash." *Hmm… well she was certainly the dirtiest of them all, after her little adventure… and some cooling river water would be nice in this heat.*

Lord he was irritating though, "How do you know?"

"Because that's what he said he was doing."

She rolled her eyes at him. Either Saul didn't see Eron for the lecher he was, or he didn't care, but there wasn't much she could do. She expected Saul to ignore her after that, but maybe he'd taken the hint better than she'd realised because he suddenly swooped her up and followed after Eron – checking that Simeon was still watching the other girls on the way past.

He was holding the rope connected to her waist,

and she bumbled along behind him for a few seconds then fell over. When Saul reluctantly turned around, he sighed exasperatedly muttering something about a fool's errand, but he did untie her feet so she could walk. He looked at the bonds he had removed for a second, now in his hands. "Well that's convenient" he said, and tied it in a gag around her mouth. *Great.*

Unable to protest verbally, she narrowed her eyes at him – which meant she was distracted when he set off walking again, ending up two paces behind, and missing any opportunity to walk beside him. He was still dragging her by the rope, but it was at least far more comfortable now she could jog slightly to keep up.

As they approached the river, Saul stopped abruptly, and put one finger to his lips to indicate she should remain silent. Carra rolled her eyes at him again, and when he remembered she was gagged he looked like he had to stifle a laugh. She felt her face flush red, part frustration, part fury. Saul hid behind a tree, from which he could achieve a decent vantage, so she followed suit.

Eron was indeed letting Sandria wash but he also seemed to be helping her, and she didn't look too happy about it either, which *certainly* didn't surprise Carra. She nudged Saul in the side. Somehow, she wasn't really frightened of him. Eron on the other hand... well she wouldn't say she was frightened of him, but he was definitely a disgusting brute.

A day of lying under their feet had acquainted her a lot more to their personalities, which was strange. She wasn't sure when she'd stopped thinking of them as kidnappers, and started thinking of them as actual people – and she definitely wasn't sure whether or not that was a good thing.

Her mind snapped back to the scene before her. Eron was certainly getting a bit... *friendly* with Sandria. He was lathering her back, but his hands were slowly sliding down to her bottom. Presumably having had enough, Sandria turned and said something like, "I can do this myself thank you," which Carra thought was awfully polite of her in the circumstances.

When he did nothing to remove his hands, she saw Sandria turn around and playfully push him away at the shoulder. It looked like only a light shove, and she'd smiled at him as she did so. Eron however, bristled immediately. He spun her to face him, then pushed her under the water and held her head there for several seconds. After about four seconds, Carra flinched in surprise as Saul gave her a kiss on the cheek, and then walked out from behind the tree.

"Stop that Eron, no need to be rough with them, we're almost at the market."

"I'll do as I please!" He let go of Sandria and she came up spluttering. She thought Saul would help her now Eron had let go – but he just completely ignored her.

"Come on Eron, damaged goods are no use to us," he came back. *Charming,* she thought.

As he'd had already proved he was apt to do when caught in the wrong, Eron turned defensive and bitter, "Why are you watching me anyway, did you follow me down here?" She saw Saul turn to Sandria and tell her to go back to the camp. Interesting… maybe her and Sandria could escape.

Carra tried to get Sandria's attention as she walked past but unfortunately, she wasn't close enough, and she couldn't make much sound through the gag. Sandria also looked in a hurry to get away from the men, who were now arguing incoherently with raised voices. It gave Carra pause to study her own predicament. She hadn't noticed him doing it, but while she had been watching Eron molest Sandria, Saul had tied the end of the rope binding her waist to a tree branch above her head.

She wrapped her hands in it, which were still tied, and pulled them downwards in an attempt to use her weight to loosen the knot. It was to no avail. After a few attempts she gave up and sat down on the forest path instead.

A short while later, the boys gave up their ranting, and she saw Eron storm off. He seemed to be taken by surprise as he walked past and saw her sitting there. Saul walked back towards her shortly after. "Did you have to let him see you? Don't you think I'd annoyed him enough as it was?" Carra shrugged, bemused. "Come on, you're a mess. Get washed now while he's gone to fetch the next girl. He seems to like you least of all, I wonder why." She gave him her best innocent look and let a victorious smile slide onto her face as he grinned back at her.

"Turn around then while I undress."

"How do I know you won't run off again?"

"You don't, but you must want us clean for some reason." Saul looked sad when she said that and suddenly, she felt really nervous. Darn it, she'd put her foot in it. He'd just relaxed slightly so she had been going to ask if she could ride in the wagon again. "Just turn around and you can keep hold of that blinking rope and then I won't be able to bolt. It's held me this long, hasn't it? Besides, I give my word I won't."

He turned as she'd asked – at which point she discovered it wasn't so easy to take your clothes off with your hands tied. "Erm...Saul?" Two minutes later, with the rope re-tied around her left ankle, she dived into the stream. It was glorious. Very cold, but oh, that was wonderful in the hot, humid environs. She splashed about.

"What's going on," he shouted.

"Calm down, everything's fine."

"Hurry up."

"Okay, okay, no need to be grumpy."

"You'll be grumpy, if Eron comes back before you're done."

She reached for the soap on the bank and scrubbed the dirt off herself. She could see it washing away in the water. Remembering her hair, she submerged it. Under the water, she caught a glimpse of the knot around her ankle. It was far too tempting to untie it and swim off. *She had given her word. They'd snatched her though! Would she* really *be doing anything wrong...*

She looked around for her clothes. Saul had moved over and picked them up – still with his back to her, she noted. *Hmmm not so dumb is he!* She walked out of the water and started towards him. "There are some dresses in the bag over there." He pointed. "There's one for each of you."

There were indeed some dresses in the bag. Identical, white, old-fashioned frocks. With laced collars and sleeves. "Who chose these monstrosities?" she asked, trying one on. The skirt was puffy too, she bet she looked a sight! She looked longingly at her old clothes, but of course they were caked with mud, filthy.

"Come on then, best get back," Saul grunted. "Wow, there is a girl under all that muck after all!"

"How about you let me wear your pants and shirt and I'll let you wear this dress? I think it'd look pretty on you."

"It looks pretty on you."

She stuck her tongue out at him, "Pretty *awful* you mean. I think this would look garish even on the princess of Florinyn."

Eron and Alliana came into sight at the end of the trail. "Come on, let's go before he gets here."

"No chance. I'm not leaving him alone down here

with Alliana! Surely you don't expect me to..."

"Okay okay," he interrupted, "But I'm not sure you're going to like the alternative much either." She didn't have time to puzzle over what that meant, because Eron approached.

"You take her back to the camp" he demanded, gesturing at Carra, "and I'll see this one's scrubbed. Go and get the next one as well, maybe bring two together next time?" He passed her rope to Eron. *Great, she didn't much like the alternative, no.*

She tried to catch Alliana's eye to smile at her, but she didn't look up. The bruising was still very visible on the side of her face, now in majestic shades of yellow, purple and black. Abruptly, she felt her body yanked backwards, as Eron started walking back. Saul threw her pumps after her and she scrambled to pick them up and put them on her feet while they kept walking. At least Alliana was safe for now – although, it was clear her idea of 'safe' had become relative to their situation.

Lo and behold, Eron *did* try to put her back in the box. She squirmed out of his grip, but he put his hand on her head and started to push. "Stop that you moron." She looked up to see where the shout had come from. It was Simeon, whom she now had a sneaking suspicion was Saul's father. "That box is filthy, and she needs to look presentable. Put her back in the wagon – it's only for a few more hours, how much harm can she do?" Carra wasn't sure which she was happier about, the reprieve from her box or the chastised look on Eron's face.

It would have been the latter, except she was starting to get claustrophobic in there. Whilst she'd never minded insects before, there was something about not being able to *see* them that had made it so much worse. She shivered involuntarily. She hadn't let herself think too much about her predicament before, and she was unprepared for the relief she suddenly felt at not having to be crammed back into that small, dark hole.

She sat on the wagon smiling while the other girls came back in turns, now clothed in their matching frilly white dresses. *Clearly a man selected these.* It didn't take long to realise all the other girls looked miserable. She studied their expressions. It wasn't just a 'weary from travelling' kind of miserable, and she was sure the unhappiness they felt at the raid on the village wasn't still showing on their faces three days later. *What did they know that she didn't?*

One more round of food was brought round the girls on the wagon and, once more, they were off.

CHAPTER 4

Now that she was back in the fresh air again, Carra was able to survey the flat, grassy plain. Unlike anything she was used to, it seemed to stretch on for miles. That patch by the stream where they had stopped and bathed had been much of an exception. For some inexplicable reason, now was the point where it was really sinking in how far they were from home. A wave of excitement washed over her. She was going to see some more of the world. It would have been better on her own terms but, even so. *Am I going crazy? This situation is awful. Although... is it really so wrong for me to try to find a bright side?*

The hours and miles rolled into one. The plants were sparse, and nothing else but muddy tracks and grass could be seen in all directions. She noticed some small birds, and of course there were more flies, but no other wildlife at all. Carra drifted off, before waking to find dusk had already fallen, and that they had finally reached civilisation once more.

Simeon was in friendly conversation with a man, who was standing in front of an exceptionally large set of gates. Speculating, she thought they must have been sixty paces high, if not more. The top of the doors pointed upwards in an arch, which somehow made their appearance even more daunting. Looming out from the sides of the iron gates, were grey stone walls of much the same height. Carra couldn't see how far they stretched. *How many people must this city hold inside it? It's completely incomparable to the three hundred back in Astonelay.*

"Have the other wagons arrived yet?" she heard Simeon ask, but the response was muffled by the sound of the wind. She had been expecting the gates to open for them, but instead, Eron drove the wagon off the path, where they waited overnight. She regretted having slept through the daylight hours, as she was left wide awake with only the chill air and three-quarter moon for company.

She watched the men at the gate, but no one else came or went, and the huge ominous doors remained closed – denying her any glimpse of the settlement or its inhabitants behind.

She watched her companions too – Alliana was sound asleep, as were the others – and she watched the stars. *They* at least looked the same as they did back home. Once again, she was reminded of her father – and then she knew for definite that she wouldn't get any more sleep that night.

Sometime in the early hours, she heard horses approaching. The city provided some light, alleviating the blackness of the night, and she could just about make out that it was another wagon. It was filled with men, and she wondered if it was the men from her village. *It must be.* She craned her neck as far as she could to try and see, but didn't overly extend herself, as she was expecting it to stop in the same vicinity. Instead, it rolled past them and kept going. Onwards, back into the night. It disappeared out of sight, into what looked like the mouth of some caves.

Some time later, she managed to join the dots between this and the conversations she had overheard. They were taking the men into the mines. It made sense these were nearby as she supposed the mass of stone around the city had to have come from somewhere.

Shortly after sunrise, the gates creaked open. The wagon was once again mobilised, and they entered the city. Instead of the fascination she was expecting, her first emotion was embarrassment. There was a certain level of humiliation in being driven around in a cage, and not one she'd want to experience again anytime soon. The residents gawked at them so much that, after turning through only a couple of streets, she felt her eyes welling up.

Her determination not to cry didn't seem to be helping. She dropped her head so that no one could see her face and took deep breaths, counting to five with each one. Her curiosity was definitely secondary to this feeling.

Once she had composed herself, she risked a glance upwards. They were travelling down a street filled with cottages. Like the city walls, these were also made of stone, but rather than imposing, they were pretty, with small gardens in the front and climbing roses curling up the sides. Now they were in a residential area, there were also less people about, and she relaxed slightly.

Whilst she was looking around, she accidentally caught Saul's eye and looked away quickly. Carra knew she had seen him watching her, but she wasn't able to determine what his expression had meant.

The cottages gave way to neat, uniform terraces, and then finally, large municipal buildings. At one of these, the wagon pulled over and stopped. The girls were led off it and shuffled into the building in a line. Carra gasped at the high ceiling, but her attention was quickly drawn away when manacles were clasped around her arms. They hadn't even untied the rope.

She noticed, then, that there were almost no marks left from that beating to her hands and arms when she'd been in trouble for talking shortly after first being tied to the wagon. *Puzzling. I guess it wasn't anywhere near as bad as I'd thought.*

They had been chained together in a linked line, each wearing identical iron cuffs, and Carra couldn't see any way to open them without the key which, conveniently, was in Eron's hand. After a short wait, they were walked in their line back out of the building, and towards what it soon became apparent was the city's market. Strangely, Carra no longer felt as though people were taking any notice of them – quite the opposite in fact – for the most part, they were being ignored, giving the horrible impression that this sort of sight must be commonplace here.

Taken to some manner of tented, holding area, they were left standing, unoccupied, for an hour or so. Although still escorted by Eron and Saul, there were now many more people busily moving about. She thought about asking Saul what was happening but the glare he gave her the second she opened her mouth made her hesitate.

When Simeon made a reappearance, it caught Carra's attention. He looked at Saul, shaking his head, "No luck."

"I don't understand. Why? Will they not protect their own?" Saul responded.

Eron spat. "All that way for nothing." He grabbed Alliana by the hair and shook her, "They're worthless." Alliana let out an involuntary squeal and Carra winced.

"Give them some more time. We can hold onto these two for another week and I'm sure she will have come to her senses by then," Saul proffered.

"Three days tops," countered Eron, "and then they go like the others to the best offer." *Even when she didn't know what he was talking about, he sounded like a real miserly grump.*

They were interrupted when an errand boy, who couldn't have been older than ten, came over and announced they were ready. Together, they were walked out of the back entrance of the tent, emerging at the side of a huge wooden stage.

Saul stayed with them, whilst Eron unlocked the

twins and led them onto the stage, before announcing, "Our first lot today, and it's a good one. We all know how rare it is to have identical siblings and here they are. Who will start me at 10 gold styles?" Carra's mouth dropped open; figuratively, at least. Getting no response, Eron continued, "five styles then... difficult crowd today! Who will bid fifty silvers?" A hand shot up in the audience, then another. In the end, a closing price was agreed of four gold styles each, and the girls were guided back off the stage.

Carra was shocked. She had heard of slavery, of course, as a concept. She had struggled to believe it was still practised anywhere – but she *had* heard them correctly on the wagon after all. Wherever they were now must be vastly different from home. Growing up in Astonelay, even the idea of servants had been frowned upon.

In Florin, the Florinyn capital, slavery had been punished by hanging ever since the revolts. Eron, of course, she had seen for what he was, but she hadn't truly believed Saul would leave them in this predicament. All for a few gold styles? While Carra had only ever seen one gold style before, a sixteenth birthday present from her father and sister, she was not daft enough to think that four styles was a significant sum. Even in North Florinyn, which was much poorer than the more populated south, messengers earned thirty styles a year.

One by one, the remaining girls were taken up and sold. Three gold styles, eighty silver, it went on – and her horror at the situation, and disgust at such a low price having been placed on their lives, did not fade. Neither she nor Alliana had been called on yet and she was sure she wouldn't stand there and allow this to happen to whichever of them got picked first. As the bidding went on, only the two of them and Sandria remained, and it was Sandria who was called up next.

Eron was still revelling in his role as auctioneer, "Our last lot goes for a grand eight gold styles! Didn't I tell you we'd saved the best for last? Join us again midweek and we may even have a treat for you." He finished with a smarmy wink and then disembarked the stage.

Carra saw Alliana was also looking perplexed at the fact the two of them had been left in their chains. She found she was clenching her fists trying not to let Saul see how much this had riled her. Despite the illogicality of it, she felt as though this was a huge betrayal from him. She knew better than to trust him, of course she did. How can you trust someone who has snatched you from your home and brought harm to your family and neighbours. Yet somehow, she had been placing the blame for that evil on Eron and the other raiders – those who remained impersonal to her. Saul hadn't seemed hateful, and his attempts at friendship hadn't seemed fake.

Eron un-clamped the chains, threw Alliana over his shoulder – her feet flailing in front of him – and walked off. Almost simultaneously, Saul grabbed her in one arm. She'd thought they were heading towards one of the municipal buildings, but he walked past it, into a small, terraced house. She'd not realised quite how strong he was – he looked slender in comparison to Eron's stocky, muscular frame.

Once inside, he carried her through a neat kitchen, which had another door at the back. Opening this revealed some downwards steps, and she soon found herself in the cellar. He then used the manacles to chain her to a duct.

She let him walk off – Carra was in no mood to speak to him, which would only have given him the benefit of seeing how incensed she was. Several minutes later, when he returned with some pie and left it on a plate beside her, she still ignored him, and ignored the pie. Of course, she ate it as soon as he left. Who knew when he would next bring her food, and it had been almost a day since she last ate. She supposed they had not bothered feeding them much, as they'd expected they'd soon be sold – becoming someone else's problem!

Carra thought she could hear someone pacing at the top of the stairs, but after a while it stopped, and she was left in silence. She was disconcerted by the fact that Alliana wasn't with her, especially when she knew that meant she must be somewhere in Eron's keeping. There was nothing she could do, but it still pained her. She had failed her sister completely.

Above her head was a small window, maybe a foot wide by half a foot long; not big enough to climb through, but she could see the light fading as the sun set. Soon darkness accompanied the silence. Just when she thought she couldn't take anymore of her despair without losing all hope, Saul brought a coverlet down to her. It was warm and she wrapped it around herself. She fell asleep even before she heard him leave the room.

CHAPTER 5

Three more days passed in that manner, and then a fourth dawned. Saul had come and gone infrequently, bringing her food, and letting her use the outhouse in the garden a couple of times a day. They hadn't spoken a word to each other. Her disgust with him had softened into a resignation, but left a bad taste in her mouth. This time when he'd appeared, she had known change was afoot, solely from the look on his face.

Surely enough, he'd released her arms, and carried her upstairs, where there was a large tub of water for her to wash. He kept trying to catch her eye, but she refused to look at him. It was far better that she didn't let him become 'human' to her again.

When she found herself being walked back to the tent, she felt emotionless. It really wasn't all making a lot of sense to her, but she surmised she was going to be sold as a slave after all.

"I'm sorry" Saul told her, and whilst she didn't let herself care either way, she thought from his tone that he probably did actually mean it. "I really thought we would be able to ransom you and your sister. That's the only reason I agreed to go along with this. It would have ended with you being better off in the long run. It should have done."

"How so..." she started to ask, but she was interrupted by Eron leading her away, and all she could do was stare back at Saul uncomprehendingly. It didn't seem he'd given much thought to all those other women, regardless of his intentions for her.

She was thrust onto the stage beside Alliana, who thankfully appeared hale. Only now could she fully appreciate just how many people there were looking at them – the audience must have gone back thirty rows. Further back, she could see market stalls, and people going about their normal, everyday business. At the other side of the stage, there were some other women lined up, all fair-haired like the inhabitants back home ,but she didn't recognise any of them.

Carra tried to move closer to Alliana, but she was standing proudly, pretending she wasn't letting this affect her. Seeing this, she tried to mimic her by doing the same.

Her distress was prolonged, as she waited apprehensively for Eron to speak. She could tell he enjoyed the power of playing to an avid audience. "I will open with the first offering of the day. Quiet... I said quiet!" She saw him regain his composure. "Didn't I tell you I had a special lot for you coming up, well here we are! Not just one, but two magicians. Two sisters with bloodlines from a powerful family." Carra snorted and Eron frowned at her.

Well really, how ridiculous. That had snapped her out of her brooding. There was no such thing as magic. Although, in fairness, there was no such thing as actual slavery until a few days ago. Even still, this was one absurdity too far.

Before Eron could formally open the bidding, someone shouted "five gold styles." Another, "five gold styles each!" The shouting continued in rapid succession, the atmosphere suddenly frenzied. Carra didn't know where to look, although she was pretty much used to the constant general feeling of discomfort by now.

She turned to the steps onto the stage and saw Saul had slunk off. In doing so, she spotted a movement in the crowd, and a man she recognised shouted, "Fifty gold." The rest of the audience hushed. She couldn't place him at first, but quickly realised where she'd seen him before - he had been down by the stream, dressed all in black, that night she'd made a run for it. It was difficult to forget a face like that, *although* she'd had other distractions at the time. She'd thought him angry before but right now, his stormy eyes glinted mischievously – Carra found herself curious to know more about him.

It wasn't over yet though. Another man, whose face she couldn't see, as he was wearing a hood, called out that he would pay eighty. Then the man she'd recognised called "One hundred gold styles." He seemed to be looking right at her and she dared to hold his gaze. Had he been trailing their wagon all this way, or had he gone on ahead knowing their destination? Or was it just coincidence… albeit a strange one.

The hooded man shouted, "One hundred and twenty gold," and she was momentarily distracted. When she turned back, the mysterious man had disappeared from sight. *Hmmm… probably just as well, given his aggression in the woods earlier, but she couldn't say she wasn't curious*. It was hard to form any opinion on this hooded man as she couldn't see his face. Carra wished she could slap the superior grin off Eron's face, though. She thought about sticking her leg out when he walked off stage, and she'd just about worked up the courage to do it, but sadly he remained where he was, with someone else coming to take them away.

No better nor worse off than before, they were led away from the market by the man in the cowl. She had a great many questions, and not just why he was wearing a hood in the heat – presumably for anonymity, but why? She wondered why in the Lord's name he had paid so much for them, unless he had taken a chance that they really were magicians…

He was going to be sorely disappointed very soon and she really hoped he didn't take out his outrage at the misconception on herself and Alliana. Maybe he'd try returning them for his money back, but that didn't sound great either – they currently had one big advantage, being that they hadn't been separated.

Once they were out of the busier area of the city, he lifted his hood and she momentarily forgot all of her concerns. She was greatly taken aback by his age – he couldn't have been older than twenty-five, and she estimated he was closer to twenty-two. He had floppy brown hair, infatuating large brown eyes and a square jaw. He held himself nobly too; he was possibly the most upright man she had ever seen – and he had to be wealthy to have that much money, so that wasn't surprising. "Names?" he asked in a deep voice. They answered, and Alliana asked sweetly what his name was in return. He responded only by pulling his hood back over his face.

They continued walking and soon reached a neighbourhood that Carra hadn't seen before. The houses here were large, and getting larger the further they walked. Three storey houses became five storeys. She didn't even try to hide the fact she was gawking. Soon they passed gated walkways; where expansive, manicured gardens sat in front of the houses. Then they passed gates leading to residences so far back from the street that you couldn't even see the actual house. It was through one of these such gates they found themselves directed.

As they walked up the path, the house which came into view was in fact beautiful. There were several front columns leading through to an open atrium. The main house behind this was a rectangular structure, with a tower either side, each made with the same grey stone that populated the village – although here it had been painted white.

After walking into the atrium area their manacles were finally removed, and it was there they were deposited. For a split second, Carra thought they had been left unaccompanied, but then a butler appeared from the front door and beckoned for them to follow him.

"You," he said pointing at Alliana, judging them based on their appearances alone. "Down those stairs. Report to Erica in the kitchen. Tell her to house you in the east wing." He kept walking, passing through an ornate dining room, then back to the mansion's main central staircase.

Carra followed him up the staircase, and down a hallway. He stopped and made an enquiry from someone, then opened one of the doors to a room containing two maids. "Where is Mistress Hope?" he demanded. One of the maids responded meekly, introducing herself as Kaitlyn, before explaining that Mistress Hope was currently absent and wouldn't be back until the following morning. "Please show this girl to a bedsit in the west wing and have the Mistress collect her as soon as she returns." He bowed and walked away, leaving her with Kaitlyn.

"Hi," was all Carra managed.

"Follow me" Kaitlyn said, then proceeded to walk down more winding corridors, up two further flights of steps, and past several doors, one of which she opened.

"Whose house is this?" Carra ventured to ask.

"Sir and Lady Strathenberg reside here with their son Nicholas. But you should only speak when spoken to. This is your room." Before Carra could initiate any further conversation with her, she walked out and closed the door. Carra stared at the door, feeling slightly aghast at just being dumped there with no further idea what was to come next.

She walked to the door and tried the handle, but it was locked. The room was not really all that different to her bedroom had been back home. There was a mattress on the floor, a basin in the corner, and a brown chest for clothes. The emotion of the last few days caught up with her, and she slumped down on the bed and sobbed. Finally allowing herself to express her emotions and feel self-pity was a relief in itself.

Once she had pulled herself together again, she got up and took a gander out of the small window situated to the left of the door. It overlooked some well-maintained gardens and she estimated she was around five floors up, and in one of the side towers. The sheer wall below her definitely wasn't climbable, however agile she might fancy herself.

There wasn't exactly ample room to walk about, but she had enough space to perform some stretches, hoping to provide some much-needed relief to her muscles. This was the first time she had enjoyed freedom of movement in a quite a while – it was absurd.

As the day passed by, with Carra still confined to the room, she fought to control her anger at what had happened to them. To begin with, she had welcomed it. She wasn't generally an angry person, but the circumstances seemed to warrant it. When she was ready, she employed the old breathing techniques her father had taught her, visualising the emotion travelling down her arms and out through her fingertips, ultimately dispersing into the air. She was so lost in concentration that the knock on the door surprised her. "Hello?"

"It's dinner time, are you hungry?" said the voice in the corridor.

"Always!" she responded, and happily found herself being led by Kaitlyn down to a servants' dining room, one floor down. Long tables with benches ran the length of the room, and at them sat women with a broad mix of different complexions and ages. Most were wearing one of two uniforms – a long brown dress, which Kaitlyn explained was for the seamstresses, or a knee-length black skirt and white blouse with a small black waistcoat, for those who were maids.

On reaching the front of the dining queue, Carra chose some boiled potatoes and vegetables, then took the closest vacant seat she could find. Kaitlyn asked the other girls to move up so that she could sit by Carra. *She must be on nursemaid duty*, Carra mused. After gobbling down her own food, Carra waited for Kaitlyn to finish and then stood up. Unsurprisingly Kaitlyn copied, so Carra let her escort her back to the small chamber. She probably wouldn't have known which room it was by herself anyway; the corridor had lots of identical looking doors, presumably with bedrooms much like her own behind them.

The mattress was soft, and far more comfortable than anywhere she had slept recently – neither the floor of Saul's cellar nor the box in the wagon had exactly been cosy – yet she still tossed and turned. Although she spent much of the night awake, she did manage some light sleep in the pre-dawn hours, and therefore found herself startled awake when someone knocked on the door.

Her visitor let themself in without waiting for Carra to respond, and introduced herself as Mistress Hope. Carra was to work under her as a household maid, one of sixteen. She explained the schedule – they would be allocated to clean either the dining room, drawing rooms and entrance hall before breakfast. Then at midday, they would move on to clean the dormitories. The more experienced girls would look after the household and any guests, the less experienced would clean the servant areas. There were fifteen main bedrooms, and around sixty servants' rooms – the duties for the latter would inevitably run right up until the evening, and if she didn't finish on time, she would be allowed to break for dinner and resume her work afterwards.

Firstly, the Mistress took her to collect a uniform. Whilst she was glad to relinquish the frilly white gown, she wasn't overly enamoured with the seamstresses, who were sniggering at her quite openly.

Although she now knew far more than she had

yesterday, Carra was still too perplexed by her situation to work out any kind of forward plan. Staying *couldn't* be an option – she needed to go back and see if her father was okay – but for now, all she could really do was wait.

Once she had learnt the routine, and the lay of the place, she hoped she would be able to figure out a viable way of escaping. So, that day, she cleaned. She didn't enjoy it, and although she was able to switch off her concerns and simply focus on the task at hand, it was arduous work. For the morning, she had been assigned to clean a couple of the drawing rooms, under Kaitlyn's supervision.

She was more than ready for a rest when they broke off for breakfast and, having not felt properly full since she was last home, she took comfort in the porridge. Having stopped moving, even if only for a short while, Carra was certain she could already feel her muscles stiffening. Maybe she was imagining it based on how she expected to feel tomorrow, or maybe a week and a half of inactivity had somehow sped up the process, but there was a definite dull ache. She shaped her hands into fists and attempted to massage the feeling back into her arms – it was likely fruitless, but it felt better to do something over nothing.

✦✧✦✧✦✧

Shortly after noon, she started on the bedrooms. She had been allocated ten rooms to clean by herself, with the promise that Kaitlyn would inspect her work later. She found herself alternating between genuinely trying to get the rooms clean and scrubbing half-heartedly while daydreaming. Her arms ached and strangely she didn't mind - the discomfort helped to provide distraction from her other thoughts, which weren't particularly pleasant.

There weren't as many high places to reach up to, which was at least one improvement on the morning's tasks, and a lot of the work involved taking the linen down to the laundering rooms and exchanging it for clean linen to bring back up.

When Kaitlyn arrived to scrutinise the standard of her work, it seemed to Carra like she had mostly met the standard required of her. There were a few extra things she needed to do, but Kaitlyn allowed her to make it down for dinner while the cooks were still providing food, as long as she returned to complete the job afterwards.

While she was eating this time, Carra found she had mellowed enough to take in more of her surroundings, and she spotted a familiar face at one of the other tables. She had to do a double take, but yes, it was Sandria! Scooping up her bowl she moved over to join her.

"How is this possible?" Carra exclaimed excitedly – then didn't actually give Sandria chance to answer. "I'm so glad to see a familiar face. Also, to talk to somebody. I haven't had a real conversation in… well… you know."

"It's definitely good to see you – though not that surprising. This is one of the biggest houses in Rivulet. Plus, Nicholas has a reputation. A certain *penchant* for selecting pretty staff."

"Rivulet," Carra rolled the name over her tongue, "Is that the name of this state?"

"Rivulet's the town. The province we're in is Pellagea. Ironically for us, it's derived from the word pilgrim." Sandria paused and Carra wondered how she'd picked up that particular snippet.

The pause lengthened until Carra managed to ask the question she'd been a little scared to, "So, what's this place like?"

Sandria lowered her voice "A lot of people didn't come by this place the way that we did. In Pellagea, poor families will receive a payment to send one of their daughters to work in a household, or a son to work in a mine. Usually, the second eldest, according to tradition. For them it's an *honour* for their daughters to be here in one of the richer, more prominent holdings. So if you're thinking of pulling another stunt, you need to be careful who you trust." Carra digested that information. She was clearly quite easy to read, and she needed to be careful to be more guarded.

"How about you? Would you be interested in making some alternative plans?" She figured had nothing to lose by asking, given Sandria already had the measure of her.

"I will help you if I can, you know I'm a friend to you. Personally, I'm not looking to leave just at the moment, though. I don't think there is anything for us to go back to. I have no family left at home. Maybe one day I will try to return, but for now it seems safe here and we have companionship from others our own age. Why don't you give it a week or two and see how you feel? Maybe it will grow on you like it has for me." Carra sincerely doubted it would. "Plus, you should see some of Nicholas's acquaintances and then you might change your mind." Sandria laughed at her own words. Given how dejected she'd sounded about Astonelay being a lost cause, Carra was glad she had cheered up slightly.

"Ha ha! I don't think I'm that flighty, but I guess we'll soon test my mettle."

They continued talking into the evening, taking a walk in the gardens after Carra had finished her tasks. Carra did her best to take advantage of the time outdoors - ascertaining that the residence was surrounded by a high wall, but she didn't manage to identify any gates other than the one they had come in via.

She sensed that Sandria may be leading her around intentionally, to show her as much, but they didn't discuss it any further. Instead, Carra explained to Sandria where she'd been for the few days after the others had been auctioned, and Sandria told her about her week as a seamstress.

Having had her fate playing on her mind for days, Carra asked about Anna, and learned that Saul had ridden off with her in the few hours while Carra had been missing. Sandria didn't know what had happened to her, but they'd speculated that he'd taken her to a nearby village to find a medic. It was a pleasant assumption and Carra, like Sandria, was happy to believe it to be true.

It was good to have Sandria around, and strangely, she did actually seem reasonably happy with her lot. Carra knew she had said as much earlier, but she hadn't quite believed it. Although, when they walked past three young men in the garden with whom Sandria exchanged a greeting, she sensed Sandria may have left out a few details.

The next morning, Carra was woken up by a bell ringing, signalling the early start to the day. She could feel the muscles in her thighs and triceps pulling, but somehow, she dragged herself up off the mattress, got dressed and went to work.

CHAPTER 6

Carra's routine continued much in the same vein for a couple of weeks. Whilst she became more familiar with the layout of the mansion, she didn't learn any new information. *Or should she say palace - she still hadn't even seen half of it.* She cleaned during the day, and walked the grounds with Sandria for company after dinner. It was already moving into autumn but, at least for now, the evenings were still warm.

Then, two fundamental things changed. One night, while at dinner, she finally saw Alliana. She was bringing a new kettle of forcemeat out to the server while Carra was queueing for some rice pudding after her dinner. Carra called over to her, but much to her dismay, Alliana simply bowed her head and walked away. At first Carra thought maybe she hadn't heard, so she followed after her, but again Alliana simply gave her a polite 'hello' and walked away.

It was only on reflection that Carra realised Alliana had been less than cordial with her for a while; that perhaps it wasn't a recent development. She asked Sandria, because she couldn't think of a reason why, nor work out when it had started – to which Sandria had replied, "Can't you?" She was still puzzling over this while they walked in the garden, so she didn't notice the man approaching them until he was practically upon them.

He bowed, his wavy tousled locks falling over his forehead, and kissed the back of Sandria's hand, then Carra's. She quickly identified him as the hooded man who had led them here that first day, and she noted he looked even more handsome now he was smiling. She was about to greet him when he spoke, "Good evening Sandria. Carra," her name sounded unfamiliar on his tongue, and his next words were spoken directly to her, "I see you have chosen your associations wisely. I trust you have found your first days here acceptable."

She was slightly astonished at the change that had come over the quiet individual she had observed previously, and only managed a nod – leaving Sandria to reply that it had been lovely to see him, as always. Then, he was gone as quickly as he had appeared.

"You didn't mention you had already met Nicholas," Sandria looked at her suspiciously.

Carra was about to refute that she had, when she realised her mistake. "He never introduced himself." Sandria laughed. *Did she sound relieved?* "He walked us back from the market on my first day here." *Surely Sandria hadn't fallen for him already... but some of her actions did make more sense in hindsight if she had.*

On a rainy morning three days later, Carra was informed of a change in her schedule. From the start of the new week, she would be cleaning the dining rooms in the morning, and Nicholas's room and lodgings in the afternoon. "He has a substantial suite," Mistress Hope informed her, "And he may likely come and go during the afternoon. He will not want to be disturbed, so make sure you remain unnoticed. If you can manage that, everything will be fine." She was also to have alternative work once a week on Lord's day, when she was to report to the stables first thing. *Great, mucking out horses sounded just like her sort of thing.* At least she'd get to go outdoors during the day for a change – just in time for the weather to turn cold.

Carra wasn't sure how she felt about being on dining room duty. It was difficult to be alone with her thoughts because there were two other maids assigned there alongside her, not to mention the hustle and bustle of kitchen workers laying the table for breakfast. The main advantage was the view out to the gardens, and she actually managed to earn herself a reprimand for daydreaming.

She was very ready to escape now – she was getting desperate – but no closer to an actual plan. One thing she did know was she needed to speak properly with her sister; and at least working the dining room shift got her one step closer to this. Carra remained optimistic she might catch sight of her again.

She sat with Sandria at breakfast, as she had been doing every day, but today she seemed a bit out of sorts. "Are you okay? You seem a bit less cheery than your usual self. Normally I'm the grumpy one!"

"I'm fine," Sandria responded, although it was obvious to Carra that something was the matter. She gave Sandria her best eyebrow raise. "Okay, fine. It's nothing. I'm just frustrated because my shifts got changed and I'm back on the servants' rooms this afternoon."

Oh, was that all. "Don't worry Sandria, I have a simple solution – I can just swap with you! You can remain your optimistic, jovial self, and I can continue doing the stuff I'm familiar with too. You're even thinking of us as servants rather than slaves so I can tell you will be fine with whatever life throws at you." *Cringey cliché Carra,* she thought to herself; the words had just blurted out of her mouth.

"That's not it. I mean, it won't work anyway but... It's just, well, Nicholas personally requests which specific maid cleans his room each week. Did you say yours changed too?" Carra now felt awkward, and although she didn't really want to say, there wasn't much choice. She explained she'd been given Nicholas's room. "Don't worry," Sandria said, seeing her embarrassment. "I'd guessed it had probably gone to you anyway. I saw how he was looking at you in the garden. No, don't look at me like you don't know what I'm talking about." Carra blushed.

That afternoon, Carra didn't cross paths with Nicholas, nor did she the next day. She did, however, manage to collar Alliana. When everyone had gone for breakfast, she had trailed behind, and surprised her in the corridor. "Sis" she called out, whilst blocking Ally's path. "Come on, tell me what's wrong. I can't do anything if you don't. I know you, you're kind and sweet, and good with people – you'll forgive me eventually, so you may as well let me help speed it up."

"I... I..." she stuttered, before gaining her composure and righting her slouch. "You left me. The day you escaped. You would have just left me."

Oh Lord. Of course that's how it would look to her. Suddenly she understood. It wasn't that Alliana had taken the fall for her that day, the bruising from that had long healed. No, Carra had been planning to go for help to rescue the others, but that had still meant leaving Alliana to endure her fate in the meantime, and worse, on her own instead of as sisters together. She didn't regret what she'd done, it was all she could have but... "I'm sorry" she said softly to the air; by then Ally was long gone. It raised an important question. Would she still escape now if she found herself given the chance – leaving Ally alone once again?"

✧✦✧✦✧

During her shift following day, she encountered Nicholas whilst cleaning his drawing room. "Hello Carra." Again, it rolled off his tongue. He said it as 'Kay- rahh' - it was annoyingly quite charming.

"I don't believe we've been properly introduced." She curtsied. *What on earth did I do that for?* He looked amused. She could tell because his eyes glinted. He did have nice eyes. They may have been his best feature.

"You just go about your business, don't mind me."

His use of the words 'your business' snapped Carra back to reality. "My business? You mean being held here against my will? Being captured and sold to the highest bidder?" She was slightly embarrassed by her outburst. Not that she hadn't spoken truly, but she'd been impulsive, and lacking in self-control.

He didn't seem riled at all. "I didn't mean to get you worked up. Families compete to send their daughters here, so it can't be such a bad place." His hand brushed her shoulder gently.

"Maybe in Pellagea or wherever this is, but where I'm from that's just not an acceptable way to act."

Suddenly his hand clasped around her arm, and he stared her down, "If I hadn't bought you, think where else you could have ended up. I'm trying to help you." She was stunned into silence.

He lounged in an armchair and began to read, while she continued cleaning – as if the exchange had never happened. Every now and then she felt his eyes on her but whenever she turned around, he was engrossed in his book. Moving to the bookcase to clean, she pretended to be immersed in what she was doing, and didn't turn around at first. Then when she did, she caught him look away quickly. *I knew it!* "Do you mind?"

"No, not at all."

"That is *not* what I meant. I'm not cleaning in here if you're going to sit and watch me."

"I'm not leering at you, I'm just curious about the magic you supposedly possess."

Carra laughed. "I'd forgotten all about that nonsense." She thought things might become awkward, but that was the end of the conversation. He got up, turned his chair away from her, and continued reading.

She finished about an hour before dinner, and he brought her over a glass of water, which she appreciated. Except, to Carra's horror, he began to inspect her cleaning efforts.

"Not the most thorough work I've seen. This shelf still has a coating of dust, and these windowpanes don't look touched. This table, you missed a whole patch here, see?" *Was he purposefully making her feel discomforted, or was he actually that meticulous?* He certainly seemed to be enjoying himself more than she thought was reasonable.

At dinner that night she questioned Sandria, but she was obtuse in her responses. Even once in private, when they took their walk in the gardens, they talked about Alliana and what Carra's options were, and there was no discussion of Sandria's interactions with Nicholas. Still, she was glad for the walk. As usual, it helped her relax. She set her mind to appreciating the autumnal shades the leaves had turned – the gold, amber and reds lit up as the sun set – and tried not to feel homesick.

Her body seemed to have adapted to her new programme, and although the adjustment had been gradual, her muscles finally no longer ached. That, coupled with her exhaustion, meant she fell straight into a deep sleep.

CHAPTER 7

Throughout the week, she'd felt Lord's Day creeping up on her, and now it had arrived. Carra didn't have to report until mid-morning, and she slept through breakfast, then had a long hot soak in the ladies' bathhouse, enjoying the quiet immensely. She felt refreshed and ready for the day, but she was still grumpy that she had to work, when previously she'd had the day free. She wondered if she was being penalised for not joining the morning prayers – but she was far from alone in that regard.

By the time she arrived at the stables, she had determined to make the best of things, but the stable master wasn't there. One of the stable hands told her he was out riding with the Master. She hadn't realised he meant Lord Strathenberg rather than his son, until Nicholas turned up. *Oh great, now he's going to know I got something wrong and turned up at the wrong place or time, whichever it was.*

"There you are angel."

"Me?" She made a show of looking around for anyone else he could be talking to. "I assume you are saying that ironically, I'm nobody's angel. Unless that's the name of your horse?"

"Of course you. Do you think I paid ten times the going rate for you just because you're comely?"

She didn't have much experience with flattery, but her gut told her he was laying it on a bit thick. It was almost like he wanted something from her. She wondered…

"Well it wasn't because I'm a magician, or I would have magicked myself out of here by now!"

He studied her face. She wasn't sure where to look. However good-looking he was, he had a talent for making her uncomfortable. "Interesting. Did your parents never discuss your heritage with you? Clearly not," he continued. "Hmmm. I was planning to give you lessons, and test your limits, but first we will have to start by investigating your talents. Back to basics."

"Well I can play the piano, but not as well as my sister, and we've established you don't think much of my cleaning skills." When in doubt... sarcasm was always a reliable answer.

"Be serious Kay-rahh. Let us walk into the woods and talk. Magic, of course, is as real as you and me. True, it is not accepted in Florinyn as it is in Pellagea, those with talent will commonly hide it from their neighbours, but I had not realised that the prejudice had run so deep as to wipe out the skills' existence from common knowledge." However sceptical she might be feeling, he certainly believed what he was saying to be true. *Should she play along?*

"So, do you also have, erm, *abilities* in that sense?"

He took one of her hands in both of his. "To know someone's power is, to borrow a well-used expression, to see into their soul. It is an intimate thing, shared only between siblings and lovers. You are mine and therefore I own the right to the knowledge. I do not owe you this knowledge in return – and you have not earned it."

"I see," she said, pulling her hand back, though she wasn't sure that she did, "But how can I discover a talent if I can't visualise it."

"I did not say that I wouldn't tell you. Rather, I was making you understand the gravity of what I am sharing with you. I do not have a strong talent, regretfully my bloodline has been weakened through the generations. My power is more of an affinity. Do you see the gardens around you?" Of course she did... but he paused, so Carra nodded in response. "The variety of herbs all growing in the near vicinity of each other?" She nodded again. She knew enough about woodlands and forests to know that the variety of plants growing in a small space, and the way the gardens thrived at this estate was not typical.

"I see seeds planted to grow herb gardens, and an estate that has several groundsmen whereas others have one, nary mind forests which have none and are left to grow wild. I don't see anything tangibly supernatural." She shook her head in confusion. "I'm sorry, I don't mean to be so sceptical, it's just a lot to take in and I don't know if I understand."

"It's okay. I'm glad we are being honest with one another. As I said, my gifts are minor and to my family's embarrassment, I was not considered eligible to study at Whistlake Academy. You may have noticed that my comrades have been absent since the weather turned, and that is because last week they were called back for the new term."

"I haven't really been here long enough... so what other talents are there, and how would I know if I had one?"

"No, of course. Give me your hands. Close your eyes." She did as she was told. "Imagine you can feel the blood circulating around your body, through the veins in your arms, through the arteries in your neck, and back to your heart. This will be your lesson today. Relax and feel the workings of your heart. Become aware as it beats." She tried to do as he said but she was far more aware of him holding her hands. She raised one of her eyelids and peeked at him, but he also had his eyes closed. She tried to slow her breathing and calm herself. Then tried again.

After a few minutes without either of them moving or speaking, she felt more comfortable, and in the right headspace to make a serious attempt at it. This wasn't so bad. Better than cleaning. She definitely thought she had grasped the feeling Nicholas had been encouraging her to look for – that sense of a flow around her blood vessels – and Carra understood what he had meant by it now. She didn't want to get ahead of herself, but if she learnt something new, it might even change her opinion on staying. The idea she might have magic sounded pretty exciting. The feeling she'd hit upon faded as abruptly as it had begun.

"You got it for a second then, didn't you? I could sense it." Nicholas asked.

"I think so, yes. It was pretty much exactly as you described."

"It's not really your blood you can feel. No one can feel their blood circulating. It's the power attached to your red blood cells that surges with the oxygen. That proves it, then, I was right." *He is obviously rather pleased with himself, but does he seem strangely excited as well?*

"You were right? How did you even know? Surely you can't have just taken it on the word of Eron, no one in their right mind would think he seemed trustworthy, regardless of whether they knew him or not."

"Eron... was he the auctioneer? Yes, I did. I believed him for two reasons – there was someone else in the audience bidding very highly for you – and the way you were looking at each other made me think he knew something – and secondly, your complexion. It's very unusual for a Florinyn peasant." He raised an eyebrow at her and Carra studied him, trying to see if that was the whole story. She felt like she was still missing something. She pursed her lips and frowned. "I may have my suspicions about your heritage as well." he added, meekly.

"They must be wrong. My father knew nothing about magic and I don't know anything about my mother except her first name and her hair colour, so how could you possibly know who she was?"

"Like I said, suspicions not facts." He put his arm around her shoulders. "Let's head back, I think that's enough for you to digest. Why don't you take the rest of the evening off. Maybe don't mention to anyone else about the magic, you wouldn't want to draw prejudice from others." He phrased it as though he was trying to look out for her, but his tone made Carra feel like it was meant more as a command.

As they walked back together, Carra saw the light was fading. She hadn't appreciated quite how long they'd been out there. They had probably missed dinner. Her stomach rumbled loudly just at the thought, and she realised she'd stupidly missed both meals today. She was contemplating how sympathetic they might be in the kitchens as they emerged from the trees. Sandria was sitting alone on a bench, and pretended not to see them as Nicholas walked off into the house. Distracted from her previous thoughts of food, Carra sat herself down beside her.

"Be careful," Sandria said, rather bluntly.

"Don't be jealous Sandria, that was not what you are thinking." *She really was rubbish with words sometimes. She hadn't meant to say that quite so... directly.*

"I'm fairly insulted that you would accuse me of envy. I'm only trying to advise you, as a friend, that materialising out of the woods with the son of the Lord here may not be too popular with others who may see you. You might want to consider protecting your own feelings as well. It is both difficult and unpleasant to be rejected by someone you have already grown emotionally attached to."

"Sorry, you're right. I know you mean well. It's been a strange day. You really have got the wrong idea though, I don't have any romantic interest in him." Sure, he had a certain appeal – and she had almost no experience with men – but she felt certain she would know if she felt anything for him.

Moments later, and thankfully before Sandria could ask her to elaborate any further, Nicholas reappeared. Carra was surprised; it looked as though he was walking towards them.

"Good evening, ladies. I seem to have kept Carra from her dinner. Will you both join me for a picnic on the lawn? I have some sparkling wine – and I know it's extremely popular at the moment." Accepting his invitation, they stood, and he linked an arm with each of them, before leading them towards the front of the house.

The first thing he procured from his basket was a rug, and as soon as they were accommodated, he poured out three glasses of the wine; it was delicious.

As might have been expected, the picnic was lavish. There were delicate sandwiches, unfamiliar fruits, and mini gingerbread pieces. Carra tried *really* hard not to eat too much in one go, but that soon proved an unrealistic goal, and she settled instead for simply trying not to embarrass herself while feeding her face. The conversation was slow at first, but the alcohol soon loosened their tongues. Carra was used to ales but had rarely experienced the luxury of wine – and never wine of this quality. A couple of times, she spotted Nicholas topping up their glasses, but he was refilling his own at the same speed.

After they had finished eating, they remained seated together, and talked. Carra commented that the stars looked just the same as they did back home. They were sparkling brightly, and the moon was only a newborn crescent. She heard Sandria craftily ask, "I do believe you're trying to get us inebriated sir."

"Two or three glasses of wine is hardly ample." he smirked. His face was a bit blurry now, but his eyes were still huge.

"Sparkly like the eyes." she heard herself say.

CHAPTER 8

When she woke up to the bells the next morning, she wasn't sure how she had ended up back in her room. Her day only got worse when she found out her shift hadn't changed, and not only that, but it was now confirmed for a full month. At breakfast, Sandria informed her she had fallen asleep on the picnic rug, and that when they had turned in for the night, Nicholas had carried her up to her room. Carra was mortified. Sandria, on the other hand, found her dilemma hilarious.

Then - having thought she'd successfully managed to avoid him - right at the end of her shift, much to her chagrin, Nicholas showed up. She should have known she wasn't going to be lucky enough to avoid talking to him; it was just one of those days. *Here it comes...*

"You were entertaining yesterday evening. You should let yourself be happy more often. I think I may owe you an apology though, I am guessing that drinking wine is not, shall we say, an acquired habit?"

"Do not think me such a peasant that I have not ever drunk wine. I am merely not used to drinking it in such quantities, especially not when someone is topping up my glass on my behalf." He really did manage to *constantly* get her back up. Carra honestly didn't even know anymore whether or not he was doing it intentionally.

"You mistake me, I meant it kindly. Working magic can leave your senses heightened to food and wine, which is probably why you were feeling the effects more acutely than

Sandria." Carra blushed at the comparison. "How are you feeling today?"

"Fine, as petulant as ever."

"The best way to strengthen character is to identify our own flaws."

"Now *you* are mistaking *me*. I am not generally petulant of character, but rather as a result of the situation I find enforced on me. Good day Nicholas." Having been so blatantly dismissed, he bowed his head to her, and left her be. Maybe she had spoken too rashly, but she was in no mood to humour him right now.

About to take her evening walk with Sandria, Carra was delighted to find Alliana coming to join them. She couldn't quite believe something had finally gone her way. Her sister was polite and well mannered. It wasn't exactly like things were back to normal between them, but the interactions were cordial, and it seemed like they were at last making proper progress on the repair of their relationship.

☆☆☆

It became a regular occasion that Nicholas would stop by and talk to Carra each day and strangely, she began to look forward to it. She didn't know many people there so it was nice to have someone to talk to, and his company was pleasant, but it wasn't just that. As she got used to his mannerisms, she began to feel as though his attention and flattery were actually a complement – even if she continued to tell him otherwise. Mainly, however, it was Lord's Day that whet her appetite with anticipation. She told herself she wanted to learn more magic – and truly she did – but she found she was also looking forward to spending more time with him.

When the next Lord's Day came around, she skipped down to the stables. Every night, she had been practising that state of mind she'd achieved the week prior, but so far, she had only managed to find it once more. She had convinced herself that Nicholas's presence was going to be helpful to her. Yet much to her frustration, Nicholas wasn't there when she arrived, and she tapped her feet impatiently while she was waiting. She was even on the verge of going to his room to look for him when he appeared.

"You show what you're thinking on your face Kay-rahh. I am only a quarter of an hour after our meeting time. Come along, we will go into the woods again where we are less likely to be disturbed." He set off, abruptly, and she had to jog slightly to catch up.

"Here, let's sit down. First of all, as much I approve of the maid's outfit – I mean, I did instruct the seamstresses myself," he paused and grinned to himself – then, seeing her reaction, added, "I'm joking Carra, I'm joking. I just wondered why you are wearing it today? Have you been doing some extra sweeping for kudos?"

"Erm. How about I don't have any other clothes?"

"Oh. Right. That does make sense, I suppose. I will have some made for you then."

"What about all the other support workers in your household? I don't want anything the rest of your staff don't have."

Nicholas started laughing. "I didn't like to say. I guess you offended someone. Everyone else *does* have extra clothes." Oh. "I'm not sure how you managed it – after all, you're always so polite to me."

"Can we talk about magic now or would you like to ridicule me some more?"

Nicholas stared at her for a few seconds, as if he were contemplating whether or not to laugh at her any further, before deciding against it. "Hold your arm out like so. Let us go back to the state we found last week in which you were aware of the magic within you. Close your eyes like before. Take three deep breaths, slowly, very slowly." She found the state almost immediately. "Good, perfect, I can sense you're there from the static, it feels like you're emitting a buzzing sensation. Now, picture the charge traveling down your arm and out of your fingertips." It happened exactly as he had described. It was like a surge of lightening running down her arm. *That was amazing.* She waited for him to speak, expecting praise. Instead, she got a, "Hmm."

"Hmm...?"

"Yes, hmm." Carra opened her eyes to see what he was 'hmm'ing' about, pulling away from her enlightened capacity. She couldn't see anything.

"I can't see anything?"

"Exactly. Something should have happened."

"I'm sure I felt something. I know I did something. Please could you show me what happens for you?" She watched, as he extended his own arm. Nicholas kept his hand clenched until the last minute, and when he opened it, the ground around his hand tremored very slightly. He pulled his arm back to his side, and much to her amazement, Carra could still see the ground shimmering slightly, in a ring around where each hand had been. Cautiously, she reached out and stroked the ground. It felt the same as any other patch of earth, except... perhaps there was a slight tingle in her fingertips where they touched. She couldn't decide whether she was imagining it.

"As I said, my power is not very strong. If you didn't have magic, you wouldn't even be able to see anything at all right now."

"It's incredible, but why did nothing happen for me?" She tried to hide the disappointment from her voice. They tried again, and although Carra could still feel something, Nicholas couldn't see it having any impact, and neither of them could see any visible remnants.

"Why don't you try doing it with your eyes open. Usually for novices, closing your eyes helps for obtaining the trance-like state, but maybe in your case, you need to visualise what you're doing." Carra continued trying, but with her eyes open she could not achieve the necessary frame of mind.

With the day now at its hottest, they stopped and had some drinks. Nicholas pulled some brandy out of his pack and poured a couple of glasses. It smelt delicious, but she wasn't too sure it was a good idea after last time. "If I drink without any food, I don't think I'll be able to keep going this afternoon." Unfazed, he pulled another bag out of his pack, and out of that, some more of those dainty sandwiches.

After they'd eaten, Carra tried again. There was some progress - she managed to produce her lightning bolt with her eyes open – but there was still no visible impact of her efforts. She tried waving her arm up and down as she did it, clenching and unclenching her hands, pressing her fingers to the ground. Even calm, serene, Nicholas started to twitch, and she could tell he was perturbed. As the day went on, the more flustered she became, and the less chatty Nicholas became. With still a couple of hours left until the start of dinner service, they decided to call it a day.

Carra stayed in her room the rest of the afternoon and didn't bother with dinner. She was annoyed at herself for doing so, as she knew Alliana would want to see her – her sister had drawn the short straw and was working that day, although she'd been given tomorrow off in its place. But she felt like she'd failed Nicholas, and somehow let him down. Rationally she wasn't sure why, because as far she could see, she hadn't done anything wrong – it was almost as though he'd projected his feelings of disappointment onto her, because she was absolutely certain that she knew what Nicholas was thinking.

✧ ✧ ✧

On Monday and Tuesday, he didn't come up to his room while she was cleaning. It didn't make a difference, Carra already knew she had been right about how he was feeling, but having to wait for him to forgive her was frustrating.

On Wednesday, he reappeared, and she thought she would have her chance.

Having walked past Carra while she was cleaning the living area, he went into his bedroom, then came back out five minutes later with a book, giving her a 'hey' as he left the room.

It wasn't until Friday, when they shared some orange juice after her shift, that he seemed back to his normal conversational self. She was still nervous about trying magic again. *What if she still couldn't do what Nicholas wanted?* She was desperate to confide in Sandria, but couldn't get past her concerns about how she would react to the idea that she was trying to perform magic. Carra supposed she could have spoken to Alliana instead, but though they were amicable again, there remained some tension between them.

She decided to wait until Lord's Day, when she asked Nicholas for his opinion regarding Alliana. "You pose an interesting question. I am pleased you have asked me for my feelings on it, and that you have been listening to my lecturing on the intimacy of this. Magic is usually only found in the eldest child of any family. In strong bloodlines, it may also be found in the second born, although almost always in a significantly weaker form. Even though magic is more openly discussed here, it is still highly coveted, and I would caution you against talking to anyone other than myself. If you did decide to go ahead, I might also advise you to wait until you can show her the product of your magic. I'm sure you can remember your own reaction when I first told you – you needed proof. Regardless of what you decide with your sister, I want you to feel as though you can confide in me."

Carra wished she hadn't asked. For some reason she couldn't shake the feeling she'd offended him. Consequently, she decided to keep quiet and let him lead the conversation as much as possible. When they reached their usual spot, he laid down a blanket for them both to sit on, and she started to relax again.

She now found the peaceful state of mind very easy to attain, but again, there was no sign of her magic actually doing anything. There was one small positive in spite of this, Nicholas was indisputably less agitated. *He must have been better prepared to see me fail.*

When they stopped for lunch, she asked him if he would tell her about the different types of magic; or at least, those he was aware of. She figured it would be interesting to learn more, but she was also harbouring a slight hope there might be a type that wasn't visible. Even better still, maybe she'd feel a kinship with one of them, and then she could visualise a specific response next time she tried to call upon it.

"The most prevailing magics are related to the elements. For example, probably the most common power is being able to exert some measure of control over the air. These magicians can produce a cool breeze, or a strong wind – there is a full scale according to ability of the user, and there are several high mages who can produce tornado-like blasts. Only slightly less common, is a sympathy for water. That power works a little differently, and these mages can seek out anywhere there is water nearby. They can also manipulate waves to some extent; again, depending on the power of the user. Earth is… well, earth is where I sit, and it's usually a weaker, less desirable power. It functions more as an affinity for nature. Then, fire magic is the rarest of the elementals. Although it can manifest strongly, using it will quickly weaken the caster, making fire mages inefficient."

"Did you say there are other types as well? Can a magician have more than one leaning?" She queried.

"Patience, Kay-rahh. So many questions. Have another piece of cake and I will continue. Yes, a magician can have more than one power, but again, this is rare even amongst those accepted to study at Whistlake. A register of high mages is kept there. Their identities are not shared openly, but I understand there are around fifty magicians classed as high mages at the current moment." He paused to check Carra was still listening as she'd stopped to look at her fingertips.

"Please go on Nicholas, it's fascinating… and the cakes are delicious."

"Any other powers are less known because, as I told you, the community is highly secretive. There are very limited exceptions, during which information might be shared. Those who are called to study at Whistlake Academy are allocated a tutor who works with them to evaluate their potential. Often students are also 'buddied' to help them develop. So, whilst there is a general idea as to what other specialities exist, few people really understand what these magicians are actually capable of.

"Sometimes, magicians are able to cloak nearby objects to remove them from sight. That's a power often found hand in hand with wind magics. I have also heard of, but never seen, magic related to heat or ice. These would of course be variations of the fire and water powers – as I say, most affinities seem to stem from the elements. There are many other, rarer powers too, but there is limited information on the extent and nature of these. Not knowledge I myself am privy to."

That was certainly a lot of new information. Carra thanked him, but needed a while to reflect on it, and Nicholas seemed to understand. When she felt ready, she tried again.

"I definitely feel as though I can imagine the magic itself more, but none of those types you described seem quite right to me yet. Maybe… what if we moved to some water? I could try blasting different surfaces?" Carra was impressed with herself for staying so optimistic. Disappointingly however, neither her suggestion, nor any of the others they came up with later in the afternoon, led to any new-found success.

CHAPTER 9

A few weeks later, Carra was informed there would be a change to her duties. She would still be cleaning the dining room in the morning but would now be cleaning some of the guest bedrooms in the afternoons.

Nothing else had changed with regards to her situation. She had accepted she wouldn't be able to leave for a while; winter was not far away, and now was not the time to be travelling. The evenings had already become cooler, and the leaves had mostly fallen from the trees. Carra and Sandria were, however, still braving their after-dinner walks, often now joined by Alliana and Nicholas, but these had been reduced to a short once-around-the-grounds. When they were a party of four, they would retire afterwards to one of the drawing rooms for a tipple and a game of whist.

She had been unable to do as Nicholas had asked regarding her magic, and they spent much of their time on each Lord's Day talking. He was doing as much as he could to make her feel relaxed, and they had developed a strong companionship, so she still found herself looking forward to their time together.

Yesterday, he had brought the shift change up during their conversation, explaining he had decided this would be a good idea to stop others becoming suspicious of the amount of time she had spent allocated to his rooms. She had been about to feel insulted when he had lent in towards her and brushed a strand of hair back from her face. Leaning backwards in surprise and pushing her back against the wall, he had arched in, placed one hand on the wall above her head, and kissed her.

It had lasted a few seconds, and she could tell from the sweet taste of his lips that he had already been drinking wine that afternoon. The weirdest part was that it felt like they'd been building up to it for a while now. The more their friendship had developed, the more she'd begun to understand his intentions.

She was still daydreaming happily as she started work in the dining room for the morning shift. So determined to do a thorough job, she ended up being caught still polishing the silver as the house and their guests arrived for breakfast. In her haste to get away quickly, she almost – *almost* – didn't notice Alliana seated at the table. She was seated amongst some of the other guests, between two ladies whom Carra didn't recognise. Before she could take in any more details, Carra realised she was gawking and hurried out of the room.

On reflection, Carra realised that Alliana had been wearing a navy frock and she wondered how she'd come by this. Nicholas had never actually come good on his offer to get her some more clothing, however after his suggestion, she had asked Sandria and through her, managed to procure a couple of simple but pretty skirts and blouses. She shook her head and dismissed the thought that was slowly building in her mind. Her sister was so good-natured, she'd probably just charmed the seamstresses. In fact, Carra reckoned they probably had loads of nice clothes available for people they actually *liked*.

☆☆☆☆

That evening, Nicholas and Alliana joined them in the garden again. They naturally fell into a two-by-two formation, with Carra and Nicholas lagging behind the others. "Kay-rahh. This is how things must be." he condescended to her. "You can join the household, take a guest suite as your residence, and relinquish your chores once you also find your magic. Alliana is now of a higher standing, but you must continue to be a maid until you can show you have the same power." His voice was soothing, and he held hands with her as they walked.

It wasn't explicitly discussed between them, but the implication was that Nicholas had also been tutoring Alliana in developing her magic. Carra ignored his lack of honesty – for the moment – in preference of a question which was currently worrying her more. "What if I'm not able to ever find it?"

"You know in your heart that isn't true. If Alliana has proved herself, it is written in the laws of magic that as the eldest sister you will be able to too. I would ask if you are sure your parentage is the same, but the two of you look so alike, I believe there can be no doubt."

"Yes, we had the same mother and father both." Nicholas ignored her use of the past tense and they continued walking in silence until they caught up with Sandria and Alliana who were sitting on a bench. They both looked up, waiting to take their cue from Nicholas, who led them all inside.

While he poured them each a glass of wine, Sandria broke the awkward silence by asking about the country's history. "Is Rivulet the largest city in Pellagea?"

"No, Rivulet is one of many cities. It doesn't have as many residents as others, but its central location within Pellagea has led to its status as a trade hub. The ruling family live in Rivulet as a result, and that is why you will find much of the country's nobility on this avenue. Unlike Florinyn though, the 'king' and 'queen' are merely figureheads here, and don't have much power. Instead, the power resides with the high mages, whose council meetings of course take place at Whistlake."

"How do Pellageans perceive the Florinyn way of ruling?" Alliana politely enquired.

"Are you sure you want my opinion on that Ally?"

"Niko, we northern defectors have no love for the Florinyn cities. Be honest and then we can have a scholarly debate." Carra wondered when Ally had started to sound so grown up.

"Yes, tell us Nicholas," Sandria chimed in.

Nicholas sighed. "Obviously, we have our reservations. Magic is a large part of our lifestyles and, well, I may not agree with the high mages on all of their rulings, but at least we are a tolerant society. The prejudices against magicians run so deep that many of us would not even venture into Florinyn."

Carra watched Sandria, but she had no reaction to the conversation about magic. She was seemingly aware of its existence, presumably from her time here, but she didn't see any indication of a deeper reaction – either prejudice or knowledge about Carra's supposed ability. "Tolerant?"

"Go on Kay-rahh. What is it you wish to say?"

"At least we don't go around kidnapping people and selling them as slaves in Florinyn! Tolerant indeed. What about the right to freedom?"

"Like I said, there are many things that I would also criticise our own State for. However, you cannot deny that punishing someone by death for being born with an inherent ability is inhumane."

"Is it true though?" Sandria came back, "I've never heard of a sentence actually being carried out. Other than the example of Prince Theodore, I've never heard of an actual conviction, and he was banished not murdered."

"Of course Theodore was banished, he was the royal

heir. No mother would condemn their own son, and she pleaded for his life. I do know of some who have been less fortunate however, as well as others who have fled over the border to Pellagea looking for safe haven."

Alliana, ever the voice of reason, asked about the administration of laws, while she stood up to pour some more wine, and Sandria passed some sweetcakes around the table.

✧ ✧ ✧

Carra had been trying for a few days to gain an audience alone with Alliana, and in the end, she was forced to sneak away in the middle of her shift. It was strange heading to Ally's new chamber; her reward for finding her magic.

Alliana seemed pleased to see her, and Carra was relieved – although it was with dismay, she realised that meant she had been apprehensive.

"I'm so glad you came to see me, we have so much to talk about that is best kept between the two of us. I'm sorry that I was cold towards you."

"Ally, no. It is *I* who needs to apologise to *you*. I was thinking about getting help and I should have realised that leaving you alone was a worse fate."

"That is all behind us now. We have other things more pertinent and more agreeable to think about. Tell me, have you discovered your affinity? Nicholas would not say. He can be rather honourable when he wants to be."

"I guess he didn't want to embarrass me further. The truth is, I'm not sure I have one. I'll show you, watch." Carra demonstrated, feeling the surge as she usually did, but producing no result either of them could see.

"That is curious. I wonder what's happening. Shall I show you mine? As Niko says, you mustn't share but, obviously I trust you... I can manipulate water." Alliana made a glass of water across the room swirl like a miniature whirlpool.

"That's incredible!" Carra pushed aside any jealousy she felt in favour of taking genuine pride in her little sister.

"Let me show you something else. I will close my eyes. Walk around the room, and at some point, place the glass of water down. Then come back to me, so I can't hear where you're standing, and I will tell you where it is hidden!" Carra moved the water, and straight away, Alliana could sense where in the room it was.

After they had played the game a few times, Alliana regained her modesty. "I suppose it's helpful when they want to establish a new town and need to find a water source. Or maybe if there's a drought? It's only weak at the moment but Nicholas thinks I can learn to control it enough to influence lakes, or even rivers. Tomorrow he is going to take me somewhere as a surprise, I can't wait to see what new tricks I can try. Oh… but Carra, can we try yours again, are you sure you can't affect something – did you try all of water, fire, earth and air?"

"It's okay Ally, I can't lament for something I never had. Besides, I'm sure I'll work it out eventually." She put on a brave face. Alliana seemed so happy, and she was glad she was being looked after. Besides, they seemed to have renewed their relationship as sisters again. Perhaps now, they would be even closer than they had been before.

"But I have an idea!" Alliana declared excitedly.

No matter how hard she tried, Alliana just laughed when Carra asked her to elaborate.

✩✩✩✩

Luckily for Carra, who still hadn't mastered the skill of patience, she didn't have to wait long to find out what

Alliana was scheming.

"Are you two plotting against me?" Nicholas asked Carra with a wink, when he found her in the dining room the following day. Carra looked at him with mock innocence. She genuinely didn't know what he was referring to – but she didn't want Nicholas to know that. "Very well. Alliana has petitioned me on your behalf, and I have accepted. From tomorrow, you will be her personal maid. You will still be responsible for cleaning her rooms, but other than that, your current duties will be relinquished and you will instead cater to her whims. This is not an excuse for you to be slack or leisurely with your time." As he saw Carra's surprise, a smile spread across his face. "Ah, so this scheme is one of hers. However, I trust you will accept your new role."

He didn't wait for her to respond, and Carra found herself left alone to weigh up the merits of her change in circumstances. It could definitely be more fun, probably not as hard work, and she would get to spend a lot of time with Alliana. On the downside, it would mean it was very difficult for her to have alone-time with Nicholas. Was that perhaps why he'd had some hesitation about the change?

It also felt strange conceptually. She was used to taking care of Alliana – without a mother-figure, the three of them had taken care of each other – but actually *waiting* on her younger sister? It felt a bit awkward to her. *I'll just have to try and impress Nicholas with some magic sometime this decade.*

That night, Carra dreamt that the house was on fire. The scale didn't really make sense – Carra couldn't imagine a house this size would go down within a matter of seconds – but then that was dream logic for you. Nicholas was trapped under the rubble, but when she tried to lift the debris from him, her arms started to burn. The fire ran across her hands, up her arms, then set her hair alight. Alliana ran in and threw a bucket of water over her, which woke her up.

She was fairly disorientated when she opened her eyes, but not wet, and Alliana – well she could have been anywhere, but she was probably still asleep in her own room, and she certainly wasn't in Carra's dormitory. In her confusion, it took her a few seconds to realise the morning wake-up bell was being rung.

Throughout the morning, she found her thoughts returning to her dream, thinking maybe it had meant something. Perhaps because it had all been so unusually vivid. She resolved that she would suggest to Nicholas she should try manipulating fire again. It felt right somehow.

CHAPTER 10

Carra adapted to waiting on Alliana more easily than she had anticipated.

Some of the maids and guards, who were also seconds like herself, stood behind their charges at the breakfast and dinner tables in order to attend on them. Carra was glad Ally didn't ask her to go that far; the tales of what Ally had eaten at each meal were enough to make Carra's mouth water, without her having to physically watch the food being eaten.

As Alliana didn't have much to do during the day, they would often sit around and gossip. She was able to leave the estate now, so they could have ventured into the market had they had a chaperone, but for some reason Ally hadn't seemed inclined to do so as yet. Occasionally other girls, friends of Nicholas, would pay Alliana a visit and Carra would be relegated again to the sidelines. She didn't mind; they would still see Sandria in the evenings, and she felt sure that this weekend would be a breakthrough one for her skills.

On the eve of the next Lord's Day, she had another dream, in which anyone who came near her found themselves burning. Her father was beseeching her for help during the Astonelay raid, except this time it was taking place during the night, rather than the middle of the day. The flames lit up brightly, incandescent against the night sky, and for some reason they now seemed alluring instead of frightening. She heard herself tell her father not to worry, they wouldn't hurt him. Dream Carra was aware this was a false memory. Even knowing it for what it was, she had no control over what was happening. Similarly to the last dream, her senses became more heightened than they should, and she felt like she was bursting with powerful magic.

When she woke up, she was veiled in a thin sheen of sweat… and realised immediately she was late to meet Nicholas. Her forehead felt far too hot, even to her own touch. There was nothing for it though; she definitely didn't have time to stop by the baths.

She thought Nicholas would be unimpressed he'd had to wait for her, but when she joined him at the stables a few minutes later, she was greeted with laughter instead. "What happened to you this morning?" Carra, unsure whether he was referring to her timekeeping or her appearance – but too excited to care – relayed her dreams to him.

"Do you think it means the same thing I do? Can we try to work fire again?"

"I have something planned for today already. I thought we could go swimming. Ironically, a bathe wouldn't go amiss for at least one of us. But… I suppose we can spend a couple of hours experimenting with fire first."

After a trip back to the kitchen to obtain some matches, small twigs, and pastries given she'd skipped breakfast, they were set up. Nicholas lit a small flame, and Carra tried her best to manipulate it into doing something… or anything…

She tried concentrating on making it grow, with no success. Then she attempted to make it sway for her. Resigned that it wasn't going to work for her anyway, she tried to put it out – still nothing. She could feel herself doing *something* though. She felt charged with magic throughout the whole session, far more so than usual, and Nicholas even said it seemed that way to him as well.

"Never mind." he proffered. "Let's not let it spoil our afternoon. Come on, follow me." He walked her down to a small lake. She recognised it as the one they had visited a while back when she had tried to summon water – although on reflection, however huge the grounds were, she would have been surprised if they'd contained more than one lake!

As soon as he reached the water, he stripped down to his undergarments, and jumped in. "Come on Kay-rahh. It's lovely and cool. Swim with me."

Without overthinking it, she jumped in, still fully clothed. They frolicked in the water as if they were children. She raced him back and forth, and found they were surprisingly evenly matched, although he did have the edge over her slightly. Finally, it looked as though she was going to have a turn at winning. Seeing this, he made a dive for her legs, splashing everything in the vicinity, then gently pulled her under the water. He was so close, she thought he might kiss her again – and she was right, he did – gently, on her forehead.

The late autumn air was chill, but he had thought ahead, having brought a cosy blanket for them to warm up with. He helped her out of the water, and then threw it around her. Nicholas was still dressed only in shorts, and the water glistened on his chest. He joined her under the blanket for a few seconds and dried himself off, then put his clothes back on.

"You're not too cold to sit out and eat, are you? Honestly, you amuse me Kay-rahh, you didn't need to stay in your dress while we swam, and I'm sure you're wearing something underneath. You have dented my pride – I'm assuming it was lack of trust in me, rather than any embarrassment on your own behalf. Although, I do think it slowed you down – without it you would have had the advantage in our little racing game, and then my pride would have still taken a beating."

Carra blushed and turned away, pretending to select a sandwich – when of course she already knew which one she wanted next, not to mention the one after that. Nicholas no longer seemed to mind that she was behind with her magic, and she felt fully at ease in his presence. When she was alone, part of her wondered if his sole intention in befriending her was to coax the hidden talent out of her, but then as soon as she was with him, any doubts over his sincerity completely left her.

He gently lifted up a strand of her hair and placed it behind her ear. "You seem deep in thought Kay-rahh. Can I share the burden?" As his fingers touched behind her ear, he let them fall, lightly skimming her neck and shoulder. He was leaning in towards her and she thought he might even kiss her again – and properly this time. She moved to make eye contact with him. Yes, she was sure he was going to kiss her.

Just as she was closing her eyes, she saw something in her periphery - a dark shape moving behind the bushes. She let out a small, involuntary gasp, her focus completely shifting from Nicholas to some topiary over his right shoulder instead.

Nicholas instantly turned around; the moment was over before it had really begun. Seeing nothing, he tried to make light of the situation. "What is troubling you? Are you eager to leave my side?"

"I saw something. Someone, I think. Moving over that way. Behind the hedgerow." She pointed in the direction she'd seen the movement.

"Wait here, Carra. Let me go and investigate." Nicholas wandered down the way she had pointed. She didn't know whether to stop him, or offer to go with him, but she found she was too scared. She appreciated him having taken what she said seriously, when he could easily have dismissed her, but by now she was already beginning to doubt herself; wondering if she had imagined it.

It wasn't long at all until he returned. "I couldn't see anyone, and nothing had been disturbed. Could you have been mistaken?" She thought she probably had been, so she simply shrugged in response. Except just as she did so, she saw it again. She blinked in surprise, but Carra didn't want him to think she was ridiculous, so this time she didn't say anything.

With most of the afternoon still ahead of them, they basked in the sun a while longer. Calmed by his presence, Carra subtly tried using magic again – if Nicholas noticed he didn't say. They didn't have much more conversation, and after a while Nicholas excused himself, declaring he had somewhere else he needed to be. He offered to walk Carra back to the house, but she politely declined.

"I think I'll stay out here a little longer. It's beautiful by the lake and it's late in the year – we may not have another warm day like this until spring." In truth, Carra wanted him to go so she could explore the area. She was convinced someone was lurking nearby – maybe even watching them – and she couldn't shake the feeling they'd been trying to catch her attention.

Once Nicholas was out of sight, she got up, and walked casually around the lake... as though she were simply going for a stroll. At the last possible second, she veered off towards where she thought the person was concealed.

Sure enough, she saw someone trying to rapidly vacate to a new hiding spot. Strangely, she realised she wasn't afraid of them. Maybe it was because of all she had been through in the last two months. Or maybe it was just because they could easily have attacked her by now, had that been their intention.

"I know you saw me see you. There's no need to be afraid. Oh. It's you." Venturing out from a few yards away from her, a sheepish smile on his face, was the man from before – in the woods and then again at the market. His face looked completely different, much less threatening, when he smiled. Despite his agreeable expression, he emitted power and confidence; and he seemed completely undeterred by the situation. "So, are you following me or chasing me?" She folded her arms over her chest and tapped her foot. "Should I be afraid?" she asked him, trying her best to sound like she was joking. Having been chased by him in the woods, she now found him rather formidable.

"I guess so." She waited for him to say more but he didn't. A man of few words then. She noted, at least, that he hadn't moved any closer to her.

"Your name?"

"It's Dom."

A noise from behind her caught her attention, and she looked back across the lake. A man she didn't recognise was approaching. When she turned back, Dom was gone. She was about to head back towards the house, to see what this new interloper wanted, when she saw something on the floor where Dom had been standing. Stepping towards it, she identified it as a piece of paper. Seeing he was nowhere in sight, she unrolled the paper. There were just three words on it: 'Tomorrow. Midnight. Here'. Carra quickly stuffed it in her pocket and walked over to the gentleman who was approaching. "Hello there, can I help you?"

"Good afternoon, Lady Carra. Nicholas asked me to kindly see if you would like me to walk you back to the manor. He was concerned about your welfare alone out here after you had mentioned seeing an animal in the bushes."

As Carra allowed herself to be escorted, she mused over the note in her pocket that her fingers were currently skimming. She knew it was from Dom, but was it meant for *her*? He might have dropped it by accident. Carra was the one who had searched *him* out not vice versa – perhaps he had been meeting someone and it was pure chance that her and

Nicholas had been nearby. Besides, this was only the second time she had been to the lake with Nicholas, so he wouldn't have known to look for her there.

Yet... she couldn't shake the feeling that it *had* been meant for her. But if, as she suspected, she *had* been meant to find the note, then she had a real dilemma facing her – whether to hold to the tryst. Really the only point in its favour was to satisfy her curiosity, and was that a good enough reason?

Carra was ashamed to admit to herself that, even though she was still adamant that she would escape this place, at the moment she was too attached to it to want to leave – assuming her inclinations were actually correct, and this rogue planned to help her leave. Although, meeting with him just to hear him out couldn't hurt. Or could it... she might just be putting herself in danger. Except, in that case, wouldn't he have made his move while she was alone by the lake? *Night would be a better time for kidnapping though, especially if no one actually knew where she'd gone...*

Carra was so lost in thought that she almost ignored her chaperone as he took his leave. She skipped up to Alliana's room, planning to discuss what she should do, and maybe ask Ally to accompany her from a distance.

However, when she walked into the room – not thinking to knock – she saw Nicholas and Alliana sitting on a chaise longue whispering to each other. She made a quick exit, before either of them managed to see her, and instead went to fetch herself some dinner.

Over a hot stew, she relayed to Sandria what she had seen in Ally's chamber. Sandria merely raised an eyebrow in response. It wasn't quite the reaction she had been hoping for.

Suddenly feeling as though she was not quite privy to everything going on, Carra decided not to mention Dom to anyone after all. They would probably only try to dissuade her from meeting him anyway, and if Nicholas heard about it, he would certainly stop her from going. Moreover, whilst Dom hadn't said to come alone, she thought it was probably implied.

Carra retired early that evening, as she was not particularly feeling in the mood to be sociable. She was hoping to shut herself off from the world entirely, to have some peaceful hours not thinking about anyone around her, but she found her sleep interrupted again. Sometime during the early hours, she had another of those strange, vivid dreams.

She was in a long, dark, stone corridor. The walls were fairly far apart, and she was walking along a thin platform down the centre, with chasms either side of her. Her dream self didn't look down to see how deep they were. Ahead of her on the walkway, was Nicholas. As she walked towards him, the walls lit up in flames, both to her left and right. Once she reached him, he stepped aside to let her pass and then followed behind her.

At the end of the corridor was a faceless man. He also stepped aside and let her walk past, then bowed to her as she became level with him. She turned to him, smiled as he became upright again, then linked arms with him. She held a flame in her other hand, and it started to grow, getting higher, and higher, and higher.

CHAPTER 11

Carra woke up to the bell feeling refreshed. Despite having again experienced a hot sweat after her vivid dream, she had been able to go back to sleep for a few hours. Hurrying to her shift, she was hoping to finish early, and have some extra time during which she could go update Nicholas on her dream. This one had been even more lifelike – more like a memory than a dream – and she felt as if she had really been there.

When she did find Nicholas later, he didn't seem to share her excitement. In fact, he was incredibly subdued – even more so than normal – and although clearly not in relation to her dream, he seemed to be deep in thought. Foolishly, she persisted. "What do you think it means though, Nicholas?"

"Probably nothing. People dream all the time."

"Not like this, it was so different. I know it was a true dream. Or some sort of, I don't know, changed memory."

"You think I should follow you around like a servant then Kay-rahh?"

"Well, no. I didn't mean it literally. I thought maybe… have you ever heard of anything of the *magical* kind that sounds anything like this?"

"No, I'm afraid not, angel," He put his hands on her shoulders. "But, don't be disheartened, there are many things I don't know. I'm sorry Kay-rahh."

"That's okay, it's not your fault."

THE LOCKET

"No, I'm sorry Kay-rahh. It thought it would work out, I really did, but I have certain *obligations*. Our lessons will have to cease. I am very fond of you, you must know that." He kissed her on the forehead and then walked away. She called out after him but he either didn't hear, or pretended not to.

She did not understand all of what he'd said, but she accepted, albeit with some disappointment, that he was no longer going to waste his time trying to find her magic. That helped explain why he was reluctant to get too interested in her dream.

Perhaps taking her swimming had been a form of goodbye. If so, she had vastly misread the situation. No, it was more likely his parents had intervened.

Carra was distracted for the rest of the day, but Alliana didn't seem to pick up on it. She knew that Sandria noticed something was wrong at dinner, but Sandria had never been one to pry – something Carra was thankful to her friend for.

In a stroke of luck, neither Alliana or Nicholas joined them that evening, which made it easy for Carra to excuse herself for an early night without any questions.

If she was honest with herself, she'd known all along that she was going to seek out Dom. It was already constantly on her thoughts - she *needed* to know why he wanted to see her.

Feeling vain, she changed into a skirt and blouse instead of the maid's outfit she'd been wearing all day. With nothing better to do, Carra thought she might as well leave now, even though they weren't meeting for another hour. At least if someone saw her, she had time to pretend she was going somewhere else, then circle back.

Having not encountered anyone she knew, Carra ambled down to the lake, admiring her surroundings. Away from the house, the main source of light was the moon, and tonight's waning gibbous was bright enough for her to easily see where she was going.

Dom was sitting crossed legged at the edge of the lake. She had a quick internal panic; she'd expected the hardest part to be finding him. She'd even had doubts he'd show at all. Now knowing the encounter was inevitable, she needed to work out what she was going to say. Her feet kept moving in the right direction, but she slowed her pace to maximise her thinking time.

As she reached him, she inexplicably felt far calmer. Saying nothing, she sat down next to him, dipping her feet into the lake. They remained sitting together just like that, without talking, for a few minutes – though it felt like longer. She paddled her feet softly. The water was still pleasantly warm from the sun's heat that afternoon, and the night was so quiet that the gentle splashing was the only sound.

"I hoped you would come." Carra let out a breath she hadn't realised she was holding. He'd basically confirmed she *had* been the note's intended recipient. "I've been searching for you."

"I noticed. I don't think I understand though... that is, you'll forgive me for not knowing why?"

"You will come to understand. We are fated to meet." It sounded to Carra like a joke, but his expression told her it was seriously meant.

"Who decides what is or isn't fated?" He laughed, and Carra let herself smile as well. That had sounded a lot more intense than she had intended.

"Fair enough. In this case, the high mages."

"Are you affiliated with the magic school then?"

"Whistlake? No, I am not. I'm just a wanderer. Not much better than a vagrant." Despite her puzzlement, he smiled like it was an inside joke.

"Oh. I see." Of course, she didn't. "So, once we meet, what do the fates say happens?"

"They were a bit hazy on that part. Actually, the high mages wanted to keep us apart. I have no idea why though, so no need to ask me." Carra frowned. Dom also looked pensive. "Come away with me." he said, suddenly.

"Excuse me? We just met! You don't even know my name." Hearing him suggest she should leave with him turned out to be very different in reality to how it had been in her imagination.

"I do. It's Carra. I heard you and Nicholas by the lake yesterday. He seems quite taken with you, is there something more between you?" She felt herself blush, but figured it was too dark for Dom to see. "There is nothing wrong with Nicholas, I'm sure he is a kind man, but you could do things so much greater than stay here as a housewife."

"I... I...," she stumbled.

"Sit with me a while. Let's get to know one another. I want us to be friends."

They talked about mundane things. It was what you'd call 'safe conversation'. She told him about the village where she had grown up with her father and sister. He told her about his parents, younger brother and sister.

However, as they grew more comfortable with each other, the conversation turned darker. She spoke of the recent raid on her village, and he told her of his estrangement from his parents. Several hours had passed before she realised how cold she was.

"Are you not cold, Dom?"

"I'm sorry, I didn't think. Here, take my cloak." She was about to refuse, but he had already removed it. Seeing that he genuinely didn't seem bothered by the chill air, whereas she was freezing, she found she didn't feel too guilty about taking it. "Let me walk you back as far as I can risk without being seen."

"Does Nicholas's family have any quarrel with you? I'm sure they could find you a room."

"No, but equally I am not acquainted with them, and don't have any desire to explain myself to strangers. However... please excuse me for not approaching you sooner. They are a good family, and I knew you would be safe with them. After I saw you at the market, there was nothing more I could do that day, not with Nicholas himself escorting you. I have actually been making good use of my time by exploring the Rivulet grand library while I was waiting for the opportunity to speak to you alone – really, I should thank you for staying behind by the lake yesterday."

For whatever reason, perhaps his articulation and vocabulary, the revelation that he could read didn't surprise her. "I nearly didn't of course. So, you did mean for me to see you then?"

"Yes, I was trying to get your attention. I wasn't sure what else to do." He sighed, then added, "Meet me here again tomorrow?" Before slinking away, leaving Carra alone, smiling to herself.

☆✦☆✦☆
✧✦✧✦

The next morning, the breakfast room was buzzing with gossip. Carra didn't notice at first, having only had a couple of hours sleep. Not to mention that she had other things on her mind.

"Are you okay?" Sandria had joined her at the table.

"I'm just so tired." she responded, assuming her friend was referring to her repetitive yawns; but when Carra looked around, she found herself frowning. In the midst of their chattering, everyone seemed to be glancing towards her. For a split second she wondered if she had been caught with Dom. She started to wonder why anyone would even care if she had been.

"No, I didn't mean that!"

"What's going on? Did they find him?"

"Didn't Alliana tell you? Hang on a second, find who?" At Carra's confused look, Sandria continued. "It's been all around the servants block since yesterday evening. Even with your early night, I would have thought you'd have heard. I'm not sure how to tell you this – and it shouldn't be me who you're hearing it from either – but, well, they announced it at dinner last night. Alliana and Nicholas are betrothed."

"No, that can't be possible." she exclaimed, without thinking.

"Oh dear, I was worried you wouldn't take it well. Here, drink some water. You look quite pale. Oh sweetheart, you must at least have suspected something?" She half felt Sandria place her hand on her back comfortingly. "For the last few weeks, every time they have joined us, they have been together. Why did you think he moved her out of the kitchens into her own bedroom? They even concocted a role for you as her maid."

Carra hardly heard what Sandria was saying. Sandria only had a small part of the story. She didn't know about her afternoons and picnics with Nicholas. Carra had never mentioned the magic to Sandria, it had felt too private. Of course, she had suspected that he had been flirting with Carra – he did so with all new maids – but all Sandria would see is that she had been a silly fool, much as Sandria had been herself until she had been replaced. She probably wouldn't even have been surprised had she known that Nicholas had kissed her.

It wasn't just that though. Despite all her naivety, Carra knew in her heart that there truly was something between herself and Nicholas; something more than friendship.

Carra replayed to herself the conversation she'd had with him yesterday, when she'd found him to ask about her dream. A little more of it made sense now. That was why their lessons had to cease. Nicholas must have known that Carra had seen him and Alliana together in her sitting room after all. She felt betrayed that Alliana hadn't told her, but that was minor in comparison to the loss of whatever she'd thought she'd had with Nicholas.

For the rest of the day, Carra couldn't shake the feeling that this had something to do with her lack of magic. At first, she thought she was just trying to find fault with Nicholas, to justify why he preferred Alliana over her, but the more she dwelled on it the more she became convinced.

Hadn't Nicholas said the magic was usually strongest in the eldest, and hadn't he also said, 'I thought it would work out'. Maybe all his attentions towards her had been fake too – but, she found that difficult to believe.

By the evening, when Alliana returned to her suite, Carra had mostly recovered from her shock. "Congratulations sister! Tell me, when are you to be married?"

"We need a little time to prepare and let guests travel over, but otherwise as soon as possible. A Winter wedding would be so pretty, don't you think? Won't we have fun organising it! Of course, you can now be my friend again instead of pretending to be my maid, but you'll still help won't you Carra." Alliana laughed. "I have also made arrangements for you to move into a room adjoining mine!"

"Of course I'll help, baby sister. It will be perfect. First though, let me ask you something, and please don't be upset with me. Are you very certain of his intentions. Has he not said several times that he wants to strengthen his family's magic and well, is there any possibility that could be his motive?"

"Are you implying, dear sister, that had you been able to access your magic, he might have been choosing between us?"

"Not exactly," Carra responded cautiously, although that was *exactly* what she was implying, and of course Alliana knew that. Nay, in fact Carra thought that as the eldest, he had originally aimed his sights at her alone.

Her words were out there now though, and unsurprisingly, she'd soured the mood – but she didn't regret them. She could never have forgiven herself if she hadn't asked. "I just mean, do you love him, and are you sure that he loves you?"

"Niko and I are very happy, Carra. Think on the estate here compared to our living back home. Even if I didn't love him, it would improve our situation, but I do. He is a good man Carra, he is even sending a doctor to nurse our father, should he be able to find him."

Carra turned to her sister and smiled warmly, "In that case, let us toast to the good news."

CHAPTER 12

That evening, they were once again a party of four; Alliana and Nicholas joining Carra and Sandria for the first time in a week. It was getting too cold to be comfortable outside, so they settled for sitting inside and taking drinks.

Nicholas had his arm around Alliana for most of the evening, and Carra was glad Sandria was there to keep the conversation flowing, as there were plenty of moments during which she found herself distracted. Although she was a bit uncomfortable at having to watch the newly-engaged couple, her thoughts were kept busy attempting to figure out how she was going to manage to excuse herself – and if possible, do so without seeming jealous.

It was strange to think that she wasn't. Well, she might have been a little jealous, but her main concerns were around her sister's wellbeing.

"You keep watching the clock Carra, do you have a secret rendezvous?" Nicholas asked her somewhat condescendingly.

"Oh Niko, you silly fool. How would she even know anyone around here?" Ally put her hand on his knee and laughed heartily. "I don't think she is cavorting with the butler!" Who was Alliana to look down on the butler like that. Never mind the fact he was from a much wealthier family than they were. Nicholas – *Niko* – seemed to have changed her sister in a way Carra didn't overly like.

"Erm, thanks Ally. No, sorry if I was being rude. I'm

just tired, I've not had much sleep. My strange dreams have been keeping me awake." Carra improvised. "Now that you mention it though, please, you must excuse me, I can't keep my eyes open."

Hopefully Nicholas wouldn't think she was upset over his engagement. Personally, she thought she should have a round of applause for her acting this evening – but having not let anyone in on her schemes, there was no one who'd be able to appreciate it. Dashing up to her room, she grabbed Dom's cloak, which she had stuffed under the bed, and then ran down to meet him. It was already half an hour after midnight.

Carra was still a little bit out of sorts as she walked down to the lake. There were too many nonsensical things happening for her to process. She was glad to know she would have company tonight, but still had no idea what Dom's motives were, and she couldn't shake off her discomfort at knowing she'd having to interact with Nicholas in the future.

Her concerns and uncertainties all vied for attention. But in the back of her mind there was a small voice, like at the bottom of Pandora's box, telling her to hope. Maybe, *maybe*, she might even be let free to leave this place. Surely, Nicholas would not be able to refuse his sister-in-law, nor keep her captive.

Dom was sitting in the same spot as last night, and as she sat next to him, he studied her – to what end, Carra didn't know. "I thought you might not come."

"Sorry, I struggled to get away. I'm here now though."

"I'm surprised Nicholas lets you out of his sight."

"And why would that be?"

"The whole town is buzzing with talk of the young Lord's betrothal. Congratulations. You must be very happy." He was very curt with his words, but he couldn't have been jealous as he barely knew her – Carra wished she had some sort of clue what he was up to.

"It wasn't something I had anticipated, but I'm sure Nicholas and *Alliana* will be very happy together."

"Alliana, who is Alliana?"

"She is my sister."

"He is engaged to your sister?" Dom did genuinely look confused, so Carra could at least surmise that he wasn't just teasing her. "That makes no sense. Unless… Is she older or younger than you?"

"I am the eldest; she is two years my junior."

"How peculiar. Yes, I thought she looked younger than you. Well, that is good news for you and me."

"How so?" Carra inquired, hoping she might finally have some insight into her new friend's thoughts.

"I have a quest for us. Before you ask, all I know is that there is something important waiting at the end of it, and that you, Carra, are key to its achievement."

"A quest? Are you just choosing that word to sound melodramatic?" He certainly made it sound exciting, but she couldn't make any sense of his meaning. "How is what you're saying possible? What makes you think it's anything to do with me. What about me would be helpful? I don't own anything of value or have any particular expertise. I don't know much about anything at all." She wasn't trying to be modest, she was quite concerned about what he was expecting of her.

"Do not play dumb with me, Carra. Surely you know the power of your magic."

"Oh." Now what. She had a predicament. *Did she trust him enough to tell him about her lack of magic?*

"So, would you tell me of your talent? What is your speciality?" Dom seemed far chattier all of a sudden.

"I thought that was something private, that I'm not supposed to tell others?"

"Perhaps that is so, Carra. However, if you want the excitement and adventure – and I'm guessing there isn't much for you to stick around for here – it might be a good idea for us to be completely honest with each other."

"We'll circle back around to that point on honesty in a moment. I guess I trust you. Trust you enough, that is. Well, maybe I don't actually trust you, but I can't think of a good reason not to tell you. I don't have any magic."

"Ha, nay be serious Carra." There was a pause while he considered this revelation. "You must do."

"No, Nicholas has been trying to teach me but, well, nothing. Nothing happens." He was making her feel a bit self-conscious now. Her insecurities whispered that Dom was going to decide he didn't want her company anymore – just like Nicholas seemed to have.

"Curious. Can show me?" Carra obliged. "I see your dilemma, but this makes very little sense. I can feel the power radiating off you. So, why does nothing happen?" She shrugged. "Your sister, Alliana, does she have magic?"

"Yes, she can use hers. I understand she is fairly strong." Carra admitted begrudgingly. It wasn't the first time she'd been left feeling like the inferior sister today.

"Nicholas knows of this?" Carra nodded. "So that is why he is marrying her not you?" Carra raised her eyebrows at him and thought that she had probably blushed slightly. She couldn't deny she felt somewhat gratified that he had come to the same conclusion as her. "Right, so Nicholas and Alliana aside, what is happening with you? Why can't you access your magic?"

"I have no idea. I only found out that magic existed when I came to this place." She raised her arm, gesturing backwards towards the house, superfluously. "Then Nicholas just expected me to have it... and it feels like I do. It feels like something ought to happen, when the power surges through me, but then it doesn't."

"Intriguing. Even if it wasn't a visible power, there should still be a shimmer."

"Yes, Nicholas showed me his." Dom arched one eyebrow.

"Carra, you come from one of the oldest, most powerful bloodlines in existence. It is *unheard* of that you wouldn't have some ability. In most families with magic, only the first-born child has any power at all. The strength of your family can be seen solely from the fact that your younger sister is also fairly strong at the arts."

"I couldn't tell you. My father has never mentioned any magic to me, and I don't remember my mother. How do you know my 'bloodline' anyway? And do you have magic yourself? What is your affinity - now that I have bared all to you?"

Dom looked at her for a few moments, and she thought that, after all of that, he might not even tell her. In the end, he simply said, "Can you not guess?" which was annoyingly cryptic. She thought for a moment.

"Should I be able to? I'm terrible at riddles. And you didn't answer the question about my family."

"Oh, I should think so, Carra. Yes, I think you know." She puzzled over it. She hadn't seen him become invisible, but given he'd kind of disappeared when she'd been with Nicholas, that was her first thought. She hadn't seen him work any of the core elements either. Unless...

"That was you?" He turned his palm over, and it

lit up in flames. Instinctively, she reached out and touched it. "Why doesn't it burn me?"

"It usually would, it doesn't seem to want to." Dom sounded amused. "Why did you touch it if you thought it would burn you?"

"I didn't. I don't know. It was just calling to me, I couldn't help myself." She reflected for a second, "The fire dreams then, they were real?"

"Not exactly. Although, I was there too, and they certainly felt real. What I mean is, they weren't real places. At least, that I know of. I'd say they were the product of our joint imaginations. They started for me around the time I first ventured onto this estate." He paused to look at Carra and she nodded in agreement. "They seem to manifest some of our thoughts and desires. I'm not quite sure how we had formed a connection like that solely from the two previous times we had met."

"Dom. That day, when you were chasing me in the woods…"

"I'm sorry about that. I knew afterwards I should have handled it differently. I was trying to be quiet, so those other men in the woods didn't hear. Plus, to be honest I never dreamt you'd managed to get away once you went up that tree." He laughed. The sound was deep and serious. "After that, I couldn't find you, so I had to take a risk and move towards Rivulet. I figured they might be taking you to Whistlake, but either way they would have had to stop in Rivulet for supplies and to unload the other girls."

"They erm… well, they put me in a box for the rest of the journey. I wish I'd let you catch me. Although… Alliana would probably never have forgiven me if I actually *had* left her there."

"She seems to be managing on her own just fine.

You, on the other hand, what do you have here? Surely you don't intend to stay?"

"I guess not. No, I mean, I never intended to."

"Let's go then." Carra looked into his eyes. He looked deadly serious.

"Whoa there, Mr. Reckless! Hold on a moment. What's the huge rush? I have responsibilities now. I can't just sneak off." She thought for a few seconds. It was with a surprising amount of disappointment that she admitted, "I probably can't leave until after the wedding. It's supposed to be this winter though, so it wouldn't be an awful amount of time to wait?" She found herself a tad worried he'd decide she wasn't worth the effort and go without her.

"No. You're right, they might send people after us. Hmm."

"Not exactly what I was thinking – which was more along the lines of the fact I can't miss my own sister's wedding – but that is also a good point! I am sure Nicholas will let me leave as soon as they are married, how could he not? I can even ask them now – but, oh… should I mention your name, or where we are going?"

"Hmm. They don't know me, and the Strathenbergs might not like the idea of their new daughter-in-law wandering off with a strange man. Do you have any friends you could say you would like to visit? Maybe you could ask to go to Whistlake to learn about your magic?"

"Maybe I *should* go to Whistlake. Where *are* we going, anyway?"

"That is a good question." The mischievous grin he seemed to adopt quite regularly reappeared on his face. "I don't actually know the location of our quest object so to speak just yet…"

"Okay," Carra sighed, "and the quest object would

be?"

"I don't actually know that either... but it's something powerful and important, and I know they don't want us to have it."

"So perhaps Whistlake would be the best place to start? They may have some record of what we are looking for. Besides, if you need me on this quest, would it not be a good idea for me to be able to use some magic?"

"Nooo, that's a bad idea. Your parents obviously hid you away in Astonelay for a reason. There are other forces at work here, and I suspect they are playing against us. I have strong magic, and yet unusually, I was denied admittance to the Academy. If we went to Whistlake, I'm not entirely certain they would let you leave again." They both thought over that for a moment. The wind had picked up and her hair blew out in front of her face. She hastily pushed the stray curls back behind her ears.

"So what do you propose? I don't see how it's possible to go on a quest where we don't know either the nature or location of the item we're looking for. You use the word quest to make it sound like we're going on an adventure, but what is the reality here? Would I be trading comfort and safety, for... for what? For sleeping on the ground with a man I hardly know for company?" Carra wondered if she might have offended Dom after her diatribe, but he just looked a little dejected.

It was a funny time for the thought to come to her, but she realised that he wasn't cold, despite the fact she was still wearing his cloak, and wondered if that was something to do with his flame magic.

She tried to sound a little more positive for him, "Okay. Let's be practical. How did you hear about this object?"

"When I left my home, there was some talk of

where I would go. In the end, it was agreed I would come to Pellagea. From what I could glean from the discussions, that I wasn't strictly supposed to be privy to, there was some objection to me going north or west." Not for the first time, Carra was slightly embarrassed about her lack of geographical knowledge, so instead of asking him to explain further she just let him continue. "I then cleverly deduced that north was off limits because that's where you were."

"So, you're saying you are originally from south Florinyn?" she asked, pleased that she was managing to keep up.

"Correct." He smiled. "I am from the capital, Florin. So, I have therefore come to the conclusion that our first step in looking for the object we seek is to head west."

"Assuming it exists, and it is an object, not a person, or say, a figment of your imagination."

"Hold on. I did ascertain more of the conversation."

"How exactly did you manage to hear this conversation if you weren't supposed to?"

He actually looked rather sheepish. Carra still felt like she was missing something. *Why did someone decide on Dom's behalf where he would go?* He seemed to sense her question, and explained that he had a friend who *was* present for said conversation, who had then updated him afterwards.

Then he *reminded* her that they'd decided where he would go to keep him from learning of this alleged fate they were trying to avoid for the pair of them – she didn't actually remember him saying it, but she decided to let that slide.

The only other thing his friend had known was that they had gone to great lengths to prevent Dom from finding this particular item. Between them, they had worked out that it must have been hidden between fifteen and twenty years earlier.

To Carra, the most obvious route choice seemed to be for them to find Dom's friend – who had stayed behind in Florin whilst Dom had sought out Whistlake in an attempt to learn more – but he seemed reluctant. "How long is it since you have seen your parents, Dom? Maybe things have changed since then. They probably miss you."

"It has been a few years. I am twenty-four, Carra and I was only eighteen when I left home. Since then, I have written to my parents several times and had no response. I'll tell you what, let's make a deal. I will consider carefully what our next move should be, and in return, you can work out how you will extract yourself from the Strathenberg family – which you are now part of." He winked at her as he said that. She almost missed it, distracted by the thought that he was five years older than her... as well as her inherent concerns about putting too much faith in what he was telling her.

He could easily be duping her. Whilst she still didn't want to tell Nicholas or Alliana about her clandestine meetings, she was starting to think she could trust Sandria. This was a situation where she needed a second opinion.

She began to imagine what Sandria would say... it's just a reaction to Nicholas rejecting you... stay away from random men who you know nothing about... Maybe those weren't thing she wanted to hear, but maybe they were things she needed to.

"One more thing," she said to Dom. "I need you to meet my friend Sandria – I want someone else's opinion before I wander off with a strange man. She doesn't know about magic though, so it might be best not to bring that up." Albeit reluctantly, thankfully he agreed.

Carra suspected Dom needed her more than she needed him and made a note to herself that she might be able to use that to her own advantage in the future.

CHAPTER 13

Despite a second night with almost no sleep, Carra managed to drag herself out of bed in time to meet Sandria for breakfast. She was acutely aware of how suspiciously she was acting, and Sandria's interest was certainly piqued when she asked her in whispers to meet her by the stables before dinner because she needed to tell her something.

"Whatever it is that has come over you Carra, it seems like a positive change."

Carra wasn't sure whether Sandria would be for or against her going with Dom, but more than anything else, she did know that her friend would be honest – and that, she valued.

As Carra had nothing to do for Ally that day, she helped Sandria with her polishing. They hoped they could finish work early, and then the pair of them could do something fun together.

Nicholas, however, had other ideas. He actually came looking for her, to tell her it was unbecoming of his future sister-in-law to be doing chores. Carra was slightly embarrassed when he dragged her away – and she realised she needed to stop letting herself become flustered so easily.

He took her up to fine one of the more experienced seamstresses, and at last came good on his promise from all those weeks ago, by instructing them to make her some dresses – in all sorts of showy colours that she would never have selected.

"Green." She managed to blurt out. "Can't we just go with the green?" Nicholas seemed a bit puzzled, but acquiesced, giving a shrug to the seamstress. "Okay good, please just make her one in the mid green, a couple in the dark green, and a navy one too, I suppose. That should do for now."

Carra left as soon as she was allowed, but he caught up with again in the hallway. "You will need to join us at breakfast and dinner now Kay-rahh. You need to look after Ally."

"Okay, Niko" she said, mimicking Ally's voice as well as her use of the familiar. "Actually," she said, becoming serious, and realising this may be the best time to broach the matter. "I was thinking that maybe after the wedding," she saw she now had Nicholas's full attention, "Maybe I should venture up to Whistlake Academy and see if they can figure out what is wrong with my magic?"

She gave him a moment to digest what she'd said before continuing, "I mean, you wouldn't need to accompany me, I'd be happy enough to go on my own – and of course if I don't have any success, I'd just return."

Carra was proud of herself. She had made an opening for herself to leave, which still applied even if she didn't go with Dom, without ever bringing his existence into the conversation. She just hoped that Nicholas was going to go along with it.

"Surely you must see that I can't let you go wandering off in the countryside all alone. It wouldn't be appropriate, never mind any concerns there would be over your safety."

"What if my father took me – presumably he will be invited to the wedding."

"Oh Kay-rahh, we don't yet know if he is alive. I'm sorry. We are hoping so. Even if he is, I am not sure he would be able to protect you. Let me think about it? I promise I will think about it. Perhaps one of the mages will accept an invite to the wedding and they could take you with their convoy."

Oops, her plan may have just backfired. Nicholas seemed to take her silence as disappointment because he continued, "Don't worry angel, we will find a place for you. I understand you feel uncomfortable around myself and Alliana given what there is between us. Tell me you understand though? I must do what is best for my family." *Had he always been this cocky?*

Carra was starting to wonder what she had ever seen in Nicholas, and reminded herself to be much more careful with her affections in the future! She felt like a real fool, but still managed to force a smile and gently flutter her eyelashes at him as if she still strongly admired him. He kissed her on the forehead and left her be. *Bleurgh.* She let her fake smile fall as she skipped off to find Sandria again, and in the end, they walked to the stables together.

Once they were sure no one was in sight, Carra updated Sandria – on Dom, on his plans, on her plans. It was surprisingly difficult to justify running off with him without bringing magic into the conversation.

"Oh Carra. I was worried about you when I heard about Alliana and Nicholas. I thought it may just be a passing affection, and I wondered how you would react once you heard it was serious, but this... this gentleman. You're using him as a rebound. Is gentleman even the right word – he doesn't have a home you say? Where did you even find him?"

Sandria did make a good point. Carra wasn't sure the explanation of 'he was watching me in the woods' was really going to help matters either. In the end, she could see no other way to get the considered opinion she needed. She told Sandria everything, right from the beginning – how she had seen Dom twice before, about the magic lessons with Nicholas, and then the way Dom had found her again in the woods.

Sandria seemed astounded. "Very well," she said eventually, "I will come and meet him with you. Tonight, you say? I think I'd better see what I think to your mystery saviour. I knew you would find a way out of this place eventually, let us see if this is it." Carra couldn't believe it – if she'd persuaded her friend, then maybe she wasn't making such a ridiculous choice after all.

Carra had to excuse herself, as she was required to join the family at dinner. She would have been a little apprehensive, but instead she was now fretting over Sandria meeting Dom – it was becoming clear to her how much she really did want Sandria to approve.

One of the gowns was ready for her when she got back to her room, so she slipped it on. It was very different from anything she was used to wearing, and between the thick velvet and long sleeves, she felt weighed down. Luckily there was one small positive; it reached down to the floor, so they couldn't see her old pumps. She made a mental note to see if she could procure some durable winter boots for her travels, but she'd probably have to wait and ask Alliana once everything had been agreed.

☆☆☆☆

Dinner was uncomfortable, however, the food was delicious. To Carra's dismay, she was seated between Alliana and Lady Strathenberg, meaning she was obliged to try and make conversation with the latter. Alliana was engaged in a debate with Lord Strathenberg, who was seated on the other side of her.

Carra waited until the Lady spoke to her first, and it wasn't until the main course that the initially stagnant conversation became more comfortable. She seemed like a nice lady, but Carra felt inferior to the surroundings.

Once they did start talking, Carra found she could hardly get a word in – but she was perfectly happy to nod her head in agreement as Lady Lucinda chattered.

"We shall have to see if someone can tidy up your hair deary. The curls are very fashionable, but only when they look as though they are there on purpose. The wild look may be attractive on a pretty young girl like yourself, but we shall attire you suitably, so you can enter our society. I daresay there will be young men queueing up. I'm sure there are many high-born families who care nothing for dowries nor magic, and just desire a handsome lady to accompany them and to birth their children. Of course, we can help you along on the money front, child if we need to. After all, you are family now."

Although this helped endear Carra to the family – whom she already knew to be kindly – the talk of her future made her long for the adventure that Dom was offering. Now she had received a taste of it, she craved the excitement. Talk of being someone's wife seemed banal.

Maybe Nicholas had put her off men entirely. She laughed at her own thought, but Lady Lucinda was still chattering and didn't notice. She was now talking about the latest cut of gowns – no she wasn't really, Carra was being harsh. She was telling Carra about other girls she might meet so that she could make social acquaintances before being thrust into a room of strangers.

It was quite sweet really, but Carra's mind was elsewhere, and Lucinda could have offered her a whole country without Carra snapping back to attention. She hoped she was at least still nodding and 'ahhing' enough in the right places to get by without seeming rude.

On the way out of the dining room, Alliana accosted Carra. She had been holding hands with Nicholas, who stepped away to grab some wine, leaving the sisters alone.

"What did Lady Lucy have to say?" Alliana asked, before adding, "She means well."

"Oh yes, she's lovely. She was just telling me about society around here and making some recommendations."

"That's so sweet of her." Only Ally could say something like that without sounding sarcastic. Carra excused herself to go and find Sandria, but Ally first made her promise to meet them in their usual spot.

The four of them shared their evening together and only now, with leaving on the horizon, did Carra realise quite what dependable friends they were. She was lucky they had been here with her. Nicholas and Alliana hadn't really ruined anything through their engagement, not if that was what they both wanted.

Carra wished she could shake her doubts. Nicholas's comment to her whilst Alliana's back was turned, about how well she was taking this, still rankled.

She tried to relax, but she was a bit jittery about meeting Dom again. Now that Sandria was in on it too, she was enjoying having a secret even more.

In order not to let on that she was up to something – to help calm herself – she may have had a couple more glasses of wine than usual.

Sandria took her leave first, with half an hour still to go before they were due to meet. Carra was glad, because they had noticed her clock-watching the night before.

Around five to midnight, Carra came up with a line about giving the lovers some privacy, then winked at Alliana on her way out. She ran up the stairs, grabbed Dom's cloak and bounced back down to the stables, where Sandria was waiting as prearranged.

"I'm so glad you came Sandria, I really appreciate

it." She was pleased to see Sandria was living up to her reputation as the sensible one, and had dressed appropriately for the cold.

"Of course. You're important to me. I want to make sure you're safe." Sandria giggled and Carra wondered if her friend wasn't slightly inebriated too.

Carra produced a bottle of wine and three stacked cups from underneath the cloak and grinned. She had picked them up as she'd left the drawing room. She suspected Alliana had noticed, but she hadn't said anything. Carra could deal with that later. "Let's go." Together, they headed down to the lake.

They weren't quite as late as Carra had been last night, but Dom was waiting again, this time standing. She introduced him to Sandria, and they shook hands. It was very formal and Carra giggled.

Sandria looked at Carra like she wanted to say something, so Carra leant in to listen. "He's frightening," she whispered. Possibly a bit loudly as Carra saw Dom frown. Carra didn't find him frightening. Although, whilst she couldn't exactly put her finger on what, there was unquestionably something commanding about Dom's presence.

Sitting down, she produced the red wine – putting slightly more in the glass she handed Dom. "Drink up friends," she encouraged. Though she was careful to only sip her own.

Carra saw that Sandria was shivering despite wearing a thick coat, and she wrapped Dom's cloak around her shoulders as an extra layer.

When the conversation slowed a bit, she asked Dom what he had dreamt last night. "I dreamt about you Carra. You were a column of flames."

"Yes, that was definitely the same as mine. Except

you missed out that I was dancing." Dom winked at her, and she knew it had been the same dream. "Incidentally, I told Sandria about everything. Oh, and I broached with Nicholas the subject of me leaving. Could have gone better, could have gone worse."

"So, you're really going?" Sandria asked. "I thought it was still just an idea being floated?"

Dom answered for Carra, "I'm expecting she'll come. There is nothing for her here. I'm hoping we can investigate her magic."

"I'd like that." she said, smiling at Dom. Carra was pleased to see that Sandria seemed a little more comfortable than she had at first. "It's weird." Carra mused, "Tonight isn't cold at all. Must be the alcohol keeping me warm."

"Possibly," Dom responded. "Although, if we are truly linked as I suspect, my internal heat may be passing on to you. Here, Carra you take my right hand and Sandria, you take my left. Do they feel hot to you?" Sandria nodded profusely, as Carra shook her head. "I'm not surprised. Carra, my hands would feel hot to anyone else, but you seem to be somewhat in tune with my flame magic. I didn't dwell on it, but it was quite unusual that it didn't burn you the other night. Perhaps we should experiment."

Dom rolled up his right sleeve and set his arm aflame. Carra, still holding his hand, felt the flames travelling up her hand, then her own arm, and up to her shoulder – in the end they were mirroring Dom's. *Interesting, is he doing that, or am I?*

"I think it's a joint effort." Dom responded, as if he had heard her.

"I have an idea!" Carra said suddenly. "Hold my hand again?" She held his hand with her left, and then tried to summon her magic with her right. She successfully conjured a flame. "How strange."

Sandria was watching them, mouth agape. Presumably it was the first time she had seen magic.

They experimented further, and Carra could do almost anything Dom suggested she tried – but only as long as she was holding his hand. She could even shoot fireballs – being careful to point them towards the lake. Dom was able to extinguish them with his magic before they set anything alight – and soon she had learnt to do that too.

"You are literally never allowed to leave my side." Carra exclaimed, euphoric from her new-found power.

"Now who's being forward?" Dom teased, but Carra ignored him. She created a rainbow of dancing flames over the lake. Suddenly it came easily to her. She made the flames swirl and sway, creating a dazzling spectacle.

Abruptly, and unforeseen by the three of them, the heavens opened. Within only a few seconds they were soaked through. The rain warred with the flames, until Carra slipped her hand out of Dom's, and began spinning around with her arms out, giggling like a child. She took Sandria's hand and spun her around with her too.

The three of them danced, and Carra would have kept dancing… except she noticed that Dom had stopped. She turned to see what he was looking at.

Standing only a few paces away from the trio were Nicholas and Alliana. Unlike Carra and Sandria, who were fairly intoxicated, the newcomers looked both sober, and severely unimpressed – the folded arms gave that away even if Carra was a little too tipsy to properly read their expressions.

Dom was looking embarrassed and Carra remembered that he wasn't supposed to be there.

The rain stopped as suddenly as it had started. "Was that you?" Carra realised that Alliana had been controlling the downpour.

Nicholas responded on her sister's behalf, "If you weren't so inebriated." Carra tried to look innocent but had to stifle more giggles, "You might have realised that your little display of fire against the black of night was strikingly visible from all of the south-facing, upper floor bedrooms."

"Oopsies." Why did Carra suddenly feel like she was the only one laughing.

"Luckily for you both, I said I would check out the source, claiming I suspected a couple of the maids had lit a fire to keep warm. Which seemed like a perfectly plausible excuse – until your rather theatrical arched display." As if deciding there was a more pressing issue, he turned to Dom, "And who is this? Are you a guest who has not been introduced or a trespasser who is trying to avoid my notice?" It sounded to Carra like Nicholas knew full well that it was the latter.

Dom coughed, clearing his throat. "I apologise my Lord," he dipped into a theatrical bow. "I am no one of any import, merely a traveller who happened upon these lovely ladies whilst they were out walking."

"Fascinating. And is one of your magical powers the ability to walk through the walls of a gated estate as if they do not exist?" Nicholas still seemed beautifully polite despite the accusation in his words.

Somehow, Dom managed to resist the urge to look upwards at the high stone walls. Carra, who on the other hand did not, tugged on his arm and pointed upwards, "How *did* you get over those Dom?"

Dom seemed to realise he was going to have to give a bit more honesty to avoid angering his unwitting host. "My apologies, Carra and I are old acquaintances. I sought her out while I was passing through, but did not wish to impose myself upon your hospitality, especially with no one here to formally introduce me."

"Nonsense, a friend of Carra's is a friend of mine, to use the old adage. Which inn are you staying at? You must bring your things here instead, and we will find you a room."

Carra wondered how Dom was going to get round the fact that he had no belongings. She suspected he had been sleeping out in the open, given he could use his flame magic to keep him warm, and to cook any game he caught. Dom however, was obviously a quick thinker, "I appreciate your hospitality. It is late, and I would not wake the innkeeper at this hour. Let us away now, and I will settle my debts at the inn in the morning."

Prompted by Nicholas, Alliana walked over to Dom so that he could properly introduce himself. Nicholas used the opportunity to sidle over to Carra. "How much do you know of this man?" he whispered. "I assume that was his flame magic. I believe he may have been sent by the Academy. From your interactions with him, can you think of any potential purpose behind this? He is a fairly skilled mage. Do I make sense or are you able to refute any of this?"

"He has no affiliation to the magic school Nicholas, he told me they didn't accept him."

"Well Kay-rahh. That is either a lie, or makes him even more suspicious in my eyes, as why would Whistlake not accept someone so skilled? I know you are not old acquaintances, dearest Kay-rahh, as Alliana has never seen him before. Contradict me if I am incorrect."

"*Darling* Nicholas," Carra wasn't sure whether that had been intended to sound sarcastic or not, "I have met him twice before he sought me out here, and it is true that Alliana was not privy to this. Furthermore, I have not seen him use magic in any way. That flame magic came from myself."

"Hmm. It sounds to me like you are trying to

protect him, and I can't help but wonder why. Has he made you a promise of some sort Kay-rahh? How is it that you have now had success in finding your magical ability? You'll forgive me for being sceptical. Are you able to show me?"

"A moment ago, you said that we were attracting too much attention. So, no Nicholas, I shan't. However, you may ask Sandria – I assume you will trust her word." Carra was really hoping that Nicholas didn't call her bluff, as she was unable to conjure up so much as a flicker without skin contact with Dom.

Not waiting for a response, she walked off towards Sandria, and Alliana – who had run out of conversation with Dom fairly quickly – took that as an opportunity to rejoin her affianced.

Unfortunately, Carra was still slightly drunk – possibly from the wine, or perhaps the combination of the drinks alongside the magic use had made her giddy. "Dom. How *did* you find me?"

"Hush Carra, you saw me in the street by the market and approached *me!*"

Carra wondered whether Nicholas was aware that her and Alliana hadn't left the estate since they had arrived. They had at least been allowed to do so for the last couple of weeks. "I don't mean just now, I mean originally. The first time we met. Did the magic school send you?"

"I did not lie to you Carra, I have no friends at Whistlake Academy or within the Council there, nor have I ever been granted entrance to the premises. The other matter we can discuss when we are alone tomorrow night."

They reached the house, and Carra was forced to bid the gentlemen goodnight as her and Alliana retired, and Nicholas found a suitable residence for Dom.

CHAPTER 14

The next morning, Carra put in her first appearance at the family breakfast, only to find Dom had also been invited as a guest. Whilst Carra felt awkward, Dom seemed perfectly comfortable. It led Carra to wonder about his childhood. Although herself and Alliana were the wealthiest residents in their village and their father had brought them up with manners above their station, as well as the ability to read and write, they were still peasants – whereas the Strathenberg family were Lords. She doubted she would ever be able to fully relax in their presence.

Glancing towards Alliana, she saw that her sister looked perfectly at ease in their surroundings. This she could explain, as she got the impression that Nicholas had done everything he could to make Alliana feel welcome.

Dom however, had been uninvited, turning up in the middle of the night. Yet he looked unfazed; by both this, and the company he found himself in. In fact, Carra would even go as far to say that he seemed in his element. His usual quiet confidence was replaced by bold charisma. He had even made plans to go riding with Nicholas and Lord Strathenberg that morning.

As soon as they excused themselves from the breakfast table, Carra found herself facing questioning from Alliana. The phraseology she used led her to believe that Ally had been in no small part directed by Nicholas. Interestingly, Carra found herself unable to answer much of what she was asked, prompting her sister to question just how well she actually knew her new friend.

"I don't trust him Carra. It's awfully strange that he would just show up in the middle of the night. He's strong magically, but claims to have never been trained. He has no home. I'm just worried he wants to use you for something." That last part resonated with Carra. She hadn't mentioned anything about Dom wanting her to leave Rivulet with him, but the more she was forced to dwell on it, the more it became clear just how little she knew about what the quest entailed – or exactly how he expected to benefit from her help.

"I understand your concerns Ally, but you'll have to trust me even if you don't trust him. Surely you see that I can't just stay here. I need to find out about my magic, and there is nothing for me here."

"So now you are talking about going away with him?" Carra didn't have a response to that. She tried to change the subject, but failed, so instead she excused herself, claiming she needed some time alone to think.

She then immediately went looking for Sandria, to see what *she* thought of their new acquaintance.

"Last night was crazy, Carra. I know what draws you to him. He is mysterious and interesting, but is the thing that attracts you also the thing that puts you in danger? Do you trust him to keep you safe? Does he have your best interests at heart? What is it that he wants?"

"So many questions and… well, you know I don't have the answers. You're right of course. I mean, those are the important questions, and I'd like to know myself too." She nodded in agreement at Sandria, knowing she was just trying to prompt Carra to consider everything she needed to. "It feels like the right thing to do in my gut, but I need to decide whether to take the leap."

"It sounds to me, Carra, like you've already

decided." Sandria could be very perceptive sometimes. "When will you leave? Will you secret away?"

Carra shook her head. "No, not unless I absolutely have to. I will be here for the wedding, and I do plan on telling Nicholas. I've already suggested to him that I may not stay. What about you Sandria; will you come with us?"

Now Sandria shook her head. "I think this is a path for you to tread alone. Plus, I'm not sure trading in these pretty surroundings to go be homeless nomads together really appeals to me." Carra stuck her tongue out at her friend, determined not to allow either Sandria's or her own doubts to consume her thoughts. Especially when she was already mentally preparing herself to leave with Dom.

☆☆☆☆☆

When they sat in the drawing room that evening, this time they numbered five rather than four. Dom and Nicholas seemed to be best of friends after their jaunt that morning and Carra couldn't help repeatedly glancing sideways at the pair of them. They played chess together while the three girls talked about what kind of wedding dress Ally was having made, and what the celebratory feast would be. Even when they joined them on the armchairs, they were deep in conversation together. Carra had no idea what they could be talking about.

At the start of the night, Carra had felt frustrated about not being able to talk to Dom alone. However, there wasn't anything specific she needed to say to him, and as the night progressed Carra had to admit to herself that part of her was just jealous she was no longer the centre of Dom's attention. He was supposed to be *her* friend not Nicholas's and she was feeling possessive. Especially as he didn't seem bothered to talk to her in the slightest.

When the ostentatious grandfather clock sounded

out its chimes for midnight, she promised Ally she would join her in the morning to help select some fabrics, and excused herself.

☆ ☆ ☆ ☆

It wasn't until two whole days later that Carra spoke to Dom again, and as it happened, she was fairly unimpressed when the knock on her door in the middle of the night turned out to be him. Folding her arms, she told him to come back during the day.

Despite his lack of welcome, Dom slid past her into the room and actually went so far as to light a candle. "You look a state! Is that why you didn't want me around?"

"Charming. It's the middle of the night. I was having a flame dream and they make me sweat, literally. You being around here seems to bring them on every night."

"Oh." He sat down on the edge of the bed.

Not bothering to provide an explanation, Carra left the room. After refreshing herself with some cold water from a wash basin, she returned, taking a seat next to him on the bed. "What's up?"

"Nothing, I just wanted some company. Things seem to be going well." Carra looked at him quizzically. "I think Nicholas is on side. It'll be so much easier for us to leave together if he thinks I'm looking out for you. At some point I'm going to suggest I escort you to Whistlake. You could even make out like you don't want me to, then he won't be suspicious."

"Who says I do want you to?" Carra quipped.

"What difference, we are not going to Whistlake anyway." Dom replied, purposefully misunderstanding her.

"Where *are* we going then Dom?"

"I thought you might be able to tell me. My plan was just to find you."

"Okay. I've been thinking about it. We go to Florin and find your friend. The one who you left listening for clues. He is literally the only information source we have. Unless you know anything else you haven't told me yet…"

Dom's grunt in response was uninspiring, so she took it to mean 'I'll think about it'. Regardless, she had more important questions to ask him, like how he came to be looking for her in the first place.

So, she asked him something that been bothering her now for a few days. He had mentioned her 'bloodline' at least twice, but it wasn't until Ally and Sandria had quizzed her that she had started wondering about it further. *What makes him think that the girl his friend told him about was me?*

"I'm surprised you don't know about your bloodline Carra. The Perywhists are the oldest line of magic users."

"Perywhists? My family name is Anson."

"It is not your father, Carra, who you inherit your power from. Your father does have some modest ability, but it was your mother who was born a Perywhist. The prognostication I received merely referred to the Perywhist heir. I had discerned you were somewhere in northern Florinyn but that was where my knowledge ended.

"After I was rejected from Whistlake Academy – that was around three years ago – I posed as a messenger and travelled the area. I had very little luck, in fact. I spent a few days in each town I visited, searching for anyone who might have heard of you. In some cases I made discreet enquiries, but mostly I resigned myself to watching the occupants.

"Your features are those of Pellagea not Florinyn. In the south, there are a wide range of blondes, redheads and even a few who are dark-haired like me, though not many. This is because anyone relocating to Florinyn from another country heads straight for the city of Florin – there's nothing to attract them to the north.

"North Florinyn is inhabited almost solely by those of a similar complexion, typically mousey brown or dark blonde with hazel eyes. As soon as I saw you, I knew. From a distance, yes, I could see your darker hair, atypical in those parts, but closer up I could also see the family resemblance."

"Did you know my mother then?"

"No, not at all, but I have seen portraits of her and other members of the family. Anyway, it was luck in the end that I managed to locate you at all. Well, either chance or fate that is, but either way." He shrugged. "Having had no success in Florinyn, I travelled back into Pellagea to stock up on supplies and see some friends. I was also wondering if your family might have re-located there. It was only on a day that I had temporarily ventured back into Florinyn that I managed to first glean news of you.

"I was drinking at a table in an inn near the Pellagean border when I overheard three men at the next table talking. Their conversation centred around two girls with magic, who they were planning to take to Whistlake college, in order to blackmail the college for ransom money.

"Stupidly, I interrupted their conversation to ask if I could be of any assistance, which did not sit too well with people who had obviously intended to keep their motives private. One of them stood up and the next thing I knew I was brawling with three men.

"I was reluctant to use magic on full display – especially in such a public place, never-mind that I was back in Florinyn, where anyone could have had me arrested for so much as lighting a candle. Plus, when it was three men, I was winning easily." He paused and winked.

"However, it turned out these men weren't alone, and were either locals, or had others who were in on the scheme – I didn't get a good look at their faces – and before I knew it, the whole inn was in chaos. Ultimately, I had to decide between trudging back to Pellagea to engage the services of a healer or keeping sight of these men.

"I risked leaving – two broken ribs and other various minor scrapes would have made it difficult to keep up with them once they moved, and I knew a healer who'd be expeditious enough that I could be gone and back in two days. Luckily, they were still there."

"I heard about that incident!" Carra exclaimed. "I thought the inn had been raided in the same way our village had."

"No, it was purely my bravado causing trouble." *Did he seem... proud of this?* "Anyhow. Luckily for me, I was able to follow them as they went on their way. There were several of them and they made no effort to move quietly, so they never heard me trailing behind them. They led me straight *to* you. The rest, of course, you know."

"All those people who were hurt – you could have helped people!"

"Carra, I understand your dismay. It was difficult to stay hidden, but they didn't kill anyone, not intentionally. I made sure of it. After they made camp, I went into the village and helped those who were left as well as I could. I put out the fires and bound their wounds."

"I saw someone die Dom, they died right in front of me. He told me to run!"

"I'm so sorry, Carra. I'm sorry you had to see that. But it wasn't me who killed him, don't lose sight of that." They sat in silence for a while, and eventually Carra fell asleep. Dom pulled the cover over her, blew out the candle, and tip-toed lightly back to his own room.

CHAPTER 15

The wedding day was approaching more quickly than she'd expected, and Carra had resorted to hiding in Alliana's living room. It seemed as though she couldn't so much as stroll the corridors without wedding guests she'd never met before wishing her well, and despite everyone looking unfamiliar, *they* all seemed to know that *she* was the sister of the bride-to-be.

The guest bedroom she was now using had been chosen for her because she was able to access Ally's suite directly from her bedroom, and today, not needing to go through the hallway was a big advantage. There were enough social situations – dinners, and evening soirées – where she was forced to make conversation that she was now avoiding being around other people whenever she could.

She was restless.

Dom had slunk off somewhere two weeks earlier, having made some sort of weak excuse along the lines of needing to tie up loose ends before leaving. Carra was suspicious. She knew he'd wanted to leave right away and had only reluctantly let her stay for the wedding. He couldn't have had anything important to do if his first choice had been to leave, although she supposed Nicholas didn't know that.

She wondered if he had decided he'd imposed on Nicholas and his family enough; she thought that was the most probable reason he'd disappeared. They had become good friends, but she remained unsure as to whether it was just an act from Dom's side. Nicholas had worked hard to persuade Dom to stay and attend the wedding, but Carra didn't get the impression he'd even considered it. *I wonder who he's avoiding - perhaps one of the high mages is attending, and he was telling the truth about them wanting to keep him and me separate.*

So... she was intentionally confined to her room, and she was both bored and feeling sorry for herself.

Sandria was being kept busy by sheer virtue of the huge number of guests. She usually spent two half-days every week weaving, but she had been roped into using this time for cleaning instead. Sandria wasn't alone in this, all of the cleaning team were far busier than usual. Rooms that were usually empty, and therefore only cleaned weekly, were now required to be cleaned every day.

Carra hadn't been close to Nicholas ever since the engagement had been announced, but that was understandable, while Alliana was just generally busy meeting people and making arrangements.

The only duty Carra had was to smile and be polite. Although, she did have her dress fitting later that day. It was a little last minute, and she suspected Alliana must have reminded Nicholas that they'd forgotten about her. She was planning to opt for something simple, assuming she was going to be given a choice.

Sandria had already helped her gather together some travelling clothes – including both a light and heavy set – and she was expecting a large, white, suede cloak with fur lining to be completed any day now. Nicholas had agreed to this luxury because part of the wedding was to be outside in the snow and she needed something to wear over her dress anyway.

Thankfully, Nicholas had also agreed to give permission for Carra to leave with Dom, albeit the date had yet to be determined. Carra was anxious to get moving but then, she was naturally impatient. Behind her eagerness, the irrational part of her worried that Dom would simply find something else more interesting to do, and leave her stuck in Rivulet.

The suite door creaked open, disturbing Carra from her thoughts. Sandria peeked round it – Carra wasn't surprised it was her as no one else other than Ally would enter without knocking.

"Carra, Alliana asked me to come and get you. Guess what!" Carra waited for her to say more, but Sandria was teasing this out. "Ha ha well come with me, and you will see." Carra stood with her arms folded until Sandria got the message. "Oh, okay spoilsport – your father has just arrived! Come on."

Carra was already sprinting out of the door and down the stairs, launching into a huge hug when she reached him, irrespective of who was watching – which incidentally turned out to be Nicholas and Alliana, who were standing together looking very formal and subdued. She stepped back a pace and took note of his appearance. *He looks so much older than last time I saw him.*

The four of them found some seats and were brought refreshments while they caught up. Carra felt slightly irritated by the presence of Nicholas, and she suspected he was probably aware of this – even though she was trying not to let it show – because he kept fidgeting, which was quite unlike him. Carra had to wait while her father and Nicholas were introduced and exchanged pleasantries, but then he finally proceeded to relate what had become of Astonelay.

"There is still a village there, although the numbers are much depleted. From almost three hundred people, just under a third remain. Several families moved away, we estimated maybe a hundred were taken to the mines or slavers, and the rest were casualties. Twenty or so were murdered, dying during the raids, and a number of others were gravely wounded. Most of those who are left are elderly folk much like myself."

Carra suddenly felt a wave of guilt about the destruction caused by these men who had been looking for her. She snapped herself out of it. It wasn't her fault that was where her parents had chosen to live. "How did you manage to put the fires out? Have you been able to rebuild the houses? Did you have somewhere to live?"

"A young man helped us – a stranger to those of us who met him. He smothered the flames himself." Carra wondered if that could have been Dom, remembering his particular talents lay in that area, and that he said he'd helped the village. She was deliberating whether to ask the gentleman's name, but something told her that might give Nicholas reason to question whatever backstory Dom had fed him. Besides, the more she thought about it, there was no real question – it had to have been Dom.

"Then he helped us move those who were injured and did what he could to make them feel more comfortable. He was a true blessing. I was able to help a little, but I'm ashamed to admit, I hardly had any of my own strength remaining. My left leg was badly broken – and actually, it only very recently healed enough for me to travel.

"For some reason he left his horse behind, which is the only reason I was able to make it here for the wedding. He said something noble, along the lines that he was offering it as 'a gift to the village who had lost so much'. We planned to repay him with our hospitality, but he had left by the morning. To be honest I felt guilty borrowing it in order to ride here, but everyone insisted."

"We really appreciate you coming all this way father." Alliana said kindly. "It means so much to me. Would your leg be okay if I asked you to walk me down the aisle at the ceremony?"

"Nonsense, of course I came. It makes me happy to know my daughter is well cared for." Carra couldn't help but roll her eyes, then realised what she'd done, and that no one else present shared her opinion of Nicholas. She was relieved when she found that her gesture had gone unnoticed.

"Father." Carra started again. "Nicholas has introduced us to magic. I'm not sure how to phrase this but, I guess, I was wondering why you never mentioned anything?"

"We moved to Astonelay, your mother and I, to put our past behind us. Magic was part of that past. With it being outlawed in Florinyn, we thought it would be easier on you and your sister if you didn't even know you had such a weighty secret to hide. After your mother wasn't around anymore, I decided to stick with what we had agreed together, and let you remain ignorant."

"Carra, do you think you should tell your father of your plans?" Nicholas intervened. However, despite phrasing this as a question, he didn't actually give her chance to respond. "Sir. After the wedding, Carra is planning to head to Whistlake Academy in order to learn more about her magic, which is slightly erratic." *Of course, Nicholas doesn't know that fire magic was only possible for me through Dom.* "One of my friends will accompany her as her escort. It is a shame he is not here to meet you, but I assure you, I would not let her go if I did not trust him to keep her safe."

Wow. Dom had clearly made a big impression in a very short amount of time. Either that or Nicholas *really* wanted rid of her.

"Thank you for looking out for her, Nicholas. Carra, are you sure you want to become more involved in this world? Whistlake has extremely high entry requirements and they are unlikely to look on you favourably given your parents' isolation from the community. You must understand, it was done to protect you. I don't know the full details, but your mother was quite adamant that you could actually be in danger should you make yourself known to the council."

It was annoying. With Nicholas there, she couldn't tell her father of her real plans, which of course would take her far away from Whistlake. "Father, I will think about your counsel, though I am inclined to believe I am more at danger if I cannot control my magic. Perhaps you can give me a day to think about this and then we can talk again?"

☆☆☆☆

Carra found dinner far more pleasant with her father there for company, and after dinner, she didn't even mind the social interaction as much. However, she still excused herself not long before midnight, saying she was tired.

She did plan on heading up to bed shortly, but first she went for a walk around the grounds. There was a light covering of snow and it was pretty despite the cold. She tried to look as casual as possible, but really, she was hoping she might spy Dom, whom she had convinced herself was keeping an eye on her.

Having found no trace of him, and given she was already outside in the cold, she decided to head through the forest and down to the lake. It was the first time she had seen it frozen over, and the ice glistened in the moonlight. Taking a second or two to admire it, she hurried back to the house. She was freezing, and she could see that Dom wasn't around, nor were there any footprints in sight.

With no magical dreams, she slept well that night.

☆☆☆☆

The next morning, after breakfast, she found she had the opportunity to speak to her father alone. "Father, I need to tell you something in confidence, and I implore you to trust me. Nicholas thinks I plan to go to this Whistlake Academy, but really, I just need to leave this house and find my place in the world. Like you, I don't think it's a good idea for me to approach the magic school."

Carra was hoping that her father would actually be happier about her leaving if he wasn't worried about her going to Whistlake. As an afterthought, she added, "If I'm unhappy I can always come back. You mustn't tell him though; please don't. If he finds out then he will keep me hostage here instead."

"Oh Carra, it's the middle of winter! As relieved as I am that you don't plan to seek out those mages, I can't say I like the idea of you traipsing about across the countryside. I don't even have money spare to give you for food. If you are unhappy here, why don't you come back with me instead? We could get you an apprenticeship. Or I'm sure you could find a kind husband, like Alliana has, if you stayed. I'm certain you'll get used to the society after a while and even start to enjoy it."

"It was really that obvious I was uncomfortable?"

"No of course not, sweetie." Except, from what he'd said, it clearly was. "Carra, is it this friend of Nicholas's that you are running off for? He can't be a true gentleman if he is asking you to run away with him."

"No, yes, I mean, it's not like that. Father, the man in our village that helped you – I think it might be the same man. There is no romantic attachment." Her father raised his eyebrows at her. "No honestly, father. You know him to be a good man. He has offered to travel with me. I think I could learn a lot from him. He can probably help me learn to control my magic as well without me having to go to Whistlake."

"A lot has happened to you in the last few months Carra. Take this week while he is not here to think about what you actually want. If this is really it, then go with my blessing – but know that I have concerns. Think properly about what life you would be choosing for yourself. Could you sleep on the ground if there was no inn? How will you pay for food? There may be extended periods where you stay in solely one town; times where hard labour is required just to earn enough money to continue this adventure of yours."

Carra jumped up with glee and kissed her father on the cheek. As far as she was concerned, he wasn't going to stand in her way – there were no more obstacles.

CHAPTER 16

The day they had all been waiting for – albeit with varying reasons – arrived at last. Carra awoke with a slight feeling of guilt over how anxious she was to see the day over. She hardly knew any of the guests attending, which she accepted was partially her own fault, but it was going to be a long day of forced smiling.

She wasn't jealous of Alliana and Nicholas like she had been at first, back when she had thought something was happening between Nicholas and herself. It wasn't that she didn't enjoy celebrations either. Her biggest issue was that she still considered there was only a limited romantic attachment between the pair.

All she could see was Nicholas marrying for the magical prowess of his line, and her sister marrying for comfort. At least, she tried to convince herself it was the latter, as she hated the idea of Ally having been taken in by Nicholas.

She wondered whether Nicholas had ever really been attracted to her, or he had just expected her to be the one with ability. Both her and her sister were attractive, but in their village, it was always Alliana that received the male attention. Carra suspected it may have been quite a lot to do with the difference in their temperaments. Whereas Ally was sweet, she was fiery and opinionated – but fun to be around in a way that she didn't overly think her sister was.

Sandria was unimpressed to find her loitering in the reception room of Ally's suite. "Carra! Why are you still in your nightclothes?" She shrugged in response. *Oh dear, I'd better snap out of this.* "Come along, get into your dress and I'll help you do it up at the back."

Carra stepped into her jade-green, silk dress and pulled it up. There were two thin straps to hold it in place, and a delicate cross-lace across the back, which Sandria tightened for her. It hugged her figure, cinching in at the waist, curving out at her hips, and then skimmed the floor, trailing slightly behind her even with her silver heeled pumps, which gave her an extra three inches of height. It was tight over her bust, but still modest – it didn't reveal any cleavage.

When she'd selected it, she'd gone for something she thought looked appealing yet demure, but having the dress on now, she realised she might have preferred something that would have better allowed her to blend into the background. At least while she had her coat over the top, she'd not have her figure quite so much on show.

Carra was tempted to leave her curls loose, but Sandria insisted on scraping them up, onto the top of her head, and she had to admit, it did look sophisticated.

Sandria was also coming to the wedding, and the burgundy gown with long brocaded sleeves she'd selected was much less showy. They smiled at each other and held hands on the way down to the ceremony. Both girls knew they might not have much more time together before Carra departed.

☆ ☆ ☆

The ceremony was beautiful. The guests stood to either side as Alliana walked with their father down a blue carpet, which had been placed over the snow to serve as an aisle. There was a silver, arched trellis for them to stand beneath when they reached the end, which had been lined with white polyanthus. It was magnificent and, Carra noted, surprisingly tasteful.

Afterwards, they were asked to make their way into the ballroom. Carra had only been in there once before, and it had been empty. Now, there were rows of tables with benches. She had to take a place at the top table, whereas Sandria was placed amongst some of Nicholas's friends – Carra wasn't sure whether she knew any of the gentlemen already, but her friend looked sufficiently at ease with the situation that she wasn't concerned for her.

There was plenty of food, and Carra found she was concentrating on eating rather than making conversation. The amount she ate raised an interesting question; making her wonder how easily she would be able to survive on whatever meagre portions her and Dom were able to carry.

Oh well, nothing I can do about it as my mind is made up... may as well make the most of the abundance while I can! She had never previously been accustomed to eating this much, prior to her time at Nicholas's house.

As soon as dinner was over, and she could leave the table without being rude, she sought out Sandria. Half of her table had decided to light cigars, so Carra knew she'd be happy to step away for a bit. "Shall we go for a walk together?"

"It's another frosty night, let's keep it brief." They grabbed their coats and wandered into the garden. "So, will you leave in the morning?" Sandria must have been waiting for the right time to ask her.

"I don't know yet, it really depends on whenever Dom gets back."

"Do you not find it suspicious that he didn't come back a day earlier for the wedding?"

"If he comes back first thing tomorrow I will! I genuinely have no idea where he has gone." They sat down on a bench. "I know you think I'm flighty, with no regard for my own safety."

"Yes?" Sandria prompted.

"Perhaps I am." She shrugged in thought.

"Oh. Is that all? No defensive explanation?"

"No, Sandria. I'm running away to find adventure. I don't know Dom, but then earlier this year I did not know Nicholas either. I'm not scared of what's out there, not after everything that's happened to us. I want to see the big cities in Pellagea and Florinyn. I want excitement." Carra paused and caught her breath. "I suppose it's not something I can really explain, it's just a gut-feeling that tells me to make one choice over another."

"I understand, and I wish you luck, Carra. I hope you find what you are looking for. I will miss you – and I will always be here for you." Sandria stood up and gave Carra a meaningful hug; not a quick take-your-leave, it was an indicator of the strength of their friendship.

"I'm glad you've been here with me, Sandria. I hope you know that."

✦ ✦ ✦ ✦

Needless to say, Dom did not come back for her the next day, nor the day after that, and Carra wasn't sure what to do with herself.

When Dom still hadn't shown up after four days, she was starting to worry that he'd forgotten about her. Her father set off for home at lunchtime that day, and she was sorely tempted to go with him. If it hadn't been for the fact he was travelling on horseback and she would have had to walk beside him, she may even have done so. He was one of the last guests to leave, and the house felt incredibly quiet after he had gone.

Trying to distract herself, she settled for a walk to

Rivulet's famous market. The market was split into sections, and she started by the food market, walked through the metalworkers' street, and found herself in the 'bits and bobs' area. A lady selling purported magical charms for protection caught her attention, but when she asked how they worked or who made the magic, the lady couldn't answer, and Carra lost interest.

By the end of the day, she had a list of items she wanted to take with her, including dried foods and nuts that were easy to carry, and a jewelled dagger that had taken her fancy.

As she made her way back to the house, Carra had the funny sensation she was being followed – but when she turned around, no one was there. She decided to walk more quickly.

The second time she looked, there was a man in a hood. "Hello? Dom, is that you?" The hooded figure paused and looked at her. "If you saw me at the market, then I know you aren't following me for my money!"

He pulled his hood back slightly, and she saw it was indeed Dom, before he covered his head once again. "Where have you been?" she asked, this time more quietly.

"Around. Are you ready to go?"

"Yes, whenever you are."

"Okay, I have two horses waiting for us, follow me."

"Right now? I didn't mean literally this second. I need to go and get a couple of changes of clothes and some food. I need to say goodbye!"

"Yes. If you prefer to do so, then of course you may. I will wait here for you." She looked at him curiously, trying to work out why he wasn't coming with her. "You may pass my regards to Nicholas if you wish, but I hardly know the fellow. I was just trying to flatter him into letting you come with me."

"I figured as much. Okay then. I will be back in a few hours, around dusk."

"Dusk? That is no time to set off on a journey. Let's meet tomorrow morning at dawn. Then you can make sure you have a good night's sleep as well." She nodded, smiling at him in farewell. "Oh, and Carra," he called after her, and she turned her head to see what he wanted, "If you're bringing extra clothes, don't forget the green dress." She thought she even saw him wink.

"All my dresses are green Dom, only my travelling clothes are brown."

"I'm sure you know which one I mean."

☆☆☆☆☆

When she got back, Carra sought out Nicholas, Alliana and Sandria. They spent the evening together in the drawing room. No one tried to talk her out of leaving, and in fact they barely mentioned it, instead acting as if nothing was about to change. She hoped that meant they had accepted her decision.

Nicholas did ask where Dom was, and she made an excuse for him; purporting that he wasn't actually back yet, but she had received a note saying where she should meet him. Carra didn't see any reason to hurt Nicholas's feelings, and besides, she might yet want to come back here.

☆☆☆☆☆

That night, Carra dreamt she was walking in the snow, down by the lake. It was still frozen but there was a line of flames across the middle of it. She was wearing the dress she had worn to the wedding, but instead of pumps, she had boots on her feet.

She wasn't sure how he'd seen her at the nuptials,

but when she woke up, she had absolutely no doubts as to which dress Dom had been referring.

CHAPTER 17

Carra left while the sun was still rising.

Dom was waiting where he'd said he would be, and they walked towards the inn. "I was wondering if we should make some purchases from the market for our trip? This is a slightly awkward question, but do you actually have any money? My father left me a silver and six coppers, but I don't think we should spend everything at once."

"Was there something in particular you were thinking of? I have already obtained food for both of us, and I'm sure you packed some from the manor before you left?"

"There *was* something that caught my eye actually. I thought maybe a dagger might be useful."

Dom actually laughed at her. "I think you would do more harm than good if I gave you a dagger. I assume you haven't used one before?" Carra shook her head. "Don't worry, I have a couple of knives of my own, see." He lifted his sleeve to show Carra a knife strapped to his wrist. "Plus, I have another at my ankle. Don't forget my talent with flames either. You'll be safe with me."

A stable hand interrupted to inform them he had saddled the horses, and Carra had her first look at their new companions. Dom had selected a sturdy white mare and a sleek black stallion – she assumed the former was for her.

Under Dom's direction, they walked the horses to the town's south-western gate. This was the gate that Carra had entered by, and the walls of the town still looked almost as imposing to her on exiting them as they had when she'd first seen them.

The guards didn't challenge them as they left, so she supposed that generally, travellers were free to come and go. It still felt strangely ominous to Carra when they re-closed the gates – behind them before they had even had time to mount up.

Having previously only ridden a horse a handful of times, she was glad when Dom helped her into the saddle, even if he did stifle a laugh as he did so. He sprung up onto his own horse as if he'd been born to it.

"These two are different breeds then?" She said trying to distract him, realising too late to stop herself how dim that question was. "I mean, obviously they are, but which breeds?"

"I'm riding Jak, who is native to Cillamon." At Carra's blank look, he added, "that's the province to the west of Florinyn."

"So, Florinyn is sandwiched in between Pellagea to the right and Cillamon to the left?"

"Maybe I should buy you a map in case you get lost." He quickly added, "I'm joking," and Carra supposed that was due to the stricken look on her face. "Okay, and your mare is called 'Hope' and she is from Pellagea. Jak is a bit of a racer, but she should be a bit less flighty and more steadfast. Don't worry though, Hope can canter with the best of them when she needs to."

"Who named her Hope?"

"I did. Why?"

"No reason. Just curious."

"Are you laughing at me?" He frowned and his forehead crinkled in a strangely appealing way.

"No, not really. I mean, maybe a little, but no, I'm not. More importantly, Dom... did you decide where we are going? Will we roam the lands aimlessly, or shall we go to your 'friend' in South Florinyn?"

"Well, Carra Anson. I have thought about it and, annoyingly, you are right. We shall go to South Florinyn – but I may need your assistance in a few matters while we're there. If we were to travel the quickest route, we could head west straight-away. It's about thirty miles back to the border with Florinyn, then maybe seventy or eighty south-west to Florin. It'll add an extra half a day, but I'm going to suggest that instead, we hug the border as we travel south, staying in Pellagea where we will attract less attention. We'd then turn into Florinyn as late as possible. In total, it should take around four or five days. If we keep up a reasonable pace, that is."

"Sounds like you have it all planned out." She gave him a thumbs up.

"I'm just hoping that when we're ready to retire each evening there's an inn nearby. We can always stop a bit early if we find somewhere; we're not in any great hurry."

After setting off, they rode in relative quiet, so Carra took time to appreciate the scenery. The wind was brisk, and even with her coat underneath it, she had her cloak wrapped tightly around her.

There was still a thin layer of snow across the ground, so they had to concentrate to make sure they were following the path, rather than straying on to the grass, which was quite slippery. Whilst the gravelly path was mostly okay, they had to be careful not to fall prey to the more treacherous patches – where holes in the road had filled with water and iced over.

Carra had no choice but to trust in Hope's ability to know where she was treading, and trust in Dom to lead them.

After only a few hours, her legs started to ache from the travelling. She rubbed her thighs with her hands to try and ease her muscles, but it wasn't having any effect. "Shall we stop for some lunch now?" she asked rather hopefully, and was pleased when Dom acquiesced.

Having dismounted from their horses, Dom showed her how to take care of them, before loosely tying them to a tree. They shared some berries and dried meat, and not being able to get comfortable, she ate them as quickly as possible.

Carra was feeling increasingly stiff, but did her best to avoid letting Dom see that she was struggling, as *he* seemed to be absolutely fine. She put her hands on her legs again, then took a deep breath to clear her head, and tried to relax, imagining the pain leaving her. When she opened her eyes, Dom was looking at her askew.

"Was that you?" he asked her. Carra looked at him, uncertain of what he was referring to, and shrugged. "Were you using magic?"

"Not that I know of! Doing what?"

"I don't know. What were you thinking about when you had your eyes closed?"

"I was just trying to ease the aching in my muscles. I'm not used to riding." She blushed.

"So how do they feel now?" Dom asked her.

"I haven't really thought about it. Better, I guess. They aren't bothering me in the same way anymore."

"I think you just used healing magic on yourself. Have you tried anything like that before?"

She had to think about it for a while. "Sort of, but not really. I've always found if I concentrate on something that's bothering me, trying to release the tension from my body helps. When I attempted healing magic with Nicholas though, nothing I tried had any effect."

"Did you attempt to heal yourself?"

"I can't remember, but maybe not. It's only sore muscles, Dom. I don't think you can read anything into it." For some reason she felt the need to change the subject, probably because she didn't want Dom to start thinking she was more useful than she was – she still didn't understand why he wanted her tagging along. "It's getting cold. The sooner we get to an inn for the evening, the sooner we can get warm again." She grinned at the thought of a beer in front of a fireplace, something that it seemed like a long time since she had last enjoyed.

Dom laughed. "Carra, did you forget? You should have mentioned you were cold, come over here and I will warm you up. With my magic, I barely feel the cold." He moved over, such that he was sitting right by her, and put his hand on her arm. She could actually feel her insides warming up, starting from where his hand lay, and radiating outwards.

"Does it not drain you, if you are using it all the time?"

"It hardly takes any energy to keep my own body warm, and besides, I *am* terribly powerful and all that." Carra waited for him to follow his gloating with a wink, and of course he did – that was how she knew that even though he said it like he was joking, he believed it to be true.

"Oh yes of course, Dom the mighty, how could I have forgotten." He didn't rise to her teasing.

They hadn't unsaddled the horses, so it didn't take long before they were on their way again. Carra's legs did actually feel better, but she wasn't sure if that was just because they'd stopped for a bit. Instead, it was now the cold she found unpleasant, which she had begun to feel again the moment she had moved away from Dom. Carra decided she needed some conversation as a distraction. "So can healers usually heal other people, or can some only heal themselves?"

"It's a lot harder to heal yourself than other people, but the stronger ones can do both. I've never heard of anyone who could solely heal themselves. I suppose it could be quite handy, though."

She paused and tried to assess his face. "So, you *do* think where we're going might be dangerous?"

"It's difficult to say. Just by virtue of us travelling through Florinyn we are putting ourselves at some risk. There is a chance I might be recognised." He paused. "It's been several years since I've been back there – maybe the scaremongering has died down a bit now."

Carra reflected over his words. "What about magic horses. Couldn't you have got us some of those or were they too expensive?"

"Unfortunately, the magic horses are really busy this time of year. They like to fly south for the winter."

Carra ignored him and stroked the side of her mare. "Well Hope, are you going to look after me, and protect me against my shifty travelling companion?" Hope whinnied, as if in response, and Carra beamed with delight.

☆☆☆

Later in the afternoon, on finding themselves approaching a village, they mutually decided they had travelled far enough that day. Carra was pleased because it was still light out and she had the chance to look around, even if it was too cold to linger outside for long.

There was only one inn, so Dom took the horses to be stabled there.

The innkeeper greeted them warmly, and happily, he had rooms available. No matter how friendly he was, Carra found she couldn't help but feel a slight animosity against the Pellageans – based on their slave trade – and yet Florinyn didn't really feel like her home anymore either.

She was looking forward to seeing Florin, the capital, but equally, was feeling slightly deterred by the fact that Dom was evidently concerned about travelling there. He instead seemed much more at home in Pellagea.

Dom asked for a room under the names of Mr and Mrs Anson and Carra couldn't help but roll her eyes.

The room was basic but very cosy, and it had its own bath chamber, which Carra hadn't been expecting.

As soon as the innkeeper left them, she turned to Dom and rolled her eyes again. She was quite good at that. "I suppose you're going to tell me now that it's safer if we travel as a married couple."

"Perhaps. I thought you would find it easier to remember if we used your surname rather than mine."

"And what do you plan to do about the fact there's only one bed and no sofa?"

Carra was a bit taken aback when Dom laughed at her in response. "Surely you trust me enough to share the bed. After all, you are travelling the wilderness alone with me and it's not as though you know me very well. I didn't have you figured for a prude." *Fair point, although he was wrong about her not being modest.*

As Carra didn't really have a good response to give him, she walked over to the bed and lifted the cover, finding that – as she had been hoping – it was actually two smaller beds pushed together to make a larger one. She methodically separated them and took the cover for herself. "It's not like you need it to keep warm so I will take this if you don't mind. Shall we go and get some hot food?" She smiled. "And beer. I've had my fill of wine for a while."

CHAPTER 18

The next two days continued in much the same vein, and they eventually reached the Florinyn border. They were along the same latitude as Florin – according to Dom – so now they just had to travel in a straight line across to the capital.

It wasn't long before the landscape changed, confirming they'd crossed into a different country; it was noticeably greener than Pellagea. Unlike North Florinyn, however, most of the trees had been felled to make way for well-paved roads, and it didn't have the same 'forested' feel that Carra realised she preferred.

Dom had been the perfect travelling companion. He was good fun but also quite protective. On the second night, Carra had been the only female in quite a busy inn, and he had actually growled at the men who had looked her way.

The snow had begun to clear as they'd traveled southwards, but Dom still regularly took her hand and warmed her. When the wind had been particularly bad, they had even slowed their pace so he could hold her hand. He had been helpful with the horses too, using his warming hands on their calves to ease their muscles.

His manner shifted as soon as they entered Florinyn.

He had tried to do it discretely, but of course Carra noticed he had immediately put his hood up; knowing it was to hide his face rather than for warmth. She wondered if other travellers would be intimidated by the pair of them. She had her hood up too, to protect from the cold, but somehow she didn't think she cut quite as imposing a figure; after all, her hood was lined with fluffy white fur.

He also became a lot less interested in making conversation, and Carra sat on Hope quietly beside him.

Shortly after lunchtime, they passed a village. It seemed early to stop, but she looked to Dom for his thoughts. "I don't know this area too well, Carra. There are three large cities in South Florinyn, and most people live in those, so there aren't as many hamlets. I don't know for certain, but I expect there will be more inns along the roads to compensate."

"I'm sure it will be fine, Dom. I'm happy to keep going. The sun is shining through the clouds and it's quite a nice day for journeying, considering we are only a few weeks past midwinter."

Although she'd spoken her mind at the time, once she'd had longer to think about it, Carra wondered if they should have stopped and spent the day relaxing – but by then they were much too far past to go back.

Both Dom and Carra began to tire before the afternoon was over, but a couple of hours passed without them finding anywhere to spend the night. It was still getting dark quite early, and before they had managed to do anything about it, their visibility had practically disappeared.

Staying close together, they still hoped to find somewhere soon. It wasn't actually that late, there were still a few hours to go until midnight, but they had been forced to slow the horses right down to a walk. At this pace, they were hardly covering any distance – not to mention the fact the temperature had also dropped, and they had to keep an awkward position; so Dom could keep her warm, but they could simultaneously keep the horses from becoming agitated.

She was finding the quiet rather unnerving given they couldn't see, and genuinely jumped out of her skin when Dom interrupted it. "At this pace, we're not going to get anywhere." Carra thought he was just grumbling, but then he continued, "The way I see it we have two options. Either we dismount and keep going on foot, or we use my tent and bedroll to make camp for the night. I know we were hoping to avoid sleeping rough as much as possible, but we may just have to brave it tonight. We do still have some food left."

It wasn't exactly what she wanted to hear, but she knew what he said made sense. They resolved to keep walking for a while, as neither of them really wanted to sleep on the ground, but after another hour they decided that it was time to admit defeat. Giving up, they stopped for the night.

Rather than making camp by the side of the road, they moved a couple of hundred paces off the path. "Should one of us be keeping watch, Dom? I don't know how safe this is."

"The horses will spook if anyone is nearby, and on top of that, I'm a very light sleeper. I've slept outside a lot over the last few years and never been caught unawares. You don't need to worry." Carra nodded, seeing that she needed to trust in Dom.

Although their food didn't need to be cooked, they had to light a fire in order to see what they were doing. As soon as they had eaten and set up the tent, they smothered it. "It's just an extra precaution, don't worry. It's very unlikely anyone will come across us anyway, the road's been empty for the last few hours. Not many sane people travel around at this time of year!"

Carra felt a bit awkward climbing into a tent with Dom, but he seemed to manage to put her at ease somehow. The first thing he did was put his arms around her and warm her up, which Carra found slightly awkward – yet she was incredibly glad of it. She could almost pretend she was in her bed back home in Astonelay with a coal fire burning.

Sleep even came easily to her. Whenever she was in close proximity to Dom, they seemed to share their dreams about fire. This time they were both riding on the same horse along a beach, next to the sea. The sun was shining, and the only flame was a tiny one that Carra was holding in the palm of her hand.

Unlike other nights, Carra was able to converse with Dom – even though she was usually partially aware, she didn't remember them actually talking in any of their previous dreams. "I've never seen the sea, so this must be your memory."

"I think it is, although it must be a memory from when I was very young. I believe this is the south coast of Pellagea."

"I like it here. It feels like we're really under the sun's rays. Can we paddle into the sea?" Dom pulled the horse to a halt, and they climbed off it. Carra tugged off her pumps and waded into the water, then turned round to see why Dom hadn't followed her. He had one finger over his mouth and was looking around suspiciously.

"Shhh, I think I heard something." Dom disappeared.

Carra was woken up by the sound of someone moving nearby, only to see Dom leaving the tent. She grabbed her cloak and peered out of the tent door. It was hard to see because there was only a slither of moon visible, but she thought there were several men outside.

Gradually, her eyes adjusted. Yes, there were three of them, and they had formed a circle around Dom. The men had their knives drawn and Dom drew his in response, though his were shorter. He spun around artfully, fending off their attacks. She had never seen anything quite so graceful. The knives clanged together, but each time, Dom made it look as though this was an intended part of his dance.

Dom rotated and one of the men went down, a slash across his stomach. Then he ducked, and threw one of his knives right into the leg of one of the others. The third tried to run, but Dom threw a knife into his back and the man fell forward.

Now the danger had passed, Carra ran out to see if he was okay. *He doesn't even have a scratch on him.* Dom however, was busy – he was using one of his knees to pin the man whose leg he had stabbed against the ground. The man twitched violently as Dom pulled the knife out of his leg, then held it to his throat. "What are you after?" Dom demanded.

The man wheezed, and a single tear fell from his left eye to the ground. "Just coins sir, coins to buy some food."

Carra could see that Dom was looking at the man with disdain. "Do you find that your targets are generally the most willing to give up their coin when you try to slit their throats in the middle of the night as they sleep?" The man's eyes darted from side to side trying to find a way out. He didn't seem to be able to think of a response.

"I'm sorry, I'm sorry, I'm sorry." Dom let out a small snort and used some rope to tie the man to a tree. Carra used to time to examine his two companions. They were both dead.

Her emotions over this were conflicted. She didn't feel sorry for the men – they would have done the same to her without remorse – but she was surprised at her own reaction; feeling guilty that she didn't regret what Dom had done to them. She was also confused from having observed her traveling companion kill two men without effort, and seemingly without feeling. It reminded her of how little she actually knew about him.

Dom rose silently, took Carra's hand and led her back into the tent, where, tired as they were, they both went back to sleep.

The next morning, the man was still where they had left him, and after they had packed up the tent, Dom untied him before mounting Jak. Carra was already astride Hope, and they rode back to the path, to once again begin their journey for the day.

Carra kept glancing backwards in the direction of the man; he hadn't yet moved from where they had left him. "Dom, I don't think he's able to walk. How is he going to get anywhere to find help?"

"Not our problem. I'm sure he'll manage to limp if his life depends on it."

"I suppose." This was a strange one for Carra. Did she really feel sorry for the man who had attacked them during the night? She was struggling to decide. She tried to put it out of her mind, but she kept picturing Dom's agility as he'd despatched the combatants. She knew he'd been on his own for a long time, but no one could learn to fight like that without training.

As if he'd read her mind, he vocalised a response to her query. "I didn't expect you to come out of the tent and see me. When I was younger, I studied the combat arts. Obviously, I had a good tutor."

"You're so vain sometimes, Dom." *And there's something inexplicably – but annoyingly – attractive about that.* She added silently.

"It's not vain if it's matter of fact. Anyway, I received schooling for several years, and it is not something you can easily forget."

"Have you been attacked before like that?" *Have you killed before?* The unspoken question she didn't dare ask, but already knew the answer to.

"A couple of times, yes. It is a hazard of travelling alone. It can attract attention. You would think people would work out that if you are travelling by yourself, it is probably because you are capable of protecting yourself, but no, those idiots just see an 'easy target'... It's not usually the brightest ones." *Hmm, not just vain, also arrogant.*

"You can think me arrogant if you want."

"Erm, Dom?"

"Yes, Carra?"

"That's the second time you've done that just now." He shrugged like he didn't know what she was referring to. "Can you hear what I'm thinking? You seem to be reading my mind!"

"No, of course I can't. Have you hit your head little tigress?" Carra rolled her eyes. It was better than 'angel' she supposed. She wondered if he had given Alliana a pet name – perhaps Nicholas even called her sister angel too. "Last night, Carra, did you notice that it was the first time we've had an actual conversation in our dreams?"

"I did, but I guess I had already forgotten with everything that went on. Do you think it's because we were making actual physical contact while we slept? I mean, it would make sense because the dreams are certainly a lot clearer and more realistic when you are nearby."

"There's one way to find out!" Dom said with a smarmy wink that made Carra want to change the subject again.

"How do you think Hope and Jak are getting on with all this travelling? We haven't given them a day off at all. Maybe we should walk today and let them take it more slowly."

"We've not really been pushing them hard. I think if we continue on horseback, we should make it to Florin by midday tomorrow – and then they can have all the rest they like." Jak reared his head and neighed deeply as if he had heard. Carra laughed, as much because of that, as from the relief of hearing they were nearly at their destination. "Can't you use your healing devilry on them if you're worried?"

"I've tried, but I can't tell if it's working. If anything, it's seemed to help them more when you've massaged their legs. Let's just keep going and see how we get on."

That day seemed to drag on even longer than any of the others. Carra suspected it was because she knew they weren't far from their destination. Not for the first time, a thought occurred to her, but this time she decided to express it. "Dom, have we got a plan for when we get to Florin. Do you know how we can get in contact with your friend?"

"Don't worry, Carra. Yes, I have a plan." That was all he said. She stared at him, waiting expectantly for him to add some more detail, but he didn't. As a reaction to his evident lack of trust in her, resentment began to build within her.

She tried to take a deep breath and wait before saying anything. She was about to give up trying when Dom started laughing. "Oh Carra, you are so predictable. I'm not keeping my plan a secret from you, I just knew that I could get a rise from you. Your angry face is adorable though... I can't keep up the ruse any longer. There is an inn I intend to head to, where one of my contacts has always been a regular. We will give them the same names, Carra and Dom Anson, and I will wait in the communal area with the hope of finding him. It is a risk, we can't avoid that, but I think I can trust him. He can then get a message to my friend."

Carra thought it over for a moment before pointing out the obvious flaw. "What if he doesn't show up? How long do we wait?"

"We'll worry about that when it happens."

"Meaning you don't know."

"I think we've been spending too much time together." Carra stuck her tongue out at him.

In the middle of the afternoon, Florin actually came into view. She was relieved to find it looked a lot less intimidating than Rivulet had, with its high stone walls. She hadn't even realised it had been bothering her so much. "How far away do you think it is Dom, could we make it there tonight perhaps?"

"We're around fifteen miles away now. Potentially if we rode quickly we might, but it wouldn't be until after midnight. I suppose we don't have any reason to be awake early in the morning."

"Would it look suspicious if we turned up then – two strangers, in the middle of the night?" Carra wasn't sure why she'd pointed that out, as she was desperately hoping they would spend tonight at an inn. She definitely didn't need a repeat of last night.

"I doubt it. Florin is a very large city. People come and go at all hours. The inn will probably still be booming with life until well into the early hours of the morning."

"Let's do it then!" She kicked Hope's flank and they started a canter. Dom's steed quickly caught up, and they sped up to a gallop for a couple of miles. Carra was enjoying herself immensely, but Dom slowed down and she reined Hope back into a walk.

"If we tire the horses out while we're still ten miles away, it'll be a long walk."

Killjoy.

CHAPTER 19

It was at the darkest point of the night when they finally entered Florin, but the city was still lit up. After having ridden through the quiet residential areas on the outskirts, they entered the city proper. Oil lanterns lined the sides of the cobbled avenues, and Carra saw rows of shops, which were all closed up for the evening. The streets with pubs and inns were still bustling.

She could tell Dom knew his way around competently, as he steered them through the streets with ease, seemingly beelining for the inn. As they approached the busier areas, they dismounted their horses, but Carra followed suit and kept her hood up over her face. "Is something happening tonight, Dom? Why is everyone out celebrating?"

Dom moved closer to her and spoke in a low whisper, "No Carra, this is what the capital is like every night. The drinking establishments become busy, and overspill into the streets."

Carra couldn't believe how many people there were. Most of them must surely have had to get up in a few hours to go to work – although seemingly there were also a lot of beggars interspersed within the crowd.

A man holding a pewter tankard bashed into her and she moved closer to Dom. "Not much further now."

As they approached Dom's chosen tavern, Carra was relieved to find it looked a bit nicer than many of the others they had walked past. She let Dom lead the way inside and enquire if there was a room available. The lady tavern-keeper was quite different from other places they had stayed.

"That will be three silvers please."

"Has the custom here always been to require payment in advance?" Dom asked boldly.

"Any who are not regulars, then yes. Many patrons are unable to settle the debt, and we *are* one of the more expensive taverns."

"We are looking to stay for a few nights but I'm not sure how long yet. Would you accept if I paid you five silvers for three nights?"

The lady thought for a while, then nodded. "I will show you to your room. My name is Kylle. Nice to meet you Mr and Mrs Anson."

They followed her up some carpeted stairs for two floors. Even though she'd seen the fancy entrance and already had high expectations, Carra was still nicely surprised when she saw the room. It was far more luxurious than anywhere else they had stayed. "Oh," Kylle exclaimed, "This room is set up with two beds. I'm sorry, this is the last room, but if you will excuse me for a moment I will have someone push these together for you."

"That's okay, we don't mind." Carra chirped, but received a strange look from Kylle in response. "I just meant, I can do that. I feel at a loss without my wifely household duties." Carra didn't think Kylle was convinced but, much to her relief, she still left them to it. Carra looked up to see Dom shaking his head at her. She ignored him and went to get washed.

"Carra. I must go downstairs and wait in case my contact shows here tonight."

She decided to let Dom continue being cryptic about the identity of his friend, as she was really pleased to be somewhere so comfortable. After all, he probably didn't even know he was being annoying. "At this time of night? How will they know to come?"

"They don't, that's why the sooner I look for them the better. He used to drink here five nights a week." Dom looked pensive. "It's been a long time since I was last here though."

"Just how long ago are we actually talking about?"

"Just get dressed and come with me. We'll attract less attention as a couple. If he doesn't show within a few days, we'll have to rethink. No point worrying about 'what ifs' before that."

They took a seat near the bar with a couple of ales. Dom wasn't in the mood for conversation, but Carra didn't mind. She was utterly fascinated by the variety of people coming and going. It was much busier than any inn she had been to before – which wasn't really surprising, given North Florinyn was only populated by small villages, and she'd never left there except to go to Nicholas's house.

Momentarily, she wondered if she had made the right decision by coming away with Dom instead of becoming a 'lady', but it was only a fleeting thought. What was done was done. Besides, Nicholas would have continued irritate her no matter how nice his family were, or how much she bonded with her sister.

After a couple of hours, she couldn't stay awake any longer and went up to bed. Dom remained behind, waiting hopefully.

✦ ✦ ✦

Carra woke up the next morning feeling refreshed. She was surprised to see that Dom wasn't there, but at least his bed looked slept in. She figured he must have come upstairs at some point, slept briefly, then decided to be up and about early. *Guess I have the day to myself.*

She was still wondering what to do with herself as she made her way downstairs, but Dom surprised her by calling out her name as she walked towards the entrance. She took a seat at his table, which was the same one they had sat at last night. "Where are you going?"

"I was just going to go for a walk. I wasn't sure where you were."

"Oh, you can if you like. I'm just going to wait here."

"Dom... do you not think you're attracting attention sitting here with your hood up?" What she didn't add was that there was almost no one around to see his face anyway, that he looked daft, and that it was obvious he was trying to hide his face. She knew he wasn't stupid, so supposed he must at least have a good reason. At least, that was what she tried to tell herself.

"I like it like that. Do you want some breakfast?" Carra sat down and let Dom call over the attendant to ask for two bowls of oatmeal. Changing her mind, she stayed with him, having suddenly lost the drive to wander around a strange town on her own.

Even though they were purportedly waiting for his 'friend', it didn't lessen the shock any when, after several hours of waiting, he actually turned up. "Oz," Dom suddenly called out. "Join us!"

A young man, around Dom's age, sat down in the free chair at their table. He didn't seem shy, or put out at being summoned over. "What are you doing here?"

"Looking for you, Oz. Desperate times. But it's certainly good to see you again. I need a favour actually." Dom leant in and whispered something in Oz's ear.

"I'll do what I can." Oz turned to look at her, as if

he'd only just realised she was there. "Who is your friend?" His mousy shaggy brown hair and kind-looking eyes gave him a friendly demeanour. He was what you'd call conventionally good-looking, she supposed.

"I'm Carra," she piped up. "Nice to meet you."

"Oswald, nice to meet you too. So, Dom, Carra, what is it that I can I do for you?"

"I need you to get a message to Jade. Can you say to her these exact words: 'Remember our last conversation, I need to know more'. She'll know what I mean."

"That's both vague and brief. It's been six years, are you sure she'll remember?" Carra thought Oz had a good point, but she decided to keep quiet and listen for now.

"Oh, this one she'll remember. Tell her where I'm staying as well. We're in room fourteen."

"Okay, I'll do my best." Oz sighed. "We, eh? Nice. Interesting arrangement. Still reddish-brown, but not quite as crimson as a certain redhead..."

"We are travelling together for convenience Oz, please be respectful."

"I'm very sorry, I certainly didn't mean to offend you. I spoke without thinking."

"No harm done. Now, stay and join us for a drink." Carra liked Oz. Matching his appearance, he was very chatty and personable. She ended up drinking rather more than she had intended to, as he kept ordering extra rounds, but it was a pleasant afternoon.

Around dinner time, Oz excused himself to 'go and perform their errand'. At least Dom seemed in good spirits. "Hopefully we won't need to stay here too much longer. I'm feeling terribly optimistic."

"It's nice to see you smile anyway."

"Have I been a bit grumpy? I was somewhat anxious about coming back."

"Don't worry Dom, it's okay here. We'll be alright. And I don't mind when you're grumpy."

"So I am grumpy." He didn't really say it as a question, so Carra didn't respond. "You and Oz seem to get along well."

"Jealous?" She put her hand down on top of Dom's, but he instinctively pulled his away.

"Oh." They remained where they were for the next few minutes in silence, until eventually Carra excused herself and went up to the room to retire for the night. Dom didn't follow her.

Sometime in the middle of the night, she felt Dom kiss her forehead. Then, presumably realising she was awake when he felt her move, he kissed her lips.

He tasted of alcohol and his stubble felt rough.

He hadn't lit a candle so she couldn't see his face, but she knew it was him from his scent and the sound of his breathing. A few seconds later, she heard him collapse on the bed next to her.

She lay awake for a while, wondering whether they would discuss this in the morning, but she must have managed to get back to sleep as next thing she knew, it was morning again.

Just like the previous day, Dom had already left his bed. Carra took her time getting washed and dressed, making the most of having some privacy for the first time in a week.

When she did make it downstairs to the pub, she couldn't actually see Dom at first – her mistake being she'd been looking for a gentleman on his own. She walked around the whole room, before eventually spotting him in a corner talking to a girl. Classically pretty, her long red hair was scraped back to reveal a slim, pallid face and slightly angular chin.

Even sitting down, Carra could see the girl was much taller than her, and she was smartly dressed. She wasn't sure what the fashions were in Florin, but to Carra the girl looked like she'd been styled, in made-to-fit expensive clothes. Worse than that, was the way her and Dom were sitting – with their heads bent in towards each other.

Dom was actually smiling.

They hadn't noticed her yet, and she decided that maybe *today* was the day she would explore the city.

CHAPTER 20

As she left through the front door, Kylle waved at her, and she smiled back. *I wonder what she'll make of Dom's present company.*

Outside in the fresh air, Carra exhaled deeply. Her interaction with Kylle had confirmed it for Carra – she felt far more at ease here than she ever had in Rivulet. But she had been cooped up in that tavern for too long.

She started walking, in order to keep warm, taking note of her surroundings so she could find her way back. Only once she'd set off, did she decide she wanted to head towards the market area, thinking that must be the most interesting part of the city.

The place was bustling, and everybody seemed to be moving quickly with purpose. She tried to amble along unnoticed, but after a few minutes she found she'd got used to the hubbub, and was able to stop feeling out of place.

As it happened, she was quite disappointed by what she found. Unlike the trinkets she could peruse in Rivulet, the stalls were all very functional. *Of course, it might be something to do with the weather being so much colder now – she'd, perhaps mistakenly, assumed the capital would have tourists all year round.*

There were lots of stands selling food, but it was mostly raw – fish, meat and vegetables were available in bulk. After making her way through a few rows of food, she reached some booths selling baskets and towels. Carra was marginally more interested in the toiletries, but decided they were a luxury that she might not even get chance to make use of.

Emerging at the other end of the market, she saw a lake in the near distance. There were lots of people sitting on the grassy embankment around it, and large torches had been placed at regular intervals to provide some warmth.

Carra made her way back to the food section of the market and bought herself a fresh pastry. She could feel the heat it was giving off, and had already eaten nearly half of it by the time she got to the lake. Most of the people were situated around the torches so it was difficult to get too close to one, but as she was on her own, she was able to skirt around a few groups, and find a reasonably decent spot.

It wasn't long before she was regretting having only bought one pastry, but she was too comfy where she was sitting to do anything about it. Plus, she was fascinated by the ice skaters. Some looked like novices, bumbling along, holding hands with a friend or partner in order to stay upright. Others glided and danced across the ice, confidently and ornately, as if they had been born to do just that.

Carra alternated between watching the skaters who were there having fun – wondering what they were thinking and laughing along with them – and watching the grace of the skilled skaters. She imagined herself out there. Perhaps if she'd had the opportunity, she'd have had a talent for it. For some reason, she thought she would have been well suited to skating.

After a while, her thoughts wandered. She began to dwell on the questions that had already been circulating in her head – such as how Sandria was getting along, whether her father had made it back to Astonelay yet, and how Alliana and Nicholas were finding married life.

She wondered whether she should go back to rejoin Dom – not just now, but at all. He might not want her back now that he had been re-united with the redhead; Carra got the impression they had known each other for a long time.

In Florin, she might be able to obtain the apprenticeship she had always intended to seek out. There was sure to be more choice here than there would have been in and around Astonelay. The idea of settling here certainly held some appeal, and Carra could feel herself getting excited by the place's potential.

The afternoon drifted away pleasantly while she contemplated her options, pleased to at last have some semblance of control over her decisions.

A shout snapped her out of her reverie.

She looked up in time to see a small, but deep, crack form in the ice where one couple were skating. The woman was directly above it, and her leg became trapped.

Carra started to stand up, somehow in the heat of the moment thinking she could run to help. A girl near her, of a similar age to her own, had stood up as if she was also intending to help.

As the crack widened, the woman found herself sinking into the water – whilst the man grabbed at her arm, trying to slow her fall, but with limited success.

All of a sudden, the ice froze back over. The woman was trapped, but had been prevented from falling further – she was safe from drowning for the moment, but her legs were still in the water.

The scene was mildly chaotic. People were running off the lake, trying to get safely to the bank in case it cracked elsewhere. Others had bravely run to the woman's assistance, and were trying to free her.

Carra was still watching the trapped woman when she noticed movement next to her. The girl she had seen before had started sprinting, but in the opposite direction to the lake, and there was a gang of people running after her.

She wasn't a particularly fast runner. A couple of the men at the front of the mob managed to apprehend her; then started dragging her along.

They were carrying the girl towards the market, and most of the people who had been sitting around the lake followed. Carra tried to blend into the crowd, moving along with them, as she wanted to see what was happening. When they gathered around the town square, she remained on the perimeter.

A hand on her back surprised her. "I thought I might find you here, given this is now where half of the city are."

She turned her head over her shoulder, "You gave me a shock, Dom." *With so many people around, how had he even spotted her?*

"Where have you been all day?"

"You seemed busy with that girl, so I went for a walk, and then sat by the lake."

"*That girl*'s name is Jade. And she is helping us."

"Either way, you seemed pretty cosy!" Carra was slightly embarrassed by the high, slightly squeaky pitch her voice had taken on, but couldn't stop herself.

"Is someone jealous?" Carra was still musing over that when shouting brought her attention back to the crowds. "Any idea what's going on?" Dom asked her. She shook her head in response, although she was starting to worry that she did have a fairly good idea.

They had carried the girl onto a raised, purpose-built platform in the square, tied her to a large stake, and were standing either side of her. They appeared to be waiting for something – Carra wondered if maybe it was for more people to arrive, to watch.

When the men started stacking branches around her feet, Carra felt herself panicking. "We need to do something."

"It'll only make it worse for her." he whispered. "If I put out the flames, they will find a more tortuous way to kill her."

"No, it couldn't be worse. I can't... Dom, I think we should leave. Please can we go back to the tavern?" She wanted to bury her head in his chest, but he was holding himself so rigidly, it didn't seem like he'd welcome it.

"I'm sorry Carra, we can't. It'd look suspicious if anyone saw us walking away now." She took a deep breath and steeled herself for what she knew was about to happen. "What did she do, did you see?"

"An ice skater was about to fall through a crack in the ice and she froze the ice back over – to *save* her. Dom, she was trying to help them! This is madness."

He put his arm around her, to lend her the support that he could plainly tell she required. "Hush, keep your voice down. I know all about it. This is how things are here. Carra, when I heard... I was worried you had done something stupid."

They both looked on as the girl was set alight. Carra knew her face was ashen and hoped everyone else was too distracted to notice. She wished she had put her hood up like Dom, but it was too late now.

A woman next to her in the crowd put her hand on Carra's arm and she jumped in shock. "You're not from around here, are you deary? It's always a shock to people the first time. Don't worry, you'll get used to it."

"I'm not, you're right. I'm from the north. This is my second day in Florin." Carra was relieved when the conversation didn't continue any further. The woman had presumably meant well, but Carra felt sickened.

As soon as it was over, Carra turned and started striding back to the inn, not waiting for Dom to say it was okay to leave. She was vaguely aware of him running after her. By the time they reached the entrance, she was in tears. She ran up the two flights to the bedroom and sat on the bed. Dom wasn't far behind her, and was soon sitting on the bed next to her, consoling her.

"I'm fine, I'm fine. I just got a surprise, that's all." she said, gasping for breath between sobs. Dom didn't respond; instead he held her even more tightly. "Please tell me we can leave this place soon."

"Yes, I promise we can. You know I'm not exactly keen to dwell here either."

"I knew magic was frowned upon, but I thought they had become more lenient. I thought... I thought... well, their son was banished not killed." Carra wished she could stop crying, she felt really embarrassed.

"Whose son, Carra? This is how magicians have always been treated here, I'm really sorry I didn't give you more warning. I see I am going to have to keep a closer eye on you, child."

"The Florindyers of course, their son was found with magic and banished."

"How do you know about that?"

"I suppose it's one rule for them, and different rules for everyone else. What do you mean how did I find out, did they try to hush it up or something? I think Nicholas told Alliana about it."

"I always thought that they had." Carra frowned at Dom in consideration. "I was here, Carra. I suppose whatever they tried to do, it was bound to get out. They strung him up just like that girl today. It took *five* soldiers to overpower him.

Then, when they tried to set him alight, the flames didn't take – maybe the wood was wet."

"Or could he, or one of his friends, have had flame magic?"

"Yes, that is probably more likely."

"Sorry, I didn't mean to interrupt you. Keep going please?"

"They all just stood around and watched him for a while. Re-lighting the flames whenever they went out. Eventually, he did catch alight, but there was no indication the flames were hurting him. The fire spread to his whole body – and if someone *had* been using magic to put the flames out, they'd stopped. The crowd became afraid.

"The city guards extinguished the flames, but it took time, and the crowd was becoming increasingly agitated. When they carried him back to the palace, the mob tried to follow… they were held back only by the closing of the palace gates.

"They beat him up badly, trying to satisfy the clamouring for retribution – while the onlookers watched through the bars of the gates. It was the Queen who intervened, perhaps the only reason he survived. She ordered that he be placed back into the dungeons until they decided what to do with him.

"Yes, ultimately, she managed to persuade her husband to be *merciful* and only banish him, but it was on the condition that the populace were left to believe he was still in the dungeons waiting justice. They supposed that, after a while, their lost prince would become forgotten."

"Then what? You can't just stop there! What happened?"

"I don't know."

"Make something up then! You can't just stop like that – right before the climax."

"Okay okay. Using rumours then... As the story goes, his father let him be bundled out of the city, and even get as far as the Pellagea border, before he unleashed his private guardsmen to hunt him down and assassinate him."

"Dramatic! What was the city like to live in while this was all happening?" A tear was tickling her cheek and she brushed it away. "Was Prince Theodore well liked before he was cast out? Is his younger brother now the crown prince?"

"So many questions Carra, as usual. I suppose the city adapted fairly quickly to the change. The Florindyers had to act quickly to ensure that no suspicion was cast on the rest of their family, otherwise there could have been a risk of revolution. If they hadn't been the only ruling family for over a thousand years – if they hadn't been so well established as sovereigns – who knows what would have happened when it was discovered there was magic in their line."

"It was the king who was a Florindyer, correct?" Dom nodded. "So, Prince Theodore's magic must have come from the queen. Okay, so remind me – it was the first queen, Karina, who gave birth to Theodore, and his younger brother and sister were both born to the current queen, Astrill?"

"Queen Karina was the mother of both Tilla and Theodore, and only Torrin is the son of Queen Astrill."

"Hmm. Seems strange. Why would Queen Astrill beg for mercy for Theodore when, by getting him out of the way, that meant her own son would become king?"

"Not everyone is obsessed with power, Carra. Theodore was never going to be king once everyone knew he had magic anyway. Perhaps Astrill just wanted to believe in the importance her husband claimed to place on family. Right, that's enough about this for today now, Carra. You've had a shock; give yourself some time to process it. If you still have questions, we can talk some more in the morning."

CHAPTER 21

Carra awoke to the sound of Dom returning – two cups of coffee and some pastries in hand. He had obviously already been to the market that morning, whilst she felt groggy enough to stay in bed till noon. *Why did I let myself cry so much? It's no wonder I feel rubbish today.* She still managed to eat though, and even perked up a bit as a result. "So, where is Jade?"

"I bring you breakfast in bed, and those are your first words to me? I knew you were jealous."

"Oh come on, Dom. Try and tell me there is nothing between you two."

"Perhaps there was. Many years ago. I've always been very charming, as you well know. You should be thankful, as otherwise she might not have been so eager to help us."

"Silly me, making you remind me of what I already know, that of course no woman can resist you." Carra gave him her best mock-infatuated smile.

"I've made arrangements for us to leave." Dom declared, instantly changing the tone of the conversation. He explained that he had gleaned enough information from Jade to know where they were going to head next.

"Okay, go on…"

"Directly south of Florin is Avo, but the eastern side of Avo is made up almost entirely of the Avonian mountain range, so I've organised for us to go by boat. It is chartered to travel around the southern coast of the desert lands, circumnavigate the cliffs that border the south coast of Avo, and let us disembark along the western shore. It will take us quite a while, but it should be easier going than by horse. They have said they will try to drop us as far south as they can, but that we can always take off with the rowboat if they are finding it difficult to dock."

"Sounds like you've had a productive morning."

"Quite."

"How soon can we leave?"

Carra was pleasantly surprised to find out the boat was setting out that very afternoon. They agreed to stay in the tavern until then; an easy decision given neither of them were particularly fond of Florin.

While they waited, Dom was able to tell Carra some more about what they were looking for, which turned out to be a large, gold locket.

"I don't get it. Why would a locket be important?"

"A good question."

"A good question that you don't know the answer to right now?"

"Precisely. I do have a description of it, however. This particular locket is a Florindyer heirloom that went missing around fifteen or so years ago. It is set with three large rubies."

"Nice – so, we sell it and have enough money to buy a large house each?"

"No, I don't think the value is in it's retail, Carra. But you're still on board, aren't you? Even though I can't tell you any more information?" Dom seemed to be having a mild panic that she'd lost interest, which she thought was understandable really. "I know you are crucial to this somehow

– and rubies are the Perywhist stone, which is a good omen."

They made their way through back streets, as Carra wanted to avoid the crowds as much as possible; she had a bad feeling about the city now. Dom tried to hurry her along, with little success, which meant they were slightly late when they made it down to the docks

When they emerged from a narrow alleyway with their goal in sight, Carra was more than a little relieved to see the boat hadn't left without them. She hadn't been meaning to go slowly, she'd just been spending a lot of time checking her surroundings.

Having been about to stride directly over to the boarding area, Dom quickly put his arm out to stop her. Distracted by her first real glimpse of the sea, she'd entirely missed the three sentries standing in front of the boat.

"Carra, I need you to go over there and ask them what's going on. Say your friend is supposed to be on the boat and you wanted to see her off." Seeing her hesitation, he put his hand on her back and propelled her forwards.

Resisting the urge to turn around and scowl at Dom, she approached the sentinel nearest to her and smiled sweetly at him. "Is there something wrong, I was hoping to slip on board and talk to a friend. In fact, I was considering travelling with her to Avo."

"Why is your friend travelling on a merchant boat?" was the gruff response she received.

"Why?" *Good question.* "Because she is the daughter of one of the traders. She thought she might be bored, so she asked me to keep her company on the trip. I'm embarrassed to say I've left it until the very last minute to decide."

The man's face softened. "Now isn't a good time, deary. The guards are searching the ship for a young man, and he is supposed to be dangerous."

Carra gasped. She hoped it didn't come across as being as fake as it had felt. "Is he trying to escape a criminal sentence by leaving on this ship?"

"He is a fugitive of some sort. Aged around twenty-five, fairly tall, muscular, dark hair. Do you know anyone of that description?"

"I don't know many people around here at all I'm afraid. I'm from the north. Would it be okay if I returned shortly then – once you have apprehended him?" The guard simply shrugged, so she walked back over to the entrance where Dom was concealed.

"You do have some ability to flirt in you after all! What did he say?" Carra relayed the comments to Dom, wondering if he would be amused, like she was, that they had basically described him. Instead, he was looking at her incredulously. She was starting to feel a bit stupid. *What kind of man am I associating with?*

He grabbed her wrist and began walking in strides, taking them away from the ship.

"Dom, why would they be looking for you? I thought you hadn't been back to the city in years?"

"Shhh. Someone must have seen me with Jade yesterday, or just lucked upon me as I was walking down to the shipyard this morning. I don't know." He rubbed his face with his hands while he thought. It was the most discomfited she had seen him. "Carra, I need you to retrieve Hope and Jak from the inn, and meet me down by the lake. We can head west and travel through Cillamon into Avo instead."

☆ ☆ ☆

When she met back up with him a couple of hours later, Dom had bought some food and, much to her delight, a map. She could finally visualise the geography that he had been attempting to describe to her.

Yet, somewhat problematically, she was now feeling rather wary of him, and they travelled the first few miles in silence. Dom rode slightly in front of her, and kept turning around – clearly trying to gauge if her mood had improved.

"What is it that you aren't telling me, Dom? You must have more information than simply that we're looking for a locket and you need my help. What is it that makes you have such conviction in this scheme? How do you know it isn't a waste of time?"

"I guess, Carra, that I just need to believe in something. If there's the possibility that there's something... anything... out there that will improve life, then I'm willing to take risks in the name of chance."

"I suppose that makes sense." *Did it? Or was she just agreeing with him to avoid the conversation becoming more awkward than it was already likely to be...* "Although, you still haven't explained why they were looking for you back there?" She spoke cautiously; she was beginning to think she wasn't actually going to get a response. Or, at least, not a satisfactory one.

"Perhaps they weren't."

"What do you take me for? I'm not going any further until you tell me what's going on."

"Carra, you saw what they did to that girl. I didn't want us to be discussing this all over again. Once they know of a magic user, they will hunt them down. There aren't too many that escape."

"You escaped?"

"Huh?"

"You just said you escaped. You never mentioned

that before."

"Of course I did. You knew I was homeless, and left my family?" Carra tried to replay their previous conversations in her head. She somehow hadn't got the full picture, and she wasn't sure why.

"You mean to say that you left because of your magic?"

"Carra."

"Six years ago. You were caught using magic and estranged from your family."

"Carra. Let it go. You don't need to say it." She had already gone white though. He moved to help her off her horse, and put a rug down for her to sit on. "Have some water." She lifted the bottle to her mouth and managed to sip some.

"You've been following *me* for six months though, don't you have anything better to do?"

"Evidently not." He winked at her. She felt lightheaded. "Don't worry, I always have this effect on women."

"Th-that's why you kept your hood up the whole time we were in Florin." She caught her breath. "That's why the girl you met was so attractive!" She could tell Dom was trying to talk, but he couldn't get a word in. Suddenly everything was piecing itself together. "Your manners. In Rivulet at the Strathenbergs. You seemed so comfortable."

He looked really exasperated with her and she started laughing.

Then suddenly, he leaned in as if he was about to kiss her. *To shut her up? To distract her?* She put her hand on his shoulder and tried to push him away, but he was strong – or she wasn't really trying? Then she guiltily realised she wanted him to kiss her, and decided that was okay, so she stopped trying to push him away.

Then she realised she *should* be trying to push him away, and used both hands to shove him off, making a show of being affronted. He slid away from her, looking abashed.

"You've made a complete fool out of me."

"I'm sorry Carra, that wasn't my intention, I can assure you. I wanted to keep you from danger. Imagine how you would have felt being in Florin had you known."

"I would have had a better idea what kind of danger I was in! Besides, don't be ridiculous Dom – you gave me a fake name long before then! Oz must have been laughing his head off at me the other night."

"I've been going by 'Dom' for a long time now. I can hardly remember a time when I wasn't Dom."

"Oh please. You mean 'please call me Dom' *isn't* what you whispered to him when he first arrived?"

"Okay, it was selfish. Be realistic, though. You wouldn't think of me the same way if I'd told you I was *disgraced* Prince Theodore. Think about it. I wanted you to be normal around me."

"I need some time to myself." They were the only coherent words she could find. "Let's get moving again. We'll talk soon. Once I've got my head around this."

CHAPTER 22

Dom respected her wishes, and didn't initiate any conversation for the rest of the afternoon. Carra was confused, but as much as she'd wanted to spend the time thinking everything over, her mind seemed strangely unwilling to cooperate. Her thoughts were incoherent and unproductive.

Rain lightly trickled down on them while they travelled. It hadn't seemed too bad – she'd just been ignoring it – but by the time they stopped again she found she was far more soaked than she'd realised. It just added to the generally miserable feeling of the day.

"There's more isn't there, Dom. I mean Theodore. Or do I?"

"Theo, and no, please call me Dom. I try to avoid thinking about that name; that life." She looked at him, waiting for him to answer her real question. "There's a little more, not much. Jade had already been engaged in research at my bequest. She had found out a few other details, but far less than I might have hoped – and worse, it's all conjecture.

"Four centuries ago, a Florindyer prince fell in love with a Perywhist. When she rejected him, he approached a magician by the name of Olivia. Now Olivia had an unusual strain of magic, which allowed her to enact curses, and he wanted her to help him exact revenge.

"Although she was magically strong, she wasn't strong enough to cast a curse that would affect the Perywhist herself – the Perywhist family being the oldest and strongest line of magicians. Instead, she offered to place a curse on her heir. In order for her curse to have any impact, it would take effect approximately four hundred years down the line.

"Olivia was desperate to help the prince, having fallen deeply in love with him herself, so when he asked what the payment would be, she asked for a kiss. Not being the brightest prince, he refused her – still fantasizing over the Perywhist for some reason, I suppose. Olivia didn't let on that she had taken offense, and asked for money instead, which she went on to use to found Whistlake Academy.

"However, having been spurned, she tricked the prince. When it came to the curse, she tied the Florindyers into it as well. Their line would be devoid of magic, until such time as the curse was invoked – the cursed Florindyer would once again have access to his power.

"He was fated to meet the Perywhist of his generation, these two being the great-great-great-great-great-grandchildren of the scorned lover and his target. Once they met, the ripple effects would destroy Florinyn."

"Literally? Literally destroy? You call that just 'a few other details'?"

"It's hearsay. I am only telling you what I was told."

"Which you weren't going to share until I forced you."

"You're right, Carra. I'm sorry. I *was* going to tell you, but I would have had to tell you I was Theo first or it wouldn't have made sense." Carra was unimpressed. There were a lot of times that Dom could have told her, and she found it hard to believe he had been working up the courage as he was implying. Avoiding confrontation, and lack of trust, were more like it.

Night fell, and though they passed a neat-looking tavern, they hadn't yet reached the border into Cillamon. Carra really wasn't keen to spend another night in Florinyn, given that there were people on the hunt for Dom, but he pointed out that the ground was too wet for them to camp outside.

Eventually she relented and they checked into an inn – as Bonnie and Sam Robbins.

"Now you have three names, Sammy." she mocked. It was the first time she'd spoken to him in hours.

✧✧✧✧✧

By the next day, Carra had recovered from her shock. *Mostly.* "Okay, come on then, let's do this. You can tell me the rest of the information as we ride." Dom looked at her blankly. "That little tale you told me yesterday has nothing to do with a locket!"

"No. I know. I haven't quite got it all figured out yet. The part about an object was something I overheard my parents and their advisors talking about when I was still at home. My parents certainly seemed convinced that I should be kept away from it, which makes me sure that it's important. Jade didn't manage to find out much more than that it's a locket and a possible location – but I'm certain this is where we should be heading. It feels right."

"Possible?" Carra could see Dom mentally retracing what he'd just said. "You said *possible* location. We could be going on a fool's errand then?"

"I didn't mean possible. I mean probable. Almost definite. I trust Jade." *Bleurgh.*

"Dom… do you miss your friends and family? At least I know I can get back to mine."

"Sometimes. It's been a few years now and feelings… well, they fade with time. There are some things that I still greatly miss. My little sister Tilla. Some of my friends. That feeling of belonging."

"You're just a big softy really aren't you."

"Leave me alone, Anson." He pointed towards the horizon. "Up ahead is Cillamon. We should reach it within the hour. You'll find it's quite similar to Florinyn, but less populated, and they hate magic a bit less."

"I've been thinking, Dom. About this whole dislike of magic. You said yesterday that before Olivia laid that curse, the Florindyers used to have magic. Do you know when this widespread hatred first started, or what happened to bring it about? I wondered... do you think it was because their own magic was cursed away."

"It would make sense, wouldn't it. That the rulers at the time were so bitter at no longer being powerful, they prohibited anyone else from using magic? Or maybe it was to protect their rule, to prevent anyone holding an advantage they could use to overthrow them. If the Florindyer line was powerful once, perhaps that's even how they gained their sovereignty in the first place."

"That's basically what I was thinking. Dom, hold my hand please?" Carra engaged her magic, now connected with Dom's ability, and threw flames into Florinyn – creating a line of fire across the border.

"Was that really necessary, Carra?" Dom sounded like he was chastising her, but she could see he was trying to hold back a smirk.

"Necessary? No, but it felt good." Almost like she'd used it as a channel for releasing her emotions.

They didn't have to ride through Cillamon for very long, just far enough to clear the mountains, and then they would be able to travel south-west into Avo.

Paying limited attention to their surroundings, and trusting Hope to watch her own step, Carra spent the whole day contemplating what Dom had been thinking when he'd nearly kissed her yesterday. Had it simply been because she was the only girl around and they were saddled together?

At the time, she had told herself he was just trying to shut her up. Or distract her at the very least. On reflection though, she thought it had felt real. Frustratingly, she didn't have a lot to compare it to. She'd only ever kissed one other boy, and that was Nicholas. *And who knows what Nicholas was thinking at the time.*

She wondered whether he would try to kiss her again, and if she actually wanted him to. He had actually kissed her before, but that drunk peck on the lips hadn't really been the same, and she wasn't sure whether Dom even remembered it.

"You're very quiet today Carra."

"I'm just enjoying the ride."

"Not thinking about me?" *Has he always been this self-centred? Oh no… is that why I'm attracted to him?*

"Only person thinking about you around here is you. Isn't that right Hope?" *Liar.*

They seemed to cover good ground that day. Carra was content with mindlessly following where Dom led. He seemed to know where he was going – or at least think he did.

Ha, maybe he's going completely the wrong way. Is it strange that I'm not sure I'm even bothered anymore? I'm getting to see new areas just like I hoped. Not to be dramatic, but it seems as though fate is interfering now – let's just go with it. I'll deal with what happens next when I have to.

They skirted their horses around a spruce, which had taken over part of the path, and something about the manoeuvre reminded her of a cut on her arm, where she had brushed against a tree. "Hey, Dom look." She thrust out her arm. It had stopped bleeding hours ago, but you could still clearly see the graze.

She closed her eyes and concentrated. She could actually feel the sensation of her skin mending. As she had anticipated, when she opened her eyes her arm had completely healed. Dom looked quite visibly surprised.

"Did you know you were going to be able to do that?"

"I suppose I suspected I could. It's not that different from what I was doing to condition my legs to help with riding Hope."

Dom looked at Carra's arm with concern, then back to her face. "I think we should make camp now and cross into Avo in the morning. I'm not familiar with the area once we leave Cillamon, so it would be wise to tackle our route plans in the light."

Carra groaned. Presumably that meant a second night out in the open.

"It'll be better this time, I promise. Plus, I looked after you okay last time, didn't I?"

Leaving the road, they searched for a suitable spot – the terrain was friendly, so they had a few viable options to select from. With the moon almost full, they didn't see a need to risk a fire, but the pair of them ended up stumbling all over the place trying to pitch the tent.

They ate some food from Dom's pack, then groomed the horses. Hope and Jak seemed to be fairly fond of each other now.

Carra climbed into the bedroll, and felt Dom climb in behind her, warming her up. He began to speak to her, but she had already fallen asleep before she could process what he was saying.

When she opened her eyes, she was back in their dream world. After waiting for a few minutes, Dom appeared.

"I guess we were right then. If we fall asleep while in contact with each other, we can control the dreams."

"I like it." Flames shot out of his hand. Carra found that she could use Dom's magic too. It was the first time either of them had been able to be free with their abilities.

She couldn't remember the last time she'd had this much fun. Before long they were competing with each other – first to make the highest flames, then to knock each other's flame towers over. She knew it was childish, but she felt happy, and regardless, Dom was grinning from ear to ear. She suddenly had a heightened awareness of her attraction to him.

At some point while they were racing each other, they collided. Dom put his hand behind her head and pulled her in towards him. She smiled and closed her eyes in anticipation as she saw his lips part.

CHAPTER 23

Carra woke up with Dom's arms still wrapped around her, feeling him stir at the same time. She immediately jumped up, with the purpose of going to check on the horses.

Dom emerged from the tent a little later and grunted in greeting, before lighting a small fire. "I'm going to see if I can catch some food, will you be okay here?" Carra nodded and he wandered off. She sighed in relief.

When he returned a while later, she had finished grooming Hope and Jak, and was sitting in front of the fire he'd left her. There wasn't much to look at where they were, just a few trees and lots of grass, but she hadn't wanted to wander off to explore any further as it would have meant leaving the horses.

Dom skinned the rabbit he had caught and cooked it over his fire whilst she watched. It didn't really taste of anything – the dried meat they were carrying had at least been salted – but on the plus side, it was satisfying to eat something hot.

Dom had pulled out the map and then begun tracing it with his finger. "What are you thinking?" she tentatively enquired.

"Just trying to work out the best route for us. See here," Carra moved so she was sitting closely enough to see what he was pointing at, "This eastern route looks to be the quickest, but then it ends abruptly in the Avonian range, and we need to go further south than that. This path in the middle will take us down in a fairly straight line but there aren't any villages on the way. There are also some points where the terrain looks difficult and probably won't be wide enough for the horses. It's difficult to tell for certain though. Then there's this third trail, which looks the easiest and does take us past a couple of towns, but it goes down the western coast whereas we need to head southeast; so it may take us an extra few days."

Carra looked at Dom to see if he was going to present a solution. When he didn't, she tried to read the map herself. It looked like lots of squiggly lines. She could see that the upwards arrows showed the mountain range Dom had described, and there were different sized circles showing the towns and villages, but she couldn't make out much else. "What will we do for food if we don't go via the villages? We can't just live off rabbit meat."

"I don't even know whether there *will* be more rabbits. This is new territory for me." He looked at her to gauge her reaction. "Let's just head for this town here. At least we can hope to make it by tomorrow evening, and then we can have some real food and get a room for the night. We have enough supplies to last us until then, but I only have what I managed to buy at the last minute. I hadn't packed much beforehand as I thought we'd have our food provided while we were travelling by boat."

As they journeyed southwards, Carra realised she hadn't felt as cold for a while. "I think the weather's changing. Is it spring already?"

"No, Avo has milder winters than we do. It'll get warmer the further south we go." Carra grinned. *That was something at least.*

Again, she found herself in deep contemplation again as they rode - it was probably natural given Dom's propensity towards silence; there wasn't much else to occupy her. She was now completely comfortable on Hope, and she also recognised how much happier she was in the outdoors than she had been cooped up at the Strathenbergs'.

Carra hoped she would still feel this way in a few days, as having now seen Dom's map, she not only knew that most of the journey was still ahead of them, but she could finally appreciate the scale.

He had insisted she continue to call him Dom rather than Theo, and not just in case someone overheard, but because he considered that to be his name now. Having grown used to the name, it was easier for her to stick it anyway. Plus, hearing 'Theo' just reminded her of all of the negative connotations associated with her companion being a prince – far above her station, far more experienced, and far better educated to name but a few.

"Dom? How did they find out you had magic?" He looked away from her, and didn't respond, so she knew she had hit a sore point – but she'd already gone too far down her trail of thought to let it go. "That story you told before, about when the fire didn't take, and they dragged you back to the palace. I didn't know that you were you back then, so I never asked you what happened before that. I mean, did you have magic for a few years before anyone found out, or did you accidentally use it because you didn't know you had it?"

Dom kept looking forwards at the road, so she was surprised when he very softly replied, "I knew from the age of about twelve. If I clicked my fingers they would spark. I used to sit in my room at night trying to make flames."

"So you never had to rely on the concentration techniques that I had to use?" She interrupted.

"No, stronger magic users usually find it comes naturally to them, so their issues are different – when it does come that easily, it's far more difficult to control. To speak plainly, the college uses those techniques that Nicholas was teaching you when kids with rich parents insist that their progeny attend the school, but they only have a small amount of latent magic." Dom looked at her, pausing his tale on seeing she was deep in thought.

"Which means I probably don't have very much magic, and that is why I can't access it?"

"Only very strong magic users can heal, Carra, and I've never heard of anyone else being able to vicariously use someone else's magic. There's something unique about you that makes you important." He sounded frustrated, rather than pleased about this.

"Presumably my bloodline? That story about the locket – maybe it just needs a Perywhist?"

Dom shrugged. "I only have my own experience as reference. I had to sneak out of the palace at night to practice. I was *terrified* I would set my room alight. I managed to get it under control purely through trial and error – then spent the next few years hiding it. It wasn't too difficult, I mean, you don't need fire magic that often in everyday life. If anyone in the palace suspected, they ignored it or pretended they hadn't noticed."

"Then what went wrong?"

"I used my magic in public. Back then, I was untrained. I couldn't do it without moving my hands."

She looked at him sympathetically, her eyes wide. "Okay but still, it must have been something serious – what triggered you to expose yourself?"

"I'm getting to that." Carra blushed, chastised. "It's just difficult to talk about. I was at the market, and they were burning a girl accused of witchery. I don't think she even had any magic, just a so-called friend who was jealous of her *sweetheart* or some rubbish." He emphasised the word sweetheart as if he found it distasteful. "That didn't matter, I couldn't stand it, Carra."

"Just like the day at the market in Florin." She said meekly.

"Exactly like that, Carra. Exactly like that. I was around the age you are now. I put the fire out. It wasn't that I did it without thinking; I knew precisely what I was doing. She was already dying when they cut her down, so they left her lying there, suffering, while they hunted me. I was strong – maybe not like I am now, but I could fight. Not the *whole town* though. There were so many people, and besides, they knew who I was. I had friends who were there that day, who saw everything. I made it back to the palace not too badly scathed, but by then there was no way to hide it; no covering it up."

Carra looked at him to see if he was going to say anymore. She didn't overly like the way he had referred to her age as if she was so much younger than him, but right then, she knew that wasn't what she needed to be focusing on. "You said earlier that you thought they'd managed to hush it up or something?"

"Not that I have magic – the whole province knew of that by the end of the week. I meant that I was still alive. I thought Theo had died that day. In some ways he did - I'm hardly the same spoilt prince I was back then. Only my good looks and noble bearing remain." He winked at her.

"It's sad. You lost so much. I lost my village, but you lost your home and your family. Do you still have contact with any of them?" He shook his head slowly. *Quick Carra, say something positive.* "Do you regret it?" *Well done Carra...*

"If you mean would I change anything, then yes I would. I didn't help that girl at all." He paused as he drew a deep breath. "What's the point in dwelling on something that can't ever be? Never met a magician who could turn back time. Not yet at least. Torrin will do okay as king." Carra jolted in her seat slightly when Dom made that comment about Torrin. He had tried – unsuccessfully – to throw it in there casually, but it showed that he really did rue the amount he had lost.

"Would succession rules mean it passes to the male?"

"I assume so. Torrin's mother, Queen Astrill, will probably outlive my father, therefore to me it seems the most likely outcome. Publicly they said my 'magic taint' came from my mother rather than the royal line, leaving Tilla 'under suspicion', which is another reason she's unlikely to be accepted as sovereign."

"I thought the reason you had magic was the curse?"

"Yes, though I suppose it's possible it was from my mother too. The populace wouldn't understand the nuances anyway, and besides, they want the Royal line to stay clean." That made sense, of course. She got the impression Dom had spent a lot of time thinking about it.

The unchanging, sparse landscape was uninteresting, and despite the temperature increasing, it was still too long until spring for the buds to have appeared on the trees. With their conversation having come to a close, the day's journey began to feel long and slow.

CHAPTER 24

It was early afternoon when the deluge started. Although the temperature felt warm, the rain was cold, and very quickly they were drenched. Carra could feel the rain dripping off her forehead and down her face.

"We are still a day away from that village, aren't we Dom?" She asked dejectedly.

"A day and a half."

She waited for him to say more, but he didn't. She didn't know why this surprised her, as it was getting to be a regular occurrence. Carra didn't usually mind the rain, but this was so heavy she felt weighed down – her clothes seemed twice as heavy. She patted Hope, "How are you doing girl, is the rain bothering you?" She heard Dom snort in the background.

They pushed onwards, but the going was slow and uncomfortable. Even Dom's warmth didn't really counteract the feeling of 'wet'. The rain soaked them through faster than his heat could dry them, and he was giving off definite miserable vibes to mirror her own.

"Please can we check the map, Dom? Maybe there is somewhere we can shelter that's closer than a day and a half away."

"There isn't. We checked. Don't want to ruin the map in the rain."

They kept going for another half an hour or so. Carra stayed quiet, waiting for Dom to come to the conclusion *on his own* that they couldn't camp outside if the weather stayed like this. *Eventually* he stopped under a tree and pulled the map out. She approached and tried to peer over his shoulder.

"Unless this dot means something here, there's nothing. I'm sorry, I don't know what we do. The clouds are so thick, I don't foresee this stopping or even easing."

"A dot you say?"

"A speck. It could be something, could be nothing. Might just be a stain or a bit of dirt."

"How far from here? Is it out of our way to stop and check?"

"It's out of our way yes, and off the path – which immediately makes me suspect it's nothing – as why would there be anything in the middle of nowhere." He re-folded the map and put it back in his pocket, which was so sodden it made Carra wonder if the map wasn't soaked through already. He looked up and read Carra's face. "It's not far though. Nothing to lose by having a look."

Carra took that to mean Dom thought there was at least a good chance there was something there, but he was downplaying it just in case they ended up disappointed. At least that was what she tried to tell herself.

Dom led Jak off the path, and she followed, looking over her shoulder several times in the hope she would be able to find her way back. Despite the scarcity of trees, the area was hilly, which made it difficult to see very far.

Carra noticed Dom had quickened his space slightly and she took that as a positive sign his disposition was improving. She was certainly getting less moody signals from him. Just as those thoughts passed through her head, he turned around and looked to see if she was keeping up with him. *He's very intuitive*, she mused, *it's like he can tell when I'm thinking about him.*

There had been a few times previously when he'd answered questions she'd been thinking but hadn't actually said out loud. Despite denying he could hear her thoughts, she still wondered if there was some way he was doing so, and keeping it secret from her.

"Dom are you sure you can't hear what I'm thinking?" She asked, but either her voice was muffled by the rain, or he didn't reply. She pulled Hope level with him. "Dom" she said, again with no response. "Dom!" He finally looked up. "Look over there do you see that?" He looked where she was pointing, but didn't seem to be able to see it. "The dome over there, that's man made, I'm sure of it."

He shook his head, but Carra was already leading Hope onwards, towards the structure she had spied.

As she got closer, she was delighted to find she had not been mistaken. The curvature rose to a similar height as many of the hills, and it did blend in slightly with the surroundings, but there was no mistaking the unnaturally smooth surface – it had been built from an emerald-green marble, with black veins running through it.

Carra lined Hope up beside it, and put her hand on the wall. Yes, it was definitely marble. Dom stopped not far behind her.

"What the Lord is this place, Carra? I'm not convinced it was supposed to be found by random travellers. It's so... *uninviting*."

"Surely they will provide us shelter though?"

"Don't be naïve Carra. They may not welcome visitors. Think about it, why would they be hidden in such a secluded place. We are not even natives of Avo. Why would they help us?"

"You are more worldly than me," *Did Dom know that was tongue in cheek?* "And normally I'd trust your judgement, but I don't see what choice we have." The rain drops fell in her mouth as she spoke causing her to splutter.

"Oh, I agree," he sighed, "I'm just beseeching you to be cautious please."

Carra walked around the cylindrical building. Reaching the point where she started, she had yet to find the door. The second time round, she ran her hands against the wall as she walked, and found the crack in the marble where it could be opened.

"Over here Dom. Should I knock?" She lightly tapped the door a couple of times. Anyone inside probably wouldn't have been able to distinguish the sound from the heavy rain, which was showing no signs of abating as yet.

Dom moved forwards and banged on the door. Thump thump. The sound reverberated. They waited a few seconds and he tried again, but there was still no response.

Carra lightly pushed the door and it started to rotate inwards. Encouraged, she pressed a little harder. With the door only very slightly ajar, she thought she heard something and turned to look behind her.

"I heard it too." The very second Dom finished speaking those four words, the noise intensified. With the volume came clarity – it was the sound of birds squawking. *There must be hundreds of them to be making all that racket.*

"Get down!" Dom shouted, and Carra felt him simultaneously push her by the shoulders towards the floor. She wasn't really sure what was happening, but Dom threw himself over her, effectively shielding her, as though he anticipated an imminent attack.

She could feel the movement of the birds all around them and Dom's grunting told her that he had been bearing the brunt of the assault. She tried to twist round to properly see what was happening, but Dom was pinning her beneath him too tightly.

"Let go, Dom." She thumped his left arm and he released it in surprise.

"Ravens," he croaked.

Now able to turn her head, she saw that the black birds – which were so close they looked huge – were not relenting. There were only about eight of them, which was far fewer than she'd thought, but they were pecking at Dom's arms and back, and he couldn't even fight them off – he was using his arms to shelter *her*.

"Dom, I'm going to break away and push the door open so we can get inside."

"Carra, no. I refuse." She tried to push him off her and he wouldn't budge. "I command you to stop that." *Command? What a dolt.*

"Dom, we have no option. Just let me go." She broke away from him and pushed against the door. It felt much heavier than it had before, and she had to push her side against it in an attempt to get enough traction.

Now she was exposed, some of the crows had moved off Dom and made for her. She ignored them, ignored the pain, and focused on the door.

Now he was no longer committing all his efforts towards protecting her, Dom managed to stagger upright to help her, and gradually they forced it open.

Once inside, they closed behind them as quickly as they could, before assessing their injuries.

Carra had a couple of cuts on her shoulders, and one on her ear – but it wasn't herself she was worried about, and she immediately moved to grab Dom's shirt with the intention of lifting it up over his head. She had to peel it off, as it was stuck down where his skin was broken. The back of it was red – not speckled, but so red that you could no longer see what colour the shirt had started. She really hoped it was because the material was so wet from the rain that the blood had soaked through it, rather than because his back was in tatters...

"I was hoping you'd be this eager to take my clothes off – and I must say this was exactly how I imagined it happening as well." Carra ignored him. It was just like Dom to feel obliged to make a joke in an awkward situation.

There were slashes criss-crossing his whole back – it was a mess – but it was difficult for her to assess just how bad the damage was. She wasn't experienced enough to know if the cuts were deep or superficial.

Closing her eyes, and trying to remain calm, she attempted to draw on her healing power. Nothing happened. She tried again.

"I'm trying to heal you, but nothing is happening." She could hear in her own voice that she sounded slightly frantic. *Were those tears welling up in her eyes?*

"Carra, hold my hand and try again? It could work, like when you use my fire magic?" His voice didn't give anything away about how much pain he was in, but she figured it was likely pretty bad from the way he was squeezing her fingers.

"It's worth a try but... Dom, please loosen your grip slightly so I can concentrate." She drew on her magic, and sure enough, she could feel something happening.

When she opened eyes, she saw she had accidentally set his shirt alight. *Good job his flames don't burn either of us.* She quickly willed it to go out.

She tried again to heal him, keeping her eyes open this time, but it was to no avail.

"It's okay Carra, I'm okay." Dom was trying to

reassure her, but she noticed that he hadn't let go of her hand. "Why don't you try and heal yourself first?"

"I don't want to waste my magic on myself, I'm barely grazed!" She couldn't help but sound exasperated.

"I think it might help you concentrate. Maybe your cuts are distracting you when you try to heal me. It might get you warmed up and help you get the feel for your magic too."

"I guess that makes sense." She drew on her magic, and she was indeed able to close up her own scratches – and with relative ease. It was a relief to take the pain away; she had been so worried about Dom she hadn't realised she was actually hurting.

Carra immediately tried to transfer the magic to Dom, but she seemed to meet with resistance. Nothing was happening. Dom didn't seem surprised. "Dom… did you just trick me into healing myself?!"

"You worked that out, did you?" He chuckled, but it was a strained, choked sound. "Normally you aren't so sharp with these things." Carra screwed her face up trying to rebut Dom's insult, but one look at the state he was in, and she realised she couldn't get angry with him.

The thought seemed to come on gradually, but both of them now began to study their surroundings. They were in a circular room that, other than the mess they had created between them from dripped blood, appeared to be bare. The inside of the domed ceiling was etched with gold leaves and vines, but otherwise the marble interior was much as the exterior had been.

Out of the rain, Carra was better able to appreciate the intricacy of the marble. It really was beautiful – before this, she'd only ever seen pictures of it in books.

She examined the walls, but the only door she found was the one they'd come in by. If Dom hadn't been so injured, she would have considered staying where they were, but there was no way he could spend the night lying on that cold hard floor.

"Dom, we're going to have to move on. We need to find someone who can help you. I think you may even be better on the grass in the rain than in here – at least we could have a fire."

"What about the ravens?" Carra shrugged. She didn't really have a response. It seemed as though the ravens could attack them at any time, but she was fairly confident in her conjecture that their intention had been to guard the door.

"Over there." Dom croaked. "In the floor." Carra walked around, looking down this time. "It's right there."

"Shhh, I'll find it."

Moments later, she had pulled the trap door open and begun making her way down the stairs – leaving Dom at the top where he lay injured.

Whilst the crack around the door had provided enough light for them to see when they had first entered the building, she soon lost sight of this.

As she descended, it became gradually darker and darker, until she could barely see where she was going at all.

CHAPTER 25

The going was slow, and the stairs had continued spiralling long after she'd expected to have reached the bottom. Carra was tentatively feeling out each individual step with her feet, and she had to hold out both her arms to the sides in order to keep her balance.

Although she was trying to not to think about what may be awaiting her, she was very aware of how quickly her heart was beating, and found herself needing to pause for a second to take a deep breath. She didn't want to move further until she managed to calm herself – she needed to be able to fully concentrate.

I hope I'm nearly at the bottom. Her fingers were starting to go unpleasantly numb from the cold of the stone. She hummed a tune to herself for a few seconds but ceased when it didn't actually reassure her.

Eventually, her foot didn't find any more steps. Facing nothing but darkness now, she shivered.

"Are you okay down there?" She heard Dom shout. The sound echoed repeatedly.

"Yes, there were *a lot* of steps!" She called back up, hoping he heard. Extending her arms in front of her, she walked forwards until she felt something.

Moving her hands up and down, she found a metal ring, which she pulled open… immediately closing her eyes in surprise, having become accustomed to the darkness.

As she gradually opened them, she saw the light

was coming from only a couple of candles, which were sitting in sconces lining the corridor. Seeing three doors along the corridor, she walked to one at random, and knocked on it.

No one answered. She was surprised to find she was relieved. Even so, she moved to another, and forced herself to knock again. This time, an elderly man opened the door.

"It's very polite for an intruder to decide to knock." His slim frame was blocking the doorway, and Carra couldn't see what was in the room behind him.

"Please, we are travelling, and we were just looking for some shelter from the rain. It is torrential out there."

The man appeared to be studying her. "We, you say? There is only one of you. Are you in your right mind, girl?"

"My friend is hurt – I had to leave him at the top of the stairs. Ravens attacked us, and he is badly injured. Even if you could please just let us use some water, so I could wash his wounds, we would be incredibly grateful for your assistance."

"Ah yes. Ravens are much easier to keep than guard dogs."

Carra was starting to wonder if this old man was in his right mind himself, when she heard a crashing sound behind her. Dom had made his way down the stairs and stumbled through the large iron door at their foot. Instinctively, she put the base of her hand to her forehead in frustration – then remembered the stranger in front of her and instead pushed it backwards, pretending she had always been intending to stroke her hair.

Their host looked as though he'd seen a ghost. She cocked her head, assessing the two men, who seemed to recognise each other.

"Flo... Florindyer" The man mumbled, and within seconds he was down on his knees, supplicated before Dom. It was a good job Dom had already admitted his true identity to her; now would not have been a good time for that particular revelation – or the inevitable conversation which would have followed.

Carra edged towards Dom, who whispered in her ear, "I don't think he knows, and I wouldn't have thought that now is the best time to enlighten him." Dom held out his hand for the man to kiss. "Theodore, eldest son of King Florindyer." He grinned at Carra. "Would you perhaps be able to assist me?" He managed to choke out before his legs gave way and he collapsed.

Carra tried to catch him in her arms. She wasn't strong enough to keep hold of him, but did manage to lower him slowly to the floor, such that she had at least prevented him from landing too harshly.

The gentleman, with unexpected agility for his years, rapidly lifted Dom over his shoulder and carried him through into the room he had come from, depositing him on a bed. *I am going to have to remember to call him Theo. No, not even that – it should be Theodore.*

The man placed a wet washcloth on Dom's forehead, and encouragingly, he seemed to pull round slightly. He beckoned Carra over to him. "Bonnie?" Dom asked – and Carra was about to worry he was delirious, when she remembered that was the name she had used at the last village they'd stopped at. "Bonnie." He repeated. "Sorry about trying to command you earlier."

"Shhh it's okay." She understood the message. Don't give away your identity was obvious, but he also wanted her to play one of his servants. "Sir" she said loudly, to try and demonstrate she'd understood – doing her utmost to resist rolling her eyes at the obsequience, which really did not come naturally to her. "We are going to have to roll you over so we can take care of your wounds."

The gentleman introduced himself as Duke Flothin,

"But you may call me Anthony for ease." Carra felt Dom reach for her hand again as Anthony turned him over. He winced as the Duke dabbed his back with a second wet cloth to try and clean the cuts. Carra tried to look away, thinking that Dom wouldn't want her to see him like this.

Anthony brought over some liquor and offered it to Dom, who drank a few sips, before falling asleep. Carra, her hand now released, helped with the binding of Dom's back.

When they were done, Anthony brought her over some soup, though he was not carrying any for himself. "Will you be okay to look after his Highness? I will check on you and bring fresh bandages in the morning. There are cushions over there where you may sit."

He took his leave and Carra realised that whilst she had felt awkward, the Duke hadn't seen her as anything other than a subject in attendance. He was below Dom in the pecking order, and somewhere, far below that, was herself.

Making sure the door was properly closed once Anthony had left the room, she lay down, exhausted, on the bed next to Dom – before remembering how wet she was, and dragging herself back up again. Stripping down to her undergarments, she changed into a tunic that she found in the room, then spread her own clothes out to dry. Lying back down again, she made sure to make physical contact with Dom by putting her hand on his, so that they could talk in their dreams.

Sometime in the middle of the night, Carra stirred. After re-orientating herself to her surroundings and remembering where she was, she realised that she hadn't had seen Dom in her dreams after all.

She rested the back of her hand against his forehead; it was warmer than she would have expected. Wetting a fresh cloth, she tried to cool him down. He didn't wake, but at least he turned his head slightly and muttered in his sleep, alleviating her fear that he was unconscious.

As she had no way to tell what time it was while they were underground, she moved over to the cushions. There would be no talking to Dom tonight, and she knew the possibility of Anthony walking in on them in the morning would be enough to keep her from being able to fall back asleep if she stayed in the bed. Propped up as comfortably as she could manage on the hard bench, she eventually went back to sleep.

When Carra woke up, she was pleasantly surprised to see Dom sitting up and drinking something hot. "Feeling better?" She asked him.

"Much." She smiled, pleased. "This is a strange development. Anthony is one of the higher-ranking Dukes; he used to be one of my mother's key advisors. After she passed away, he left the palace, but I never knew what became of him."

"What is he doing out here in the middle of nowhere?" Carra wondered out loud.

"That's the big question, isn't it. Let's ask him when he returns."

They didn't have to wait long.

Carra had to stifle a giggle when she saw that Anthony had neatened his beard, and dressed in what was probably his most formal clothing, aged though it was. He insisted that Dom let him check his wounds before he would engage in conversation. Carra watched in silence, wincing at the scratches, even though she was relieved to see they looked a little less raw than they had the evening before.

Eventually he spoke, addressing Dom alone. "I suspect I don't know as much as you are hoping I do." He paused and let out a small sigh. "I have been waiting an awfully long time for you. It is rather unfortunate that our protection backfired, and I can only apologise – should anyone have had enough foresight to realise you would bring a companion with you, the guardian spell might have been constituted differently.

"As it was, the ravens were set to stop anyone other than yourself from entering the dome. It was inevitable that you would not travel here unaccompanied even if we asked you to come alone – yes of course, a maid makes perfect sense." He cleared his throat loudly. "Perhaps you might ask her to leave so that we might converse in private."

Carra tried to put on her best 'innocent' face while Anthony was gesturing towards her, but as soon as he looked away, she shot a glance at Dom that she hoped he knew meant 'there's no way I'm leaving'.

"Anything you can say to me, can be said in front of my serving girl." Carra raised her eyebrows but then donned a fake smile. "Continue, old friend, tell me of your purpose."

"Okay, then I shall begin. Please stop me so that we may ask her to leave when you feel it is appropriate. Although... firstly, could you help me to understand what went wrong? I expected you several years before now. I do not mean this as a complaint, it's just that I thought that you would get here more quickly once you received our message."

"I must stop you there and apologise, because I received no such message." Dom interjected.

"Then how came you by this place? No," he tutted, "You must have received our directions?" Dom shook his head slowly. "On your twenty-first birthday, a gift – a chest containing coins – was to be delivered to you by your friend, Lady Lintel-Dern. Through my written correspondence she was privy to everything... please don't tell me that something happened to her, which prevented this?"

Carra frowned at Dom, who appeared dumbfounded. After hesitating for a second, he turned to Carra and explained, "Jade."

Suddenly that incident at the harbourside made a lot more sense to Carra. She wondered if Dom was having the same revelation, or whether he still felt inclined towards trusting his *friend*. "Nothing happened to Jade, no. Not *yet*." she sneered.

Dom interrupted her. "I have been out of the capital of late."

"For several years?" Anthony looked rather confused, but Dom urged him to continue and, whilst he seemed uncomfortable, he was clearly reluctant to disagree with him. "I am sorry for the pain that telling you this may bring you, but it was your mother's dying wish that I retreat here, and wait for you until you set off on your search. We were concerned that there must be the utmost secrecy as to our location.

"So let me tell you what I can. The letter said:

For you to fulfil your true potential, you must retrieve the treasure they have kept from you. Seek out the location marked on the map below. Travel alone.

"Many were against our purpose – our main goal being to free magic. Your mother and I created this refuge – intended as a stopover on the way to your true destination – long before things actually came to a head. Very few know of its existence, and even fewer its actual location."

Anthony pulled an iron key out of the pocket of his robes and handed it to Dom, laying it across his palm as though he were afraid it might snap. Carra peered over. It was a fairly small key, with a circular handle, but otherwise unremarkable.

"On her deathbed, your mother gave me this. It's a key, of course. We didn't want anyone to find you with it, so we kept it here. Only you were supposed to have the map, so you knew to leave the path and find me.

"If you continue your route south, then hopefully its use will become apparent. Your mother tried to explain to me what it unlocked but I'm afraid it didn't make too much sense to me. Something about a desert mirage. Oh dear, I *am* sorry, I haven't spoken aloud to another soul in almost twenty years." Dom moved to put an arm around Anthony just as she could have sworn tears were forming in the corners of his eyes. "So very sorry." he said again.

Dom tried to get up to let Anthony lie down, but he wasn't strong enough. "Bonnie, help this man to a chair." After a slight delay, she realised that meant her, and jumped to Dom's command. All these pseudonyms were getting confusing.

Carra was perplexed by what had just happened. Moments ago, he had seemed fine, and now he looked as though he had aged another ten years in the space of minutes. She was desperate to ask him to elaborate on the words 'route south' but she could hardly do so now.

"He's been saving his strength, waiting for me." Carra lifted her head, but neither Dom nor Anthony looked as though they had spoken. *Must've imagined it.* Although, Dom *was* looking at her as though he was trying to tell her something.

Perhaps he was simply asking her to attend to the Duke, who was looking increasingly unwell. She thought he might even collapse, but after sitting for a while he seemed to recover slightly, and on finding the energy to rise, he excused himself from their company.

CHAPTER 26

Carra immediately hurried to Dom's bedside, expecting they'd talk through the information they'd just learnt, but he already seemed deep in thought. "I wonder why Jade never gave me that message. I mean, surely she could have given me the chest when I returned last week."

Is it not obvious? Carra thought to herself. Jade clearly wanted Dom for herself as opposed to helping him bond with Carra.

"It's not obvious to me, no." Dom replied to her unspoken question.

"How do you do that?" Carra asked him. He frowned, seemingly confused by her question. "Sometimes when I'm thinking, you respond to something I haven't said out loud."

"Nonsense Carra. You're imagining it."

"I thought so too at first!" she said indignantly. "Why did you just say that out of the blue then, about it not being obvious to you – implying it *was* obvious to me." She could see him thinking back over what he had said.

"I've no idea... your facial expression probably showed what you were thinking. Right now, we have more important things to think about." A grin lit up his face. "We're obviously going the right way! He mentioned the desert as well, which confirms that the nameless Desert Lands to the south of the Avonian range are our correct destination. Jade was telling the truth about that much at least."

"I *suppose* she thought we would be apprehended at the ship, and if by some miracle we weren't, that we wouldn't get very far without that key. What a wasted trip it would have been if we'd got all the way there without it!" Carra had to admit she felt slightly vindicated, now she actually had a valid reason to dislike Jade. "It's going to be a while before you are able to travel though, Dom?"

"I'll be okay soon. Why don't you go and explore this compound, given I am unable to? I would appreciate you checking on Duke Anthony to see if he has regained his spirits. I have a feeling he has been clinging to this world solely for the purpose of awaiting my arrival."

On that solemn thought – and obvious dismissal by Dom, who clearly wasn't going to discuss the matter of Jade's betrayal with her any further – Carra wandered out of the room, and back into the corridor with the two other doors.

She opened the one nearest her, which gave way to a fairly large storeroom. There were some items of clothing, a couple of bedrolls, a dagger, a crossbow and various sacks of dried food, nuts, and seeds, as well as some grain for the horses. It would certainly enable her and Dom to stock up before they went on their way.

Although the room was reasonably large, the storeroom didn't allow for much exploring; the huge sacks and stacked crates prevented her from walking too far into the room.

Back in the corridor, Carra approached the other door more cautiously, knowing that Anthony must be behind it. After receiving no response to her knock, Carra edged it open.

There was a fairly comfortable living area with a kitchen and some chairs. Sprawled across one of these chairs was Anthony himself, and it dawned on her that he must have given over his bedroom to Dom last night. She rushed over to check for a pulse. It was faint, but there, and Carra heaved a sigh of relief.

Aware she was standing over him, he opened his eyes and smiled. "Tell him, I'm glad I made it long enough to see him again." Before Carra could take in his words, Anthony had faded from the world. "Dom" she screeched, "Dom help." Reluctantly she let go of Anthony's hand and ran back to Dom, who had sat up in the bed.

"Are you talking to me? *Theodore*?" He emphasised the latter in order to correct her mistake.

"Theodore." she mimicked, "I think Anthony is gone."

"He's run away?" Dom said confused.

"No, I am trying to tell you he's gone; no more. I think he's died." Once she got her breath back, she told him Anthony's last words, whilst Dom hauled himself out of the bed. With his left arm around her shoulders, she carried him through to the living area.

Agreeing with her assessment, Dom gently closed Anthony's eyelids. "Let's go. We start back on our route, right now." He proclaimed.

"Dom, I know you're upset but we need to bury him, and besides, you're in no fit state to travel anywhere!"

☆ ☆ ☆ ☆
 ✧ ✧ ✧ ✧

A few days later they were both well rested and fully packed up with the provisions needed to resume their journey. They had buried Anthony outside, away from the dome; the protection over which had been relinquished since his passing.

Dom's back was much improved, although Carra

could tell it was still bothering him. With the amount of food saved up – of which they had only taken a small fraction – they would no longer need to stop by any villages.

She wasn't sure if that was a positive or a negative.

As she saddled up Hope and then Jak for Dom, Dom marked their current location on his map more clearly, so they could stop there again for supplies on their way home. *Home, where even is home?* She screamed inside her mind. *We can't go back to Florinyn!*

The temperature was far more bearable now, and well... she seemed to have, if not forgotten, at least forgiven and put to one side, her annoyance with Dom from the previous week.

The rain had stopped two days earlier, so the ground was no longer as boggy, and it only took them a couple of days to traverse the rest of Avo – fairly uneventfully. Although they passed other people on their route, no one seemed either particularly friendly or noticeably hostile so, happily, they kept to their own company.

As they arrived at what Dom informed her was the southwest coast, Carra found it difficult to contain her surprise. The cliffs stood hundreds of paces in the air, with a sheer drop down to the sea. The height alone was enough to make her shudder, but Dom dismounted and strolled right up the edge as if there were nothing frightening about it at all.

She moved towards him, though not nearly as close to the drop as he was standing, and peered over. The sea was smashing vigorously against the cliffs below. The first time she'd seen the sea, back in Florin, it had been calm and still. She could appreciate, now, how boats in stories were smashed against the rocks and torn into thousands of pieces. She was mesmerised by it. Huge waves rushing towards the coast were crashing against the rocks, and the roar boomed all around her until she wanted to cover her ears.

Her mind conjured an unwanted image, forcing her to envision what would become of her body if she fell. Blinking to rid herself of the thought, she decided to take a few steps backwards and return to the horses.

After a few minutes, she realised Dom had moved to stand next to her. "Ready?" He asked her.

"For what, Dom?"

"We're going to abseil down." She looked at him as though he had gone mad; perhaps he had. Turning to their supplies, she wondered where Dom had hidden the rope – although she couldn't actually remember seeing him pack any. "Oh, I'm only joking Carra. Come on, there's a way down."

"Down to where? Isn't it just sea down there?"

Dom retrieved the map, and showed her where they were. They had taken a path ending to the south-west of Avo, despite the Desert lands being to the south-east. If they had headed straight for the desert, they would have had to either scale these cliffs, or cross several miles of the Avonian range. A few miles may not have sounded like much, but Dom assured her that would have meant climbing at least two, maybe three of the mountains.

He explained that, although they had travelled several miles out of their way, from this position there was a way down to the beach. In low tide, this would allow them to enter a tunnel network through the caves down there. These tunnels would take them out just at the point where the Avonian range met the desert – a good place to start their search.

"Don't the tunnels flood from those enormous waves?" she asked him.

"Nope. The caves are sealed. We'll go through a watertight door, and close it again behind us. See that lighthouse over there – that's where we can climb down."

They made their way over to the lighthouse, and as Dom had promised, there were indeed some steps – although to Carra, they looked worryingly steep.

With a short wait ahead of them, they ate a little earlier than usual. Carra fidgeted anxiously, in anticipation of the moment Dom would indicate the tide was low enough for them to begin their downwards climb.

With no other choice, they set Jak and Hope free. They left a sack of grain by the lighthouse in the slim hope they might return there to feed, and therefore be around for the return trip.

Somehow it felt slightly lonely now it was only the two of them, but Carra was distracted from her melancholy by the stone staircase, which took her full concentration. Not only were the steps narrow and precipitous, but they were slippery.

Although Dom had tried to reassure her by going down first – in case he needed to catch her – she was incredibly worried she'd slip and thereby be the end of both of them.

It wasn't the second time she'd been miserable as a result of some stairs recently. The irony was, while she should be thankful it was at least light this time, all it served to do was show her quite how high up she was – and how far she had to fall.

As they safely reached the bottom, Dom put out his hand and helped her down the last two steps. "I hope you haven't had your fill of adventure yet," he joked. "There's plenty more to come. Based on the amount of time it took you to come down those steps, I estimate we have about five hours to find this door before the tide comes in and we have to climb back up again, so let's get going!"

Carra didn't like to ask if he was joking. In fact, she knew he wasn't, but she wanted to pretend that he was. The idea of going back up those steps again and doing this all again tomorrow… she genuinely couldn't stomach the thought of it.

Even with what Dom called 'low tide', they were still wading a foot deep in water. Yes, the waves were much lower, but some of them were easily reaching the height of her waist. Carra wondered how Dom would be able to tell when the tide was coming back in because, whether it was solely in her imagination or not, she couldn't help but feel like those waves were becoming increasingly vigorous.

Thoroughly soaked through, by the time they found the entryway she was shivering, despite the sun shining down on them.

Dom heaved the door open, and she helped him close it behind them – although it was so heavy she probably didn't make much of a difference.

She remained sceptical the large, stone door was actually watertight like Dom had claimed, but at least it seemed to be sufficient to prevent the tunnels from flooding.

The last slither of light disappeared as the door fit in place and they were plummeted into a darkness that was so complete she couldn't see her own hand in front of her.

She felt Dom grab hold of her wrist – both surprising her and causing her panic, because she thought it meant he must be nervous. A flame spouted up in his other hand and after blinking a couple of times, suddenly she could see again. "Dom you scared me!"

"I didn't want to burn you and I couldn't tell for certain where you were." He'd clearly forgotten his flames didn't harm her.

She lit her own small flame too, mostly to give her an excuse to keep hold of Dom's hand, but also because she was wet and cold, and there was something reassuring about its warmth.

Around four strides wide and six strides high, the tunnel stretched out ahead of them, seeming endless. She felt reassured by indications it was manmade – it looked to have been chiselled out – but she wasn't sure how long ago.

"It's centuries old," Dom declared. "These tunnels were made five or six-hundred years ago. Look." Sure enough, there was a date plaque on the wall by the entrance. Carra frowned. *So can he hear my thoughts then, or not?*

"No, I can't hear your thoughts." Dom said, "You're just predictable."

"You… but you just…!" she stammered.

He put his hand to his chin, "Yes okay, I see your point. Tell me if I do it again?" *Well, that was disconcerting.*

CHAPTER 27

The tunnels twisted slightly, but generally they seemed to be leading them the same way, and Dom was confident they were heading east as he could see the trail marked on the map. It was of some comfort there were no forks – no difficult choices to be made – but Carra had lost all sense of time and direction.

Sometimes her and Dom talked, but mostly they were just accompanied by the sound of their footsteps, which echoed slightly. She knew she wasn't badly claustrophobic, but with the amount of time they had been down there, she was starting to feel as though the weight of the stone above was pressing down on them. Every time she saw a loose stone on the ground, she began to hallucinate about the ceiling caving in.

She had grown up in a forest and spent most of her time outdoors. The air down here felt different, stilted, as if it was low on oxygen content.

Aside from finding breathing less comfortable, and the unavoidably unpleasant atmosphere as a result of being underground, Carra thought there was something generally eerie about the place. Some areas had dense moss and others had none, but otherwise the passages had no distinguishing features, so she couldn't quite put her finger on what it was specifically that made the tunnels quite so unnerving.

Perhaps it was the sameness of it all. Everything was grey. Some avenues were narrower, some were wider, but they were all the same dull, cold chiselled stone.

It wasn't until she heard an incongruous noise that she realised just how quiet it had been. She stopped, somewhat suddenly, in response. Except for her intermittent conversations with Dom, the only sounds had been their own breathing and their feet moving; she was *sure* she hadn't heard anything else before now.

When Dom turned to look at her, she put one finger to her lips to stop him from speaking.

There was complete silence. He shrugged.

Maybe an hour later, she heard it again. It was almost like a scratching noise, although it was very faint. "Dom, is that you?" she whispered.

"Is what me?"

"That scratching."

"I don't hear anything."

"Listen for it. Please? I don't like it."

"Okay, I will keep an ear out if it makes you happy. I'm absolutely certain it's just this place making you imagine things. It's… creepy down here."

"You're supposed to be the brave prince, don't tell me you're scared?" *No really, please don't.* "The only thing reassuring me, keeping me going, is that you're here to save me!"

"I said creepy not scary. Don't worry, I don't get scared. I'll listen out for your mouse – real *or* imaginary."

"Thanks." She wanted to be reassured but… *would there really be mice down here? It doesn't seem very hospitable.*

"I didn't literally mean a mouse, Carra – but I'm sure it's a rodent or creepy crawly of some sort."

Carra heard it at least twice more before Dom admitted that he had heard it too. "Now you've got me hearing things, Carra."

"Oh yes, totally. It's my fault."

"Just keep walking. Everything is fine. This place is getting to you."

She tried to do as he said... tried to keep walking *without* thinking about what might be lurking down there, as yet unbeknown to them.

But then Carra heard the noise again, and this time it was much louder. She gripped Dom's wrist tightly.

It sounded like something was clawing at the rock. Maybe it was even trapped down here. Perhaps they were about to reach a dead end, or they'd fall into a pit, and that would be it – they'd be entombed down here with it. *Breathe Carra, breathe.* She let out a deep breath and visualised her fear leaving her through her fingertips – then realised she had been using magic to control her emotions all along.

"Dom."

"What?" he almost snapped at her.

"Nothing." *Never mind.*

"The closeness down here is getting to me. I'm not meaning to sound angry with you. And I want to hear what you were going to say."

"I think I have been using magic." He frowned at her in confusion. "I think when I concentrate, I can release my emotions. I've done it a few times when I've felt afraid, and it's calmed me down. Does that sound silly? I probably just want to believe it's happening, because I was feeling scared, and I don't want to anymore."

"Emotions are linked very closely with magic. Many healers can sense their patients' feelings through their magic. It's entirely possible you have some power in that respect." He seemed pensive for a moment. "If, as you suggest to be the case, I keep responding to your thoughts as well, then maybe you are actually transmitting them."

That gave Carra something to think over. She couldn't quite believe Dom had accepted what she'd said as a possibility – it made her feel the most positive she had since they'd been down there.

Her assumption had been *he* was the one listening in to *her* mind, it hadn't occurred to her that it could be something she was doing – and she really liked the idea she could banish her fear. Regardless of whether it was only a placebo, it calmed her.

She had almost relaxed, when her relative serenity was interrupted by a loud bang. It sounded like something large had fallen, which would have been frightening enough, if it hadn't been followed by a scuffling sound, and after that, a second, smaller bang.

She gasped.

Instinctively, Dom put his light out, so she did too. He pulled her against the wall, and they both pressed their backs flat against it. For several minutes, she listened to the sound of Dom's breathing and held tightly to his hand – whilst trying to ignore the cold seeping through her.

Nothing happened.

She leant her head against his shoulder, and they waited a bit longer.

"How far along are we?" she whispered.

"Past halfway, I would guess, but I can't say for sure. At some point the path diverges, and we need to take the right-hand path. I'll be able to gauge our progress once we reach that fork."

Once the panic they'd felt had passed, they began walking again. They moved slowly and kept their lights small.

Every now and then, Carra was convinced she was hearing scratching, or scuffling. Sometimes there was also a clinking – but they didn't see anyone, or any*thing* else down there.

Both her and Dom stepped as quietly as they could. She could tell he felt unsettled, and that knocked her own confidence in return.

In order to distract herself, she started to think through a song in her head. She dared not sing it out loud, and played it in her mind instead. After not too long, Dom started humming the tune she'd been thinking about – at least until she shushed him.

"How long have we been down here, Dom? Has it been days? I can't tell."

"I don't know... but I do think it's possible we haven't slept for a couple of days. Maybe that's why we're going a little stir-crazy. Why don't you sleep for a few hours whilst I keep watch, then we'll swap over?"

Carra looked around her. The tunnel was not particularly wide, but it wasn't exactly as if they'd passed anywhere that would make a better place to stop and rest. "How did people do this, Dom – when they travelled through here? What am I missing?"

"It's a good question, but one I am unable to answer. This tunnel was only ever used by slaves. I don't know if anyone ever asked them how they felt about it."

Dom began humming the tune she'd been thinking about again, while he laid out a bedroll for her. She laid down, wondering whether she would actually manage to fall asleep in this accursed place. Dom took a seat, cross-legged beside her and stroked her hair. It was soothing – either that, or it really had been two days since she last slept – and she quickly fell into a deep slumber.

Her sleep was laced with nightmares. As Dom was

still awake, keeping watch, he didn't join her – and she didn't have any control over what was happening.

Unfortunately for Carra, in her dreams she was walking through the same tunnels – unable to escape these surroundings, even in a setting created by her own mind. Except, despite Dom not being there, she wasn't alone.

Emaciated men, with shackles around their ankles, walked beside her, watching her. Their chains jangled intimidatingly, and it became apparent to Carra they were moving them purposefully so.

She stopped walking and pressed her back against the wall to let them go past, but instead, they stopped and stared at her. She put her hands out in front of her to try and keep them from approaching. The scratching noise she'd been hearing began, and one of the men began laughing. She flailed her arms wildly in front of her until… until, Dom woke her up.

"My turn." She put on a brave face, or at least she hoped she did, while she moved to let Dom lie down.

Maybe it just wasn't light enough for him to tell she was so distressed. And afraid.

As she sat there in the darkness, feeling alone and defenceless, she couldn't shake off the imagery from her dream. *Get a grip Carra.*

The only sound she could hear now was her own breathing, which seemed hurried. She consciously tried to slow it down with some, limited, success.

Taking Dom's hand, she lit a small flame for herself. The flickering created moving shadows on the wall that were unnerving at first, but she managed to get herself accustomed to them. The flame was gently swaying, despite the lack of airflow – although she *was* holding it in her palm, so maybe it was her own thoughts and feelings making it move.

The shadows replicated, and several now danced,

enticingly. The longer she was sitting there, the more she became hypnotised by them.

The next thing she knew, Dom had his hands on both of her shoulders and was shaking her, somewhat energetically. She frowned and looked up at him. "Oh thank the Creator, I was worried I'd lost you." Carra shook her head trying to bring herself around. She looked up at Dom questioningly. "It was like you were in some sort of trance. What happened to you?"

"I couldn't really tell you. I think I was just freaked out from my dream, and the darkness. Perhaps from being alone as well." Dom had wrapped up the bedroll and was rummaging around in his pack, so didn't immediately respond. She was about to berate him, when he passed her some peanuts, and she realised that was what he'd been looking in the bag for.

"I think it might be quite a while since we last ate. As we've discovered, it's hard to keep track of time in this place. Maybe you fainted from lack of energy?"

"Let's just get moving and get out of here. I'm not sure how much more of this place I can take. I'm completely losing my mind."

Neither of them were in particularly high spirits as they continued, but they did pick up the pace a bit, so they must have been at least partially refreshed. At one point Carra thought she felt a breeze on the back of her neck, but otherwise the next few hours were fairly uneventful. That was, until she started hearing her name being whispered.

"Can you hear that, Dom?" He shook his head, so she tried to ignore the beckoning voice.

The susurration was faint, softly spoken, but it was definitely *her* it was summoning. Then she thought heard the word "wait" shouted in a different voice, but she was already following the call. It was dark, but that didn't matter anymore, because she was following the direction of the voice.

As Carra glided towards it, the clinking sound became increasingly louder, but she wasn't afraid anymore. She needed to help them.

She placed the palm of her left hand against the tunnel wall to feel her way. After she gained some confidence, she began to only skim her fingertips along the stone. She kept going, even though the voice had now ceased. The further she went, the more light-headed she felt.

Eventually her foot hit something hard, and at almost the same instant, her hand hit a bar, which was blocking the way. The passageway was closed off.

Grabbing one of the metal bars, she tried to pull or push it, but the gate wouldn't budge; so she tried to shake the bar loose – again, with no success. Somewhere in her mind she registered that it was ice cold against her hand.

Carra bent down to see what it was she had stumped her toe on and felt more metal. Exploring the floor around her, she discovered several sets of iron chains, with shackles at the end of these.

The clanking noise when she disturbed them brought her back to her senses and, at last appreciating her situation, she screamed – but no sound came out.

Now that she was aware again, free of whatever spell had carried her here, she realised she was freezing. *I need to go back, but where has Dom gone? How have I managed to lose him?*

She knew she needed to retrace her steps in order to find him, but she found herself frozen rigid, unable to move from where she was standing. Her limbs didn't want to obey her. *Maybe not entirely free of the spell then.*

The chains she'd found abandoned on the floor

seemed to be convulsing, and she could have sworn the gate had started creaking too, as though someone was trying to open the old, out-of-use portcullis.

Creak. Creak. Creak. The groaning of the gate as the machinery was slowly coming to life – for the first time in who knows how long – was such an unpleasant sound that it sent further chills through her.

She tried to lift her leg, but it felt weighted down. The dreadful noise was beginning to dull all her other brain functions.

This time when she opened her mouth, a real scream came out.

There were footsteps and suddenly a light – Dom appeared, panting as though he was out of breath from running. "You slipped my hand!" The sudden, very welcome, appearance of Dom shook her out of her antithetical reverie. She sighed in relief, and very almost laughed.

"Just get me out of here. The way is blocked. I don't know what we should do!"

"You went the wrong way. I even told you beforehand that it was right at the fork, but then you suddenly sprinted on ahead and I couldn't keep up, nor find you further down the route. I didn't expect you to have taken the left path – but once I realised that's what you'd done, I doubled back to look for you."

Once she was within his reach, Dom took her hand, which seemed to breathe life back into her. His approach had lit up the area, and she could see now that the gate *had* in fact been descending into the ground, and worse, there were piles consisting of what looked like human skeletons on the other side of it.

Making eye contact with Dom, one glance was all it took for them to communicate their intentions and both break into a run – Dom overcoming his breathlessness from a few seconds earlier out of necessity.

They didn't stop running until they had made it back to the fork.

"I didn't see there was a split in the path before. I didn't have any light," she admitted, "and I really don't understand how I could have covered such a long distance."

Once they had both recovered from the shock, they speculated on what had happened. Neither of them could come up with any plausible suggestions as to who – or what – had raised the spell, nor why it had targeted Carra, and *only* Carra.

After their strange experience, Dom seemed increasingly worried about her, and kept his arm around her rather than just holding her hand. She preferred to assume he was trying to be protective of her over the alternative – that he might himself be just as afraid as she was.

"It's not far now, I promise." Carra didn't ask him how he knew that; she wanted only to believe it was true.

☆☆ ☆☆ ☆

He'd spoken honestly. A few hours later, they started to feel a light breeze, and not long after that, there was a thin sheen of water on the ground.

At long last, they approached the mouth of the tunnel; although as it was night outside, it took them a little while to appreciate exactly what was ahead.

When Dom dimmed his flame, and they could suddenly see stars ahead, it was a very pleasant surprise to both of them.

CHAPTER 28

To say Dom was pleased to leave the caverns would be an understatement, but on stepping through the entrance he felt something odd. He would have described the sensation as the air rippling around him – but it passed so quickly he decided he'd only imagined it.

Carra had stepped through a second ahead of him, but she was already nowhere to be seen, which didn't bode well at all.

He was reluctant to light a flame, not knowing what creatures it might attract in these parts, but she hadn't left him much choice. *What is it with that girl and running off?*

He started with just a small flame, and didn't stray too far – doing his utmost to keep the cave entrance in sight. Calling her name proved fruitless. Eventually, he realised he was going to have to make the decision between venturing further and potentially becoming disorientated, or camping until morning.

Having no knowledge of the desert lands, and no idea which direction Carra might have gone in, calling it a night won out.

☆☆☆☆☆☆

When Carra emerged, all she wanted to do was get as far away from those abhorrent tunnels as possible. She walked out a few steps, savouring the fresh air; it was musty and dry, even though the night itself was cool.

Feeling like celebrating, she looked up at the dark sky, held her arms out, and span round and round until she was dizzy. Laughing, she looked around for Dom, but he was suddenly nowhere to be seen.

Typical she thought, *is he perhaps surveying where we are? But surely that can wait until morning.*

As she had the tent in her pack, she set it up in what she thought was a suitable spot. It made sense to camp near the cave, so they didn't lose their bearings, and she was sure Dom would feel the same. He could just lay out his bedroll and climb in once he got back.

She didn't light a fire as the air was warm enough – although this would mean *she* wasn't able to see *him*, she assumed his flames would light up the area enough that he'd be able to find where she'd set up camp.

Although she tried to wait for him, it was half-hearted, and Carra – who was exhausted – was very soon fast asleep.

☆☆☆☆

Morning didn't bring any clarity.

Sitting up, Dom looked around. He wiped his eyes with his sleeves, to remove any residue of sleep, but the haze he was seeing didn't go away. The air was thickly saturated with sand particles.

It was how he would have imagined the aftermath of a sandstorm to be. Holding his hand out in front of his face, he could only just make out his fingers. He racked his brain for any relevant knowledge on deserts he might have, but nothing was coming to mind.

Going through his backpack, Dom found his spare shirt, and tore some strips off it to tie around his eyes.

He tried calling out for Carra, but there was no response. Giving up, he reluctantly used a few drops of his water to wet some additional strips, before tying these around his mouth.

✯✯✯

Carra woke up and felt around, unsuccessfully, for Dom.

She still couldn't see him when she looked outside either, so she packed up their tent and snacked on some dried meat.

There was a path snaking through the miles of sand, and she decided this was the most likely route Dom had taken – she didn't understand why he would have wandered off without her but, well, this seemed like the only remotely plausible way he would have gone.

It had been clearly demarcated with rocks; the sand left no signs of use so it wasn't possible to see how well trodden the route was, but someone had clearly decided it was important enough to go to the effort of lining it with stones every few steps. She couldn't see where the path went, as it disappeared over a hill, but she could see a reasonable distance – Dom must have already travelled pretty far to already be out of sight.

Carra felt instinctively that this was the right way to go. Surely it would lead her to civilisation sooner than her wandering around aimlessly, and she didn't have enough water left to remain put. She couldn't think of any good explanation for Dom's absence, but there was absolutely *no way* she was going to head back the way they'd come, especially not alone.

After several of hours of walking, Carra was desperate for the last drop of water in her flask. Her willpower was resting entirely on her hope that once she rounded this hill, there would be something to see... but there wasn't.

She flopped on the floor, glad that Dom couldn't see her right now, mid-tantrum, and drank whatever was left. It was so little that it wasn't even remotely satisfying, and she irrationally flung her water bottle away, trying to throw off her bad mood.

Carra was staring aimlessly at the path ahead when, out of the corner of her eye, she saw something moving in the distance. She quickly jumped up and brushed the sand off herself. As she was about to wave her arms and call out to Dom, she realised it was both too tall to be him, and somehow the wrong colour. He only wore black clothes and this creature appeared to be sandy-brown.

She didn't need to look around to know there was nothing for her to hide behind. Her panic quickly ebbed away when she recognised it was actually a camel – something else she'd only seen before in picture books! – and moreover, it was riderless.

As the camel approached her, it slowed to a halt. Unable to stop herself, she held out her hand and stroked its flank. It turned to look at her, then sat on its hind legs.

Bemused, she glanced around to see if anyone was watching her, as she felt her new-found reckless side returning. *The reckless instincts I've started having since meeting Dom...* she mused to herself. After walking back to gather her flask – she hoped she would at some point be able to refill it, and didn't want to regret having carelessly discarded it – she climbed on the camel's back.

Almost immediately, he jumped up, then turned around, and began to stroll in the direction she had been travelling. The way he stuck to the path amused her. Carra stroked his neck, "Are you someone's pet? You're awfully tame to be out here alone. Where are you taking me?"

The good news was that *surely* she would catch up with Dom now she had a speedier means of travel. *Why in the kingdom had he insisted on going so far ahead?* "Have you seen my friend, little one? He has dark hair, broad muscular shoulders, and about six days' growth of facial hair." *Over his strong jawline hmm, below his big dark grey-blue eyes. And why am I asking the camel?*

The camel was surprisingly comfortable, but it wasn't until it was starting to get dark again that Carra realised she could make out a town in the distance. Dom couldn't possibly have got this far without her catching up, but hopefully the people there could help her look for him.

The distance was too far to cover before nightfall, and it wasn't much longer before the camel stopped and crouched down to let Carra off. She didn't bother tying him up to secure him. She was close enough that she could reach the town on foot tomorrow if she needed to, and more pertinently, there was nothing to tie him to.

The night air was nice and cool, *almost* a cure for her insufferable thirst, and she lay down in her bedroll rather than erecting the tent.

On waking, Carra was glad to see that her friend had remained by her side. She laughed to herself as an image came to her mind of him sitting on guard vigilantly while she slept. Climbing back up on his back, they continued their journey. At this speed, they'd make it to civilisation before the sun was at its meridian.

As they got closer, Carra could see that the hamlet was only slightly bigger than where she had grown up. As they got even nearer, she started to worry that they may think she'd stolen the camel. After all, it was probably owned by someone in this village.

Unfortunately, unless he stopped to let her off, she

was left with no choice but to continue. She hadn't really thought this through – but equally, she was so dehydrated, it wasn't like she'd actually had a choice.

Although travelling faster than she could astride Hope, she was also higher up – a little *too* high to jump off. Clearly this new adventurous, reckless, Carra had its bounds.

There were no walls or gates to this small community, and the camel wandered freely down the streets. A few people came out of their domiciles to stare at her, and she had a flashback to her uncomfortable entrance to Rivulet – then shook herself out of it. She was being silly, there was nothing unfriendly to be found in their expressions.

With her mahogany brown curls, she had always had hair darker than others, but these people had black locks at least as dark as Dom's, which flowed in big loopy waves. Carra realised she was staring back.

The camel chose the middle of the street to stop and let her alight.

"Excuse me," she said to the nearest person, a girl of around her own age.

The girl nodded and put her hand on Carra's shoulder. "Gabbie."

"I'm Carra. This isn't my camel." *Why did I say that?*

"Welcome to Savarah. Please come with me." Carra – who was amazed that they spoke the same language here – followed a couple of steps behind, as Gabbie turned and walked towards what looked like a town square.

"How is it that we understand each other?"

"We fulfil the need we need to fulfil." Carra obviously wasn't satisfied by such a cryptic answer, but this warred against her need not to insult her host, and the latter won out.

Gabbie led her to a small wall with a hole in the centre, from which water was flowing. Gabbie put a small amount in her hands and drank, then gestured for Carra to do the same. She didn't need much encouragement, and after a couple of handfuls, she filled her flask – then drank three-quarters of it and filled it again.

"Have you seen anyone else travelling through here? A man." Carra realised, looking around, that she could only see females, "around this high" she said holding her hand a foot or so above her head.

Gabbie shook her head. "No, you are the only stranger that has graced us in a long while. Will you join my family for a meal and tell us your story?"

Carra followed Gabbie into one of the larger dwellings and directed her to have a seat. She was introduced to a couple of older women, Gabel, and Petra, and watched, feeling useless, as Gabbie helped them prepare and serve a meal.

The hut was of a comparable size to the home she had grown up in, but that was where the similarity ended. The edges of the living area were lined with three wide, low benches, which were covered with large, brightly coloured, mismatched cushions. Whilst this area was spacious, the kitchen was cramped, and there was only just enough room for the three women to stand at the counter.

When they were finally done, they joined her on the benches. Carra studied the food being served, trying not to look ungrateful. It didn't look particularly appetising even though she couldn't remember the last time she'd eaten.

Before tucking in herself, she waited for one of her hosts to start, then braved a mouthful. The food was as plain as she'd anticipated, but still pleasantly satisfying to her empty stomach.

She was careful to eat slowly, giving herself time to think about how much of her tale to relay to her hosts. She concluded that, seeing as she would need help for the next stage of her journey, she would have to include the part about the locket – and if she was revealing that part, then there wasn't really anything else worth hiding.

She was reassured in her decision by how isolated this community seemed. *Although...* she still didn't see any need to mention Dom's previous identity.

While she relayed her story, her three companions sat quietly. They were more patient than she would have been herself; Carra knew if their situations had been reversed, she would have been interrupting with questions throughout.

Once she had finished, she looked around at them expectantly. They appeared deep in thought.

It was Gabel who at last interrupted the silence, "Thank you for sharing your journey so far with us. We can now reveal our own gifts to you. This town is here and also it is not. We are on the cusp of the world – both within it and outside of it. It has appeared to you because you called for it. This may sound strange to you, and we do not expect you to fully comprehend this. Nor is it easy for us to help you conceptualise this.

"It is likely that your chaperon has been kept behind the curtain of the mirage, unable to see through it. This means that this part of your quest must be yours to complete alone. We will see that he is provided with water as this desert is not self-sufficient for travellers.

"Tonight, you will stay with us and rest, but tomorrow you must embark. It is not healthy to stay here in the in-between for too long. We are tasked with guiding you to your next destination. Please step outside with me?"

Carra did as requested and walked with Gabel into

the cool night air. Gabel raised her arm skyward and pointed to a huge stone tower. "This is where you must go." She couldn't understand how she hadn't noticed it before.

"We will provide you with food supplies, and you can refill your flask before you leave in the morning. Pyjo," Gabel gestured to the camel, "Will be waiting to guide you back to your young man should you succeed."

The words reverberated through her and Carra shuddered, unsure whether Gabel had meant that to sound *quite* so ominous.

Surprisingly, the rest of the evening was fairly relaxed, and Carra fell into an easy conversation with Gabbie. She was both interested and particularly horrified to discover this desert was home to copious numbers of scorpions – and was equally relieved she hadn't encountered any yet.

Enjoying the company, she even felt reluctant to retire for the night, but knew she should be using the opportunity to refresh herself, as Gabel had suggested. Gabbie had explained that the longer you stayed in Savarah, the more difficult it was to leave, and she could well believe it to be true.

CHAPTER 29

The bed they had provided her with was extremely comfortable, and she woke to find herself feeling fresh, and so re-energised, that she couldn't find any excuse to justify prolonging her stay.

Walking into the living area she discovered that Gabel, or someone assisting her, had already packed a bag of breads, crackers, and fruit ready for her departure. Gabbie, Gabel, and Petra were even waiting for her outside to see her off – Gabel bowed to her in farewell, and Gabbie walked her to the edge of their village, via the water fountain.

"Come with me?" she blurted out.

"This task is for you alone to achieve, friend."

"Come with Pyjo then, and join me as I travel home?" She could see Gabbie wanted to.

"It is not my path. Gabel is my grandmother, but also my mentor. Soon I will take on the mantle of Guide; although the role is so much more than that one word conveys." Carra nodded in understanding. She was disappointed for Gabbie as much as for herself – she knew how much seeing the world outside of Astonelay had meant to her. *Even though I didn't know that while I was actually living there!*

As she neared the tower, Carra turned back and waved. She thought she could just about make out Gabbie waving back.

Re-focusing on the present, she craned her neck upwards. The tower could easily have been twelve storeys high. She wondered why the locket was hidden in such an obvious place.

There was a slight creak as she forced open the door, and bracing herself, she stepped inside.

It soon became clear why this 'hiding' place had been chosen. The whole building was thick with magic, it was palpable in the air.

The interior was nothing like she had anticipated, or at least would have anticipated had she spent any time thinking about it. There were three, arched doorways in front of her, each with a sculpture above the entrance – one with a rose, another a sword, and the third with an eye.

Pausing before she approached any of them more closely, she considered each in turn: the rose was yellow, in full bloom, and beautiful; the sword was sharp despite the hilt having been designed to appear old and worn; but the eye... the eye was disconcerting – it almost looked as though the iris was tinged with red.

On further examination of the iris, she thought she could identify red stones interspersed amongst the blue. The resulting colour was spectacular. Hearing Dom's voice in her head describing the ruby as the Perywhist stone, she cautiously approached that third arch.

As she put her hand to the door, intending to push it open – hoping she may even get a glimpse inside before she had to commit to a choice – the door disappeared, revealing only a black nothingness.

Taking a deep breath, she walked through the space where it had been.

It was as though she had been transported back outside, albeit not to anywhere she recognised. She was in a forest, but the colours were unrealistically vivid, and the population of trees was reasonably sparse. Their trunks were long and thin with green bushy leaves at the apexes.

Between the trees were flowering shrubs of many varieties. Some were fantastic due to their colour alone – fluorescent pinks, lilacs and oranges jumped out at her; some had striated petals, blended so seamlessly she could barely distinguish the individual colours. Others were beautiful by virtue of being so unusual. She saw those she recognised – foxgloves, honeysuckles, and ramsoms were easily identifiable – and others she didn't; there were some plants she wasn't even sure existed outside of this unreality.

Above her, she saw blue sky, peppered with wispy, cirrus clouds, which formed pleasing shapes but didn't obstruct the sunlight.

The temperature was unusually pleasant, and it made her slightly sleepy. She was strangely tempted to lie down and bask in the sun.

After taking a few steps forwards, she was assaulted by the most wonderful smells. She walked at a snail's pace in order to properly take in and admire her surroundings, and had to keep reminding herself not to relax and instead stay on her guard.

The fresh air was blissful in comparison to the desert air, the oppressive caves, and the cold winter chill she'd been subjected to before those.

After an uncertain amount of time, she came across a small grassy knoll, which somehow looked perfect for a nap. As she climbed it, she came across a grey and white chequered rug, laid out on the grass next to a picnic basket.

Seeing there was no-one else around, she laid down, and peeked into the basket. There were sandwiches, scones, and sparkling wine. She felt sure it had been left there for her, but – by virtue of the same reasoning – she knew she should keep moving. It felt wrong to linger and enjoy herself when she needed to complete the Tower.

As soon as she stepped off the hillock, she felt herself being whisked away.

She was indoors once more, and with the blast of hot air that hit her face, her first thought was she'd been lucky enough to find herself inside a furnace.

As she re-orientated herself, her eyes adjusted to the smoke and the absence of natural light, and she found – much to her surprise – that she actually recognised the room she was in. *It's where we were in my dream. I had forgotten all about it, but that faceless man was Dom – I didn't really know him yet then!*

The corridor was long, with drops either side – and unnervingly, Carra couldn't see how far down the bottom was. As she peered over the side of the pathway to look, flames shot up. She darted backwards quickly and managed to avoid being singed. Her heartbeat seemed to rapidly speed up in the process.

Apparently, she had set off a chain reaction, as flames sprouted up on both sides from the chasms ahead of her. She turned around in retreat but there was a solid wall behind her – nowhere to go but forwards.

Without Dom's flame magic, the heat felt far more intense. Or perhaps it was because the other had only been a dream. Either way, it was unpleasant, and a stark contrast that that fresh forest air from moments earlier. She struggled not to cough. *So, was this the true test she now faced?*

She paid heed to her balance as she started down the path, which was around half a pace in width. She wanted to extend her arms out to either side, but the flames were too high.

Walking between them was not an experience she'd ever ask to repeat.

Ordinarily, she would likely have been able to keep to a straight line more easily, but the smoke was making her slightly dizzy.

After a hundred paces or so, she approached a gap in the path. It was around a stride in length, and it was just far enough that she'd have to jump to get to the other side. Even worse, there were flames in the gap. Okay, so they were lower than the flames either side of her, – which reached to around the top of her head – but they were still about the height of her waist.

She really wasn't sure how to proceed. Panicking slightly, she turned around – but somehow the solid wall was still directly behind her. *Magic.* She rolled her eyes.

Concentrate Carra. You're going to get burned whatever you do, so the important thing is to make sure not to let that distract you from landing on the path the other side.

Taking a deep breath, she leapt.

She cleared the flames, for the most part, and landed on one knee, with both her palms flat on the stone path. It hadn't been intentional – she'd meant to land on her feet – but actually it turned out to be a good way to stabilise herself.

As she, unsurprisingly, approached another such gap, she aimed to land in the same way. The path wasn't quite shoulder width, so she needed to stagger her hands slightly for it to work.

The third time, her jump wasn't high enough and her leggings caught fire. Carra hurriedly patted out the flames, and luckily only her thighs ended up singed, although this left her hands fairly sore too.

A little further on, the path narrowed to such an extent that she was required to walk with one foot directly in front of the other. Inevitably, she came across another gap. Carra stood in contemplation for a short time – partially frozen in fear. There was no way she could risk jumping this one, she had no chance of landing successfully on the other side.

She could *possibly* make it across if she took a large stride – directly through the flames.

She knew she was just going to have to go for it. The longer she remained still, thinking about it, the more smoke seemed to clog the air – as if this place was reacting to her progress slowing. Besides, there was nowhere else to go.

With no choice now but to put her arms out for balance, she placed her right foot as close to the edge as she could. Cringing slightly from the flames, she tried not to think about the pain, then held her breath whilst extending her leg and striding across.

She made it; but both her legs and arms came out quite badly scalded.

Carra might have despaired but after having cleared that last gap, she could finally see her goal up ahead. The path culminated with a circular stage, seated upon which was a small platform.

Wobbling a bit from the pain, she made her way towards it. There was a crystal atop it, which she reached out to touch. The second she did, the room faded away and she felt herself being transported physically. Whereas previously she'd felt her surroundings moving around her, this time it seemed like *she* was the one being displaced.

It was a strange sensation; she felt like she was moving very quickly, but there was clearly also magic working to dull the whole experience.

☆☆☆☆

Carra found herself in a grand hallway she didn't recognise. The stone floor was carpeted with a lavish cerulean rug, tasselled with gold along its length. In both directions, the end of the corridor seemed to branch out both left and right, giving her four possible routes.

At one end, there was a large statue of a muscular man holding a sword and shield, with the sword pointed downwards as if he was about to take a killing blow. At the other end of the corridor was a tapestry of what appeared to be a town surrounded by hills – but she wasn't close enough to see if she recognised it.

There were stained glass windows to either side of her, but they were too high from the ground, so she couldn't use them to look outside.

Hearing footsteps, her heart started racing. She stepped off the rug, and flattened her back against the wall, out of the way of whoever approached – but there was nowhere for her to stand so that she wouldn't be noticed.

As the person came around the corner, and into sight, she saw that it was Dom. "Carra, what happened to you? You're covered in wounds." Then, in a whisper, "Is something wrong with your healing magic?"

Embarrassingly, it hadn't actually occurred to Carra to try and heal herself. Inspecting her hands, she could tell her magic had already been working away by itself, which was probably why the burns hadn't been overly bothering her – but it didn't take her much effort nor time to focus properly and bring her skin back to normal. She then quickly directed the healing to her arms and legs.

Dom watched her with a puzzled face. She was about to explain what had happened to her, when she was distracted by a girl who had followed him around the corner, and Dom spoke before she had chance.

"Nancy, what is Carra wearing? Please make sure she's dressed – and choose something green." He winked at her. Nancy looked her up and down, apparently mortified by what she saw, then curtsied and took Carra's arm. Carra was about to object, but Dom shooed them away with both his hands telling them to hurry up.

Carra almost had to jog to keep up with Nancy.

"Sorry miss, we should have had you dressed by now. You must let me do something with that hair – whatever has happened that it could have ended up in that state? Never mind, hurry along."

Carra placed Nancy's age at around twenty-five. She was dressed smartly, in a plain grey tunic, with a black plaited ribbon tied around the waist. After following while she briskly wound her way through several passageways including a flight of stone steps, Nancy unlocked a large wooden door, and they entered a chamber together.

"You have until I count to a hundred to strip off, jump in that tub to get the dirt off, and dry off again. We cannot forgo this bath with you in that state, but there is no time for you to relax. Quick, quick. Clothes off."

Carra obliged. The bath was reasonably warm. It would have been nicer hot, but she supposed the water had been sitting there for a while. It was nice to be clean, but as she'd promised, Nancy dragged her out of the tub before she'd had time to enjoy it. She was promptly dried off using a rough towel that Nancy scrubbed at her with.

After briefly leaving the room, Nancy returned holding a dress. "Arms up!" she called and placed it over Carra's head. This was nothing like the dress she had worn for Ally's wedding. Yes, the colour was similar, but whereas that had been a thin but tightly fitting layer of fabric, this was a corset with a puffy skirt.

"Breathe in!" Was Nancy's next command, and Carra felt the back of the dress being laced up. She intentionally let go of the breath she'd been holding before

Nancy could finish, to make sure it wasn't done up so tightly she couldn't breathe.

She was then led to a chair to have her hair styled, which basically consisted of her curls being thrown over the top of her head and tied up there. "No time for anything else." Nancy said with a shrug when Carra looked at her.

If she hadn't been so desperate to find out from Dom what was going on, she might have objected; but as it was, she didn't care what she looked like. She was even satisfied with ignoring the dress. It wasn't *that* bad she supposed, it just didn't do anything to flatter her. *It's probably the fashionable thing to wear, who knows?*

Nancy led her back through the palace and down to the ground floor. They went back up some steps – a different set to the ones they'd come down – and emerged on the balcony of a large ballroom.

There were twin staircases leading down to the dance floor. The banisters were glass, and each step was mirrored. The effect was breathtaking.

Carra walked over to the balcony's edge and surveyed the scene below her. There must have been almost two hundred people below! She could at least see that her dress didn't look out of place. Interestingly, the men were dressed in colours as bright as the ladies – it was not at all what she had expected, given Dom's penchant for wearing black.

Dom was seated in a chair on the dais. *Or should she say throne?* To his left were a lady and gentleman aged in their early fifties, and on the other side of them was an empty chair. On his right there was a handsome girl, who looked around her own age.

As she was walking down the stairs – trying to remain graceful even though she had to hitch up her skirt slightly to stop herself from tripping – Dom beckoned her over.

She was forced to weave in and out of the people conversing on the edge of the dance floor, to reach him.

"Curtsey!" Nancy whispered in her ear. Carra turned and saw Nancy had bowed her head. She curtseyed as told. Rather than introducing her to his family as she expected, Dom stood up, and walked towards her.

"I need to tell you what happened to me, Dom." He smiled at her and nodded as he led her to the middle of the room, "I didn't find the amulet, but... it was really strange. I went into this tower, and I had to walk through flames."

Dom put one arm around her back, and the other on her shoulder, and started to lead her through a simple four-step. She concentrated until she got the hang of it, then looked up from watching her feet to scan his face. "How did *you* get here though? I was brought here by magic but," Dom put his finger to her lips, cutting her off.

"Shhh, later. For now, dance with me. I've missed you."

So, she danced with him. She certainly deserved to relax for a while; to enjoy herself, even. She couldn't, however, stop her mind from turning things over for long.

On surveying the room, she saw some people watching them, but most were either dancing themselves or talking to other guests. "It's strange to see you reconciled with your parents. I assume that's who they are, and is that Tilla, your sister? Where is Torrin?"

Dom looked into her eyes, and she stopped talking. But after a while, she couldn't help herself from blurting out, "What happened while I was gone? I don't understand how..." He lent in and kissed her.

For a fleeting moment, she returned his kiss, earnestly.

Then she returned to her senses, suddenly feeling

as though something was terribly wrong. She released her arms from their dance hold, and with one last glance at Dom, she ran.

The only way out seemed to be the way she'd come in. Her exit was therefore forced to be both undignified, and incredibly public. There was nothing she could do about it now – she'd already committed to her decision.

All she needed was some time to collect her thoughts. She could always make things right again later. Probably.

The second she stepped back out of the ballroom, everything went hazy.

☆☆☆☆

When she regained consciousness, the haze hadn't lifted. Not the haze over her thoughts – although that was still there too – but rather the walls, ceiling and floor of the room she found herself in were what she could only describe as blurry.

It was as though she were in a box, but the sides were made of static, and moving in waves that confused your eyes if you looked at them for too long.

The room... cage?... was about ten strides wall to wall, and maybe half that from floor to ceiling. There was no obvious exit.

Carra staggered to one of the walls and studied it. Up close, it appeared to be shimmering. She thought perhaps there was no door because she could walk right on through. It looked ethereal; certainly not solid. Hesitantly, she reached out with her right hand to touch it – and was rewarded with a strong static shock.

"Dom?"

"Dom, Dom, Dom, Dom... Dom... Dom... Dom," the room echoed back, so loudly that she recoiled.

Carra sat down on the floor to consider her position. She thought over what had happened, step by step. It was as though, on leaving the ballroom, she had been knocked unconscious... and then what? *Someone had carried her into this room.*

In which case there must be a way in, and therefore a way out. She spent a while lost in thought. *Unless the room is magic, in which case the exit has simply been sealed. I don't know enough about how magic works to figure it out.*

Carra determined that if she was being held here, her best option was to wait until whoever had put her there came to collect her.

☆☆☆

Waking up in the same position as where she'd curled up on the floor, her first thought was that no one had come for her after all. Her second was that it was a very long time since she had eaten anything. She no longer had her bag with her water flask, and Carra was unable to remember the last time she had even seen it.

Pacing backwards and forwards across the cell, she resorted to trying the other three walls, but of course nothing happened – except Carra being left with slightly raw-feeling fingertips.

Sensing she was destined to just keep repeating the same actions – sitting and pacing, sitting and pacing – she sat down again. She tried to picture the other guests who had been at the dance. There certainly hadn't been anyone paying particular attention to her, at least that she'd noticed... but then she hadn't really been looking.

Was it more likely that someone from Dom's

family was keeping her here? Motive-wise that seemed more plausible, but supposedly they didn't have magic. Would they have risked hiring a mage given their hard-line stance?

Any line of thought she could muster just seemed to just reach a dead-end. She hadn't known anyone there, other than Dom, well enough to assess whether they would have any possible interest in her.

It seemed strange Torrin had been absent, but she couldn't get her head round how he could have known she'd run out at that particular time. There was the possibility it was a mere chance encounter, but if that was the case, how had he even known who she was?

If it wasn't personal – if she'd simply stumbled across someone doing something they shouldn't have been – that could be a motive, but she couldn't figure out why they would go to the effort of keeping her in a cell rather than just killing her.

Carra felt like she was missing something significant. *If I'd actually puzzled things out correctly, I'm sure I'd know that I was on the right track. Nothing I've come up with so far sounds remotely plausible.*

Changing tact slightly, she tried to relay the events of the dance in her head, including any conversations she could remember, as slowly as possible. It was already a little blurry, but something had felt vaguely wrong about Dom, and that was why she'd left.

The more she thought about it, the more questions she felt were as yet unanswered. In particular, how had Dom known where she'd be transported back to after the tower? *It was like he'd been expecting me in time for that dance but... how was that possible? Why does he no longer seem to care about the locket?*

She felt as though she was on the brink of some sort

of revelation. Magic sizzled in her fingers at the thought. She pushed herself further.

It doesn't make sense that he had suddenly reconciled with his family. The connections in her brain seemed to surge with energy. *What if... what if I never finished the quest?* Yes! That felt right somehow.

The stone she touched had transported her, but what if she had never actually left the tower.

Carra could almost imagine the walls starting to gain some clarity in response – as though the shimmer was starting to fix in place.

In which case... that wasn't really Dom? She felt a slight panic and the shimmer came back as she lost concentration.

Now confident that she wasn't imagining it, she placed her hands either side of her, and tried to transfer her magic to the room. It was the part of her magic that she used to release her emotions and helped calm her.

Gradually the room solidified around her – mirroring the understanding also currently solidifying in her brain.

The ballroom had been one of her trials, just like the fire walk had been, and this room was now. As that final piece of the puzzle clicked in place, a door appeared.
Feeling a little light-headed, and fairly low on energy, she walked over to the door, turned the knob to open it, and passed through.

CHAPTER 30

Dom had been about to run out of water when a camel appeared.

If the timing hadn't been strange enough, there was also the bizarre question of how the area around the camel seemed to be unaffected by the sand saturating the air. This dust-free pocket moved with the camel. Clearly some unusual magic was at play here.

When the camel sat down a few steps away from him, the relief was instantaneous. He removed the dusty strips from his eyes and mouth, and breathed in the fresh, albeit humid, air.

Dom looked at the camel, and it looked back at him. He cocked his head to the left, and the camel moved its own to the right in imitation.

After a short while of suffering Dom's observation, the camel harrumphed and turned to the side, revealing a satchel. It tilted its head backwards as if gesturing for Dom to take a look – to which he politely obliged.

It held three flasks. Picking the nearest one and looking inside, he found it to be filled with water. Dom couldn't help but grin.

He sneaked a glance at the camel, who was watching him. Rooting around further in the satchel, he found some flatbread and an assortment of vegetables, including a pumpkin and some tomatoes.

Deciding the easiest thing to do would be remove

the satchel, he unhooked it from the camel's saddle. In Dom's position, survival had become more important than worrying about where the food had come from – or whose it was.

Apparently not planning on lingering, once he had stepped away from the camel, it stood back up and walked off. Once it had travelled more than a couple of paces, Dom could no longer see which way it was heading.

Luckily, the area around him remained free of the sand saturation, and he decided the magic must have been sent to help him – as possibly the food had also been. It was a pleasant explanation, regardless of any doubt he might have over the credibility of it.

With a clear circle of around six paces in diameter, Dom had the sense he was supposed to continue to wait here for Carra, but it was vexing not knowing where she was – and not being able to do anything useful.

There was nothing for it. He helped himself to some water and sat back down on the sand.

✫✫✫✫✫✫

Carra found herself back in Astonelay, although she now knew this to just be another of the Tower's mirages. The strong sunlight revealed it was the middle of the day, and the village presented to her was still intact. There was no reason they would have rebuilt it in full, given the significantly reduced occupancy, so this was designed based on Astonelay before the fire had devastated it.

Tentatively, she walked across to her old house, and made her way inside.

Seated around the dinner table, she discovered her father – who looked as healthy as ever – Alliana, and another lady. She studied the features of the stranger closely to be sure, but yes, they resembled her own. This lady was an older, sterner version of the mother that had left her when she was small.

Her father turned towards her as she sat herself at the table with them. "You're late," he scolded as he passed her some bread. Frowning slightly, she poured herself some water, then finished both her drink and the bread before selecting some fruit, meats, and cheese from the plates in the centre.

Carra wasn't sure whether to let the scenario play out, or to speak first and prompt the conversation. She decided to eat and see what happened – fully accepting that her hunger may have had something to do with this choice.

As she was lifting a piece of cheese to her mouth, her mother waved her arm and a plate of bread moved towards her. Her jaw dropped. "Is that... that's air magic?"

Her mother frowned. "What kind of question is that girl? Since when have I used any other kind?" Carra stumbled over her words as she tried to mutter a sensible response. It made sense that her mother would have magic, and that she would know what kind of magic she had, given she was close family – but it was strange seeing it being used in such a mundane way.

Her introspection was interrupted by a knock at the door. She turned around, but didn't get up from her chair, expecting someone else to answer it. "Carra. Aren't you going to greet Frederick?" Her mother's tone was sharp. "You only begged and begged us for these lessons for weeks. Have you lost interest already – before you've even started?"

Carra got up and went to the door. She looked over the boy who was standing there. She supposed he was around her age, although with his soft reddish-blonde hair and light freckling, he looked rather baby-faced in comparison to Dom. He blushed, and she realised it was because she'd been staring at him while she made her assessment.

Unsure what to expect, she followed him. He led her to a small open area and handed her a wooden baton. Carra looked it over, trying to work out its purpose.

"It's best to start with something simple so you can focus on the best stance, and I can show you how to hold it properly. After a couple of sessions, maybe only one if you take to it well, I promise we can move on to practice swords."

They spent the rest of the afternoon together. He positioned Carra's arms and feet in different ways and made her repeat the poses until he was happy she had them right. It wasn't particularly fun, but her interest in learning meant she was determined to do well.

It made sense to Carra that she would have insisted her parents give her sword-fighting lessons, although she *was* surprised they'd actually agreed. It was something that interested her, and had for a while, but it had never occurred to her to ask her father until after the village had been attacked, at which point it had been too late.

As the sun set, Frederick walked her back to the house and bid her good evening. Inside, her mother was preparing their evening meal, so she silently went over and peeled potatoes in assistance.

Carra opened with a simple question, "Where is Alliana?"

"She is having dinner with Niall's family tonight." Of course, the man Ally would have married if they hadn't left Astonelay. It was strange to think this might have been her future. Would her sister have been happy if it had been? *Yes*, Carra thought she would have been.

"How was your first lesson?" her mother continued. She came across as blunt in her mannerisms, and the way her dark brown hair was scraped tightly back into a bun only accentuated the impression of her harshness. However, Carra was growing more used to her tone, and could see that there was *some* feeling behind the persona she presented.

"It was good, thank you mother. I know I can learn a lot from Frederick."

"So you said, although I do hold out the hope it will help resolve your girlish fancy of him!" Carra grimaced. She supposed maybe Frederick was the sort of man she could have seen herself with once upon a time, but she hadn't even remotely looked at him in that way.

"I'm still not sure what use you intend to make of these skills, but it never hurts to be able to have the means to protect oneself better I suppose. I assume you will still make time for your magic lessons?"

"Of course, mother." Carra was reminded that, although she knew she was living out a fake scenario, she hadn't yet deciphered exactly what she was meant to be discerning from the situation.

There was a strong temptation for her to stay here, surrounded by family. It seemed like a win-win. She would get to know her mother, study magic, and learn the sword-skills she coveted. Maybe she could stay for a short while, and *then* go on to finish her quest. It almost seemed too good to be true.

Her heart sank. *It is too good to be true. That's because it's not true. In fact, for the Tower to create a scenario this good, it must really really want to distract me and keep me here… which at least suggests the locket is worth pursuing.*

Perhaps she *could* stay just a little while more though?

She thought about Dom waiting for her somewhere in the desert. It wasn't fair to leave him any longer. Who knew how much time had passed in the real world, how much food and water he had left, or even whether he would continue to wait for her? He probably wouldn't even be *able* to wait –

regardless of whether he wanted to – if his supplies ran out.

Carra took a deep breath and tried to release her emotions to steady herself. She gave her mother a farewell hug and walked out of the house. She kept walking until she had left the village.

Surely enough, her surroundings dissolved around her. She couldn't help but feel a strong pang of regret. Forcing herself to stay strong, she kept to her resolve, and didn't look back.

Carra walked out of the simulation into the sort of room she would have expected to belong in the tower, given the exterior architecture. The design was similar to the entrance where she had come in, but that had been far grander in both scope and size. Instead of being presented with the choice between three doors, the room contained only a large window, and a single trapdoor, which she assumed led to a downward staircase.

A sudden movement startled her – but when she turned towards it, there wasn't anything there; not really. *Is this another test?*

Gradually, the shimmer in the air became more pronounced, until it was almost *person-shaped?* It started to elucidate into a female form, and Carra gasped – it looked just like Gabbie. Frowning, she maintained eye contact, "G... Gabbie?"

"You have made it all the way through the tower, Carra. Yes, it's me." She smiled, warmly. "I was entrusted as the guardian. Before I explain your challenges, to make sure your lesson was complete, first let me go back to the history. When those responsible created this locket..." She held up an object on the end of a gold chain.

Carra started to reach out for it but, no, Gabbie wasn't relinquishing it. At least, not quite yet. "It was because they had been unable to destroy its contents. They used the locket instead. As a small object, with a familial link to you, this made it suitable for their purpose – and their intention was to keep it concealed. Luckily, they approached us to assist in their scheming.

"We rejected the idea that it should be buried in the desert. Firstly, our role as guides means we would still have been required to help you in the same way we did on your arrival to Savarah, and that would have meant leading you straight to the locket.

"Therefore, instead, we agreed on a series of challenges, which were intentionally difficult, but would prove to fate whether you were worthy of the prize." Gabbie paused – for dramatic effect, Carra thought.

"Your first trial was selecting which arch to enter, as this determined the type of challenges you faced." Carra was intrigued – she had forgotten all about the archways.

"The eye denoted sensitivity to emotions and thoughts. It was therefore the most suited to your type of magic. I believe you were subconsciously aware of this and that's why it attracted you.

"The rose represented nature and would have been more suited to those who have earth magic, or any affinity for the elements. The sword, more obviously, was geared to those who excel in strength and skill. Although we had our inclinations, as the locket wasn't hidden until after your birth, we didn't know exactly what kind of magic you would have.

"This brought you into the forest. The path to completion consisted of three 'life scenarios', and two further challenges in total – the forest was the first of the life scenarios. These were designed to tempt you, by showing you possible futures you might desire.

"The challenges of the fire walk, and the boxed

room were interspersed between the life scenarios in order to distract you – by encouraging you to think these were the real test, and thereby making the simulations more effective.

"Through the forest, the tower was showing you a life where you could relax and enjoy the slow pace. The magic chose this setting because of your upbringing, which has led to your love of the outdoors. You can see why it would have been easy for you to have lingered and enjoyed the picnic, leading to you losing track of time. The longer you lingered in any one scenario, the more you would have begun to confuse fantasy with reality.

"The fire walk, simply put, was to test your bravery. This challenge was unique to the path of the eye, and considered appropriate for someone with healing magic. Had you fallen from the path, you would have been allowed to continue; only if you'd tried to run, or spent too long in indecision, would you have been disqualified.

"Following this was perhaps the most difficult challenge. It was designed to make you think you were no longer in the tower." Carra nodded her head in agreement. "This is the life you could have had, if Dom didn't have magic, or was not estranged from his parents because of his magic.

"Of course, you would never have met him if that were the case, or perhaps you might have met at Whistlake – but the way the magic worked was by taking your current circumstances and bending them to a possible truth, based on your existing knowledge. You passed this test again, by resisting the temptation and remembering there was somewhere you needed to be."

"The box trial required you to figure out you were still in the tower and understand the ballroom hadn't been real. Once you recognised this for the challenge it was, you were able to rationalise that you needed to use your magic to dissolve the box.

"This was by far the closest you came to failing, as you spent two days in there. In fact…" Gabbie paused at that moment in consideration, then held out her hand. Carra's missing bag appeared in it. "Perhaps you might like to eat something while I finish. The food you ate whilst under the tower's thrall provided no nutritional value for you.

"By the final situation, you were of course aware it wasn't real, which is why the Tower had to entice you with something you really wanted. This scenario wasn't there to mislead you into thinking it was real. Instead, like the forest, it aimed to delay you. As you know, you were offered both the opportunity to spend time with your mother, and to learn swordsmanship.

"It was the life you could have had and might have chosen – had your mother stayed; had the assault on your village never happened. Had you lingered, it would have become increasingly difficult for you to ever leave.

"Which brings us to the close of this stage of your journey. I can now present you with this locket. Dom was correct when he told you this was the item you sought. Now, I would advise you travel to meet him; I believe he is still waiting for you. Pyjo is here to carry you, just as we promised."

Gabbie clicked her fingers, and the next thing Carra knew she was blinking from the sunlight, as they were back outside. "The click was just for dramatic effect, but in all earnest we must now part. Perhaps I will see you again some time, should you ever call upon the help of Savarah in the future."

"How can I do so?" asked Carra, eagerly.

"You cannot, unless your situation requires it. We understand and anticipate needs. It is the nature of the magic surrounding our existence."

"I'll miss you Gabbie, I hope we do meet again."

Somehow, Gabbie's words had led her to believe they would, so she didn't question her any further. Instead, Carra reached out and gave her new friend a hug. After a few seconds, they both pulled away and she climbed on the camel.

She turned around to bid a last farewell, and saw Gabbie at the foot of the tower, waving goodbye – but the second time she looked back there was nothing there.

CHAPTER 31

Carra relaxed, enjoying her ride on Pyjo. It felt amazing to be letting all her tension go. She was excited to see Dom, expecting him to be proud of her – and let's face it, she was genuinely proud of herself – but she also felt relieved to be back in the real world. Although… soon they would probably have to go back through those awful caves. *No, I mustn't think about that. At least, there's no need to do so right now.*

She found Dom sitting cross-legged on the ground, right by the entrance to the caves. She wasn't sure what she had expected, but it definitely hadn't been that.

"Hello?" she said tentatively. She detected some nervousness in her voice and realised it had been a while since she had seen him. Something akin to surprise lit up his face.

"You came back! What happened? You just disappeared."

"It's quite a long story, but..." Her brow furrowed. "Were you just sitting here the whole time?"

Realising his story was going to be shorter, Dom explained first. It was strange how he described only being able to see sand. He hadn't even been aware that he was merely five hundred paces from the sea – there were no cliffs at this shore, just a slight descent and then water.

Carra looked around, surveying the area. "Should we stay sitting here, or should we set off for home while I tell you about my adventures? It's going to take me a while."

"It's nearly nightfall, Carra. Whilst it will make no

difference in those caves, I suggest you might want to use this opportunity to sleep. I know I want to – I have spent most of my time trying to keep my eyes open, watching for you."

What Dom said made a lot of sense, so they apportioned themselves some food, and made camp for the evening. Pyjo had been back and forth in her absence, so they had some food for the return journey, but they would have to ration it very carefully. Carra had been carrying the tent, but Dom was far more rested, so he offered to put it up by himself.

As it happened, they ended up talking well into the evening. Carra told Dom everything she could remember. Although some of her memories were slightly blurry, she thought she covered the key aspects of most of her experiences.

"Can I see it then?" Carra handed him the locket. Dom frowned, so she moved closer to him, so she could look as well. She hadn't actually had chance to examine it yet.

There was a long gold link-chain with a chunky cube at the bottom. It didn't look particularly expensive or desirable.

Dom lifted it up to the air. "Are you trying to reflect the light through it? I don't get it. It's not really the right time of day."

"No, I'm inspecting the different sides of it. This isn't the locket."

"Of course it's the locket – when Gabbie gave me it she literally told me it was the locket!" Carra was starting to worry she'd been duped, that their search wasn't over, and worse, that she had embarrassed herself in front of Dom.

"No, I mean, this part is not the locket." He inserted the small iron key. She hadn't even noticed a keyhole. The key released the true locket from what she could now see was just a cage.

"It still doesn't seem like anything special." It was traditional looking, with a gold case of two halves – nothing she hadn't seen before. The front was encrusted with a large ruby, circled by three smaller ones. The other side was plain gold, but with a swirling letter 'P' engraved in it.

"Is there anything inside it?" Dom studied the clasp.

Carra opened her mouth as if to protest, but he turned to her before she could speak, "You should do the honours. You've earned it."

He passed the locket back to her. She was excited now. She unfastened the gold clasp and prised the shells apart. Inside there was a drawing of a young child. She squinted. It almost looked like herself, at an age of maybe two.

Coming back to herself, she lifted her head – Dom was sitting there very patiently, but his anticipation was clear. She passed it back to him. "I think it's me. I mean, it looks a little like me. I guess it could also be an ancestor with a strong resemblance."

Dom frowned. "Is that it? How does this help us?" He studied it for a few minutes, then passed it back to her. Carra put the chain over her head. Wearing it around her neck seemed the safest place for it, but she hid it underneath her tunic. "We'd best call it a night. Stay near me for warmth." She was happy to oblige.

☆ ☆ ☆ ☆ ☆

The next morning, an unexpected sight greeted her – a boat! She looked around for Dom, but he had disappeared again!

Perhaps he was worried they were looking for him. If that was the case, she should be the one to investigate. She felt sure he'd be watching from some convenient vantage nearby.

First things first though – she ate the small breakfast he had set aside for her, then proceeded to pack up their bedroll. Concerned what might be awaiting her, she knew she was intentionally delaying the impending encounter.

As she was still busying about, two figures appeared on the horizon, coming from the direction of the sea. She looked away quickly on instinct, but of course they could still see her, so she looked back. *I may as well give myself time to assess them as they approach.*

A few moments later, when they were sufficiently close, she realised one of them was Dom, and the other... Carra ran forward and wrapped her arms around Oz in a huge hug. She pulled away and blushed, slightly abashed.

Dom broke the silence by exclaiming, "She wasn't that happy to see *me* yesterday!"

If she hadn't already been blushing, she would have been now. "I am just so relieved that the boat is here, and it's a friend not someone hunting down Dom – you're not, are you?! – and... and best of all, we don't have to go back into those horrid, awful caves!"

Dom raised one eyebrow at her, so she rolled her eyes at him. "Carra, I've just been updating Oz on our journey, I hope you don't mind. Oh, and yes, your assumption was correct – they are able to take us back to the civilised world. In fact, we've just come back to collect you." He shrugged, "I mean, we debated it of course, but then Oz pointed out that you have the locket."

"May I see it?" Oz turned to her and asked sheepishly, "If that is okay?" Carra pulled the locket out from under her vest and lifted the chain over her head. She had already grown comfortable having it there and it felt a little strange giving it up.

It was actually Dom who reached out and took it

from her, before showing it to his friend. "It's the right locket, of that I am certain – look, it displays the Perywhist insignia and the rubies. However, when you open it, nothing happens." Dom paused and demonstrated opening the locket.

Except this time, nothing *didn't* happen.

All three of them were thrown backwards. Carra hit her head as she fell.

☆☆☆☆

She opened her eyes to find herself lying on her back on the sand. Dom and Oz were leaning over her, staring. "Carra. Carra!" Dom shouted placing his hand on her shoulder, and then turning to Oz, "she's awake."

"Hi," she heard herself say. "I'm okay." *Am I okay?* She turned her head slightly and it felt a bit sore, but she could move it like normal. Her arms and legs felt really heavy. "What happened?"

"We're not sure. It was like a dust cloud came out of the locket. We were thrown too but I guess the force wasn't strong enough to actually knock either Oz or myself over. So… we had a chat while you were out." Carra frowned at him.

"Don't worry it wasn't that long, but we should keep you awake now, in case you are concussed. Anyway, we think that maybe that reaction was because *I* opened the locket this time? I'm afraid it's the only theory we have. I had the key, and, to put it rather bluntly, otherwise it doesn't make sense that I even needed to be involved."

"Sure. Assuming I accept the rationale – that part seems less important anyway? – what has actually happened differently when *you* opened it compared to when I did? It can't have just been meant to knock me out?"

"We don't know."

"Right." Carra tried to push herself upwards but was struggling a bit. The two boys helpfully stood by and watched her. It was a bit embarrassing, and she wasn't sure whether to keep trying. Her limbs did not seem to want to obey her.

After watching her fail, for what felt like quite some time, Oz made a suggestion, "Shall I carry you to the ship? Our doctor can have a look at you. If you didn't mind, we could still set off on our journey." Carra nodded in ascent.

It was Dom, rather than Oz, who scooped her up and carried her over his shoulder, in what wasn't the most dignified position – but it wasn't uncomfortable, so she didn't really have any grounds for complaint – at least not ones she was willing to admit to.

Carra studied the vessel as they walked – and she involuntarily bounced along. The four large masts stood high and proud. It didn't look like there was much room for living on it though. Also, as she got closer, she could see *a lot* of men.

"There's far more space below deck, Carra. I'm sure Oz can find you somewhere you can have a little privacy."

"Oh yes!" Oz jumped in enthusiastically, "The ship holds sixty people but we staffed it with the minimum crew we could, so just over half that. There's plenty of room on board."

She had almost no knowledge of boats, having only seen one for the first time when they had been in Florin. It wasn't a mode of travel she had thought she'd ever get to experience. Aside from the obvious relief at not having to go through those tunnels, she was quite looking forward to it. She liked being outside and the boat would offer her fresh air.

Oz led them to a small rowboat, which he paddled up to meet the main ship. Once they'd been hoisted aboard, Dom picked her back up, as she was still incapacitated.

He took her directly to the doctor, who couldn't find

anything wrong with her, and decided – contrary to what Dom thought – that the best thing she could do would be to rest and recoup.

"Follow me," Oz asked Dom, "I'll take you to her room."

"I'm right here you know!" *Why am I snapping at Oz?*

They went down two floors below the deck. It was a small, claustrophobic space, but easily preferable to the tunnelled caverns. Her room contained a small bed, maybe two-thirds the size her bed had been at the Strathenbergs', and a table just wide enough for a small tray of food.

Dom placed her down; not particularly carefully.

"Now we're somewhere private, we can have a quick chat. I'm not sure if anyone would have seen the explosion from the boat – but maybe you two want to have a think about what we should say it was if anyone asks." Oz didn't pause for long enough for either of them to proffer a suggestion. "I'm sure you're both wondering what I'm doing here?"

Well yes, Carra supposed she *should* have been, but the truth was she had been too happy to see him to question it, and then she'd been distracted by her fall. Oz laughed, "Well, the amazing thing is, a lady who said she was from the mythical town of Savarah appeared and told me to bring a boat to you!

"I was sceptical at first, of course, but she described the pair of you so well – and last time I saw you I could tell you were up to something – so eventually I agreed to commandeer a ship. The crew don't know anything by the way, I even paid them extra for a 'no questions asked' service... you're welcome by the way.

"Even more strangely, she told me that *Jade* of all people had the funds to pay for this, but not to tell her what they were for. She was most put out when I demanded the coins from her," Oz laughed and Carra was most gratified by the fact he clearly felt the same way about Jade that she did, "But she did hand them across, just as the lady had said she would. Don't worry, there's plenty left still." He frowned. "Dom - did something *odd* happen with Jade?"

Dom nodded, letting out a sigh. "Yes, we believe Jade betrayed my identity, preventing us from boarding a boat to travel here from Florin. I didn't entirely believe it until we discovered that she had in her keeping not only the chest of coins you're referring to, but also a letter from one of my mother's advisors, which she had never passed on to me. Well Oz, I'm certainly very happy to see you."

"You saw someone from Savarah? That's where I was in the desert." Carra chirped up. "Was it Gabbie?"

"She didn't give me a name. Wait you saw the actual city? That's amazing Carra! If I hadn't had that encounter myself, I don't know if I would have believed it was a real place"

She promised Oz she'd set aside some time to tell him all about it.

CHAPTER 32

When Carra woke up, she wasn't sure how much time had passed. Dom and Oz had left a small oil lamp burning on the table, but there was no window, so she couldn't see whether it was light or dark outside.

She left the room to search for somewhere she could have a quick wash before she made her way upstairs. Down the corridor, she found a small inlay with a bucket of water next to a basin. She splashed her face and neck, then tried to do something with her hair, wetting it and using a piece of cloth to tie it out of the way. *It'll have to do. At least there's no mirror to show me how much of a mess I look.*

It felt a bit strange walking on a moving boat – they'd evidently set off while she'd been in her room – but Carra assumed she'd get used to it. The stairs, at least, had a handrail.

On reaching the deck, it became obvious it was sometime during the night. There were several sailors nearby, but they were all engaged in tasks. Unsure how she would locate Dom or Oz otherwise, she attempted to determine who looked the least likely to mind being interrupted.

Just as she went to take a step forward, the boat stooped. Carra went flying. On reflex alone, she managed to get her hands out in front of her in time to prevent herself falling flat on her face.

Her left hand hit the ground first, and where it did, the wooden plank gave way – her hand went straight through the floor.

The edges of the wood were jagged, and as she pulled her hand back through, she held her breath as she waited to see what kind of mess it would be in. Her wrist was badly cut, and the numerous splinters would have to be removed before she could use her healing magic.

Carra felt a bit woozy, so while she still wanted to go and find Dom, instead she sat down cross-legged, hoping she would regain her balance. Her head continued to spin.

Even though the sea looked calm – she couldn't see any big waves at least – the boat felt like it was rocking and tipping turbulently. It was quite an unpleasant sensation. She put her hands down on either side to steady herself, and pain jolted through her injured arm.

Dom's face appeared in front of her. "How did you manage to break the boat." Was he…? Yes, he was definitely more concerned with the boat than with her! "No really, the shipbuilder needs to be brought to task over this. Jeoff," He turned to the crew member who must have gone to fetch him for her. "Please can you inform Oz of this incident, followed by whoever you have that can do the repair."

He sat down next to her, and she thought he was going to comfort her, but he just kept turning back to the hole in the deck and frowning. "That really is badly damaged considering the circumstances. It's not like you weigh as much as the rest of us. Makes you wonder about the safety of the rest of the ship."

While Carra was wondering exactly how worried she should be, Oz came running over. "Carra are you okay?" She was about to explain she could heal it, when she realised it was important no one overheard her discussing her magic. She pursed her lips instead. "You don't quite look yourself. Hmm." He said pensively, and then ran off again.

Carra held up her wrist and pulled out the largest of the splinters, grimacing as it came out. *Only about six more to go.* Dom seemed to lose his fascination with the floor and remember she was there.

"Here, let me do that." He took her arm. It didn't hurt any less when he did it, even though he could use two hands, but at least she could look away.

He was already removing the last splinter when Oz came back. He handed her a peeled ginger root – she could tell what it was by the smell. "It's all you can try really. Either the sea sickness will go away once you've got more used to the motion, or you'll be stuck with it for the journey I'm afraid… but sucking on the ginger is supposed to help."

Carra's brain took a little while to catch up to his words, but she sighed when they did. She tried to stand up and a new wave of dizziness came over her. She wasn't aware she'd fallen, but Dom seemed to have caught her. He helped her over to the side of the boat so she could lean on it.

She had assumed that once her balance was under control, she'd be able to heal her wrist, but nothing was happening. "Dom, I can't heal my hand, it's not working." she said under her breath, trying not to panic.

"Are you doing anything different to usual? Could the sea sickness be affecting you?"

"I don't think so. Usually, my body starts the process of healing itself naturally anyway, but it feels different now. Come to think of it, if it was working, wouldn't it have been subconsciously healing my sea sickness too?" She lowered her voice. "It's difficult to describe… it's like the magic is hitting a block and rebounding instead of flowing."

Her eyes widened; they both seemed to reach the realisation at the same time. "Has the locket stopped my magic somehow?" She hoped she'd managed to keep the trepidation out of her voice, or at least, most of it – that was something she really needed to work on.

"Right," he said – and Carra was pleased that he was taking charge. "I'm going to suggest you stop trying for a while so we can work this out. For now, we need to get that wrist wrapped up before it gets infected and you end up back with the doctor." As she was unable to stay stable while walking, Dom had to go fetch her a bandage. It felt sore as he tied it, but she would probably still be able to use her arm almost as well as normal.

☆☆☆☆☆☆

As she walked up to the Captain's cabin for dinner, Carra reflected on how slowly the last few days seemed to have passed. Although she really enjoyed the feeling of being completely surrounded by the sea, the sea sickness had for the most part stuck with her.

Finding she preferred standing in the breeze up on the deck over being in her room, she had even taken to sneaking up there at night with her bed sheets to sleep. Sneaking so Dom didn't see her, at least, as quite a few members of the late-shift crew knew of her habit.

She still hadn't been able to heal herself, and she also hadn't spent much time alone with Dom – she only really saw him for meals, when they joined Oz, and the ship's captain, Rej.

Even more frustratingly, things kept seeming to break around her. As puzzled as everyone had been by the hole she'd fallen into, there had been similar incidents on another two occasions. Oz had tried to blame the boat's construction, but she couldn't deny the common factor in each incident was herself.

She only had to look at Dom's expression to see that

his mind was at work trying to figure out what was happening.

The second incident had occurred when she had been leaning over the side of the ship, watching out to sea, and it had suddenly collapsed beneath her. Her heart had started racing afterwards, once she'd realised just how easily she could have toppled over, but luckily, at the time, she'd managed to react quickly, and grab hold of part of the still-intact hull.

The third time, the cabin wall had spontaneously opened up. There had actually been other crew members closer than her – but she had still been in the general area. Oz had asked her where Dom was, and strangely, just as she had pointed towards the direction from which he was approaching, a mini implosion had happened. Right behind where Dom had been standing. As if by pointing at the wall, she had sent a bolt of lightning into it.

Carra liked to think *she* had been avoiding the crew members, for their own safety, since then – but the truth was they weren't exactly coming anywhere near her if they could help it either. Unhelpfully, the sea sickness had distracted her from being able to focus on worrying about what was happening or why.

Loathe to admit that the locket might somehow be causing the problem, she still wore it around her neck, and was increasingly aware that she had grown some sort of peculiar attachment to it. She had even developed a nervous habit of holding it and rubbing her fingers across it as though it were a good luck charm.

As the last to arrive, she took her usual seat at the table quietly. The three men were already deep in conversation about cross-border trade, so she studied her food and tried to listen to the bits she could understand.

Seeing Dom watching her out of the corner of his eye, she tried to make a bit more effort to stop sulking and be pleasant.

The food was very plain fare, which she was given to understand was the staple for sea journeys, and the crew had needed to stock up in advance for both the journey to collect herself and Dom as well as the return trip, so there was nothing fresh. She still had the bag from Savarah in her room and between meals she'd been snacking on the provisions they'd given her; these were still fairly bland, but it was good to have the slight variety in taste.

Her thoughts were interrupted with a voice inside her head. *"Trust you to be thinking about food when we're discussing something serious."* Did she also hear him roll his eyes? She looked at Dom and they instantly locked eyes.

"How did you do that?" she blurted out – quite rudely interrupting Rej mid-sentence, she realised only afterwards.

Dom glared at her. *"No discussion on magic in front of Rej"* he reprimanded in her head, and then asserted, "We'll talk later." out loud. It seemed like Dom had some semblance of control over it. Maybe this was another type of magic he had, but hadn't told her about. *Was that how he was reading my mind before!*

"I told you, I'm not reading your mind, Carra!" And then he had the nerve to continue the dull dull dull conversation about shipping versus land trading options.

Carra had to take several deep breaths to calm herself throughout the remaining duration of the meal. Her patience was really being tested, and all the various ways Dom could have managed to deceive her were floating around in her mind.

Just when she thought the men's discussion was finally going to come to an end, Rej proposed they joined him in a nightcap. Luckily for Dom, he politely declined. "Sorry Rej, but I think Carra's head is going to explode if I don't let her offload whatever is bothering her."

They could hardly dismiss Rej from his own quarters so Carra and Dom, having finally broken free from the small dinner party, crammed themselves into Carra's cabin. The second the door closed, Carra confronted him, "What is going on? Why didn't you tell me you can hear my thoughts? How are you doing it?" She frowned at Dom's expression. Was that... *amusement?*

"Your magic is broken." Her eyes widened at him. it was hardly the response she'd been expecting. "That's the short version, but I needed to get your attention. Maybe now you can start acting rationally."

"Of course my magic is broken, it always has been." She clasped the chain of her locket. "I can take this off, I guess. I did try one time, but I still couldn't heal myself." They were both sitting on her bed, and he edged closer to her in order to put his arm round her. Her mood was foul, so she was tempted to shrug him off, but she didn't want to deter him from sharing whatever explanation he might be able to give her.

"I don't know enough about healing magic to help you, but I can tell that your malfunctioning is causing the 'issues' which keep occurring around you. Oz and I have discussed this and I'm afraid we think it would be best if we took you straight to the Academy. The boat will still dock in north Pellagea as originally planned, you'll just have to wait a bit longer before going to visit your sister."

She gently nodded in understanding. She had been looking forward to seeing Ally but she had to admit the idea of the magic school excited her – even if she was rather unimpressed Dom and Oz hadn't seen fit to include her in their discussion. "Thanks." Dom looked confused. "I'm glad you decided to make this decision without bothering to include me. Please leave now."

"Leave, Carra? A minute ago, you were desperate to

talk to me."

"A minute ago, I didn't realise what a complete jerk you were. Here, take the damn locket. You've used me to get it for you, and I'm sure now you no longer have need of me, there won't be any issue with me being deposited at the Academy." Even if that *was* exactly where she wanted to go. If she was destined to fail at using magic she supposed she'd now find out sooner rather than later.

Dom let out an exasperated sigh. "That's not it, Carra. I've known Oz a long time and we were catching up. The conversation just naturally turned to the present. Besides, that locket is yours, not mine – and unless you plan to sell it to pay the Academy's entrance fee, I think you have need of me for a little while yet."

That did make sense she supposed… but… remembering her initial anger, she opened her mouth to confront Dom again. He cut her off. "I can't read thoughts. When will you finally believe me on this? If I could read thoughts, it would work with everyone not just yourself. It's you, Carra, not me. My theory is that, as a healer, you're projecting your emotions. Remember I said the two disciplines were closely tied? I can only hear you at certain times. Maybe when you're most…." He paused to think of the correct word. "Emotional?"

Dom's surmise reminded her of when they had discussed this before, although that felt like a different lifetime. He thought she'd been projecting her thoughts the whole time. It had just never previously been as clear as it was now. Dom's actual voice had been inside her head. "How do you figure I can suddenly hear your replies then?"

"That, I'm afraid, I don't know – but I'm sure someone at Whistlake will be able to explain your specific speciality. We just need to keep you out of trouble until we get there." He turned towards her abruptly and studied her face.

"Think you can manage that?"

It was then that Carra realised Dom's arm was still round her. They'd lost some of their closeness in the last few weeks, whilst in the desert and then on the boat. At one point it had seemed like, maybe, there might be something happening between them. Right now, all she felt from him was friendship.

Carra cringed. Could he hear her current thoughts? He was certainly pretending he couldn't if he could. "Dom, have you ever heard my thoughts when I haven't been in the same room as you?"

"No, Carra. Until recently I could only detect a sort of image you were conveying. For the last day or so, it's been more like you were having a conversation with me, but it hasn't ever been one-sided." That was something at least. Dom leant in, she closed her eyes, and he kissed her on the forehead then stood to leave the room. "Goodnight Carra."

As soon as he left, the seasickness came rushing back to the forefront of her mind. *Broken magic hmm. It's just as well I haven't tried to use his fire magic – I don't think that would work too well on a boat.* She could have sworn she heard a chuckle from somewhere in the distance.

CHAPTER 33

Carra was not sorry to be leaving the ship.

Her head span as she stepped out onto the dry land, the feeling of being in constant motion not immediately dissipating.

Only herself and Dom had disembarked – Oz and the crew were returning to the port at Florin. Whistlake was around a day's walk, and they expected to arrive in the nearest town before it became too dark.

She turned to her companion "So… I guess… sorry? That you've got stuck babysitting me?"

Dom sighed. "Is that really what you think Carra? After all this time. Because if it is, then frankly I'm a little insulted."

Oh bother, I can't say anything right. "Sorry. I just meant that, well… the locket didn't come to anything. After we went through all that to find it. I'm not sure I've mentioned this in the last few minutes, but the worst part was the tunnels." She shuddered and Dom raised his eyebrows.

Carra removed the locket and made as if to hand it to him. "Maybe someone we meet at the school will be able to tell you what its use is. Or you could at least sell it – I know you said you have money, but at some point, that will run out."

He pushed her hand away. "Keep it. I've told you. It's your family's and it should stay with your family. It is right that you should look after it. *You* shouldn't sell it either, Carra."

"What will you do once we reach Whistlake?"

"That will depend on what they say. Although I wasn't accepted there, I should be able to stay nearby until term starts." That raised so many questions she didn't know where to start, but Dom kept talking so instead, she listened. "Each school year is made up of three terms, with a four week break in between them, and a longer eight week break for summer. We're now approximately two weeks before the second term starts, but given the unpredictability of your magic I want to get you seen by someone as soon as possible."

"Like a magic doctor?"

"No, like a teacher who can assess you. Even if they don't accept you into the school, they should be able to help you control your outbursts." She growled at him. "Okay bad choice of words but you know what I mean. You had the whole crew perplexed as to how the boat kept breaking, never mind how it was being caused by someone as slight as yourself."

She looked down at herself and realised she had actually lost a lot of weight – and she hadn't been overly heavy to start with. She hadn't appreciated how unhealthy she was looking. Dom also looked like a more gaunt version of his usual self – the shift had been so gradual she hadn't been consciously aware of the changes in him either.

They made eye contact for a few seconds. "It's good to know you think I'm looking so handsome at the moment. Maybe we ought to treat ourselves tonight. We need to find a pub near the Academy where we can stay until term starts as anyway." He chuckled to himself. "At least you have the decency to blush this time."

Carra wasn't sure whether Dom thought she was blushing because he knew she'd called him gaunt, or at the idea of staying together again - from the way he'd said it, she was relieved he'd implied the former. *Yes, definitely the former.* At least they still had plenty to talk about after so many weeks together.

A realisation – that for some reason had evaded her while they were on the ship – came rushing back to her. "Hope!" she gasped, "and Jak. Dom we never went back for them!"

By his lack of reaction, this had evidently already occurred to Dom – and frankly she was ashamed that it had only just now occurred to her. "There's nothing we can do, but they will have found their way back into the grassier areas. In fact, I'm sure someone will have claimed them by now."

Carra, firmly of the opinion that he was just trying to reassure her – however rational he was being – felt slightly miserable for the rest of their walk. The area where they'd left the horses had seemed to be only sparsely populated, and she'd always expected they would end up going back for them; even though it would have meant braving those awful tunnels. She couldn't help but fixate on them whenever she looked back over the last few months. She wasn't sure how she'd *ever* managed to get through them.

The weather in Pellagea was freezing, although Carra supposed it was inevitable she'd feel cold having come straight from the desert lands. If the Academy were on their winter break, that meant they had missed the very coldest time of the year, and she was currently experiencing the lower temperatures typical of late winter, very early spring. The lack of trees and vegetation, which seemed to be typical of Pellagea, delightfully enhanced the feeling of inclemency.

The few hours they'd spent together since being back on land had brought her closer to Dom; or at least, she felt more comfortable with him again. It was nice to be sharing his fire magic for warmth once more, and she was really looking forward to their evening together – *real* food, a *real* bed, and even just each other's company whilst in slightly more comfortable surroundings.

Dom had informed they were heading to a town named Paragon, and despite its small size, it apparently boasted three inns, of which one was far superior to the others. After how much he'd been talking it up, she was going to be very disappointed if it didn't have any rooms free.

Carra was *more* than ready to have a break by the time they approached – her feet were really quite tired. In spite of this, she soon forgot all about her exhaustion, when they received their first proper visual of the Academy.

She had seen countless stone buildings – made possible because of the area's surplus of stone – when they had been in Rivulet, but the way the stones had been used in building the magic school was something different entirely.

The main part of the complex was like a grand castle, with four turrets, but that wasn't the whole of it – there were many side buildings with their own turrets or spires, and even one with a dome that made her think back fondly of Duke Flothin.

For her to be able to see them at this distance, she knew the size of these buildings must be colossal.

Far less impressive, was the small town not overly far to its east, at which they had just arrived. The natural light had almost faded, and the candles she could see through the windows were making a pretty effect, but this was easily eclipsed by the grandeur of the Academy.

The streets had cobbled stone paving, and the houses looked well kept. Many had wisteria growing up the sides, and there were blossom trees where the roads met. It was clearly a prosperous place, and Carra could appreciate its quaint sort of charm.

She tried to picture how the town would look in late spring, imagining the trees in bloom, and the sunlight reflecting off the cobbles. Dom sent a slightly different, and presumably more accurate, mental image back to her – he'd obviously been here before, during warmer weather.

Happily, he was making straight for the large Bed and Breakfast that Carra had been so impatient to get to. *"Might as well give our real names this time, the school will know we're here by tomorrow—and of course magic is actually legal here."* Dom said in her head. *"My real name as in 'Dom' that is."*

It dawned on Carra that she was both apprehensive and looking forward to tomorrow. Stupidly, she got so preoccupied by the thought, that she slipped on the cobble stones and fell onto her knee.

Dom put his hands under her arms and lifted her back up. "Are you okay?" She shook her head, but in embarrassment rather than to say she wasn't okay. "The cobblestones are..."

"Slippery – yes, I'm aware. I just stopped paying attention for a second. I'm a dolt, I know." Her knee actually felt rotten from the fall, to the extent she even felt slightly nauseous. Just as rapidly as the pain had begun to bother her, she'd started healing herself – before she'd had chance to remember she wasn't supposed to be using magic.

Apparently, her magic was okay when she used it subconsciously.

"Don't worry about it. It's dark and you don't know your way."

They didn't have much further to walk, so it wasn't long before they entered the inn. It didn't disappoint; it was indeed far more luxurious than any of the others they had been to, and whilst she had been expecting something similar to the large cold stone interiors in Rivulet, that hadn't been right at all.

Wooden beams in the ceiling had been used to

support the structure, and the same wood had been employed to create a large arching, spiral staircase. Unlike in Astonelay, where wood was the only material available and therefore used out of necessity, here it had clearly been used as a design choice. Someone had painstakingly painted all the surfaces with varnish to keep them in good condition.

Carra was sufficiently distracted by her surroundings that she'd hardly listened as Dom had made the arrangements with the proprietor. She mindlessly followed them up the staircase, through a heavy arched door, and into a comfortable room – and was immediately struck by how immaculate it was. "I think I'd better wash before I sit on the bed!" she exclaimed.

"Yes, go ahead, we will leave you to it. I will show your young man friend to his room and see you shortly for dinner." She blinked as they exited. It hadn't occurred to her that Dom would ask for individual rooms, but of course it made sense. It was actually going to be quite nice to have her own space.

Her thoughts were interrupted by a knock at the door, signalling that someone had already been sent up to fill the tub with lovely, hot water.

Submerging herself in the bath was bliss. Even after her toes had wrinkled, she continued to lie there relaxing. Her eyes started to droop, and when they shot open again, she wasn't actually sure if she'd fallen asleep – and how long for – because, she admitted to herself, she more than likely had done. It was pretty foolish of her, and she could just picture Dom chastising her. Hoping she wasn't already transmitting what she'd done through her thoughts, she tried to think more quietly... if such a thing were possible.

When she stood to reach for the towel, she realised she felt a bit dizzy. The heat had relaxed her muscles, which must have been aching from the journey more than she had realised. It was *almost* too much effort just to get to the bed and collapse upon it.

✶ ✶ ✶

She opened her eyes to nothing but darkness and silence. The inn had obviously closed to non-residents for the night.

No longer feeling tired, she lit the candle by the bed, and found that a plate of food and jug of ale had been left on the desk. Either the innkeeper *or* Dom could have left it there, so it was lucky she had wrapped herself in the towel before drifting off! The food tasted mediocre cold, but she still managed to empty the plate – it would have been delicious while hot.

She found herself contemplating how much more time there would be for her to spend with Dom now they'd reached Whistlake, and a guilty thought crept into her mind. Dressing, she crept downstairs and managed to locate the night porter – and yes, he did know which room her companion was in…

Returning briefly to her own room, she removed most of her clothes, before creeping across to Dom's. Not bothering to knock, she edged cautiously inside. Removing the rest of her undergarments, without pausing – in case she talked herself out of it – she pulled back the covers and climbed in.

He shifted slightly, leaning his nose up against her hair. He didn't stir again, so she pressed her cheek against his and then gradually lowered her arm over his chest. *Hmmm, he was also wearing very little.* She moved her arm downwards to check just how little – but he did have shorts on.

He turned towards her, meeting her for a kiss while still half asleep, but then he woke up, and returned it even more vigorously. With his arms around her, he flipped her from on top to below him. His arms stroked her stomach and gradually moved higher. His mouth moved onto her neck, and she felt his tongue caressing her.

There was an explosion across the room. The tension dissipated entirely.

They both looked around in panic, but it was Dom who sussed it first. "This wasn't a good idea. You need to get your magic under control – and I was right, there's clearly some sort of emotional trigger."

Carra, glad of the cover of darkness, was sure she had turned an exotic shade of red.

After an awkward moment of indecision, she grabbed her clothes, held them over herself, and muttered 'goodnight' as she left the room to sprint back to her own.

Thankfully, it turned out the explosion hadn't been heard across the whole inn – but someone from the neighbouring room *had* come out to investigate. She pretended not to hear his whistle as she shot past.

☆☆☆☆☆☆

It got better.

When she went downstairs the next morning, Dom was in conversation with the innkeeper – she never had caught his name – offering to pay for the damages. *Oops.* To add even further to her embarrassment, he then proceeded to ask them to leave. It seemed totally unnecessary as they'd only requested to stay the one night, but he was clearly trying to make a point. Loudly.

Dom, however, apparently had no qualms about staying for breakfast.

As they sat down, a tall man she vaguely recognised

from last night winked at her. He was actually quite good-looking.

Then she remembered he'd seen her bare bottom and cringed.

Dom looked at her questioningly, so she did her best to smile mysteriously. Luckily, he decided to let it go. For now, at least…

CHAPTER 34

By the time Dom had walked her down to the college, all thoughts of the previous night had been banished from her mind – temporarily, at least. Dom headed straight for the welcome desk, and she let him speak while she assessed the place.

The floors and walls were a cream-coloured marble with grey flecks. Three open doorways led on to unremarkable corridors, with the entrance hall's only real features being the main stairwell, and the four suits of armour guarding it. At the top of the stairs, there were several further doors, which were all closed.

Dom didn't appear to be getting very far. She was telling him they were part way through the year – on month four to be precise – and admissions only got taken in the first week. In return, he was throwing words like 'dangerous' and 'uncontrollable' around to try and make his point. Carra wasn't sure that was exactly the first impression she was aiming for...

Having apparently reached some sort of compromise, the secretary disappeared into a nearby side room. Dom took a seat and motioned for her to copy. Eventually, with Carra's patience having been tested to its limit, despite Dom reassuring her that everything was 'fine', an elderly gentleman walked down the stairs – doing so surprisingly quickly given he was using a stick for support.

"What is this kerfuffle, my friends?" He inquired, kindly.

Carra opened her mouth, but Dom seemed to have decided he was going to be speaking on her behalf. "She recently came into her magic. It's strong, and she is not in control of it."

"With whom am I speaking? I also sense strong magic from yourself, but I do not recognise you as having been a student here."

"I did apply to study here. However, my application was rejected." Dom sounded like he was challenging the gentleman, but he merely raised his eyebrows. "This is Carra, she is Florinynian."

"You may refer to me as Professor 6C for now." At Carra's puzzled look, he explained, "We refer to ourselves first by the level of expertise and power we have attained, and secondly by the sector of the college we are responsible for. Now, please explain the encroachment." *What a ridiculous naming system.*

This time Carra stepped forward to answer for herself. "I have only suddenly come into magic, and I don't know what it does – other than four times, when I have caused random explosions entirely by accident. Before that I could heal myself, but that was my limit."

"What is it you want from me? Applications open next winter."

Hmmm, that didn't actually sound like a question. "Well, I need control. I'm worried I might hurt somebody!"

"Don't use magic then."

"Were you not listening? I can't help it! I haven't been *trying* to use it. In fact, quite the opposite, and I've been doing my best not to. It just… happens." The pleading tone she could discern in her voice made her inwardly cringe.

"How intriguing."

And...? Is that it? Carra reckoned she should keep quiet and wait for him to speak again. He didn't.

"I trust you understand the seriousness of this," Dom piped up after what seemed like forever.

"I will consult with my fellow faculty members." Silence again.

"So, should we wait here?"

"No no, there is a meeting tomorrow. Come back then. But after lunch." Carra found the idea of waiting until tomorrow deeply unsatisfying, but even without Dom's telepathic instruction to just agree they'd wait, she could see from his face he was happy to comply. Patience really didn't come as naturally to her as she supposed it did for others.

☆☆☆☆☆

The next day, they turned up as prescribed. The accommodation had been nowhere near as nice as the night before's, and she hadn't slept very well – although Carra figured there were probably several reasons why that was the case. She was even more apprehensive than she had been the previous day, if that were possible.

The lady at the welcome desk begrudgingly called Professor 6C. This time he appeared quickly and wasn't alone. A tall, stern woman wearing tailored grey trousers and a white blouse, with her hair tightly scraped back from her face, accompanied him.

Carra shivered involuntarily as recognition set in, and as the green eyes almost matching her own, albeit lined lightly in kohl, narrowed to a squint, she knew the feeling was mutual.

"Mother." was the only word that came out of her

mouth; but one was better than nothing. Professor 6C looked distinctly uncomfortable. Dom looked intrigued. She wasn't sure *how* she felt. Once again, as she had been in the Tower, Carra was struck by how she could still see her mother in this person she barely knew, having not seen her for so many years.

"Yes, well." The Professor broke the silence, "You didn't mention anything about your mother being here. Very inconsiderate of you not to say. Professor 7T here had kindly volunteered to assess whether you will be ready to join the rest of the first years despite having missed three months, and to catch you up on training if so. I'm not sure where this leaves us now."

"Had my *mother* not disappeared almost fifteen years ago. Had I known where she was. Yes, had I had any inkling at all she might be here, I would have deigned to let you know." *Keep calm, Carra.*

"Everything I've done, I did for you." the woman seemed to impulsively spout out, whilst still managing to sound angry. Somehow the words didn't quite ring true.

"Very well, very well. What now?" The Professor stammered. Carra looked questioningly at her so-called mother.

"You are not supposed to be here. How is it you have magic?"

"Don't yourself and father both have magic? Is it not logical that myself and Alliana would? Remember Alliana – your other daughter?"

"Carra!" Dom chastised. She was about to ask him what *he* had to do with any of this, but managed to stop herself when she remembered that he wasn't exactly on good terms with his own family. Estranged even. More importantly, he was her only ally here.

"We can discuss this later." Carra could see how

other people would be intimidated by this person but honestly, she felt almost nothing. "We will start this afternoon. Follow me." Carra was about to do as she'd been told, when her mother abruptly turned back towards the Professor. "The tuition fee…"

"Settled." Carra, in the process of being marched off, barely had chance to wonder at this; one glimpse at Dom's face, and she realised he'd used his inheritance money.

They reached a classroom and her mother sat down at the front, gesturing for her to take a student's seat in front of her. It was slightly awkward with only the two of them in the room.

"So, how much do you know about magic?"

"Maybe start with the basics?" Anyone who hadn't been paying close attention might not have noticed the small exasperated sigh she received in response, but to Carra, it was loud and echoing. However, her mother did oblige.

The only part she had already known was that elemental skills were the most common. The grading system, set up by the college to give them an easy way of understanding magical prowess, worked such that you were allocated one point for each new type of magic, or for each power increment of an existing type of magic.

It was rare to have more than one type of magic, so most people didn't surpass what the college would have assessed as a rating of two or three. Professors were mandatorily at least a five.

Her mother was therefore extremely powerful, even for a professor.

Generally, applicants weren't admitted to the college unless they could demonstrate they could attain at least a grade two.

"So, what is your other type of magic?" Carra thought out loud.

"Excuse me?" *Oops. Her mother looked quite put out.*

She'd already backed herself into a corner, so deciding she may as well continue, she asked, "Your main type of magic is air magic, but what is your other type?"

"That is extremely irresponsible of your father. We agreed that he would not discuss magic with you, and to tell you my speciality on top of that is uncouth and ill-mannered."

"It had nothing to do with him." *And maybe you should wait for the facts before criticising people so harshly.* Carra managed to hold her tongue, recognising she had more to gain by avoiding an argument than by instigating one.

The rest of the afternoon was taken up by Carra explaining where her magic came from. Every now and then, her mother's face twitched. She wasn't sure if she should mention Gabbie and Savarah, but it all came pouring out. As she brought the tale to a close, they both looked at each other awkwardly.

"It seems as though my efforts were fruitless. There is no point in disguising the truth now. Yes, we locked your magic away in that locket and attempted to hide it. The reasoning was the apocalyptic nature of the prophecy Dom obviously caught wind of and relayed to you. You are destined for destruction, child." She almost sounded endearing... until she began tutting to herself.

"We tried to prevent it from happening in the only way we could think up. The sad truth is that your father and myself moved to Astonelay after you were born in order to distance you from both magic and any knowledge of it. It seemed remote enough there to keep you sheltered.

"One day, when you're older, you will understand why I had to leave. Your father is mediocre – he could ignore the pull of magic, ignore its promise – but I could not live with the magic withdrawal." Carra bristled at the words but knew better than to say anything. She hoped she would be showing her maturity by remaining impassive. Her mother, after all, did not seem to have any regret lacing her blunt words.

Time had run away from them, and her mother dismissed her, presumably expecting her to have somewhere to go. Dom, however, hadn't waited for her.

The welcome desk, which seemed to be staffed at all times, informed her she'd been assigned a room in T block. She rolled her eyes but, given her mother was training her, she supposed it made sense for Carra to be within her remit for accommodation as well.

Having in her possession only a satchel with one change of clothes, she headed straight for the room. It was well signposted so, despite being left to her own devices, it wasn't too difficult to find.

Within T block, there was one girls' floor and another for boys. Each had ten rooms, of which roughly half were locked, and the other half were empty. No one had remained behind after term had ended.

The room itself was pretty much what she had expected – a bed, a desk, and a medium-sized window. Her floor also had a couple of lavatories and a wet room.

Finding nothing else worth exploring, Carra went looking for food. She figured, given there were still Professors here, there must be somewhere serving meals. Hopefully for free.

Her prayers were answered – the tuition fee did indeed cover food, and she took a perch in the empty cafeteria, tucking into a piece of chicken and several potatoes. Naturally using the quiet downtime to reflect on the day, she realised that while the theory side of magic had been really interesting, she was no closer to control.

Hopefully she wouldn't blow anything up in the

meantime. Although she had been managing okay for the last couple of weeks, with her mother here – and no Dom to keep her calm – things could be more... unpredictable.

Wherever Dom was currently, it was apparently too far away to respond to her thoughts.

Her sleep was fitful that night. The bed wasn't uncomfortable, and although she'd overeaten, she didn't she had done so excessively. No, she wasn't going to try and deny to herself that it was probably because she missed Dom.

Deciding in the early hours that lying there any longer would be unproductive, she crept out for a walk around the campus. She wasn't actually sure there was any reason she *shouldn't* be wandering around, but it did make it seem more exciting if it was clandestine.

Although the buildings were interesting to look at, sadly they all seemed to be locked. The one she did find which wasn't, turned out to be just another block of bedrooms.

Giving up, and heading back to her room, she did manage a short nap before the sun came up.

CHAPTER 35

When Carra met her mother the following day, she was greeted by a frown. "You wore that yesterday."

"Erm, well yeah. I don't exactly have a lot of clothes." she replied sheepishly.

"I will arrange for you to be taken to the market." Carra was almost gobsmacked at the thoughtfulness until her mother added, "I really can't have you being such an embarrassment to me."

Buoyed by her tone, Carra was more confident speaking this time, "I don't have any money."

"Yes, fine. I will provide credit for you. My assistant will organise it – and I'm sure she can advise you on what to purchase as well, so you don't end up with more of the same." Carra crossed her arms defensively, then forgot to turn away before she rolled her eyes.

At least the rest of the day went better. Her mother asked her to call her Alexandra, which was a huge relief, as '7T' was just awkward – and if you asked Carra, pretty dumb sounding. Apparently, students always called professors by their first names – she also learnt that Professor 6C's name was Bart.

Each year there were three twelve-week terms of teaching. Carra had already known she'd skipped the first three months, but her mother refused to fill her in on what she'd missed until she'd first gone over the 'basics'.

At the end of each academic year, there was a

grading test to determine what power level each student had attained. The result of this directly impacted their ability to continue on to the next year of learning. To be accepted for a second year, a level '3' needed to be achieved, which Carra didn't think sounded too difficult.

Most students studied for two years, with about two thirds making it to level 3, however only about one in ten had the option to stay at the school after that. This ten percent needed to reach level 4 to continue learning and, on admission, would then undergo a further two years of intense training, enabling them to excel in their chosen area.

Not everyone opted to stay on for the further two years who could, although most did, and there were three scholarships available for those exceptional students who wanted to, but couldn't afford it. These were rarely used, as most families with strong magic were among the wealthy, however it did occasionally happen that a student from a previously weak or null line showed promise.

In effect, this meant that students in their first year could potentially have a broad range of power levels, and wouldn't have an officially graded title until they demonstrated their prowess at the testing.

Noticing the hour, Carra realised that lunch was *not* going to be a feature of her lessons – so she tried to focus on listening, and ignore her grumbling stomach. It was so loud she was sure her mother had heard, but determined not to show any weakness, she soldiered on.

"As you know, the most common specialisms pertain to air, earth, fire and water. The next most common skills are healing, augmentation, and necromantic. The least common are spirit and clairvoyance. We haven't had a clairvoyant here during my lifetime. Occasionally we have seen spirit manifesting as a secondary talent, but this inevitably means it manifests weakly at best."

At Carra's raised eyebrow, Alexandra explained that necromantic skills didn't mean the ability to raise dead bodies, rather, it meant communing with spirits. Apparently curses, something Carra could claim first-hand experience with, also came under their remit.

"In that case what is spirit magic?" Carra asked, confused.

"Spirit magic is focused on the living. Those who believe in such a thing, would say it centres around the soul. Spirit wielders can influence the emotions of those around them."

That gave her food for thought.

She debated whether to say anything, but her mother had already continued talking. Eventually, she stopped to take a breath and Carra, who had now had time to weigh up the best way of phrasing her next question, took a risk.

"Is there such a thing as magic changing through physical contact?"

"I'm not sure I follow what you're asking. Speak clearly, girl."

"If you were making physical contact with, say an air magic user, and then you could access their air magic?"

Her mother seemed to think for a minute. "Yes, I think that would be an example of a more advanced spirit user. Where did you dredge that question up from? Never mind, I doubt you'll ever come across any situation where you'd need to worry about that." Carra made a mental note to find a book on spirit users. Assuming there was a library here... and no one checked up on what books each student had been borrowed.

Each type of magic could be more or less powerful. Achieving a certain amount of power would enable you to step up a level, but also the more powerful you were, generally the more things you could do with the magic.

Her mother used the example of water magic – which only served to distract Carra, by reminding her she hadn't been able to visit Ally.

All water users could manipulate water. The weaker ones could just about manage to fill or empty a beaker, whereas the more powerful ones could create their own currents on lakes. However, there were also additional skills that meant a water user was more advanced. The most usual of these constituted being able to breathe underwater, by parting the water to create a pathway of air.

Interestingly, advanced air users also had the same ability, by essentially manipulating the oxygen within the water to be more concentrated. A strong air magician could even draw oxygen down from the air above a lake or river, in effect surrounding themselves with an air bubble while swimming.

More advanced water users could also solidify water into ice, or evaporate it into a gas; being able to do one of these didn't necessarily mean being able to do the other.

Earth magicians didn't have one particular starting skill that was more common than others. Generally, they could do one or more of three things: cause tremors in the ground; nurture plants to grow; and create holes to assist in digging tunnels. The most advanced earth magicians could also heal diseased plants and trees.

Fire magicians were more unusual, being the least common of the elemental types, and were generally strong by nature – evaluating as a level 2 at a minimum. The first skill they manifested was the ability to manipulate flame, and the second was to create a flame from nothing – and it had never been documented that a fire magician had been unable to create a flame.

Augmenters usually found their first ability was being able to increase another magician's strength – it was easier to make people stronger, for example capable of lifting a heavier weight, than it was to instil weakness. Augmentation was usually a secondary skill, so most magicians didn't develop it past this point. Those that did advance, were able to make other magicians more magically powerful, not just physically. She understood this could be very helpful for learning and experimentation.

Healing was also usually a secondary skill – and her mother couldn't resist commenting on how strange it was for this to be Carra's primary talent. She was a little surprised when her mother admitted she'd had to research skill levels in healing as preparation for their lesson.

First level healers could encourage wounds to heal more quickly, whereas second level healers could actually initiate and control the healing process. Other healing skills included being able to heal yourself, immunity from diseases, and destructive magic – or 'anti-healing'.

Carra took advantage of her mother pausing for breath to interrupt, "That makes no sense though. I can't heal others, I've tried."

"Have you tried since the locket released your powers? I understood you had been careful not to use any magic, in order to avoid accidentally using destructive magic."

"No, I suppose not." H*mm*, "So why is it I could still heal myself, even before finding the locket?"

"If I had to hypothesise, I would imagine there was a flaw in the magic worked, being that the locket only captured your magic up to the level of those who enacted the spell. Your ability to heal yourself must have been able to surpass this in some way, and thereby remained with you."

"I suppose that could be a possible explanation…

and then did you say the reason things keep exploding around me is some sort of super healing? How do I control it? Isn't that the most important thing?"

Alexandra sighed in a way that did not inspire confidence. "Yes, tomorrow we will discuss control of your magic. We do not have any healers at the Academy who specialise in anti-healing skills, which is the formal name for it. However, I will do my best to instruct you in the way we teach beginner students to first use their magic.

"I should have time for some further reading this evening. In the meantime, be conscious that the trigger is your emotions. Once you can control yourself you will be able to control the magic. Do you think you can manage to keep your temper in check?"

Carra growled in response. Her mother had already begun walking towards the door, so she took that to mean her lesson was over for the day. Evidently, they weren't going to discuss spirit or necromanctic skills.

A flash of inspiration came to her, and she followed Alexandra, who – as she had suspected she might – led her towards the library. Noting its location for later, Carra of course went in search of food first. She hoped that, if she was lucky, her mother would have left by the time she returned.

Going via the front desk she enquired whether Dom had stopped by, but no one recalled having seen him.

Alexandra must have taken some books with her as, even though Carra had rushed her food down, the library was deserted. She was surprised to find that there wasn't even a librarian monitoring it.

Unsure where to start, she paced up and down the aisles until she located the beginners' section. Finding a basic book on skill types, she leafed through it, skipping pages until she found the ones that interested her. Unfortunately, there was very little information on spirit magic, and she found nothing beyond what her mother had already told her.

She was going to have to comb the aisles – apparently, she was searching for a more niche subject than she'd anticipated.

It took her quite a while to find any books that looked even vaguely relevant – and by the time she did find something that at least looked worth reading, she had lost the light. There were a couple of lanterns lit in the entrance, but they weren't sufficient to enable reading, so Carra decided to take the book to her room for another time and call it a night.

☆☆☆☆

Sleep had been marginally better that night, but she couldn't say she felt well rested when she woke. She still hadn't had any contact with Dom, and was struggling not to fall further into a bad mood – until she realised she might finally get the chance to do some magic, and the whole day seemed to brighten.

She turned up to the classroom twenty-five minutes early, then watched the clock tick by. It passed the hour they were due to meet, and after waiting half an hour further, she went to check with the office. Apparently, she'd forgotten to mention some appointment.

It was almost lunchtime before they were able to begin. Carra was desperate not to let her frustration show, but then it turned out the lesson wasn't even new to her. Alexandra had her doing exactly the same exercises Nicholas had demonstrated.

Regrettably, her mother hadn't had the foresight to have her practising outside, and this time when Carra channelled her energy through her body and out of her fingers, she managed to create a small explosion. After the smoke had cleared, they discovered she'd left a deep dent in the floor.

Alexandra's glares informed her, belatedly, that giggling hadn't been the appropriate reaction.

Learning from their initial mistake and moving to the grass, Carra repeated the exercise over and over. Encouragingly, her control had vastly improved by mid-afternoon. She hadn't been able to practice any aspects of her healing ability, but at least she now felt confident that she wasn't going to accidentally explode anything. Or anyone.

Alexandra obviously agreed, because after another three days of theory, interspersed with repetition of this exercise, she announced she was leaving for a few days. She didn't deign to tell Carra where she was going or how long she would be gone for, only stating she would be back for the start of term.

She left Carra with only the vague instruction of 'keep practising'. Despite this, she made it clear there was still a lot for Carra to catch up on; she would therefore be required to attend evening lessons to make sure she wasn't 'unworthy of her place at the school'.

Not quite knowing what to do with herself, she stuck to her routine and went for dinner – performing real magic had made her even hungrier than usual, not to mention in need of a good sleep.

☆☆☆☆☆

She sensed the exact moment Dom returned.

Even though she was asleep, it suddenly seemed as though he was in the room with her. A moment later – in dream time – he appeared.

Apparently now her magic had been returned to

her, she no longer needed to be in physical contact with Dom to call him into her subconscious – just in close proximity.

Their dream was also far more vivid than those she had experienced previously, and she was able to play around with the landscape.

Sensing Dom's impatience she stuck her tongue out at him – before settling on a woodland theme, which was fairly unimaginative, and essentially just grass and a few trees placed at random.

"Where have you been?" she asked him.

"Around. Scoping out the political situation here, and in Florin."

"Spying." Carra surmised. Dom simply shrugged, so Carra told him she was at a loose end for a few days.

"Let's go visit your sister then."

Her face lit up, "That's quite a good idea actually!"

"I'll stop by in the morning. Pack a bag."

"Okay, will do. I need to be back the day before term starts to make sure I have chance to buy some suitable clothes. Also… so it looks like I've been here the whole time practising control."

"We can do that on the road, and then you genuinely will have been practising."

"If you insist…"

CHAPTER 36

Dom arrived the next morning, as promised, with a couple of horses in tow. She remarked upon how placid they seemed, so Dom explained he'd rented them, and they were therefore used to lots of different riders.

As soon as they were away from the town, Carra brought up something that had been bothering her.

"I asked my mother about your rejection from the Academy. She didn't give me a direct answer, of course, but she heavily implied it was due to who you are, rather than your strength in magic."

"That is not exactly a revelation Carra," Dom condescended, "The question in my mind was whether the problem is whether that means who I am – an exiled prince, or who I am – prophesised to be." Carra shrugged. In her mind they were one and the same, and she said as much.

"Not at all. Either they don't wish to antagonise Florin by having anything to do with me, or they are afraid of me. There's a huge difference, and I far prefer the latter." He smirked.

Carra really wasn't sure what she saw in him sometimes; she evidently projected this thought, as he promptly informed her, "I'm incredibly charming."

It was a fairly easy path from Paragon back to Rivulet. Pellagea was well developed and there was a well-trodden, demarcated trail. Better still, there had clearly been a man-made effort to flatten the ground for the ease of travellers.

Other than when they passed a few groups of people heading in the opposite direction – which made a pleasant change from their previous travels, during which they'd encountered almost no one – there wasn't much variety to their journey, and Carra found very little in their surroundings to interest her.

Mostly to pass the time, she relayed everything she'd learnt to Dom. She got the impression that very little of the information was new to him – and anything that was related to the Academy, so was therefore largely irrelevant.

It wasn't at all far to the Strathenbergs, so instead of stopping for the night, they pushed on. By the time it would have been too dark to see, they were close enough for the lights of Rivulet to provide enough illumination for their journey – and much to Carra's disappointment, they didn't even need to make use of Dom's flame magic.

Arriving at the manor brought back a not unwelcome rush of memories, particularly the happy ones involving Dom and Sandria. Other than the steward, no one was awake – but luckily, he recognised them well enough that he, albeit slightly reluctantly, agreed to provide them rooms without waking their hosts. Much to Carra's chagrin he did, however, have to rouse a few of the maids, as Dom insisted on staying in guest suites rather than servants' accommodation.

Before Carra knew it, it was morning. She'd slept solidly from the second she'd laid down on the bed, until the sun had not too recently risen. Making use of the basin, she washed her face and made herself presentable, before heading down to where the family were breakfasting.

Luckily, they had been made aware of her arrival; and not only was she relieved not to be catching them by surprise, but a place had already been set for her. Dom wasn't present and, seeing her looking around for him, Nicholas informed her he was still in bed. She politely thanked him and sat down, reaching for some bread and a knife.

In contrast to Nicholas and his parents, who maintained their usual formality, Ally was surprisingly animated. Feeling a little unsettled at first, she hadn't been paying as much attention as she usually would have been. When she finally looked at her sister properly, she started at what she saw beneath the table. Her mouth must have dropped, quite literally, as Ally broke off from whatever she'd been saying.

"Yes," her sister's cheeks blushed as she spoke, "It happened almost straight away after the wedding. I'm between four and five months along, it's really only become noticeable very recently."

"Congratulations!" Carra squeaked, hoping very much that she didn't actually sound to the others as high pitched as it had seemed to her. At their talk of the baby, she saw Nicholas' face light up, and she relaxed slightly. Maybe he really *did* care for her sister.

When Dom sauntered in, she loosened up even further. She smiled at him as he took a seat, and he winked at her as he reclined against the chair's back. It was difficult not to make the obvious comparison to Nicholas.

One example was the quite different ways in which they exerted their dominance. Nicholas maintained an air of superiority and held his body stiffly 'on duty'. However, Dom was the one who actually had the powerful presence – he naturally exerted his authority; effortlessly.

She snapped out of her contemplation when she realised everyone was looking at her. "I asked you how long you were staying for," Ally chattered.

"Probably three days?" She tried to gauge their reaction. "If that's okay? I've been enrolled at Whistlake and start courses next week." After a few seconds of puzzled reactions, Dom laughed. In fact, it was more like a giggle, which Carra found quite amusing, but didn't have time to dwell on once she realised she'd put her foot in it.

"We… I… thought Dom had taken you to Whistlake straight after the wedding?" Ally stammered.

"Ah, yes I did. However, we missed the initial entrance period so had to reapply for this term. Given we needed to equip Carra with supplies, and she had some reading and practising to do anyway, the time was well filled."

Carra, albeit mildly impressed at his quick thinking, took note of how smoothly Dom could spin a tale – just in case she ever found herself on the receiving end of one.

✧✧✧

Ally and Carra managed to grab some time alone in the sitting room that afternoon. It was nice to catch up, but it also highlighted to Carra the fact she actually found Dom a lot easier to talk to. Probably because she could be more open with him.

Ally kept asking about 'her and Dom', which only served to make her uncomfortable. Whilst she felt like there was *probably* something between them, Carra definitely didn't want to tell Ally that in case she was wrong. She did her utmost to dismiss Ally's questions, but then Ally wanted to know why they *weren't* together.

Yes, it was lovely she was pregnant and married but she didn't need to interfere in *her* personal life – and Ally was the *younger* sister! Where did she get the right to be so condescending?

Having gritted her teeth throughout the conversation, one thing did finally catch her interest, and made her realise she may have been a bit harsh on her sister –

who was really only trying to be friendly.

"So, I can hardly do any magic now. We're not really sure what happened. One day it came easily to me, and then poof." She motioned with her hand – holding out her fist then opening it – to demonstrate, "I can still move water in a basin, but anything bigger than that is too much of a strain."

"I'm sure it's nothing to worry about. In fact, it's probably just due to the pregnancy – because all your energy is going towards the baby at the moment."

Ally moved her voice down to a whisper, "It didn't happen when I got pregnant though… it was a few weeks ago… and it was so sudden. We were actually quite worried about the baby, as I was bed-ridden for a few hours afterwards." Carra opened her mouth in concern, but Ally reassured her straight away. "He is fine, I can feel him kicking strongly, and the midwives have checked me over repeatedly."

She wasn't really sure of the right thing to say. "How strange."

"Nicholas tried to research it. We actually have lots of books on magic here." Ally was still whispering, and Carra couldn't help but suspect Nicholas had specifically instructed Ally *not* to tell her about this. The more she thought about it, the more likely that seemed. "He couldn't find anything about this happening. I think at first he thought I was just doing it to get attention, but then he remembered that's not really in keeping with my personality."

No, Nicholas did not know her sister very well if he'd thought she was doing this for attention.

Having only had a short amount of time to process Ally's dismal revelation, Carra made the snap-judgement it would be best if she didn't divulge quite how strongly she'd come into her own magic.

Later, when she managed to find Sandria and get

her released from her duties for a few hours, she found conversation between them flowed naturally; it was if they'd last seen each other only yesterday.

It wasn't hard to come to the realisation she'd simply grown apart from Ally. Nor was it a surprise; after all, their current situations couldn't have been more dissimilar.

※※※※※

The three days in Rivulet were a welcome break, but they passed quickly. Carra didn't mind – she was looking forward to starting classes.

The idea of meeting the rest of her peers didn't make her nervous like she once would have been, even if they *had* already had a full term to get to know each other. She was used to dealing with the upper classes now. The thought made her laugh to herself, although she realised she was picturing the men – she probably needed to focus on making sure the women accepted her first.

As soon as she had some time alone with him, Carra told Dom about Ally's issues with her magic. Ally hadn't specifically asked her not to, but she probably would have told Dom either way - that was simply where her loyalties lay.

Dom was nonchalant. "Sounds like when you came into your power, she lost hers. Seems logical enough." *Did it?* "Younger siblings are never as powerful. In fact, it's rare for any other than a firstborn to even have magic. It's only because you come from such a strong line that she can even tap into a stream of power."

The road was far busier on the way back, and most people were travelling in the same direction as them. Carra presumed they were also heading to Whistlake, in time for the new term. Whilst most were accompanied by one or two servants, some of the students seemed to have a whole entourage with them. Carra began to feel quite proud that she had Dom as her escort.

"Thank you," she blurted out before she could stop herself.

"For being so wonderful?"

"Well, yes, I suppose. For everything. You know what I mean."

"Maybe I'd like to hear you tell me. You always seem so unimpressed, whatever I do."

"Well… you got me out of Rivulet."

"Away from Nicholas you mean. Yes, that's a good start. What else?"

"I hadn't finished! Okay, and you got me my magic back. Actually, I had to do that dumb tower, but you helped at least. You got me to Whistlake – and paid." He raised his eyebrows at that. *How should she phrase the other thing…* "And you're always, you know, there."

"So, you have noticed then? I wasn't sure."

There was an uncomfortable silence while Carra searched for something to say. "What will you do while I'm at Whistlake? Where will you go?"

"Do you know what? I'm not entirely sure. I'll keep an eye on you every now and then though, don't worry."

Carra suspected he might be planning to take another trip across the border, to find out what his family were up to. "You'll be careful, won't you? If you go into Florin."

They both knew that wasn't really a question, and that was where the conversation ended. Still, something had shifted between them slightly. When Dom dropped her at the Academy, he caught her by surprise with a long deep kiss. She could still feel it on her lips while he rode off on his horse – hers in tow – without turning back.

With nothing else left for her to do, she took a deep breath, and went inside.

CHAPTER 37

Apparently, her mother had given her assistant *very* clear instructions on what clothes Carra was supposed to have. She wasn't even sure why she'd been required to be present.

Unlike Rivulet, the shops were permanent fixtures rather than market stalls. This was a novelty at first, but she soon lost interest regardless. Luckily, there weren't many of them, and she was back in time for dinner.

The dining hall had a somewhat different feel that evening. It was still only about a quarter full – from what Carra had gathered, the school itself was only at about half its capacity – but people were huddled in small groups, and she felt compelled to find a seat against the wall, away from notice.

Most of those around her were of a similar age to herself, although a few were several years older; she supposed the professors must have a private dining room. Having eaten without anyone attempting to engage her, she made her way directly to her room.

It wasn't until the next morning that Carra realised her slightly embarrassing oversight. She'd assumed she would head to the classroom where her mother had been lecturing her, but on route from her bedroom, she overheard enough snippets of conversation to realise this was unlikely to be correct. It sounded as though there were lesson timetables, and the topic of study changed every half-day – presumably along with the class location.

Unsure where to go, she instead made her way

to the front desk. Thankfully, there was a pack of papers waiting for her – including, unsurprisingly, her schedule. Her discovery wasn't, however, made in enough time to prevent the awkwardness of walking into the classroom several minutes after the professor had already begun.

Even worse, her first class was – *of course* – being run by her mother, who was less than impressed by her lateness.

"Nice of you to join us." She didn't even try to disguise the sarcasm lacing her tone. "As you are a new student, I will excuse your manners, this once. Please make sure you are prompt in future." *Yes, I get it.* "Now, introduce yourself to the class."

Thanks mother, nice way to skirt around the fact that we're related. Or indeed. that we've even met each other before. Having been forced to stand and give her name, she was actually quite pleased that her surname, Anson, didn't reveal she was any relation to the Perywhist line.

With there being nothing further she felt inclined to say, she took the nearest empty seat, which was in the second row. Only then did it occur to her that the whole time she'd been standing at the front of the class, she'd been staring at the back wall; in her discomfort, she hadn't registered a single thing about the others in the room with her. It was too late to gauge their reactions to her presence now, she'd have to wait and see whether anyone tried to speak to her; the thought of making an active attempt to ingratiate herself didn't overly appeal.

Giving only the direction, "Please return to what you were doing." her mother made no attempt to explain what she'd missed, so Carra waited awkwardly, in the hopes this would soon become clear.

It transpired this was some sort of strange, meditation-based class, where they spent most of their time feeling and understanding their power. Being able to start with something she was already quite good at was something of a relief to Carra, who'd expected her first day to be rather intense, given she'd be meeting the other students for the first time. Finding it relatively easy to block out her surroundings, she quickly settled into her practised state, where she could sense her magic travelling round her body, in the way she imagined her blood cells did.

She was intrigued to find out that the more she did this, the more she would build up her power levels. It was a slow process – slower than actively using magic – but it also helped make their bodies stronger when it came to *containing* the magic. This particularly suited Carra because, being a healer, her specialism wasn't as easy to practice as the elemental magics were. At least... not without exploding things and destroying the place.

She was actually rather enjoying herself, when a noise behind her caught her attention. Alexandra was chastising someone for talking – but it wasn't that which shocked her, it was the sight of the boy *next* to them. Feeling like she was going to be sick, she ran out of the room.

Not being sure where the nearest lavatory was, she at least managed to find her way outside before she actually threw up.

Feeling only marginally better, she righted herself, to find the instigator standing right behind her. Saul had the cheek to reach his arm towards her shoulder as if he was going to *comfort* her. Carra stepped backwards, actually lost for words for once. Her entire body shook as she tried to control her anger.

As if things couldn't get any worse, her mother appeared behind them – just as Dom leapt over a nearby wall, charged across, then stood protectively between her and Saul. She instantly felt braver as a result of his presence.

"What is going on here? You have been at this

school less than a day and have already caused disruption. I suggest you come to my office this evening and we can discuss whether you have a future at Whistlake." Alexandra showed no emotion, despite the words being directed at her own daughter.

Saul responded first. "It was my fault, Professor Alexandra. Please excuse us, I gave her a fright."

"It must have been a pretty bad fright to elicit such a ridiculous reaction." Her mother visibly softened and Carra frowned. Dom was still glaring at Saul – although Carra couldn't think of a time the two of them had ever met. "Given I trust my favourite student." Carra felt the bile rise back up in her throat. "I will accept your explanation. For now. Girl – do *not* try my patience again."

With that, she turned and marched back to the classroom. Carra supposed they were supposed to follow. Instead, she waited for Saul to leave so she could speak to Dom – but he didn't seem to be moving.

"I'm sorry." She looked at him blankly. "Can you give me a chance to talk to you? After classes today. At least listen to what I have to say."

Carra didn't like it but, as far as she could tell, she had two options: either spend the next couple of years avoiding him; or to talk to him and try to put the past behind her. So, she nodded. Then she nodded at Dom too – to let him know she was okay – and walked with her head held high back to the classroom.

Her concentration for the next hour certainly wasn't as good as it had been before. It probably didn't help that a lot of her classmates – three other girls and seven boys – seemed to be staring at her in curiosity.

At lunchtime, when they stopped for a free hour between classes, she had worked up the courage to try speaking to the other girls. They seemed to be pretty happy as a threesome, and she found she wasn't able to make eye contact and join in their conversation.

Left standing on her own, she made her way to the dining room, picked up a plate of food, and sat on one of the benches feeling uncomfortable. She hadn't really experienced anything like this before.

Someone took a seat next to her. Apprehensively, she turned towards them, and saw that it was Saul of all people. She continued eating in silence, and thankfully he didn't make any attempts to converse.

She was about to clear her plate away when she turned to him, "Do we keep with the same class all week?"

She was almost amused at his surprise. "Yes, we stay as a year group. Except for one day a week based on our specialisms."

The afternoon's class was called 'practical', which she supposed told her everything she needed to know. Examining the week's schedule further, she saw with some disappointment, that this morning's conditioning class seemed to have been an exception. The next three days were labelled as 'theory' in the morning and 'practical' in the afternoon, and the fifth day was 'specialism' – helpfully, Carra's schedule had the tutor for that day listed as unassigned.

☆☆☆☆☆

As the week progressed, Carra came to understand the day-to-day differences, which they hadn't bothered to explain in the brief descriptions on her schedule.

One of the weekly practical sessions was focused on problem solving – and disappointingly, was very much desk-based. They were given scenarios in teams of two or three and asked to find a solution. Sometimes they were given specific specialisms to work with, and in other cases they were asked to use their own.

Another of the schedule's practical sessions turned out to be about learning to care for, and ride, horses; nothing to do with magic. Most of the students could already ride, and Carra figured this had been scheduled with the intention of giving them time to keep up the hobby.

The third practical session was learning everyday uses of magic. This was interesting because it actually involved demonstrations, but equally frustrating, in that it seemed to revolve entirely around the elemental magics.

The final practical session was centred on team building and involved outdoor games, which saw half the class pitted against the other. Carra found she was quite enjoying the first session, until out of nowhere she remembered she wasn't yet accepted by her peers, and quickly lost her focus.

Of the three theory sessions: one was the history of key magicians, alternated with the study of various specialisms and the development of these; one was geography and map reading; and the third was a free session that they could use to either practice conditioning, or study in the library. Carra suspected a number of the students used it to catch up on sleep.

She gathered through hearsay they were never actually tested on the theory side; that the end of year test considered solely whether they were powerful enough to continue on at the Academy.

Carra had been informed they hadn't found her an appropriate tutor, so she had nothing scheduled for day five as yet.

It was a surprise, albeit a very positive one, to find her mother had seemingly forgotten about her threat to use her evenings to help her catch-up on what she'd missed. Her primary concern was it would have meant missing dinner... Carra wasn't planning to remind her unless it turned out there was something really important she was struggling with.

On the two 'free' days there were additional sessions you could sign up to but, for at least now, Carra hadn't identified anything she was particularly interested in. The choice included higher mathematics, history of language, and study of poetry. Carra supposed they supplemented what most students had learnt at school.

She'd garnered that in Pellagea, there was a set curriculum followed across the country; there had been nothing of the sort in Florinyn – Carra had been lucky her father had even been able to afford a school place for her, as most children in her village hadn't had the same opportunity. The local school had been focused mostly on practical activities, with reading and writing being considered the 'higher' skills – *not* the kind of educational experience the students here had obviously received.

Thankfully, it wasn't affecting her capability in the compulsory sessions. What she lacked in practice compared to other students, she seemed to make up for in power.

She did, however, find it difficult to spend so much time sitting silently, keeping still, and listening. Even when they had received desk-based lessons growing up, the pupils had been encouraged to participate as much as possible. Whenever she began to fidget, Carra had to remind herself to use her emotion-calming magic, which she had become overly reliant on, out of necessity.

Strangely, she was no longer feeling apprehensive about meeting with Saul. Carra had asked him to give her a couple of days to get used to the idea of talking to him, so it wasn't until the evening of her fourth day of classes that she met him after dinner.

Not being warm enough to sit outside, they found

a deserted classroom. Belatedly, it occurred to Carra that if anyone saw them, they might jump to a very wrong conclusion about what they were doing – but by then it was too late to do anything about it. They didn't light any additional candles, and as luck would have it, she didn't see anyone walking past who appeared to notice they were there.

It was actually Carra who broke the silence "Well?"

"Sorry. I'm thinking where to start." He looked decidedly uncomfortable, which put Carra a little more on edge. "It wasn't supposed to work out how it did. Obviously, you are aware of what we did. Edon's father, and my father, sat on the town council that decided to instigate it all.

"My father, I think, was motivated by his knowledge of how much I wanted to study at Whistlake. He had somehow become aware of you and your sister's existence, but on that part, I only have minimal details – he said he'd overheard two professors gossiping about Professor Alexandra's estranged children. Once we were over the border and into Florin, it wasn't too hard to *persuade* someone to tell us where you were settled.

"I'm not explaining this very well. I just... I need you to understand that you weren't supposed to get hurt in the process. Our plan was to inform Professor Alexandra of your ransom. She would pay for her children – and everything would have worked out okay. You would be safe, albeit now with your mother rather than your father, and I, ashamed as I am to say it now, would have had the tuition fee for the Academy."

"Saul, I don't even know where to start with how much this disgusts me. No one get hurt? What about all the families you separated? The women sold at auction? My sister and I may be okay, but we were incredibly lucky with where we ended up in comparison to everyone else!"

Cognisant of the look of disdain she'd given him,

not wanting him to stop providing information, and not really stopping to think about the implications of her question, she asked him, "Why did the ransom never happen?"

He squeezed his eyes closed and rubbed the palm of his hand over his forehead. "Well, that's the most embarrassing part. The Professor, your mother I mean, said no. There was never meant to be any auction. The plan was for the men to be offered work in the mines, and the mothers and children to be relocated with them. The girls you were with, well… Edon lost his temper at your mother's refusal. The rest you know."

That was more than a little like a slap in the face. "You're saying that your father and Edon acted on your behalf?" Carra raised her eyebrows.

"My father, yes. Edon had his own agenda. After all, it was a lot of money."

"Did it not occur to you that if the plan had actually worked, my mother would enrol me, and you might see me here?" That seemed to stump him.

"I guess I didn't realise when we started out that we were going to be the same age. I was expecting two young children from the description I'd been given."

"That's sickening."

"I wasn't exactly the mastermind. My father and Eron decided they could use the village raid as a cover for their own separate side mission. In fact, I'm not convinced they didn't encourage the raid exactly for that purpose."

"Pathetic. Accept some responsibility, Saul. You'd have me believe you were an innocent bystander? Honestly, what do you take me for?" However unmannerly her tone may have been, in that moment, Carra felt proud to be standing up for herself.

"I made a mistake."

"A big mistake."

"I'm sorry."

"I'm sure." She raised her eyebrows. "So how did you even end up at the Academy?"

At least he had the decency to look bashful as he responded, "I received a scholarship." As if the thought had only just struck him, he suddenly asked, "How did *you* end up here?"

"You have not earned the right to that information!" Carra snapped.

"Sorry. You're right. That's true. But how can I make it up to you?"

"Why don't you try very hard, and we'll see." Really, she had no clue what to say. The irony wasn't lost on her that Saul was the only student who had spoken to her all week. Having had the last few days to mull it over, she'd decided she'd be in a stronger position if she didn't alienate him.

Saul had sat himself next to her at lunch and dinner each day, and although she didn't actually want to speak to him, his presence was comforting. It distracted her from Dom's absence. She had considered using her magic to dull the emotion of missing Dom, but for some reason she didn't want to... she knew it wasn't *quite* the truth when she told herself she was worried it might backfire and explode something.

It had been a small consolation, but at least Dom hadn't been particularly far away. Occasionally he made sarcastic comments when she transmitted her thoughts too loudly in lessons, and Carra still saw him in her dreams. She'd even begun to hope her suspicion he was planning to head back into Florin had been unfounded. However, he'd now told her he'd be going 'away' for a few weeks. Their connection was very unlikely to reach that far, and not only would she miss him, she knew she was going to be fretting over his safety.

As well as providing her the opportunity to see him, her dreams had been giving her a distinct advantage. Being alert at night was effectively gaining her extra practice time, and she wasn't sure how this would work once Dom wasn't around to share them; Carra knew, in all likelihood, it wouldn't.

CHAPTER 38

When their designated 'specialist' day came around, Carra found she was simply left to her own devices. She would have been tempted to go to Paragon and find Dom, but he'd told her during the night it would be *this* morning he was leaving. She'd decided to stop short of begging him to stay, seeing as her main reason would have been her own amusement.

Carra was walking aimlessly around the grounds, when she suddenly remembered the book on spirit she'd hidden under her mattress just before their visit to Ally. This would be the perfect opportunity to delve into it.

The days had become warm enough for her to sit outside comfortably – as long as she wrapped herself up in enough layers – but she wasn't sure she wanted anyone to see what she was reading, so she propped herself up on her bed instead. With the sunlight falling in on her, it was very tempting to be lazy and have a nap, but once she mustered up the willpower to open the book, she found herself immediately enthralled.

Flicking to the inside back cover before she became too engrossed, she saw this book had only been checked out once before – by a professor, just over three decades earlier. That was, of course, not including anyone else who had failed to adhere to the library rules, and had just walked off with it, like she'd done. This lack of usage by other students cemented her theory that she shouldn't mention her interest to anyone else, at least until something changed to mean she had a good reason to do so.

Unlike other textbooks or reference books she'd come across, this book had been adapted from the journal of a spirit user. However, whilst the journal was now two hundred years old, this book had only been authored eighty years ago – so its writer hadn't actually collaborated with the original magician. Rather, he had built upon the journals, using his own research of other spirit users through the ages.

The first skill discussed, and the usual starting skill for spirit magicians, was one she'd known about but as yet never used – altering other people's emotions. It was described as gradual in effect, akin to alleviating the pressure in someone's mind. Spirit users could also do this to their own emotions but that didn't generally count as an extra power point, it was just a slight enhancement to using the same skill on others.

Reflecting on this for a moment, Carra began to wonder whether spirit users *weren't* as rare as everyone seemed to presume. Perhaps it was just they didn't necessarily *realise* what they were doing.

She quickly flicked through the book to see if she could confirm a suspicion she'd felt lingering for the last few days. Her mother had thought it likely, but that hadn't been enough to confirm it for Carra; now she knew for sure. It was a spirit skill to be able to use the magic of a person you made physical contact with.

This particular individual lamented the limited application of this ability, noting they had found themselves restricted to only being able to use the magic of those they already had an emotional bond with – in this case his wife, and eldest child. He had also noted that the level of magic was dependent on the third party rather than the power of the spirit user – so, Carra for example, could only ever be as powerful as Dom in her usage of flame magic.

From what she was reading, it seemed fairly strange that she'd been able to use Dom's magic so early on in getting to know him.

Scanning the pages again, she was a little disappointed to find there was almost no information on dream sharing. The closest she was apparently going to get was a quote from one of the historians the author claimed to have interviewed, who had speculated that bringing people into your dreams or entering other people's dreams was theoretically possible.

It wasn't very clear how he'd come up with this hypothesis or why he hadn't been able to provide any more information on the subject. Presumably, it was purely hearsay. Carra was reasonably confident he didn't have any actual experience in this area because of how specific her dream sharing seemed to be. She didn't, for example, think she would be able to gate-crash other people's dreams – although she did make a mental note to pat Dom's shoulder if she ever saw him sleeping to see what happened.

The dream sharing sounded as though it was going to be another skill that only worked where there was an emotional, or possibly familial bond in place.

Having assuaged her curiosity, she went back to the beginning of the book and began to read it properly.

None of the spirit users were identified as having a secondary power, like her healing ability, but they unanimously seemed to have claimed to be incredibly powerful.

One final thing particularly caught her interest. Some spirit users noted being able to sense magic in others – the strongest ones could not only recognise what another magician's specialism was, but they could also gauge how powerful they were. In fact, it claimed the end of year

Academy test had been devised by a spirit user. Carra wondered if it was still the same test –that *she'd* now be facing. There hadn't been a spirit user studying there for a long, long while.

That evening at dinner, the other first year students all seemed particularly sluggish. Several of them even just took plates of food directly to their rooms. She couldn't help but ask Saul if this was normal.

"They've spent all day using their magic, it's inevitable they'd feel fatigued. That's why we have two days off before lessons start again – tomorrow is affectionately nicknamed 'recovery day'. If it weren't so important for them to eat, most of them would probably go straight to bed."

"You seem fine though?"

"I do feel a mild exhaustion, but not enough to render myself bedridden. How do you think I got my scholarship? Generally being more powerful means suffering less in the magical fatigue department." He frowned in contemplation. "How do you not know this? Have you never felt tired after using magic?"

No, not really. "I only recently discovered I have magic. I haven't had much chance so far to actually practise using it." She couldn't help but add, "I didn't even know magic existed before your, erm… *intervention*."

"Alright. I get it. I'm a horrible person. From what I can see you either get over it and we can help each other out, or I'll leave you alone."

Carra looked at him, studying his face. She'd already decided it was helpful to have an ally – but one more powerful than the rest of their class, now that could *really* work to her advantage. Probably. He wasn't particularly accepted by the other students. She didn't think he was actively disliked, he just didn't fit in all that well. Possibly because he also wasn't from their same, elite background.

"Okay. We work together. What's your specialism?"

"Wow, straight to the point." Carra cocked her head, but didn't otherwise respond – deciding instead that her best option was to wait and see what Saul came out with. "Okay. I'm an air user." Now that could be interesting... she certainly wouldn't mind understanding some more about what her mother's capabilities were.

She looked at him again, raising her eyebrows. "I'll tell you my secondary specialism later," he assured her. "You haven't even told me your primary one yet." Touché. Carra decided to whisper 'healing' in his ear – mostly for dramatic effect – and his reaction made it worthwhile. "No wonder you haven't had much chance to practice!"

☆☆☆☆☆

With nothing particular to do the next day, they decided to spend their time learning from each other. Choosing a remote spot within the grounds, they compared their abilities.

"I think I've finally worked out what I can do to make us even." That got Carra's attention. She'd already moved on from their past – she wasn't the type to hold grudges – but she was very curious as to what he was about to say. "I'll injure myself and you can heal it."

She'd shown him the destructive magic, and they'd experimented with smaller and larger explosions, but she hadn't yet been able to practice healing anybody. Saul had only demonstrated one skill so far too – creating stronger and weaker winds – as that was what his assigned tutor had tasked him with improving.

"I appreciate the offer, but what if I accidentally anti-heal you, and blow your arm off or something?"

"I trust you. It's not like the Academy are giving you any opportunity to practice. If we're going to team up, you need to be able to use your magic."

Carra wasn't overly sure what he meant by team up but didn't want to push it. After all, he knew Dom existed, having seen him leap to her rescue. "I don't think it's about trust, I honestly don't know if I can control it. It's simply too risky."

"Maybe trust was the wrong word then. I meant it in the sense that I trust in your ability to be able to do it. I tell you what, we've both been doing a lot today and we're exhausted." Carra blinked, taken aback; she wasn't tired at all. "Take the next few days to think about it. We'll reconvene same time next week and, assuming you're feeling brave enough, you can try it out then." Despite his words, his tone implied he was assuming she'd decide to go for it – and if he was willing, then maybe she should.

☆☆☆

The next day, she felt a bit of a buzz. It felt as though she had more power running through her. Describing it to Saul at breakfast, he explained she was feeling her body charging up. It happened whenever the internal power capacity of a magician improved.

Essentially, her magical fitness level had increased from yesterday. Whilst it didn't occur that frequently for most people, it made sense for Carra to be experiencing it, considering she was relatively new to using her magic and had quite a lot of catching up to do.

As she mulled over Saul's offer, it occurred to Carra that she had neglected to tell him she could heal herself. Now she was thinking about it, she realised she didn't actually want him to know. She was too enthralled by the idea of being able to try healing someone else, and didn't want to give him the opportunity to retract his offer.

Being too embarrassed to tell him she was at a loose end again, after breakfast, she wandered off by herself. With nothing to do, she decided to browse the library and see whether she could find anything of interest. Another book on spirit would be great if there *was* anything, but Carra thought it more likely she'd find something useful on healing – which could turn out to be very handy in helping her advance.

Given she was here, she figured she may as well embrace the learning aspects, and aim to better herself. Carra already had an intuition she was more powerful than anyone else here.

☆ ☆ ☆ ☆

Having managed to avoid seeing her mother since last week's contemplation lesson, it was now that time of the week again. She couldn't really complain – it had been such a busy week, the previous lesson felt more like it had been a month ago.

This time she sat next to Saul by choice, and happily, the two and a half hours went by fairly uneventfully. Her concentration level probably reached about sixty percent – so it could have been more productive – but she thought she did quite well considering.

That was, until, the end of the class, when she found Alexandra blocking her way. "So, so." she said, condescendingly, "What was *that* all about last week then? Some sort of lovers' tiff?"

Carra couldn't help but laugh. "Really mother? That just demonstrates how little you know me at all." Carra saw a rare glimmer of emotion flicker across her face. It was swiftly gone again. "So, tell me then mother, why?"

Silence.

"Why, mother," she spat out the last word, "Were myself and Alliana not worthy of your ransom money?"

"The answer to that is simple, darling *daughter*," The sarcasm lacing the term of endearment was not lost on Carra, "You were not supposed to be anywhere near magic. If you remember, we had gone to all that effort to prevent you even knowing about it. Taking parental responsibility for you as a professor of Whistlake Academy was simply risking too much. It would have brought the prophecy far closer to completion."

"Yet here we are."

"Quite." There the conversation ended. Carra replayed it in her mind as she walked away, trying to find some remorse in her mother's words, but it simply hadn't been evident.

Her anger started to boil over – after all, not three weeks ago she had told her mother the story of herself and Alliana being bought by Nicholas, without a whisper of indication from Alexandra that she not only knew about it, but could have prevented it.

Annoyingly she had also tipped her hand – she hadn't asked about the prophecy, and it was now presumably clear to her mother that she was already aware of it.

She tried to recall Dom's words. It was almost laughable the Academy had taken something which was so ominously facile, so seriously. Once her and Dom – well, Theodore – met, 'the ripple effects would destroy Florinyn'. Why did they even care about Florinyn in Pellagea? Florinyn's laws were deadly to magicians.

Carra then did something very out of character and

missed lunch. Instead, she used the time to go outside and release the anger from her body. She could almost imagine she could visibly see the sparks flying from her fingers, so prolific were the levels of toxins she let go of.

She did, however, manage to pull herself together in time to attend her afternoon problem-solving practical. Saul had even sneaked a piece of bread and an apple out of the food hall for her.

CHAPTER 39

Expecting to find her specialism day once again free from any scheduling, Carra was dismayed to discover a note had been pushed under her door, explaining she needed to meet with Professor Sila first thing.

Her disappointment quickly turned to excitement when she realised she was going to practice actual healing magic. She was already familiar with Sila, who taught the theory session on history and specialisms, although she didn't have any particular opinions – positive or negative – on her as yet.

She thought Sila probably hadn't noticed her in class, and wouldn't know much about *her* either, so she determined she'd try and make a good impression.

The morning was laidback, and fairly pleasant; they started out by spending half a day just getting to know each other. Much to Carra's excitement, she found out that healing was actually Sila's secondary skill; she hoped she might have the opportunity to learn more specifics on one of the elemental magics too.

Sila was limited to healing others and healing herself, but these were the two areas Carra was most interested in developing anyway.

Interestingly, it sounded like Carra's destruction magic was reasonably rare even amongst healers – Sila had taught at the Academy for thirty-eight years, so had seen a lot of different students' skills.

She was also able to tell Carra about several of her ancestors who had attended the Academy, both on the Perywhist side, and on the weaker, Anson side. She was careful not to mention Carra's mother, so it seemed likely someone had forewarned her about the fragile nature of their relationship.

She did feel slightly awkward for a moment when Sila commented on how strange it was that Carra didn't have a secondary skill, given how powerful she was. Carra felt she managed to deflect the comment as well as she could have done – by saying she was relatively new to this, and something might materialise later. She was probably just trying to be polite but, conveniently for Carra, Sila responded by saying healing was quite a rare specialism and maybe that had something to do with it.

Carra discovered Sila was surprisingly knowledgeable about the other students, and she tried to prompt her to talk about them without being too obvious. Seemingly only four members of her class had a second skill – five if you included Carra. That meant those were the five mostly likely to progress to second year, along with maybe only two or three of the six others.

Each of the fellow students in her intake had an elemental-type primary specialism, which was why there were four other assigned teaching groups, and they'd had to draft in an additional professor for Carra.

Students' secondary skills were basically ignored until second year, as generally there was already more than enough for them to learn on their respective primary skills.

As it happened, Carra wasn't completely certain whether her primary skill was healing or spirit – although healing did seem more likely, as her destructive magic meant this ability was quite a high level. Even so, usually it was more obvious; and usually, the elemental power. When a user had two different elemental specialisms, she was given to understand they could physically feel the strength of one over the other.

After lunch, Sila asked Carra to demonstrate her destructive power, saying it was the easiest one to start with in the circumstances. Carra suspected it was more to do with her professor's curiosity as to how it worked. Regardless, she could see no reason not to oblige, especially if she hoped to achieve anything out of the mentoring relationship.

Sila regularly offered her unnecessary breaks to recoup her strength, and Carra was becoming increasingly conscious of her lack of fatigue while performing magic. If her instructor had noticed, she had yet to say anything.

As the afternoon went on, Carra began to act as though she was more tired than she really was, pretending to need the rest periods to recuperate. She wished she'd done so a little earlier, as she couldn't help but fear the faculty already saw her as a threat simply due to the prophecy. If she was significantly more powerful than the other students... well, that would just add fuel to the fire.

As the day's practice came to a close, Sila set out her forward-looking lesson plan. The Academy had made arrangements for something slightly unusual – although honestly, it irked Carra they hadn't consulted her first.

A message sent to the residents of Paragon had apparently requested that anyone who had any minor ailments in need of healing, should please come to the Academy, where they would be attended to.

Sila reassured Carra they had made it clear they were offering the services of a novice, so any assistance provided was at their own risk.

Although she had initially been taken aback, on reflection it seemed entirely possible this would be the best learning experience she'd gain from these sessions – while she'd enjoyed spending the morning chatting, during the afternoon *she'd* mostly been the one doing the demonstrating.

✧ ✧ ✧

During dinner, she had to put up with Saul being unusually perky. Their time practicing together had obviously paid off for him. She hadn't asked – he told her anyway – but apparently, he'd really impressed his professor today. When he let slip this was Alexandra, it very nearly soured Carra's reasonably good mood.

In earnest, Carra was beginning to wonder how much she was actually going to learn from Whistlake Academy. She had mastered control, and wanted to practice healing, but anything more than that, she was struggling to envision. Still, the theory and practicals were interesting – and presumably, would be more useful in the future than she could currently appreciate.

Unlike the other students, she didn't have a clear conception of what she wanted to do. She knew she was basically alone in this respect, because in Sila's demonstrations class that week she had asked them all how they saw themselves practically using magic in the future. Carra had been the only person well and truly stumped by the question.

Intriguingly, one of the students had mentioned he was considering the role of a medic – so she assumed his secondary skill must be healing. Carra was, however, no closer to finding out Saul's secondary skill. Or Dom's. *If he has one.*

It was strange. She had *used* to be the sort of person who planned ahead – but life clearly seemed to have had other plans for her. When she tried to picture herself as an apprentice to a scribe or bookbinder as she'd once expected to be her lot, she could no longer do so.

She made a mental note to ask Sila what sort of thing magicians did after Whistlake. Besides becoming a professor there of course, which at present, she had zero intention of doing.

It might have been psychosomatic, but Carra didn't think she had been sleeping as well since Dom had gone away. She regularly found herself lying in bed awake, trying to picture what he was doing. Since she'd grown more confident with the layout of the school, she'd even got into a bit of a habit of wandering around in the dark once everyone else had retired for the night.

Having discovered that, more often than not, the dining area was left open, she headed that way on the off chance she'd be able to scavenge some of the leftover cake or buns. The library also seemed to be accessible at all hours, but she rarely felt like reading when she couldn't sleep, and tonight was no exception.

Going outside for fresh air did at least help clear her mind a little. The lawns were well-maintained, but the dearth of trees or shrubs meant the gardens provided limited diversion. She was certainly having limited success at taking her mind off her Dom-related worries.

It wasn't just that she didn't like the idea of Dom putting himself at what she considered to be unnecessary risk – regardless of how many years ago it was, he'd been quite the public figure before his banishment – his presence itself helped her feel more at ease. Selfishly, she also wanted more time with him, to try and unravel how he felt towards her, which was ridiculous given how much time they'd spent together.

Truth be told, she was also getting a little bit bored. Daytimes were okay, but she had nothing to do with her evenings. She suspected some of her peers frequented the taverns in Paragon, but Carra had never been extended an invite. So, unless she wanted to spend some more one on one time with Saul – which, she didn't – she was finding there was an excessive amount of enforced solitude.

Yet he'd given her no indication of when he was going to come back to Paragon, and the thought that he might not be back until the end of term made her feel a bit sick.

Carra had already managed to spend a number of nights second-guessing herself. Part of her wondered if he'd left in order to have some space, and time away from her. She kept trying to work out what she could have said or done differently – revisiting any conversations she could remember, to see if she'd said something stupid or put him off in some way.

She hadn't come up with any answers, but then she didn't exactly have vast experience with the opposite gender. Although she did suspect Dom might be a bit of a case unto himself anyway.

Maybe she just wasn't good enough for him. She wasn't even nobility in the way Florinyn measured it. In Pellagea, she knew that her family were considered important in some way, but she hadn't explicitly laid claim to her lineage. She didn't overly want to acknowledge her mother as being such, and *somehow* – Alexandra wasn't exactly subtle – she got the impression the feeling was mutual.

CHAPTER 40

Dom quite enjoyed the thrill of sneaking into Florin and trying to avoid detection. The reality was probably simply that nobody cared, or perhaps even remembered him, but he was not such a fool as to let down his guard.

Travelling across Florinyn barely troubled him, but actually entering the capital – that, he found exciting every time. It was getting warmer now, too warm to keep his hood up without drawing attention, so he'd had to find an alternative disguise.

He rather liked the idea of baiting the public by walking around so out in the open, but there were still some people he knew in the city, and he now had the additional concern of running into Jade – who had shared his usual haunts, and knew about his occasional visits. There was also no way he could get as close to the palace as he intended unless he found a way to go incognito.

So, he'd slicked his hair with grease and combed it to the side – a style which he couldn't help but laugh at. Sadly, outside of the room in the inn he'd rented, there weren't very many mirrors around to admire himself in.

He'd also tried to find some spectacles, but given he didn't really need the magnification, they had made his eyes blurry, so he'd had to settle for some sunshades. Hopefully, no one would ask him to remove them while he was indoors.

Dom's main reason for visiting was to see what his family were up to. He didn't like to be too removed from the current politics – he still had the intention of returning here for his 'rightful' position one day.

Part of that meant a lot of sitting in taverns, drinking ale, and listening to drunkards rant about their living situation. Sometimes he even pretended to join in.

During the day, he lurked around the palace exterior; watching, and listening to the conversations of whoever was coming or going.

On previous visits, he'd played games – walking alongside groups of ladies he saw, often his sister's friends, and daring any of them to recognise him and then point it out; all the while having a good flirt. Although he'd been looking, on this trip he'd yet to see anyone he thought was worth chatting to. He had wanted to take his mind off Carra, but it seemed his standards had become much higher recently.

Which brought him to the other reason for his visit – he needed to be sure what he wanted before he progressed things with Carra. He'd grown up considering himself a precious commodity and Carra certainly wasn't the royal connection he'd expected to be matched with.

He also knew that if something happened between himself and Carra, then that was it; they were together forever. He thought that was *probably* what he wanted, but he needed to know for sure. Assuming at some point he was, then being in Florin would also provide a good opportunity for him to find a ring – however, he needed to leave that until just before he left the city, as spending that much money was certain to bring attention to himself.

So far, he hadn't learnt anything which would actually justify his visit here. The most he'd achieved was hearing some gossip that Torrin was engaged to be married – to Jade of all people. Not hugely surprising, and it was of a little consequence in the grand scheme of things, but he felt quite sickened by the idea, nonetheless.

He was struggling to suss out the allegiances of Torrin and Tilla. Obviously, he knew Tilla better, having grown up with her, but she wasn't the one now in line for succession. So – whilst he thought she would probably support him – what he really wanted, was to find out more about Torrin and judge what kind of king he would be.

Torrin's ties to Jade certainly gave him doubts regarding Torrin's judgement, but it was hard to know where the line was between his own bias, and his desire to find flaws to justify his own superiority. After all, for a long time, he had also trusted Jade.

When it came down to it, all Dom really had to rely on was his own gut feeling that Torrin wasn't competent enough, nor sufficiently fair-minded, for the role.

✧✧✧✧✧✧

On his third day in the city, Dom managed to catch a glimpse of the now elderly man who had once been his father. He wondered whether this was the same strange feeling that Carra got when she saw her mother – curiosity, detachment, and regret, all inseparably interlaced.

It was tempting to walk up to the man and confront him; maybe even challenge him on what he apparently considered to be the appropriate treatment of his own family – but of course, he didn't. Instead, the encounter led to him making his way to an inn a fair bit earlier in the afternoon than usual.

Assuming he was mistaken at what he thought he had seen, Dom had to look twice. In his desperation to escape to the nearest tavern he hadn't considered his proximity to the palace. It was the first time in a *long* while that he'd seen Tilla.

She was surrounded by people; so, however tempted he might be, at least for the moment there was no chance of approaching her. He settled for studying her body language, whilst trying to overhear any snippets he could – which, regrettably, turned out to be very few.

He did his best to keep his head down, in attempt to avoid attention. When he *did* look up, he saw something unusually serious in her expression. She was plotting something, and he wanted... *needed* to know what it was.

When she finally left, he followed at a distance... and ended up lost – he both didn't know where *she* was, and didn't know where *he* was. Which was strange, as he had thought he'd known his home city inside out.

The buildings in this area were much older than those in the Palace district, and he found himself lingering to study the architecture. A stone archway, with a small, ugly, squatting gargoyle at the apex, particularly caught his interest, and he couldn't help but wander through to see what it guarded.

Entering the building behind it, he discovered he had wandered into a library. The inside was eerily similar to the marble dome back in Avo - *too* similar to be a coincidence, he decided.

Many of the books looked extremely old, to the extent he was worried if he touched one, it might disintegrate.

A young slender girl stepped out from behind one of the shelves and startled him out of his fixation. He frowned at her. The girl, on the other hand, seemed bemused. *Damn it, I'm pretty sure she recognises me.*

"Dani. I'm the librarian." She held out her hand to him. "Would you like a warmed ale?"

Thrown by the whole situation, he found himself accepting her invitation. She wasn't as young as he'd first thought, and yes, she definitely knew *exactly* who he was.

Having somehow been roped into an intense

conversation, he found himself divulging all sorts of personal information. They seemed to have a naturally good rapport, and it had been a long time since he'd discussed any of his 'secrets' with anyone other than Carra. Even with Oz, he had tried to remain somewhat guarded.

She was strangely interested in his and Carra's journey to the Tower and kept probing him for further details. He couldn't figure out why until she started fixating on Duke Flothin, and he gradually made the connection. "Duke Flothin built this library, didn't he?"

"Don't be daft, it's much older than him. He did lay the marble though – he always did lean towards the eccentric."

"You're his niece, Danielle. I remember you now!" She smiled. Dom felt reassured. He had instinctively trusted her, and now he knew his impulse had been correct. She wasn't likely to alert anyone to his presence in Florin.

Since they had already embarked on the subject, he ended up relaying the whole story to her, from meeting Carra, until the Tower. She was fascinated by the Tower's trials, and grew frustrated when he couldn't adequately describe them. It became obvious that he hadn't asked Carra nearly enough questions about what she had gone through – something he was determined to rectify when he next saw her.

Dani, clearly having decided she'd heard everything she was going to about the Tower, turned the conversation back to the tunnels that Carra had so despised. In fact, the whole encounter was making him think about Carra an awful lot.

He discovered that Dani had been storing some useful knowledge. Having made out as though she was going to fetch another drink, she'd instead pulled a history book off the shelves, before presenting Dom with it.

She'd opened it to a specific page, about two-thirds

of the way through. "See here," she pointed at the text, "it's all about Olivia – the necromancer Olivia, who cursed the Florindyers. Your family used to use those tunnels for transporting slaves from the desert, up to Florin. Selling them to Avo and Cillamon too." Dom cringed. "It's written as a fairy tale. I remember my father reading it to me when I was young, although... it's quite dark. She went down to those tunnels after being spurned by the prince and, well, she killed herself."

"Are you suggesting that those clanking noises, and the spell that seemed to come over Carra, were because of some curse that had been lurking down there, waiting?"

"In effect, yes. That, or some lingering magic. In the past magicians were far more powerful than they are now, and she was *particularly* gifted. In the tale, her traumatic death, and dying promise to haunt the Royal family, echoed through the tunnels. It wasn't too long after that they were abandoned." She snapped the book closed. "Of course, we also gained access to boats, so they weren't needed anymore – and this is just a tale to frighten children."

Dom couldn't help but wince and, lacking his usual subtlety, he shifted the conversation. He was going to have to tell Carra that maybe she *hadn't* imagined the whole hearing voices thing after all.

✧✦✧✦✧

It took two more days before he managed to glean anything which might give him an insight into Tilla's plans. Seeing her servants buying travel equipment, he surmised she was planning to leave Florin.

Whilst he could have stayed longer, to find out where she was heading, he was itching to get back and check on Carra. Knowing she was surrounded by hostility – from both her mother and that boy she'd had a confrontation with – was bothering him.

He wished he could have watched over her discreetly – he didn't want her to feel like he thought she couldn't cope on her own – but inevitably, the night after he returned to Rivulet she'd know. On the other hand, now he was ready to declare his feelings to her, it seemed like no moment would be too soon.

Ready to head back to Pellagea, he decided to take a different route to usual, travelling directly north towards Astonelay. It was only polite for him to check on the rebuild process… and he also had an important question to ask Carra's father.

CHAPTER 41

The next three weeks were fairly uneventful. There were no changes in her routine, and Carra had become accustomed to the other students in her year. Even so, with the exception of Saul, she still hadn't spoken more than a few words to any of them outside of the group activities they engaged in during some of the classes.

Her interest had been gradually waning, and she'd almost stopped taking any notes in her lessons – until, her geography class renewed her enthusiasm, with a debate on Savarah.

Enraptured, she intentionally let the debate as to whether it did or didn't exist continue for half of the time slot, before she piped up with, "It does exist, I've been there." She kept her face as serious as possible, despite finding it *really* difficult to restrain from smirking.

Only one person's jaw actually dropped, and she was surprised to find that it was Saul's. Possibly because he was the only person who believed her…

Unfortunately, the professor in that class was Bart. He was more than just a little old fashioned, so she had no chance of his support on the matter. Carra didn't really care. Well, actually, she was glad Saul believed her, it would have undermined their burgeoning friendship if he hadn't – he knew how honest she was.

Everyone just kind of stared at her for a while, presumably waiting for her to say more. She really had no reason to, so she pursed her lips, and forced her expression into one of disinterest.

Let them judge her.

She was happy to answer questions – if they asked any – but she didn't need to justify herself. She sat back in her chair and put her hands behind her head, whilst looking around the room. The silence was actually broken by Saul who let out a sudden, but jolly, chuckle.

"Yes, yes." said Bart, although he wasn't really saying 'yes' to a question, that was just how he spoke, "Make your point Carra."

"I'm not making a point, Professor. It was a simple statement of fact."

"For pity's sake Carra, tell us more," Saul declared, just as another student questioned whether it had been in a dream. Carra had been too busy listening to the students' debate to consider how she was actually going to give an explanation – that is, without mentioning certain things that were really no one's business like Dom, the Tower, or the locket.

"It was while I was in the Desert lands. The people were really nice, they made me dinner." Finally realising she wasn't going to be particularly forthcoming, they plied her with questions – how did she get there, who did she meet, what did she eat, and the one she did her best to circumvent, why did they let her enter.

Apparently, as rare as it was for someone to *meet* a resident of Savarah, it was practically *unheard of* for someone to actually go there. She was under no illusions; Carra knew they didn't give any credence to her claims. *Although...* Bart, at least, seemed to change his mind when she mentioned a few names. The one he seemed to particularly dwell on was Gabel.

"How curious. Maybe you could have a chat with

Professor Charing, who has claimed to have met Gabel too." Whether intentional or not, Bart's intervention managed to add some credibility to her story. They still didn't believe her – after all she could easily have heard the name anywhere and 'dropped' it into her story – but suddenly they weren't sure either way.

"It can't be that strange. Gabbie said this Academy had contacted them before. She didn't explain how, but she did also say I would potentially be able to contact them again at some point in the future." She frowned. It was interesting that her mother hadn't reacted even remotely, when Carra had told her about her visit there.

Somehow, the conversation took a turn, and Carra found herself being ridiculed. Apparently, Savarah wasn't necessarily in the desert, it was somewhere 'in between' here and not here, so could appear anywhere it was required.

On reflection, that almost made sense; it had been an incredibly strange place, and there was a time when Gabbie had appeared out of thin air. Presumably, it had turned up in the desert because that was where they'd chosen to hide the locket, or the location of the Tower, or some such.

The head of the Academy, Carra was yet to meet Professor Charing, and however much it intrigued her, she certainly didn't fancy approaching him to talk about Savarah. The idea that he may have been directly responsible for her magic being taken away made her uncomfortable, and she felt certain anyone whose confidant was *her mother* would be someone to avoid.

Having somehow recognised she was withholding information, it transpired that Saul actually thought she was going to fill him in afterwards, once they were alone. Her facial expression when he said as much was clearly enough for him to be set straight on the matter. He'd have to find something else for them to talk about over lunch.

Having arrived back in Paragon, Dom timed his trip to Whistlake with the intention of surprising Carra at lunchtime. He positioned himself in a spot behind the wall nearest the dining hall while he waited, laughing to himself about how much this reminded him of when he'd spied on her at the Strathenbergs.

He was expecting to surprise her any second, but when he did catch a glimpse of her, she was accompanied by the man with whom she'd been arguing just before he'd left. *Their relationship certainly seems to have shifted drastically.*

The more he watched, the more unsure he felt as to whether his feelings for her were returned. Carra perhaps wasn't being quite so open about it, but her companion didn't seem to be making any effort to conceal where his affections lay. Dom couldn't help but conclude that Carra must have given her new friend some reason to believe there was something between them.

Feeling dejected, he left them to it.

Carra suspected Dom was back, but felt a bit awkward that he hadn't come to see her yet, especially when she knew he was likely to be called into her dreams.

Fleetingly, she wished she could control it – that she could *decide* whether she wanted to summon him or not – but... really, it was better this way. At least while it was out of her control, Dom wouldn't know how desperate she was to see him.

When she awoke in the early hours, she realised she'd been in quite a deep sleep. It appeared as though she must have been wrong about Dom being back.

Yet, when she fell asleep again, he did appear, and she realised he must have just had a late night. She didn't have to spend much time wondering what he'd been doing, as he had clearly gone to bed inebriated, and could barely string two sentences together.

"What is *wrong* with you?"

"Just had a few drinks with some new friends." Carra rolled her eyes, consciously changing the surroundings to bright sunlight. Dom lifted his arm over his eyes. "Stop it, you sadist." Waving her arm, mostly just for effect, she swept in clouds to cover the sun.

"What is the matter with you, Dom?" she repeated. "You're acting out of character."

"I get drunk."

"I meant, undignified."

"Saw you. With boy." She shrugged her shoulders. There was no talking to him like this. "He likes you. Happy?" She put her hand on his shoulder, and Dom, catching her completely by surprise, lifted his head up and slowly kissed her. He *really* kissed her.

She stumbled off balance and had to right herself. Encouraged by her kissing him back, he put his hand behind her neck and deepened the kiss.

It was with regret that she pushed him away. "Come and find me in real life, Dom. No more of this using dreams as a cover to protect yourself."

She couldn't help but wonder if he'd actually remember what she'd told him when he woke up.

☆☆☆

She didn't have to wonder for long. The following evening, when she returned to her room, he was there waiting for her.

Carra had spent a good part of the day considering whether she was ready to take things further with him… and if she *was*, whether it would be a good idea to do so. It only took one look at him for her resolve to weaken.

"If we're going to do this," she said, gently resting her hand on his arm, "We're going to do it properly."

Disappointingly, they spent the evening talking. As much as Carra was interested in hearing about his trip, she was finding sitting on the bed, in such close proximity to him, really distracting.

Things were different here. When they'd shared a tent, it had been out of necessity. This felt more like a choice.

At some point during the night his arm had appeared around her shoulders, and not much later, they had fallen asleep next to each other.

Dom then had to wait until classes had started the next morning in order to sneak out. Carra watched from the window of her first lesson to see if she could catch him, but he was surprisingly stealthy.

They had agreed to spend some time together on her two free days at the end of the week; he had even promised her a trip to a travelling fair, which she was inordinately excited about.

She found the lessons that day slightly more tolerable.

CHAPTER 42

By the time the end of year tests were approaching, Carra was getting bored with Whistlake. She wasn't sure how she felt about coming back for another year of this but, optimistically, she hoped the few weeks off following the tests would help change her mind and renew her enthusiasm.

Dom had been right about Saul... Luckily, they'd still managed to stay friends, of sorts, after he'd tried to kiss her. Dom had been slightly prickly with her about it, but even he had to admit that there wasn't anything Carra could have done about it. They'd simply been practising together one afternoon, as they often did, when Saul had made his move.

In the break between the second and third terms, Carra had taken a trip with Dom up to the northern seacoast. He'd said his inspiration was the beach scenes she kept creating in her dreams.

Slightly less romantically, it turned out their getaway destination was also the location of one of Pellagea's three hospitals, which he'd insisted she visit every other day to see how she could help.

As much as she'd enjoyed complaining about working during her time off, the result had been an almost unbelievable increase in her internal magic capacity. She'd even gained an additional spirit skill as a result – the ability to sense magic in others.

Initially, she had struggled to adapt to the different mental impulses she'd been newly receiving. With practice

– something she'd been forced to do for three days straight, before she could walk around again without feeling dizzy – she'd honed the ability to focus in and out of the skill; and eventually, she'd learnt to shut it off.

Using it on the general public, she'd expected to see a small level of magic running through the veins of a lot of people, but instead she'd discovered that only maybe one in twenty people had any capacity for it at all. Of those who did, less than half had anything more than a flicker.

The more she'd forced herself to use the spirit sight, the easier it had become, and her ability had continued to develop at a steady pace for the several weeks following. More recently, she'd become able to sense specialisms as well; these were represented by different colours.

One of the best things to come of this, was the discovery that both her mother and Saul had a second specialism of necromantic arts. It made her wonder if *that* could be why Alexandra favoured him so much.

Having tried to research which colours corresponded to each of the specialisms, she'd found there was nothing of use in the school library, and had therefore been left to figure these out by the process of deduction.

Elemental powers were displayed as one of four, core colours. There were a number of different shades of blue, which Carra assumed indicated whether the wielder's inclination lay towards air or wind.

Broadly speaking, water displayed itself as silver, Earth as various hues of green, and fire as orange.

Carra's healing talent presented as lavender-purple, and her spirit magic was grey; having studied Sila, she had been able to determine which was which.

Once she'd assigned those specialisms she knew about, there had been two colours left over. One of them, a reddish magenta, had been attached to Saul, whereas the other had resided within Dom. As she was confident Dom had no necromantic talents, the revelation that *this* was Saul's second ability had been the only logical conclusion.

More importantly, and with much greater potential as far as Carra was concerned, was the discovery Dom had a secondary skill. The yellow-gold aura surely meant he was an augmenter.

Dom had pretty much laughed at her when she'd first suggested it. He'd said yellow and orange were close enough she'd just been seeing the various strands of his fire magic. Carra knew they were distinct as they ran through him as two separate, discreet veins, but when she had attempted to describe this to him, he'd remained unconvinced.

After sneaking Dom into the library at night so they could both read up on it – amongst other things – he'd begun to come around to the idea. On further experimentation, they discovered he'd been using the talent subconsciously.

Ostensibly, Dom's augmenter talent, combined with the amount of time they'd spent in physical contact, had led to her magical capacity being somewhat extraordinary.

✫✫✫✫

One evening, while Carra was staying over at the Inn where Dom was renting a room, he finally brought up in conversation the subject they'd been skirting around for weeks. "When do you think you'll be ready?" he asked.

For all their courting, they still hadn't taken things as far as they could. It seemed clear they were both waiting for the other to make the first move and neither wanted to break the stalemate.

"I need to know that we're in this for the long run, I guess."

"I'm committed to this. I want to know if you are too." She nodded hesitantly. He got down on one knee. It turned out he *wasn't* talking about sleeping together after all. Pulling out an emerald ring he looked up at her, "Will you marry me, Carra?"

"Yes!" How had she not even had the slightest inkling this was happening?

"I need you to accept all of me. You know what my plans are. You know... what I aspire to."

She almost laughed. "Yes Dom, I know. It's all you talk about some days. I don't like the way things are in Florinyn either."

They did take things further, then. Twice. She felt like a different person in the morning.

The end of year testing was nothing at all like she'd been expecting.

With the number of people suddenly coming and going across the college grounds, she had been beginning to think Whistlake was going to make a spectator sport of it. Seemingly, it was conventional for students' families to stay in the area for the entire week.

It mostly worked in her favour, as it was much easier for Dom to come and go from the college without turning heads, but she *greatly* begrudged the much longer queues at mealtimes.

In addition to the eleven first years, there were seven second years being tested. Sila was Carra's sponsor, which she was glad of, but even her favourite professor wouldn't give away any real details. She simply stuck to the line, "They're going to see how many skills you have."

Carra wasn't particularly apprehensive, as she figured she would pass comfortably with her healing skills alone. She still hadn't mentioned about her affinities on the spirit side of things to anyone other than Dom, and he fully supported her decision on this; his being the only opinion she felt mattered.

Set-up within the grounds were three tents, and she was instructed to enter these in a specified order. The first two were small gazebo-type constructs, but the third was much larger, and looked to be of a more semi-permanent nature.

She wondered if they might transport her elsewhere, as the Tower in the desert lands had – but even if they did, the trials she was about to face were unlikely to be anywhere near as taxing. So, whilst the thought had, for a moment, made her anxious, it instead became something which reassured her.

As she was still using her father's name, she had the pleasure of being first alphabetically. 'Carra Anson' was announced over the loudspeaker, Sila patted her on the back, and in she went.

The first tent was occupied by a nurse, who used a syringe to take some of Carra's blood. Carra thought, satirically, that this might be a test of being able to keep still under bizarre circumstances. Even with the lady holding her arm down so that Carra didn't dislodge the needle, she suspected it was going to bruise later. The medic said thank you, and that was it. She was asked to leave.

Carra considered asking if she'd passed, or what the test had been, but she didn't manage to summon the courage; and once she'd walked out, she had already missed the moment.

Shortly afterwards, Carra was directed to enter the second tent. There, Professor Charing was seated at a small, square table. A second, empty chair, faced him.

His condescending expression reminded Carra that he was the only professor who insisted on being referred to by his surname – he clearly thought this would set him above his peers in some arbitrary way. Carra took a deep breath and, for some reason, thought of Dom as she sat down. She certainly preferred Dom's quiet superiority to this man's need to throw his influence in your face.

"My name is Professor Charing. I am here today to talk to you about your magical abilities. Please start by introducing yourself." Even the way he spoke to her was patronising. If she'd been more susceptible to it, she would have been made to feel like a small child.

"My name is Carra Anson. I grew up in Florinyn and I was admitted to Whistlake at the beginning of the second term of this school year."

"Anson," His eyebrow twitched. "I knew your father. Who gave you permission to enter this Academy?"

Not so close to her mother after all then. That was an interesting development. "I was struggling to keep my magic under control, and I was worried I might harm someone, so I came here seeking help."

He paused in thought for an unreasonably long amount of time. Carra stared at her nails uncomfortably, running her fingers along their edges.

"What's done is done. For now, we shall continue with the test, and at a more appropriate time I suggest we meet to discuss whether it is suitable for you to continue to be enrolled at this respected Academy."

Carra, not one to sit back and let herself be offended in such a way, had a dilemma – did she continue on and try to pass the test, or did she confront him. Her inner nature won out.

She never had been good at holding her tongue.

"Excuse me, but how do you expect me to maintain a civil conversation with you after you have spoken to me as such?"

"Child, I am many years your senior in terms of experience and knowledge. Do not try my patience."

"If that is so, then you should know how to be polite, and how inappropriate it was to be so rude."

"Excuse me one second." He stepped out of the tent – which suited Carra perfectly. Moving to sit on the floor, she straightened her arms and took a deep breath.

She couldn't help but laugh when, upon opening her eyes, she saw the floor was slightly scorched in two parallel lines where she'd released her frustration. When she moved back to the chair, she felt far more at ease.

Carra wasn't left on her own for long, and when Professor Charing returned, he had Sila in tow. Sila was carrying a chair with her, which she carefully placed on one of the unoccupied edges of the table. Carra was pleased, considering this to mean she wasn't taking sides.

"Let us continue amicably. Sila will be here to bridge the gap between us. We shall now commence the examination." Carra *almost* rolled her eyes. "Tell me about your magic. I want to know your various skills and how advanced you are in each."

Carra proceeded to do as requested, at least, to the extent she was willing. She told him she could heal others to a high standard, heal herself – albeit only to the limited extent which had been required of her so far – that she rarely contracted diseases, and saving her favourite until last, described her destruction magic. His eyebrow raised again at that point.

"How big an explosion are we talking about?"

"About an arm-span wide would be my largest to date, *Professor Charing*."

He seemed unsure how to phrase the next question, "And, is that because you haven't *tried* to create a larger explosion, or is that the limit of your current power?"

"That would be the limit of the size of explosion I can *control*." she said with a sly smile on her face.

Carra was a little surprised when she was dismissed from the second tent – and a bit put out that Sila had remained behind with Professor Charing. When she finally reappeared, she didn't have much to tell Carra, other than that he'd asked about her lack of a second specialism and had been particularly interested in her anti-healing.

She had been informed she'd have to wait until the afternoon to find out what awaited her in the third tent, so she whiled away the time by pacing between Dom and the buffet, impatiently. Dom clearly had nothing to helpful to say and, sensibly, had the tact to stay quiet.

Saul was nowhere to be seen, so she had been unable to find out what his take on the experience had been. She didn't even know what his surname was, so she had no idea where he'd be in the running order – for all she knew, he might not start until tomorrow.

When she heard her name called for the final component of the assessment, and made her way across to the testing area, the cause of the delay became apparent. They had been reconfiguring the area's set-up specially for *her*.

At least this part looked more like a real test.

She didn't recognise the two professors observing, but it was Sila who briefed her.

Firstly, she was directed to someone with a severe

cut in their leg, whom she was to heal. Secondly, she was to heal someone with a pox. Thirdly, she was asked to create three controlled explosions, in varying sizes and perfect circles. All of these she did with relative ease.

Expecting that to have been it, she thought she was simply waiting for the nod that she could leave. Instead, one of the judges gave her the option of proving she could perform self-healing. Considering for only a second, she agreed to the additional evaluation – although when they approached her with a knife the length of her forearm, she began to have second thoughts.

Despite how it had first appeared, the attendant simply made a small, shallow cut in the palm of her hand, which barely drew blood before it had closed over and disappeared. The two judges conversed between themselves for a few moments, then nodded.

Sila led her to the exit and her first year at the Academy was officially over.

Walking back towards Dom, Carra shrugged her shoulders. She was glad she hadn't wasted any time going back over what they'd been learning in class.

CHAPTER 43

True to his word, a week and a half after her testing, Carra was called before a conference of the professors, spearheaded by Professor Charing.

She was led by one of the administrative assistants to a pair of large bolted, wooden doors, and instructed to knock.

On entering the chamber, it became evident from the empty mugs that the group had been communed for a while already. They were sitting around a large circular table, and she was asked to stand against the middle of one of the walls. If not all the professors were in attendance – she wasn't certain, as all those she had met were present – then this was at least a very good representation of them.

"Good afternoon. Welcome Carra Anson." He paused, waiting for her to say something.

"Good afternoon…?"

"We would like to discuss the uncertainty around your continuing education at Whistlake Academy in light of the proposal which has been put forward requesting your expulsion. This is in the context of the risks inherent in both your magical development, and our risk in allowing an association with you. I appreciate that this issue is in no small part due to your entry not having been brought to my attention on your arrival, when it first should have been, therefore I will give you the opportunity to provide a defence. Do you have anything to say to your own merit?"

"Yes, quite simply this. You do not need to worry any further, as I would like to register my voluntary withdrawal from Whistlake Academy." There were *many* other things she could have said. So many it would have been difficult to choose the most fitting. Instead, she waited to see their reaction. One lady let out a small gasp, a couple looked mildly flustered. Professor Charing, however, did not look surprised.

Alexandra looked at her intensely. "That decision would not seem to be within your best interests *before* you have heard what we have to say. Is this an impulse reaction to some perceived slight at being called to this summit, perhaps?"

"I can see why it would appear that way." Carra kept her head held high, "However, I have been considering this very question for some time now. I came here to achieve control over my magic, so that I wouldn't accidentally hurt anyone. My goal has therefore been achieved."

"It is not as simple as all that." Professor Charing continued. Carra frowned. "There is another matter we have called you here to discuss. We would like to try and make this as easy as possible. Is there anything you would like to, as they say…, *come clean* about?"

Not particularly, she thought – and certainly not without a bit of context. *Are they talking about something to do with Dom? If they know his identity, then why do they need me to tell them about it? I don't see how his proposal to me would affect them.* She twiddled the ring now adorning her fourth finger.

What else could they be referring to? On the one hand, she was acutely aware of how uncomfortable the silence was becoming, but on the other… she could hardly be seen negatively for *not* knowing what they were talking about. It would add credence to the fact she wasn't trying to deliberately conceal something. "I'm afraid I don't know what you're alluding to."

"Unfortunate, most unfortunate." Carra knew without looking that this was Bart, so didn't feel overly perturbed by it.

"The results of your testing were... unusual."

"I'm not sure I follow, Professor Charing. I explained each of my healing abilities to yourself, and then demonstrated these. How was the test graded?"

"Ah." He placed his elbow on the table and rested his chin on his hand. "You do not know the nature of the testing. If you think back, you may remember we took your blood. This is used to test your magical capacity and register you on the power spectrum.

"In most cases, students are then able to accurately predict what their level is, within an error level of one point either way. When students are learning, they may conceivably find they gain a skill or two as their capacity increases, but by the time they graduate from the Academy, the skill level is inevitably fixed. As you know, mine can best be represented as a number eight."

This prompted Carra to turn on her spirit sight, and she quickly tried to memorise firstly the colours of all the professors, and then secondly, the intensity of these.

"An eight is *extremely* powerful. Professor Alexandra is ranked as a high seven," Her mother was smirking at this point, which was irritatingly distracting. "As is Professor Leo. The other Professors have all attained a level six. Which brings me to you. You disclosed healing skills that would register a level four; maybe five at a push. Your blood test, however..."

"Oh." Bother. Carra had almost been too distracted to notice that, based on the expressions of those around the table, this was clearly news to most of them. If she had to guess, she'd say only Sila had been aware in advance of what

Professor Charing had been about to say.

"Might I assume from your reaction that this is *not*, after all, a surprise to you, Carra Anson? What do you think your test might have registered?" Carra shrugged non-committally. "It was an eight."

Briefly, she considered whether she ought to pretend to look surprised - but quickly thought better of it. Carra was actually quite impressed he didn't sound more annoyed, given he was alleging she was just as powerful as he was.

"Carra." Her mother stood from her chair in disgust. Aha, so there's one person in here who is clearly angry. "You despicable girl. Tell Professor Charing how you cheated the test." Carra crossed her arms defensively.

"Alexandra, be seated. The nurse confirmed it was Carra's blood she took. She tested it immediately and brought the results directly to me. We do not suspect any tampering."

Plus, I just demonstrated I had no idea what the blood was being taken for anyway?!

"Maybe I'm an augmenter and not aware of it?" *Aargh, why did I say that? Now I've put the suggestion in their heads that I know how the augmenting skill works... and likely know someone with that specialism.* It probably didn't matter, and she was probably overthinking it, but it still felt like a minor betrayal of Dom.

"Interesting... but inaccurate. As you well know. Now, Carra, there are some buildings on this campus that you haven't have access to. Within one of these there is a library, which is provisioned solely for the use of those under my employ. I suspect you can imagine what sort of delights can be found there. Much more interesting things than the book we found under your mattress."

He raised his left eyebrow and Carra almost snarled

at him. "Amongst these treasures, is a book that was left to us by one of our predecessors. In fact, this was the very person who designed the test. Can you see where I might be going with this?" Carra nodded but only partially managed to stop herself from rolling her eyes.

"Using her knowledge of both earth magic and spirit magic, she was able to create a formula for a liquid, which essentially imitates spirit sight. Helpfully she also left a key to de-coding it." He adjusted his spectacles, purely so that he could look down his nose at her. "By your lack of questions, I assume spirit sight is something you are familiar with. Now would you care to explain. The truth this time, if you please."

"I mean, not particularly." Carra frowned. "If I'm leaving the Academy anyway, I don't see that it's anyone here's business."

"Incorrect." This was the first time he'd actually raised his voice. "You are a threat to us, and you are most probably a threat to yourself!" She felt that was a little extreme. "Now you can either cooperate – or we will be forced to take any measures necessary."

"Fine. Tell me what you want me to do. I don't see that it matters anyway."

"When we observed your healing magic you registered a four. Broadly speaking, a summary of your talents would be as follows: healing both minor wounds and serious illnesses; thirdly, destruction magic; and fourthly, healing yourself and immunity from disease. The immunity you possess wasn't yet sufficient to be classified as its own skill point. I hope you can see that by providing you with this information, you are obliged to us."

She really wished she had known about this meeting in advance – she would have insisted Dom be allowed to accompany her. Although, that wouldn't have helped her with gaining their acceptance, she supposed.

"Yes, Professor Charing. I will comply – and disclose what it sounds like you already know, given there are only four spirit skills within living knowledge. In the future I will be more careful about being asked for my blood."

She looked at Sila in order to calm herself. "I would suggest the four remaining skill points are as follows: firstly – I can manipulate emotions. I want to be very clear on this that point - I have never tried this on anyone other than myself."

"Not consciously." Carra reluctantly turned to Sila at her interruption, feeling her last vestige of support slipping away. "Please continue." Maybe best not to mention that one of her skills had developed into being able to communicate with Dom telepathically then – if she could get away with it.

"Secondly – I can use the magic of another, if I have a connection with them. Thirdly – using the same connection, I can converse with another in their dreams." And outside of dreams. "Lastly, I have very recently developed the ability to use spirit sight."

"This may be a good thing Charing. She can help us update the test. She could work with new students to help them find their potential." Carra tried to contain her horror at Sila's suggestion, which would require her to remain here, tied to the school.

"Absolutely not." her mother commanded, as she walked over to where Carra stood. "I remain unconvinced. Prove you can use my magic and I may believe you."

Carra didn't need to initiate any physical contact, as her mother grabbed her by the arm. She tried to access her mother's magic – more as a result of having the opportunity, than because it was being demanded of her – but nothing happened.

She tried again, not putting in as much effort the second time, as she already knew it wouldn't work, whilst looking beseechingly at Professor Charing.

"Alexandra, cease this nonsense. It requires an *emotional* bond not a familial bond. You are embarrassing yourself."

"The only embarrassment here is my so-called daughter." Her mother spat out.

Carra was really starting to get frustrated now and Professor Charing clearly sensed as much. "This session is ended. Carra, you are to be returned to your room. I suggest you behave yourself or there will be consequences." He directed two of his colleagues to accompany her.

In the short time she had been gone, someone had actually added three deadbolts to her bedroom door. On the wrong side. They had been spaced apart in such a way that if she wanted to get free, her destructive magic would have to break through metal, which it couldn't do. *Although... maybe with practice...?*

They'd been busy – once inside, she discovered a metal bar had also been placed across the window.

Had she been determined, it would have been difficult, but certainly not impossible, to break through the stone exterior walls. On only the second floor, she wouldn't have been too high up to jump. What stopped her was a lack of confidence she would be able to do so without bringing the ceiling down on herself.

Amusingly, someone had placed some books on the bed to keep her occupied. They were a mix of factual histories and stories, and all distinctly non-magical. She opened the book on the political and economic history of Florinyn and sat on the bed.

Either Dom was going to have to turn up soon and sort this out for her, or she was going to be here a good while. *So much for being one of the most powerful magicians in Pellagea.*

CHAPTER 44

Dom was quite a while in returning. Fifteen nights to be precise. During that time, not a single one of the professors had been to visit her – which Carra took to imply they were planning for her captivity to last quite some duration.

On the morning of her arraignment – which Dom hadn't known was happening – someone had left an anonymous note at the inn where he was staying, informing him his father had died. When he'd first told her, Carra had assumed it was a dirty trick – that he'd been purposefully sent on a false errand while they decided what to do with her – but it hadn't been.

Florin was in disarray, and the news was quickly spreading beyond the capital. The princess had disappeared, and Torrin was already arranging his coronation. He needed to be crowned urgently if he hoped to re-establish order, but his move was widely being interpreted as both cold-hearted – given the funeral wasn't going to take place for a week and a half – and inappropriate, with Tilla not being there to attend.

Dom had told her all this through the window.

Apparently, there were two guards posted on her room, who'd been instructed to raise an alarm as soon as they saw anyone try and approach her door. Dom knew this, having already been taken completely by surprise, and then questioned by Professor Charing.

It transpired that, whilst they were perfectly happy

to keep *her* locked in a room, they didn't dare do anything with Dom. They obviously knew his real identity, as they'd left him that note – the timing was too much of a coincidence – and presumably that was why he'd been refused the opportunity to study at the Academy in the first place.

Dom waited until it was late evening to break her out. Carra felt this was purely for dramatic effect.

He created a large fire down the corridor from her room, to distract the men they'd hired solely for the purposes of watching her door. Carra had to give them some credit – at first, they had resisted the natural impulse to go and investigate. Once the floor had filled with smoke, putting their lives at risk, they gave in.

It was at this point, that Dom strolled down the corridor like he owned the place. At least, Carra couldn't actually *see* him – or perhaps, Dom was sending her a mental image – but that was how she imagined him coming for her. It was inevitable they'd know it was Dom who had helped her – but regardless, Carra thought it was rather cocky of him to flaunt it *quite* so much.

The second he opened the deadbolts, Carra was out of the door. She over-dramatically swooned for her rescuer and they both laughed. "Do you know what Dom? I think I'll miss this place."

☆☆☆☆☆☆

The days seemed to be moving along rapidly, hurtling Carra headfirst into the inevitable.

After stopping at the market in Rivulet to buy more appropriate clothing, and travelling south through Pellagea, they had reached Florin the day before the funeral.

Sadly, they couldn't stay at the same inn as last time, but Dom still managed to find somewhere opulent enough to suit Carra's expensive tastes. "Aren't we supposed to be keeping a low profile?" she'd whispered to him, but he'd simply grinned in response.

They were travelling under the pseudonyms of Hope and Jak – which made her smile every time she heard it – and this time they only needed one room. She was enjoying herself so much she *almost* felt reluctant to go through with what they had planned next, but with the coronation approaching, time was of the essence.

They had dinner at a small kitchen, which had tables spilling out onto one of the cobbled streets. The evening was still quite light, and the weather was warm enough that she was comfortable outside in just her dress – they'd both donned formal wear to make a special evening of it. And of course, it materialised that Dom knew the owner. They were presented with course after course, whilst being fussed over profusely.

Her dream skills, which had previously just seemed like a harmless bit of fun, were really starting to come into their own. They could discuss things between themselves with the guarantee that no one else would overhear. This was especially handy on that particular night.

He hadn't mentioned anything to Carra about it, but once she overhead some of the whispering at other tables and questioned him, Dom admitted that during his stay in Florin the previous week he'd been spreading rumours regarding Theodore's return.

Several of the other patrons had been looking over and Carra thought maybe they recognised him, or at least were trying to work out why he looked familiar. She smiled at them, relishing the attention.

Carra had decided she was pretty disgusted with how she'd been treated of late – her village had been burnt to nothing, she'd been forced to work as a maid and toyed with by

Nicholas, and to top it off, the Academy – where the Professors should have known better – had kept her locked alone in a room for two weeks.

Sitting here with Dom, the only person she now considered her equal in power, she felt strong. She felt free. This was how things were going to be from now on.

It was one of the best evenings she could remember having. She almost skipped back to the hotel, light-headed from euphoria and sparkling wine.

☆☆☆☆

They dressed in black.

Although it was, of course, custom to wear black for a funeral, usually cobalt blue was worn for a Royal funeral. That was tradition, and the way it had been for his mother's, Dom had said pensively. Only Royals wore black on a day like today.

Carra felt enjoyably scandalous, as she donned the floor-length, slinky, black dress they'd purchased in Rivulet. Dom smiled at her in appreciation.

He himself looked captivating in his black trousers and jacket, with a dark grey shirt underneath. He pulled up the zip on the back of her dress, and placed a necklace around her neck, before fastening the clasp. It was a chain of small emeralds to match her ring and she'd been looking forward to having the opportunity to wear it.

He had even managed to plan a surprise – keeping it a secret that he'd asked someone to come by to style her hair right up until the knock on their door.

When they stepped out of the Inn, Carra truly felt as confident as she needed to. She walked arm in arm with Dom, and they walked slowly, so that as many people might see them as possible. In fact, by the time they reached their planned spot, they'd already attained quite a bit of the attention they desired – and more than a few people were trailing them in curiosity.

They didn't head to where Dom's family were standing, just outside the gates at the foot of the Palace – this wasn't the right time to approach them. Instead, Dom led her to the centre of town.

It was the perfect position – the procession would pass through there several times on its route around the city – and Carra only felt herself shaking *slightly* as he helped her climb up onto the platform, where almost a year earlier, they had seen a girl savagely murdered for trying to help save someone from drowning.

Yes, Dom was certainly choosing to make a statement.

It was the first time she'd ever seen him quite so unsettled – and she only knew he was because his palms were sweaty. Had she drawn attention to it, he would have pretended it was from the heat, but she knew hot weather had no effect on him.

Their approach had been discussed beforehand – Carra would adopt a half smile and stand demurely whilst Dom greeted people and waved. However, during the procession itself, they would stand to attention in respect of King Florindyer.

People had travelled from elsewhere in Florinyn to be there today, and not everyone had been able to afford new clothes in the correct, azure colours. Yet, Carra noted triumphantly, she hadn't seen anyone else wearing black.

She turned on her spirit sight. Part of their plan during the procession was that she'd assess any potential threats in the city. There were far fewer magicians here than in Pellagea, but she did determine there were a handful present who could boast to have reasonable strength. Obviously, none of these could match herself or Dom; she estimated there were maybe a couple of level threes at best.

As the procession passed for the first time, Carra clenched Dom's hand tightly and he did the same to hers in return. He appeared to be okay, but she could only imagine the emotions he was going through right now.

It was unlikely Carra and her mother would ever have had a relationship, even under different circumstances, but he had at one time been relatively close to his father. His death had taken away any chance at reconciliation.

Carra personally felt nothing but hatred for the man and what he stood for – but it wouldn't have helped Dom to say as much.

The next few hours were remarkable only in how uneventful they were, given the situation. When the procession ended, they descended from their spot on the pedestal.

Carra's heart began pounding with excitement when the crowd parted to allow them to pass through. Many people shook Dom's hand as they walked past, and a few even shook hers too.

Every now and then, she heard scornful words being shouted, and to the extent she could, Carra took note of their faces.

They continued walking until they reached the edge of the town, then spent several hours in one of the taverns there. It was important no one was able to trace where they were staying, or they wouldn't be safe there.

It turned into quite an enjoyable afternoon. For the most part, the only people who dared approach their table were a number of the capital's richer nobles, and Dom endeavoured to work his charm on them. The majority of them he had actually met before, so he drew them in by relaying memories of them from his childhood.

Having now announced their presence, they slept uneasily that night – always half on guard.

By the next day, the atmosphere had shifted. The Royals had been alerted to their presence, and the streets were lined with soldiers. As they approached the Palace, the density of soldiers thickened.

They've mobilised the army overnight.

Carra repeatedly reminded herself they had planned for this. Dom intended it to work in their favour.

They walked a long route, all around the centre of Florin, in order to garner as much attention as they could before they approached the Palace.

Today they wore more practical clothing. Dom was still wearing his black trousers, but with a loose black shirt. She was wearing a red tunic with a thin gold belt, and black pants underneath – the sort of clothing she was accustomed to, except *this* tunic was expensively made.

They were still at least five hundred paces from the palace when they reached the point at which there was no longer space in the road for them to continue; too many soldiers were blocking their path.

It was Dom's responsibility to act first. He created a circle of fire surrounding himself and Carra, controlling the flames such that they were kept from rising above their waists – thereby ensuring their faces could be seen.

Next, he used his augmenter ability to increase the volume of his voice. This one had been more difficult to perfect, but they had practised as much as possible – while they'd been travelling through the more deserted areas, on their journey to Florin.

They lifted their clasped hands; joined to ensure their power was at its strongest, and to demonstrate their unity. Carra shivered with anticipation.

This was it.

"Listen to me." The crowd calmed slightly. Dom waited, allowing it to quieten even further.

Only once it was merely a susurrus did he continue. "I am Theodore." His decision not to use an honorific was bold. It meant he wasn't labelling himself a prince, and thereby declaring himself to be less than a king.

"I have returned, and I am here to lead you – alongside this lady, Carra, who will be my wife." They raised their joined hands further in the air. "Some of you will support me outright. Some of you will oppose me. Others of you will not, presently, have an opinion, thinking the kingship to be of little consequence to them. You will come to love us. I hereby assert my right to the throne."

He paused, to allow Carra to point at a nearby statue. Having scouted the area in preparation, this one had been chosen specifically. It was high enough that most people would be able to see it, and importantly, the impact would avoid the walls of any buildings. If any structures came down on the crowd, it would likely turn against them.

"Any who would challenge me, first heed this warning."

Carra raised her arm and pointed at its neck. This was actually the thinnest point, so required the least power for her to explode it, but the effect was terrific. Her blast was so precise that the, still intact, head rolled around the floor at its feet.

Once the resulting commotion had died down –

which took a good few minutes – Dom continued, "I bear no ill-will to any amongst you who are soldiers. You should be commended for doing your duty to my family. I merely ask that those of you who do not deny my position, stand aside." He made it sound so reasonable.

As he waited for each soldier to make up their mind, he enticed the flames surrounding the pair of them to flicker more highly.

Then, as if Dom was doing so merely to relieve his boredom, he created a second circle of flames a pace further out than the first.

To make doubly sure his control was indisputably conveyed, he kept a flame burning from his left hand – being the one which Carra wasn't holding.

Carra was convinced they just needed a few brave soldiers to step aside, and then the rest would follow suit. Going slightly off plan, she raised her arm out –as if getting ready to strike again – and that seemed to do the trick.

They were forced to scramble over each other to get out of the way, as the whole area was brimming with observers, and there was limited space for the army to reposition. Somewhere between one in three, and one in five, of the original horde remained to oppose them.

Once they had waited long enough to establish no others were planning stand down, Dom amplified Carra's voice for her. "You have one more chance to leave. Remember this. Yes, you are protecting Theodore's family, but *they* will be shown a mercy that none of *you* will be entitled to if you stand in our way." She paused for breath, to give them time to reconsider – even though she doubted they would – and to be thankful she'd at the last second remembered to say Theodore rather than Dom!

It would have spoilt the effect somewhat if she'd

stumbled over his name.

"If anyone else, outside of the army, would also challenge our rightful place, I implore you to do so. These men do not pose any threat to us, so do not cower behind them." Surprisingly, a few nobles actually drew their swords and stepped forward from the crowd. Carra suspected they were Torrin, or even Tilla's, friends by the way Dom flinched.

At least his sister Tilla was not going to be present at what was about to be a massacre.

Dom had offered to do the *unpleasant* part alone, but Carra had refused – they were in this together. Part of her relished the opportunity to feel powerful instead of small. This was who she had been forced to become. She had no respect for this town.

She could feel Dom's magic burning within her, wanting to be let loose.

They opened fire. Two of them against the remaining force standing against them. She felt alive. She knew it was wrong, but for the first time in her life she felt in control of her choices – and the guilt fuelled her power.

She thought she felt Dom flinch beside her in response to her determination, but at this moment, the only thing that mattered to Carra was herself. Her strength. The way she had been pushed about and used. They had made her this way.

Perhaps this version of herself had been there all along and they'd inadvertently released it, or perhaps she wouldn't have had it in her otherwise; but whichever one of those was the truth no longer mattered.

While Carra had commenced by firing explosions at individuals, Dom had been throwing fire at open spaces – they were hoping more would abandon the fight. She'd rather they lived, even if any men who only yielded because they were cowards had no place in any future army. Some did, but others continued to resist, and in fact, she had a begrudging kind of respect for all of these men who were clearly extremely loyal to those they had sworn to protect.

With progress being too slow, and men starting to fight their way through Dom's flames, they upped the ante. Letting go of each other's hands, Carra threw destructive force out with impressive speed, hitting several men in each throw. She was ashamed to find herself hesitating, on facing the first woman she had seen in the fray, but calling Jade's face to mind helped renew her efforts.

With their change in tack, they advanced on the palace easily, leaving a trail of ashes and craters in their wake.

Maybe she had done her best to temper her adrenaline to start with, but after a while she had stopped wanting to. This was it, what they'd been building up to, and it was working out exactly as they'd hoped.

It didn't abate until they'd removed almost all of their opponents. Torrin didn't call an end to it, and Carra knew with absolute certainty they'd been right to have doubts about his ability to make the correct decisions.

When they reached the gates, Carra held her breath as Dom called out for the crowd to bow to their King and Queen.

They did.

Dom instinctively bowed his head in return, and together, they entered the palace.

CHAPTER 45 - EPILOGUE

Astrill, Torrin, and Jade had retreated inside the Palace. They'd lingered, bashfully, inside the foyer rather than attempting to hide; they simply hadn't wanted the ensuing scene to be public.

As Dom had accurately predicted, Astrill had immediately bowed to him, declaring her allegiance, whereas Jade had just as quickly sworn she never would. As Dom had the utmost confidence in Astrill's word, she was welcomed by him as the mother of the King – her position no different to the one she would have held should Torrin have worn the crown instead.

Jade had been escorted directly to a prison cell, to which would have been the case regardless, given her past actions. Neither Dom nor Carra felt the need to engage in any attempts at conversation with her.

Torrin was a more difficult conundrum. They hadn't been sure how he'd react, especially once his fiancée had been 'removed'. He had asked for time to think, and Dom had graciously allowed him one week – whilst confined to his bedchambers.

In the end, Dom had to make his way up to his half-brother's rooms and push for his decision, as Torrin wasn't pro-active enough to assert one for himself.

Torrin had decided to swear allegiance to Dom, and

later, Dom made him do the whole thing again in public, at the coronation.

Carra thought it was the only sensible outcome, as Torrin's options were either prison, or to live in luxury, albeit not as king. It worked in their favour too – an imprisoned prince could have provided an opportunity for someone to back Torrin in a power bid sometime in the future. Dom didn't have any adverse feelings towards Torrin anyway, other than a slight lack of respect, and – much to Carra's amusement – the only condition he imposed on his brother was to forbid him from visiting Jade.

As Torrin had already made arrangements for his upcoming coronation, it hadn't difficult for Dom to make use of these, and he was crowned far sooner than either of them could have anticipated.

Between herself and Dom, they made sure to spend time meandering the streets of Florin, meeting people, in order to garner as much goodwill as possible. They wanted to be seen to care about their country. Given they were both more than capable of defending themselves, they didn't have to move around with any guards, which Carra thought created a much better impression.

Dom seemed to have an easier time integrating than she did herself. They had known him before, but she was an unknown quantity – and one whom they'd seen kill people at that. They treated her with a considered respect, careful not to offend her but reluctant to receive her attention. Carra continued to do her best outwardly, but inwardly, she determined she didn't *want* their friendship.

She was a leader and their sovereign.

☆☆☆☆

None of the classes at Whistlake had been aimed at

preparing Carra for ruling a country – something that would have been very useful. She had considered asking Sila to come over as an advisor but sadly, had decided she didn't trust her enough.

Her first job, therefore, had been to hire people who *did* know about these things. Foremost, she appointed three accountants – just one and she wouldn't trust them not to embezzle, two could collude, and well, four seemed excessive.

Secondly, she chose six legislative advisors – three for herself and three for Dom, because it seemed as though she'd now decided three was a good number; except Dom tended to rely on Oz and herself for advice more than the team, and it was usually Carra who ended up consulting all six of them.

They were managing, but it wasn't until Gabbie came to visit her that things really improved.

In addition to her help and support, Gabbie brought with her somewhat of a revelation about the prophecy – which made Carra feel foolish for not having asked her before.

Apparently, the line, 'ripple effects destroying Florinyn' was the result of paraphrasing caused by the prophecy passing from person to person over the years – the original prophecy had referred to the destruction they'd *already* enacted on the city.

Better still, they now had the opportunity to make real improvements – and changes to Florinyn's anti-magician rules sat at the top of both Dom and Carra's lists.

Dom rather cleverly decided to start with what he peddled as a minor rule amendment. He commanded that any magicians were to be reported to the crown, instead of executed.

This gave him the chance to make use of their talents and win their loyalties, whilst not completely overhauling the opinions of the majority, who still considered magicians to be dangerous. Of course, their little *display* hadn't exactly helped with that; so it was important they did some good, and quickly, to turn their subjects' sentiments to respect instead of fear.

Luckily, most of the nobles knew him sufficiently, or had heard enough about him, that they were aware of his character. *Strong, proud, and powerful.* The rest of the population were able to see he had won the nobles over, which meant the peace had generally been kept – but everyone was watching, to see what happened next.

Ally and Nicholas had visited them for a few weeks to attend the wedding, giving Carra the opportunity to meet their daughter Danni. As had Carra's father but, despite her attempts to convince him otherwise, he insisted his home remained Astonelay. She invited Alexandra too, just so she couldn't complain to all and sundry that she hadn't been welcome, but sadly, she didn't make the trip.

Their wedding was held in front of the palace. Due to the destruction they'd wreaked, it had been necessary to invest a substantial sum of money rectifying the area, and that had given Carra the opportunity to create her own beautiful setting without doing something considered overly vain and excessive.

The day itself had been perfect – a short ceremony, followed by people throwing flowers at them as they rode on horseback through the city.

She had even found herself able to build a good friendship with Astrill, and could tolerate Torrin quite well. Gabbie visited every few weeks and gave her advice, whether she wanted it or not.

Dom had been a little surprised by her actions during their public stunt, but their relationship was as strong as ever. They worked well together, and even when they were too busy during the day to have time to themselves, they more than made up for it in their dreams.

It had been a difficult journey, and she continued to face new challenges daily, but yes – Carra found she was happy with the way things had turned out.

Printed in Great Britain
by Amazon